Very Heaven

Very Heaven

by

Anthony Taylor

Very Heaven

Spiderwize
3rd Floor
207 Regent Street
London
W1B 3HH

www.spiderwize.com

ISBN: 978-1-908128-34-8

Dedication

To Linda,
and my sisters, Pat and Jill,
for their support and encouragement

Saturday, 14 June

A t nine in the morning the sea is already a sparkling blue.
Golden dots of sunlight dance on its surface and
interlacing wavelets splash the sand and glide up the beach.
Under an airy expanse of sky the promenade sweeps in a
smooth crescent along Marine Terrace, from the University at
one end to Alexandra Hall - 'Alex', the women's hall of
residence - at the other. Guest houses, hotels and holiday and
student flats make up a gently curving façade of vanilla, varied
by the occasional turquoise, soft green or yellow.

The promenade is deserted apart from, in front of Alex, two
students who have idly strolled its length. The academic year is
almost at a close, examinations are done with and Geraint and
Rob can taste the freshness of the summer morning air. Ahead
of them is the prospect of a relaxing day that this sea and sky of
carefree blue promise.

The tide laps in and lazy ripples play along the sand. They
lick the ankles of the body that lies there. It is face down,
uncomfortably so, spread-eagled on the grey polished pebbles.
Its arms reach out in front of it as if it's trying to swim. It wears
a slightly ragged dark-blue T-shirt and crumpled jeans. It has
socks and matt black casual shoes.

Geraint and Rob gaze. Odd that it should be stretched there,
its nose pressed against the shingle, early in the morning. A
post-exam prank to wind them up. It wants to entice them down
onto the beach. It will wait until the very last second and when
the terror grips them and they are looking petrified at each
other, it will jerk its head up, laugh monstrously at them and
exclaim, 'I really put the shit up you guys!'

1

All is peaceful, including the body. It is lying impressively still. Everything is still. Only the water around its ankles is moving - and, further out, the constant swell and heave of the sea, lilting patterns of currents in a gentle restlessness.

Do the two students recognise the figure? From where they stand they can't tell the sex. It looks male but they can't be sure. All they can see is the top of the head and the back of the clothed torso and limbs. But the arms - they look a strange colour, a ghoulish chalky-white. Is it make-up, to add to the realism?

Geraint and Rob look at each other. And, as they watch and wonder, a creeping recognition starts to fill each mind. *Isn't it...? No, it can't be.* A sense of incredulous dread is rising slowly but unstoppably in each stomach. This might begin a film or a novel.

But not a summer's day, on North Beach, in Aberystwyth.

The sense of dread lessens. It can't be true This can't happen to them. Why should they be the ones to find something like this?

The awful sensation returns. Each is now tight-mouthed. Each wonders, if he was on his own, would he turn back into the town, to lose himself and leave the discovery to someone else? Or let someone else have the grim joke played on him, because that is what it must be...?

Thursday, 26 September

Nine months earlier and the same sea, in a different mood. Ranks of waves curl in along the crescent of the bay, lashing the pebbled beach. White foam seethes to its crest, tumbling down like flowering snow and sucking back out. Gus watches the waves rear up and spill over themselves in their downward rush to burst in soft explosions on the sand. Now he is out of reach of all that has gone before. His parents are a hundred miles away and it feels like a joyful million. They are on their planet - now he has his own. The clear vastness of sky and sea stretches away before him like the future, an immaculate, empty, undiscovered territory waiting to be explored and filled with joy and light. Time opens out before his eyes into a tapestry of colour and fulfilment, supreme with beauty, love, delight. The confines of school and home have slid from his shoulders.

He is just above medium height, but his frame - lean, angular, but erect - makes him look taller. At eighteen his body is just beginning to broaden out to catch up with his adolescent spurt of upward growth. His face is narrow with gentle, musing eyes topped by soft, mid-brown hair starting to lengthen about his ears and neck.

There is a wild joy inside him that he has never felt before. Perhaps it is the sight and sound of the sea spread immensely in front of him, and the oddly-shaped university building behind, and the girls who saunter the seafront, and the sense of an adventure about to be undertaken, of mind and body, and something imprisoned in his soul that has now been released and can run free.

The labouring six-hour train journey from Cardiff, in the shape of a figure 7, climbing from the bottom north-east out of Wales to Shrewsbury, then back in and westward at last, the train chugging contentedly along, has made him feel he has reached the furthermost point of something - something brilliant and exciting, though he can't quite define what, which is part of the excitement.

Gus's lodgings are in Gwylan House, a tall, narrow, cream-painted guest house with doors and window frames of flaking maroon, halfway along the promenade. Above him as he strolls back for his first evening meal, the seagulls bank and career, their flights seemingly haphazard, as if done on a moment's impulse for no purpose, their cackle and shriek piercing the peace of the sky. He can taste the tanging freshness of air in his nostrils, cleansing his whole being of what has gone before.

His room overlooks the sea and he will be sharing it with Nick, a tall, well-proportioned boy from Pontypool with a broad face and a sportsman's good looks. His build is solid but athletic and his eyes have a sparkle that is both mischievous and friendly. He, like Gus, intends to study English and the occasional look of pained sensitivity comes over his face when poetry is mentioned. Another first-year student is fortunate in having his own room. Dermot, a History student from Builth Wells, is an overgrown untidy youth with uncombed hair of shiney jaundiced colour that falls randomly across his brow, and a large shapeless mouth. He has the mysterious, romantic-sounding attic room.

' "Gus?" What's that short for?' Nick's friendly, forthright manner as they sit down for the meal eases the usual embarrassment Gus feels about his name and he can reply quite calmly.

'Augustus.'

'Does that mean you were born in August, or - there was a Roman emperor, wasn't there?'

'Yes, I was born in August.' Gus wishes he could think of a joke to enliven the bald, boring statement.

Nick gives a chuckle. 'That means I should be called June - doesn't sound right.'

'Hey Gus! Bet your middle name's John!' Dermot laughs at his own joke.

'Yes, it is.' Gus feels his face reddening.

'Augustus John? Wasn't he some sort of painter?' Nick asks.

Dermot pushes back his hair. 'Yeh, he did that flowery picture of Dylan Thomas - golden curls and all that. So are your parents artists?'

Gus laughs inwardly at the thought. His mind goes back to the morning, his father looking in on his bedroom at six o'clock before leaving for work, mouthing 'all the best, Gus,' in a hoarse whisper. Then his mother, moving anxiously, wordlessly, about the kitchen as he prepared to leave home for the first time.

'No - I was born in August and my mother likes the name "John". She's not very imaginative. It's just coincidence that it happens to be a famous painter.' Gus hopes this will end the conversation.

They begin to dab at bowls of scalding soup, brought in for them by the landlady, Mrs Morgan. It is so hot that Gus feels the first spoonful spiking into the skin of his mouth, as he holds it there in an agonised gargle to avoid the even more painful option of swallowing it.

Nick cries out. 'Jesus, this soup is hot. And it's only the first course.'

'More like an assault course,' Dermot says.

Gus looks questioningly at the room's faded walls. 'D'you think she's given us paint stripper by mistake?'

Before they have completed the first-course ordeal, Mrs Morgan marches determinedly back in with the main course - brimming plates of lamb, carrots, onions, potatoes in mahogany gravy, steaming menacingly like the soup.

'Come on boys! Keep going! Don't fall behind!' She is like an officer urging the troops onward through a hail of bullets. She is an ample woman in her early sixties, wearing a butcher-like striped apron over a brown cardigan. On her feet are furry slippers of bright pink. Her laugh is a series of sharp staccato cackles, like a stick across railings, or a cawing seagull that has thrashed into the room.

'This'll warm up your innards!'

Gus is seriously wondering if his innards still exist.

The main course proves less arduous; the ice-cream that follows is a cold paradise.

'Now who's for coffee, who's for tea?' she bawls. 'I've only got normal coffee. None of that decapitated variety.'

The boys glance at each other, furtive grins assuring them they've heard correctly.

'So it's just the three of us, is it, Mrs Morgan?' Nick asks in his amiable way.

'No. There's another boy still to come - from Essex.' She adds the county pointedly, as if it is a little-known distant land. 'His mother phoned to say he won't be here until Saturday night. Simon, his name is.'

'Saturday night,' Dermot repeats when Mrs Morgan has left. 'So he'll miss Registration, Freshers' Disco for all us first-years. That's strange.'

'Probably can't face the prospect of meeting us,' says Nick, with a rollicking guffaw that resounds around the room.

Friday, 27 September

In the night, the ceaseless serenade of the sea continues, a constant plash and sluicing of waves upon the shingle. From dawn onwards the seagulls scream like feuding children. Their cries, repeated in echoing overlaps of calls, cut across Gus's sleep. He looks out of the seafront window at a sky that is a pale faraway blue and as soft as petals, with clouds of cottonwool white ghosting along it. The sea unfurls gently along the sand in white foaming frills.

Gus is up, dressed, washed and ready for breakfast by seven forty-five. Nick yawns and stretches luxuriously in his unfamiliar bed.

'Come on, Nick! You can't miss the first breakfast!'

Nick turns over with a contented smile. 'Ahhh - eventually I might sit up. You know what?' His voice emerges in a muffled moan from beneath the bedclothes. 'I might ask the landlady if I can have breakfast the night before, to save getting up in the morning.'

'You're joking!'

'No - I think staying in bed is good for you. I did it all summer.'

'What - as a kind of hobby?'

'Yep - a self-improvement exercise - like watercolour classes or learning a foreign language.'

'But do you *always* feel like doing nothing?'

'Not always. But I tell myself that, once I knuckle down to it, I'll feel its benefit and get over the initial stages of reluctance. You know what a teacher wrote on my report once? "Nicholas has an almost limitless capacity for doing nothing." And I do it with a bit of style. Boy - I can pack an awful lot of doing nothing into one day.'

Suddenly, as if vaulting a hurdle, Nick leaps out of bed. He examines his hair in the mirror. 'God, I'm going thin on top!'

'That's nothing to what's to come,' says Gus. 'Just think, one day when you're older, you'll look back at photos of yourself and say, "Mmm, I had quite a lot of hair in those days!"'

'The future,' Nick replies, 'who knows what's going to happen? In thirty years' time they'll have invented authentic replacement hair.'

'You'll probably be able to replace your entire head.'

The morning is taken up with Registration in the Old College building on the seafront, where the Arts subjects are taught. On Penglais Hill above the town is the newer site housing the Sciences and Economics departments. The Old College reeks history and its Main Hall, also known more ominously as the Exam Hall, where Gus now waits among milling groups of first-year students, has a cold magnolia décor. Spaced along the high, overbearing walls are equally cold photographs of past vice-principals, with stern, imposing, ancient faces staring down at him. It is a crowded chaos of forms to be filled, of queuing, of hasty chats with lecturers about which three first-year subjects to study. Gus notes the sheer number of unfamiliar faces among the students. Some are enviably composed, some full of a nervous humour. Some look bored, stoical or defiant, others appear lost, awkwardly aloof, or worried. Some look reassuringly young, others more intimidatingly adult. Some of the girls have a visionary beauty that sets his desire racing and the blood thumping through his veins. He is staggered by the range of different accents. Apart from the varied strains from North and South Wales, he can recognise from television those of Birmingham, London, the West Country, the North-East, but others mystify him.

The Head of English, Professor Arnold Savage, known affectionately to the students as Sewage, flits busily about the room. Senior Lecturer Dr Brian Parker-Hurst, his academic gown enveloping him like a shroud, sits dispensing weary advice on the relative merits of combining Philosophy or History or Classical Studies with English, peering at the students through the ashen undergrowth of his eyebrows. Younger lecturers like Peter Strutton and Gerald Bailey look more welcoming, less forbidding, with friendly smiles and a more engaging manner.

Outside the Main Hall the quadrangle is filled with the stalls of the various student clubs and societies, as noisy and bustling as any market, except that the wares are not fruit, vegetables, cheese or flowers, but music, religion, French, politics. 'Y Ddraig Goch Ddyry Cychwyn! It's A Great Time To Be Welsh - But Then It Always Is,' announces the red banner of Geltaidd, the Celtic Society. The Astronomy Society displays a large photograph of Armstrong on the moon with the caption, 'Take One Small Step - Join Us.' The Socialist Society proclaims, 'Don't Get Left Behind - Join The Revolutionary Left - Do Something Positive In Aber.' The Caving Club canvassers wear lamp-adorned hard helmets, while six Bellringers peal and chime their Society's invitation.

'We'll have to join the English Society, I suppose,' says Nick.

Dermot's eyes gawp in wonder at the array of activities.

'The brochure says there are sixty-four societies,' he shouts to Gus.

'And I think there are about forty sports and games clubs,' Nick adds. 'They're all listed alphabetically, so Tiddlywinks is next to Weightlifting. Boxing's next to Bridge. When will we find time to do any work? Hey! There's a Surf Club! I'm gonna try that in the summer. Riding those waves! Wow!'

In the evening Gus, Nick and Dermot sit in the Angel, the pub at the top of the town. In term-time loud and lively, tonight it is quiet, with most second- and third-year students not having arrived back, and only a handful of first-years having so far discovered it.

Nick slaps Dermot familiarly on the shoulder. 'Okay then, Dermot, do you think Aberystwyth is the dreamlike romantic existence I'm looking for?'

Dermot leans back in his chair. 'I should think it's a good place to dream dreams - it's not exactly the thriving metropolis. And if you think how long it takes to get here and get out of here...You have a feeling that you're a long way from the rest of civilisation.'

'Or from civilisation,' Nick adds.

Dermot ploughs his hand through his hair, his fingers disappearing into its yellow thickets. 'If you can call it civilised, when you think of Vietnam, the apartheid situation in South Africa, the trouble that's flaring up in Northern Ireland. Yeh, if you're not careful, you could easily lose touch with reality up here. There's nothing to dilute the student atmosphere. You can't escape - except into the sea.'

'Sounds ideal. That's exactly what I want,' Nick responds. 'I don't mean escaping into the sea. I mean, student atmosphere, unreality.' Gus is thinking the same.

'I remember reading,' says Dermot, 'that places on the west coast of America are thought to have a higher ratio than normal of eccentrics, radicals and plain nutters because that's the farthest west people can venture before dropping into the sea. I wonder if it's true of Aber as well.'

Nick's brow creases and he leans forward gravely. 'Somebody told me there are a lot of third-year students who just wander round on their own. After three years up here, they're bored with everyone else, there's nothing to do and no-one to do it with.'

'That's rubbish,' Gus says. 'There's so much going on . It must be because they're introverted - weird. They'd be the same in a big city.'

'Maybe this place does attract more dreamers,' Dermot continues. 'I wonder if there's a higher percentage of them here than at other universities. Someone should do a statistical survey.'

'How do you define a dreamer?' Nick asks.

Dermot sniggers. 'Anyone who studies English!'

'Oh yeh, just because you're a historian, dealing in cold boring facts!'

Dermot strokes his chin. 'History's very inventive. Most of it is made up… I think Jane Austen said that.'

Nick turns to Gus, who has said little so far, concerned to bring him into the conversation. He uses mock schoolmaster tones. 'So how do you see *your* future, young man?'

'I think of the future as - a limitless expanse stretched before me.' Gus smiles a long satisfying smile to accompany his vision.

'The trouble is that limitless expanses are usually deserts,' Dermot retorts. 'People are always asking me what I want to be. "What do you want to be when you leave school?" By *be* they mean *do* - they don't realise the difference. " What do you want to be when you leave university?" My answer is exactly that. I want *to be*. Full stop. If you feel that the sentence is incomplete, you can just add *alive*. The beauty of being. Just being. The French have a word for it. *Etre*. After all, we're called human beings, not human doings.'

'I suppose,' says Nick, 'if you spend enough time dreaming, you don't need to face reality at all. Dreaming becomes a continuous reality and there's no time for the real reality, so to speak. University doesn't prepare you for the real world anyway. Subjects like English, History, Classics. What good are they unless you want to teach them to others, who then teach them to others in turn. So the subject is never actually *used*. It's just taught from one generation to the next.'

Dermot is suddenly loud and passionate. 'What do you mean by the real world? There's more than one real world. There are lots, depending on what you want. There's a real world where people become obsessed with thinking about money, and getting on, and becoming imprisoned as husbands and wives, mothers and fathers, which is the one you're probably thinking of. But that's not the only real world. There are others in which people are not obsessed and incarcerated by these things.'

Gus looks stunned and a little fearful at the outburst, but Nick smiles in playful approval and there is a burst of clapping from the next table.

'Bravo!'

'Speech!'

'Stand up all you anti-materialists!'

Two boys lurch uncertainly in their chairs.

'Did you know, there are thirty-six chapels and thirty-seven pubs in Aberystwyth?' says one, wild-haired and thin-faced.

The second boy, fingering a wispy, struggling beard, thinks deeply. 'No - isn't it - thirty-six pubs and thirty-seven chapels?'

This annoys Wild Hair. 'Rubbish! The se-, se-, secular has to triumph over the religious.'

The second boy turns in appeal to the others, spreading his hands and raising his voice as if addressing a large audience. 'Well - there's only one way to find out - visit all the pubs.'

Nick laughs. 'You sound as if you already have.'

Wild Hair seems to contemplate standing on his chair, but thinks better of it. 'No - patience - that'll take a few days yet.'

'Or you could visit all the chapels,' suggests Dermot. 'You'll have to do that anyway, to count them.'

Wild Hair's eyes gleam with the certainty of one who has just solved a challenging mathematical problem. 'No we won't. If we do all the pubs and find there are - thirty-seven, that means there's got to be - thirty-six chapels, or vice-versa.'

'Or alternatively, you could do a pub immediately followed by a chapel and see which type is left over at the end,' Dermot says sagely.

The two boys seem bemused by the sudden range of options open to them. Wild Hair is thoughtful. 'No, I think we'll stick to our original plan - except I can't remember what it was. Oh yeh - the obvious. Do all the pubs. My name's Geraint.'

'Take life one pub at a time, that's my philosophy,' says Wispy Beard.

Geraint introduces him. 'This is Rob. We're from Carp.'

'Carp?' repeats Nick, with puzzled visions of a fish.

'Carpenter Hall, on the seafront.'

'Oh, the boys' Hall of Residence. That's just up from us, in Gwylan House.'

'And just down from Alex,' Geraint adds.

The room in Gwylan House that Gus and Nick will share is large, rectangular and spartan, with ugly brown furniture, a narrow bed at either end and one wash-hand basin. The carpet is a worn colourless fawn and the walls an uncomforting off-white, but each has his own wardrobe and small desk, and the window is filled with a view of the sea and a panorama of the whole grand oval of Cardigan Bay. They have already drawn an imaginary line bisecting the window and running down the middle of the room, with an unspoken arrangement that each will keep his own things in his own half.

'Hey, it's a bay window with a view of a bay,' Nick quips as they lounge on their beds. He puts his hands behind his head and stretches.

'Ah, Freedom! That bloody train yesterday. Were you on it? We must have come via Edinburgh. Talk about picking daisies - you could watch the buggers grow. My mother wants me to go home halfway through term. I'm not paying that bloody fare. And my parents can't afford it. My dad's just been laid off.'

'What does he do?' Gus asks.

'Gas fitter. Puts in fires and things like that.'

Gus feels both comfort and disappointment in Nick's words. Comfort, that Nick's father is an "artisan" like his own. Disappointment, that he is not sharing the room with the son of a teacher or architect or some middle-class professional, which would truly signal a new experience.

'What does your dad do?' Nick asks.

At least Gus feels no embarrassment now in replying. 'He's a miner. Works underground.'

'Ah, my dad used to do that. He managed to get out. Yeh, mining runs in our family.'

Gus nods. 'Mine too.'

'But that surprises me, about your dad,' Nick continues. 'I thought he might be an accountant, or teacher, or something like that.'

'What makes you think that?'

'You seem very well-read - more so than me.'

Gus shrugs, trying to disguise the pleasure he feels in having impressed Nick.

'Oh, not especially.'

Nick raises himself up on one elbow and peers out of the window. 'When you think about it, we're completely cut off up here. If anything happened to us, it would take days for news to reach my parents. They don't even have a phone - or a car.'

'Same here,' Gus says.

Nick laughs. 'I think this is a crazy place, full of crazy people. I think we could be in for a few adventures. Those two guys in the pub!'

'And there's Dermot,' Gus adds.

'Yeh - what was that outburst all about? All that stuff about the real world - and being?' He adds in a deep, sonorous voice, '*Etre.*'

'Should be interesting. The three of us. What'll we all be like by June?'

'Walking into the sea, I expect, as Dermot mentioned.'

'And there's our mystery man still to arrive.'

'Oh yes. The man *from Essex*.' Nick mimics Mrs Morgan perfectly. 'What was his name? Simon - wasn't it? I wonder why he missed Registration. He might even miss the disco tomorrow night. That's unthinkable!'

Saturday, 28 September

This is the night of the Freshers' Disco. The unfamiliar figures and faces that floated dreamlike before Gus's eyes in registration, that he has seen colourful in the autumn sunshine about the town and university, will take on a darkened mystery in a wartime-like blitz of blacked-out dance floor, flashing tracers of white light and the booming rhythms of the music. Gus has never been a disco fan. He enjoyed school dances, sanitary affairs enriched by the pleasure of viewing girls released from their uniforms, and by the breaking free from home and parents for an evening - yet with the comfort, unacknowledged at the time, of knowing they were nearby.

But this will be in a vast hall, overflowing with unknown forms of life from the four corners of Britain. The spectrum of emotion before those school hops, along a scale from mild anticipation at one end to slight apprehension at the other, feels somehow now suddenly, violently, widened, so at one extreme is a wild heart-spinning expectation and excitement, and at the other a paralysing fear, with the arrow indicator of his mind swinging crazily back and fore across the scale like seagulls wild across the sky. He has browsed through a book of Dermot's on the Napoleonic Wars and he feels how a raw young officer must have felt as battle lines were drawn up, watching the sweeping ranks of the enemy steadily coming into view, thrilled by the resplendent blues and whites and glinting helmets, filled with terror by their relentless march towards him.

Seven-fifteen in the evening. Nick applies finishing touches to his hair in the mirror of their room. His mind is calm and focused. There is a cool determination about him.

'I'm looking forward to this. Some of the girls I've seen around are - wow!'

'Got your eye on anyone?' The pendulum of Gus's emotion swings a little towards the enthusiastic.

'No. It's a cattle market, isn't it? Just see what takes your fancy. Then go for it.'

Dermot wanders in, in a stiff new bright blue shirt. Gus feels the battle-preparation syndrome. The troops are moving into position around him. He looks out of the window.

'I think I'll nip out for a stroll along the prom.' Gus hopes neither of the others will offer to come with him. He is confident about Nick, less so about Dermot. Neither makes a move.

'You're not coming to the pub first?' Nick looks at Gus with eyebrows raised.

'No -.' He lets the word drag out nonchalantly. 'I'll get some fresh air before all that sound and fury.'

'Signifying nothing,' adds Dermot, completing the Macbeth quote with satisfaction. 'I don't blame you. But the lure of a pint is stronger than the call of the sea at the moment.'

Far out at sea the horizon is like the rounded rim of the world, edged amber-red with the sunset. A narrow carpet of gold stretches across the water, unrolled by the lowering sun, and the sea lies peaceful in the gathering cool of the late summer evening.

Gus walks along the promenade and past the pier and the Old College. From the headland by Castle Point, that separates north and south beaches, he looks back to the long curve of the seafront, with Alex in the distance and the mysterious dark green mass of Constitution Hill rising over it. The distant northern cliffs of Aberdovey and Towyn are dim lavender shadows under billows of flossy white cloud.

He would reach out and embrace the whole sea, take it in his arms. This entire world, in front of him, all around him, all is his. Everything in his mind shines with the brilliance of newness. A new place to live, new people to meet, new subjects, new writers to study, new teachers, new experiences, new adventures, a world that glitters fresh as if polished. And yet - alarming in its unknownness.

South Beach is a mosaic of beige, white and grey, sand, shingle and pebbles, as the evening draws in and the sky begins to darken. Overlooking the beach are four-storey apartments and guest houses, a tapestry of pastel shades. In one top-floor window a girl leans on the sill and looks out to sea. Her room is full of orange lamplight. Who is she? Second year? Third year? She looks serene, unreachable.

Time to retrace his steps to King's Hall on the seafront for the disco. The darkness closes in. The ocean becomes inky-black, lipping the dim shingle with a more sinister siphon and suck. He nears the hall. A long queue straggles its length. The shadowed faces look tense, unjoyous, dutifully doing what they feel they should.

He can't see Nick or Dermot. He doesn't want to stand in that file, next to a girl, hands in his back pockets, not knowing what to say to her, or behind a group of lads who nervously laugh and joke, he feeling obliged to smile at their wit for fear they should think him a bit strange if he doesn't.

Once inside - will he meet someone? Will he talk to her through the blockade of music which he can hear blaring forth?

He strays down towards the beach. He looks back at the high looming walls of the hall, the small figures waiting patiently in line below.

He turns and walks away, along the seafront towards his lodgings, to the quiet and security of his room.

A shape on the beach catches his eye. Someone is contemplating the sea, someone whose collar is pulled up high against the darkness and whose shoes kick absently at the pebbles. The shape gazes into the water, turns and wanders along the shoreline.

Gus reaches Gwylan House. He glances out of his bedroom window. The form he saw on the beach is making its way up to the prom. It vaults onto the pavement and crosses the road, head down, hands deep in pockets as if trying to make itself as small as possible against the night air. Gus can see now it's male. The figure moves directly below Gus's eyes into Gwylan House. It must be the new boy, Simon. Gus hears him treading quietly up the stairs and into the room opposite.

Sunday, 29 September

B reakfast at Gwylan House consists of fruit juice and cereal followed by Mrs Morgan's unpredictable range of cooked dishes, all of which contain egg in some incarnation. Today it is scrambled egg and tomato on toast. Nick drowsily surveys the mixture of yellow and red on his plate.

'Look at it. Looks like an abortion.'

Simon smiles nervously as he gives his name in response to Nick's introduction of himself and the others. He has a small, tense face and dark wire-like hair that looks as if it might draw blood if anyone should touch it, and is combed straight down over his forehead, turning up at the edges like a much-thumbed magazine. His shoulders are hunched and his eyes have an inward look about them, unwilling to contemplate the outside world, but they start if he is looked at or spoken to.

Nick turns to Gus with concern and surprise in his voice. 'Hey, didn't you make it to the disco, or did you crash out early? You were in the land of nod when I came in.'

In fact Gus had heard Nick lurch into the room and stumble about around midnight but had decided to feign unconsciousness.

'Oh - I felt a bit tired. Wanted some fresh air, so I walked the length of the prom and came back for an early night.'

'Fresh bloody air! You've certainly got it in this place - tons of it!' He looks to Simon for confirmation as he speaks. 'Anyway, you didn't miss much. Nothing special. Some decent talent there, mind you.'

Gus is relieved at Nick's casual acceptance of his absence. He feared a reprimand, or, worse still, a quizzical look that might brand him different, an oddball. Already he's regretting his timidity. He should have gone. Showed his face. Let it wash over him. Taken it in his stride. All the phrases that signify unconcern.

Dermot seems equally unenthusiastic. 'It's strange - discos. It's where you're supposed to meet people. Yet everything conspires *against* you meeting them. You can't see them - they're just vague outlines in the darkness. You can't hear them, because of the volume of noise. You can't smell them because of the smoke and alcohol in the air. Yet you know they're out there, somewhere. It's like guerrilla warfare. As Shakespeare once said, "Partying is such sweet sorrow."'

The other boys groan in unison.

'Well there's only one other way to make contact! You have to grab them - grope them!' Nick looks again to Simon for a response, but all he gets is a rather frightened grin.

Mr Morgan comes in for a chat. He is probably in his early sixties like his wife, but he shuffles wearily about in contrast to her decisive stride. He usually wears a dark V-neck pullover with a battered, sad-looking maroon tie knotted at varying daily angles to his sagging shirt collar. He likes to peer out of the window each morning and give gloomy forecasts of the weather. Today the sky is metallic grey and misty drizzle sweeping in from the sea dampens the sand to a dark brown.

'I think this rain's in for the day. They say it'll brighten up by late afternoon. By that time it'll be getting dark. Welcome to Aberystwyth, boys!' He turns to them and revolves his false teeth thoughtfully in his skull, a manoeuvre that causes Simon to quickly choke back a heave that threatened to recycle his scrambled egg.

Mrs Morgan brings in a large, smoking pot of tea. 'So you're all enjoying the egg!'

'Lovely, thanks, Mrs Morgan,' says Nick with a quick grin at the others. Dermot is not certain if her words were a comment or a command.

She folds brawny arms and stands headteacher-like over the boys. 'So another English student,' she says, scrutinising Simon, who gives an awkward nod in reply. 'Isn't that funny? You come to Wales to study English. That makes three of you, doesn't it? I like to read - a ferocious reader, as they say. But especially, a good romance.' She glances out of the window. 'Holiday season over now! How time flies. It'll be Christmas before we know it!'

'So do you manage to get away for a holiday at all?' Nick asks the couple.

'Yes,' says Mr Morgan, 'we always take a few weeks in summer. Went to a place on the Italian Riviera last year. The wife didn't like it mind.'

'It was all right,' says Mrs Morgan. 'Not enough shops, though.'

'Honestly. That's all she looks for wherever she goes. Shops. If she went on an expedition to Everest she'd look for shops.'

'And I was ill one night!' she moans. 'O-oo-h, we had these very spicey Italian sausages. I think they were called - tsunami sausages. I had the runs all night. I wasn't dry till the day after! And then the year before we went to that village in Spain. What was it called now, Griff? Boredom - that was it. Very nice beach -'

Mr Morgan interrupts with calm exasperation. 'Benidorm, love.'

'That's what I said, didn't I? We had a lovely time. Went to a bullfight and all! Oooh it was a bit nasty. I didn't like the bull being killed. But the matterhorn was very handsome. The way he stood there in all his finery...'

Nick turns to Simon when the couple have left, and does a perfect imitation of Mr. Morgan. 'Welcome to Aberystwyth!'

Simon smiles, looking a little more at ease.

Thursday, 3 October

Gus gazes up at the amazing spectacle that is the Old College. The standing joke is that its designer must have just managed a third-class degree in Architecture. Gus has heard one student call it a Gothic monstrosity. Yet it is the sort of building that, once seen, is never forgotten. Light sandy-brown in colour, it sprawls along the promenade like a huge prone leviathan washed up from the sea. It consists of a jumble of geometric shapes, thrown together like gigantic ill-fitting jigsaw pieces - a large triangle at one end, rectangles, squares and an assortment of circular towers in seemingly random positions.

Yet it possesses its own eccentric dignity. Though originally an hotel, bought unfinished after its architect had gone bankrupt, and completed with money raised from the public, it somehow looks an imposing seat of learning. Gus thinks it resembles the chambers of the mind of a scatty but creative genius, with its medley of large and small rooms, narrow castle-like winding stairways, secret passages and corridors, its great echoing inner quadrangle and seaview library bulging with books. It seems incongruous, and at the same time appropriate, that next to its commanding South Tower should be the 'crazy golf' course.

They all sit waiting, perched on hard chairs arranged in a rough semi-circle facing a desk with neat stacks of papers and books. There is an air of hushed expectancy for Dr Strutton to appear and begin the seminar. Eight students pack into his room in the English department opposite the Pier. Through the window Gus notices a sheen of glowing silver-grey on the water. He looks around at the other students. One girl is named Amy - he heard someone call her that in the Students' Union canteen. She has a pleasant face but with dark, doleful eyes that seem to be contemplating some endless sadness of the world. He also notices Simon, hands clasped tightly together, and he has met two other boys - Josh, light-skinned, freckled and ginger, and Dafydd, swarthy and unshaven.

One chair among the students is unoccupied, but it has a rumpled pile of papers on it. A girl waltzes briskly in, pushing long dark wavy hair back behind one ear. Subjected to the eyes of the other eight, she is unconcerned. Her quick, concentrated glance about the room reveals no empty chairs, so she moves swiftly to the one laden with papers and places them deftly on the corner of the desk.

'I'm probably disrupting some - terribly intricate filing system,' she blurts breathlessly, turning laughing to the others as she lays the papers down. She waves to Amy and flops into the chair, brushing back her troublesome dusky hair again with a quick flying hand. Gus envies her articulate confidence, her easy humour in front of unknown faces.

Peter Strutton ambles into the room. In his late twenties, he has a youthful appearance, with an abundance of fair hair that falls across one temple almost to his eyebrow. He looks relaxed in a light jacket and pale blue shirt; calm, summery colours that make him seem less imposing than some of the lecturers who stalk the corridors in dark suits and vampire-like academic gowns. He has also, in contrast to other English lecturers, published his own poetry and a collection of short stories, which gives him special status in the students' eyes.

'...So, there he was. France, just after the Revolution. A young man not much older than yourselves...,' Dr Strutton's eyes pan around the room to take in each student, '...in a foreign land, learning the language, drinking in the experience. Then suddenly all around him erupts this ferment of anger and hope. The country is in the grip of a transformation both dizzying and exciting. The old order of misery and repression will be overturned forever. A new world, of liberty, equality, fraternity, is promised and proclaimed. Put yourself in Wordsworth's position. No wonder, years later, looking back on it all, he writes:

> *Bliss was it in that dawn to be alive,*
> *But to be young was very heaven.*'

The October mid-afternoon is tranquil and still. The students stare down at their *Selected Poems of Wordsworth*. Gus glances around at the attentive heads. He is curious about the dark-haired girl, so unselfconscious, moving confidently towards adulthood, and about Amy.

'Notice,' continues Dr Strutton, 'how Wordsworth reverses the word-order and the normal iambic foot to give that thundering emphasis on *Bliss* at the beginning of the line, and how he uses assonance to draw out the syllables - *ve-e-ery he-e-ave-en*. And *in that dawn*. A new day, a new era, is commencing, flooding the horizon with light.'

He looks searchingly around at the class. 'Another point worth contemplating. What phrase is repeated in those lines? Think of Shakespeare.'

The students rummage through the lines. Gus knows the answer. But if he speaks, all eyes will be upon him, all minds will be assessing him, all will be noting his embarrassment. Some may even recall the moment in years to come and he will be the timeless object of mockery and smug recollection. He glances quickly around. Amy is busy reading. Simon, like him, has his head down, pretending, Gus judges, to be thinking ardently, careful to avoid direct eye contact with Dr Strutton.

Finally, the girl with dark wavy hair looks up. '*To be.*'

Dr Strutton leans back in his chair. 'Exactly. And what was your name again?' He has the list of names in front of him but likes to be certain who is who.

She tosses her head back and smiles confidently. 'Fiona.'

'Thanks, Fiona. But whereas Shakespeare links the repeated phrases with *or not*, Wordsworth uses an intensifier - *but*. Hamlet is weighing a positive against a negative. *To be, or not to be*. He's thinking, should I carry on living - or should I kill myself?' He looks around again. 'Wordsworth is giving us two positives about life, and the second *to be - to be young -* is even more intense and affirmative than the first, *to be alive*, which was already *bliss.*'

Gus glances at Amy while her eyes are cast down in thought. He likes her mouth, innocent and sensitive. He looks out at the shimmering steel-coloured sea. The wide sky dips gently down to touch the water as if forming the edge of a flat planet. Above their meeting place lies a range of clouds like soft white mountains. You feel that if you sailed out far enough, to the point where heavens and sea merge, your boat would take wings, soaring you up into that billowing white ether.

Saturday, 12 October

Saturday night in the crowded bar of the Angel. Warm bright noise of chatter and laughter circulates in the crammed atmosphere. Gus, Nick, Dermot and Simon shoulder through the press of bodies to where a large group of first-years squash around two tables pushed together. Nick finds himself next to Fiona. The girls are evidently discussing parents. Fiona lets out a loud sigh. 'With my parents, you just can't win. They worry if I'm unhappy, because they wonder what's wrong, and they worry if I'm happy, because they wonder what I've been doing…'

'So what are you studying?' Nick asks her.

She inclines her body invitingly towards him. 'History, English, Philosophy, but I'll probably do History for my degree.' Her face is attractive, with its fullish lips, clear tanned skin and dark eyes. But she is big-boned and strikes him as being snobbish and superior.

'Oh - I'm interested in history,' Nick says. 'My father fought at Waterloo.'

She eyes him curiously, her mouth forming the start of a smile. 'What are you talking about?'

'Waterloo Station about ten years ago. He got into a fight with some rival supporters after a football match.' He gives a loud laugh, notices Fiona's distaste and his face takes on a more serious look. 'So why History?'

'It's a family tradition,' Fiona says casually, as if it is the most natural thing in the world. Apart from mining, Nick cannot imagine doing anything, least of all studying, as a family tradition. How strange for it to be normal! He envisions a line of Fionas, stretching back through the past and reaching into the future. Fiona can see her future waiting neatly for her, bound up in a series of parcels to be delivered at set intervals in her life. Nick inwardly shudders at the prospect.

Gus too feels ill-at-ease with her. For a moment stabs the realisation of how alone and unsupported he is. But then the glorious feeling of adventure crushes it. He will have the chance to study authors his family have never heard of. Names revolve in his head - Keats, Chaucer, the Brontes, Byron. Had he been born in any previous generation, in his family and background, he, like Nick, would have had no chance.

Fiona turns her head in search of more elevated conversation.

'Fiona's met the Queen,' nods Tessa, a small eager-eyed girl with large, dangling silver earrings.

'My father received an award,' explains Fiona, 'so she came around and chatted to us after the ceremony.'

'How does *one* address the Queen?' asks one of the girls.

'You just say, "very honoured to meet you, ma'am."' Fiona bows her head as if curtsying, in a surprisingly elegant way.

'That's what we call our mother - mam,' shouts Nick.

Fiona gives a brief dismissive chuckle. 'This is a little different -it's the royal "ma'am".'

'That's what I said. I wonder what her kids call her, if everybody else calls her "mam".'

'You're talking about the Welsh "mam,"' puts in Geraint, the wild-haired boy they met in the Students' Union, who'd expressed the ambition of visiting all of Aber's pubs. Rob of the wispy beard sits next to him.

'Same spelling, same word,' Nick answers.

Dermot's voice can be heard from down the table. '… It's the fact that they have all that wealth and fame when they haven't done anything to achieve it apart from being born, which the rest of us have also done.'

Fiona glances around. 'Who's that boy - a socialist in our midst?'

Gus has been watching Amy. She is attractively quiet, with soft, chess-black hair and eyes. She looks gentle and beautiful. Her face can be reflective or animated. She looks out of place among the hum of voices, but seems at ease, turning her head to left or right to catch the flow of conversation.

Fiona's voice is high-pitched with animation. 'Yes - this theory that English lecturers get to look like the writers they lecture about, just as dog-owners are supposed to grow to resemble their pets - there's definitely something in it. Take Parker-Hurst. He's exactly how I would expect the Ancient Mariner to look - tall, thin, those sunken eyes…'

'What about Sewage?' Gus says. 'He looks like pictures of Chaucer with his neat little beard. I can imagine him in a medieval smock, dark stockings, funny shoes.'

'Not only is he middle-aged - he's *from* the Middle Ages,' Nick adds.

'But what about - Peter Strutton?' Fiona's eyes enlarge with awe. The girls take over the conversation.

'Definitely a romantic poet,' Amy says.

'But not Wordsworth. He was dull and ate porridge three meals a day.'

Fiona is thoughtful. 'I would say - Shelley. "A bright but ineffectual angel", someone called him.'

'A bright angel, certainly, but not ineffectual.'

'I would say he's probably very - effectual!' Fiona giggles.

'Or Rupert Brooke - he was described as "the handsomest man in England." "A young Adonis, golden-haired"!'

'Or Peter Strutton could be Keats. I can just see him in one of those lovely baggy nineteenth-century shirts. Curly hair, sensual lips…'

'And all the people you've mentioned died young,' says Fiona. 'Definitely romantic!'

'And from what I've heard,' says a girl named Glenys, conspiratorially lowering her voice, ' - he has an eye for the girls.'

'Who'll be the lucky one this term?' says Tessa.

Fiona shuffles excitedly in her chair. 'He asked me my name in the seminar!'

Nick watches Lorna, a fragrant, blonde beauty, light a cigarette. She inhales on it in a calm kind of rapture, her lips pulling on the tip in a sublime satisfaction.

The drink is liberating Simon's tongue. He begins to confide in Lorna. 'I want to be less the centre of my own universe.'

She nods seriously and sympathetically. 'So what do you want to be, then?'

'Well - really, I want to be a novelist. But as soon as I think about it, doubts begin to assail me and I think, there just isn't enough inside me waiting to come out.'

'Nonsense,' Lorna says, 'anyone who can use a phrase like "doubts begin to assail me" in normal conversation must be a novelist. You need to unfurl your sails a little more, let the wind embrace you and carry you forward.'

Simon looks doubtful.

Nick watches Lorna come back from the toilet. He is fascinated by the way she sways her shoulders as she walks, in a slow, smooth rhythmic motion, undulating her whole body, like a fashion model.

At closing time, the group ramble and skip down Pier Street. After laughter, chat and goodbyes, the girls head off back to Alex. The boys linger on the prom. Simon looks disconsolate, idly kicking pebbles and stones back onto the sand below while the others laugh and joke. Nick goes up to him. 'You all right?'

'Yes,' Simon murmurs, as much to himself as to Nick. 'It's - oh, I don't know. I wish I could just talk easily, like that girl Fiona, or Lorna, or you.'

Nick tries to sound comforting. 'Well, I talk mainly rubbish! Anyway, people who talk a lot don't necessarily have anything worth spouting. They just feel this need to communicate. People who don't talk much just don't feel this need. It's not that they don't have anything to say.'

'Yes, but I want to communicate. I feel as if I'm on a desert island. Anyway, thanks.' Simon gazes at the sea, its white foam luminous in the dimness of night, curling and crashing, its sound a soft echo all along the shoreline. 'I think I'll just walk down on the beach and let the breeze take me.' They all jump down onto the dark sand. 'Once more unto the beach, dear friends!' Dermot shouts, laughing.

Nick thinks of Lorna. He remembers the flourish with which she held and drew on a cigarette. She had a lawless look in her eyes that entranced and enticed him. That undulating, underlying movement of her body, like a walking dance, a slow, endless rhythm. Lagoon-blue eyes. Her wide white laughing smile. Her blonde hair, short but thick, in soft clusters.

'What do you think of Lorna, then?' Nick asks Gus.

'I don't like people who know they're sexy,' he answers. 'I much prefer people who don't realise they're attractive.'

'Like Amy,' Simon says.

Oh, so you noticed her too, Gus thinks. He may have a rival. He can see why Simon would like her. She is undemonstrative, unassuming. Worryingly, she might like Simon.

Nick does a little dance on the sand. 'Wah! Lorna knows she's sexy, all right! And I don't give a shit! I could eat her, I could gobble her up!'

'Stop making her sound like a packet of biscuits.'

'She's more like a tart, if you ask me.'

Geraint had left them to rush into the off-licence in Terrace Road. He reappears swinging a red-labelled bottle.

'I reckon Dermot fancies Fiona,' he shouts.

'Oh yeh, what a snob,' says Nick. 'Did you see that look on her face when I made that joke about "mam"?'

'No way would I fancy her,' Dermot protests. 'She's a snob all right - the sort of person who thinks sandwiches taste different according to whether they're cut diagonally or in squares. She's stunningly ugly - apart from anything else.'

'Oh, I wouldn't say that. She's got her good points.'

'Especially the two that stick out in front,' Geraint adds.

'What we should do is raid Alex,' Nick suggests.

Geraint swings his bottle. 'That place is like a fortress. There's a curfew from eleven-thirty at night till ten-thirty in the morning - but a few clubs and societies hold meetings there. We could infiltrate them and stay on afterwards.'

'I think it's Tiddlywinks, Bridge Club and Philatelic Society,' Dermot says. 'I can't imagine Lorna playing tiddlywinks - unless a bedroom version's been invented.'

'Curfew!' Nick repeats with disgust. 'What'll they do if they catch you? Shoot you?'

'I think you get hauled up before the Senate. Or you might escape with a warning the first time. It's like a nunnery.'

'Probably the most promiscuous nunnery around,' Dermot says. 'Perhaps we should just "kick the bar," as they say, and go to bed.'

' "Kick the bar",' says Gus. 'I've heard of that. What is it?'

'It's an age-old Aber ritual. You walk the length of the prom and kick the bar of the railing across the road from Alex.'

'I thought it meant hitting a pub,' shouts Nick.

'Apparently it started when a visiting Royal put his foot on the bar while admiring Constitution Hill,' Dermot says. 'A more plausible theory is that it provides a good excuse for loitering outside Alex.'

'Or it could be a test of sobriety,' says Simon. 'Can you stand on one leg long enough to kick it?'

'I think I might fail that one. Anyway, I've got a better idea.' Geraint brandishes his bottle. It is vodka.

Nick rubs his hands together. 'Well, let's have a beach party!'

Dermot is less enthusiastic. 'Better count me out. I've had enough for one night.'

'Me too,' says Simon. He half turns, waiting for Dermot.

'Come on boys,' Geraint urges. 'The night is young.'

'I'm suddenly feeling old. See you tomorrow. Coming, Gus?' Dermot turns away, followed by Simon.

Nick slaps his arm around Gus's shoulder. 'No. He's staying with us! Come on Geraint. Break it open!'

Gus has never tasted vodka before. The name has an exotic, romantic ring and the cheerful red-and-white label excites his curiosity. He takes a gulp as Nick passes the bottle to him. It is a strange taste, not like liquid at all, but like pure heat being poured down his throat.

'This is like Mrs Morgan's soup,' he shouts, struggling to regain his breath.

'Not a comparison that would have occurred to me,' Nick answers.

The sky hovers dark above. They can hear the water chopping and munching through the shingle.

'Let's go in for a swim,' Nick shouts.

'That's a bit risky,' says Geraint. 'It's going to be cold in there.' Gus is grateful that Geraint may be more sensible than he appears.

Nick is annoyed. 'Aw, come on. I've always fancied that - a midnight swim with something warm inside you. This is the perfect place.'

Gus looks out at the sea. The black water lies as if in waiting, the incoming tide prowling along the shoreline. Nick is already fingering his jumper, about to pull it off.

'I agree with Geraint,' says Gus, coughing some of the heat out of his chest. 'Probably not a good idea.'

'Well, you boys!' Nick protests. 'I thought you were romantic!'

'Mmm, not my idea of romance.' Geraint flings his head back to inhale the vodka.

Nick folds his arms and looks disappointedly at the water. 'Well, some other time then. We must do it before the year is out. I know, we'll save it for the summer - June - after the exams.'

Sunday, 13 October

G us wakes up with the stale taste of alcohol, like rotten unswallowed food, in his mouth. He raises himself near-upright in his bed and his head thumps in protest as if he has smacked it on a beam of wood firm against his eyes. His stomach feels as if it holds an alien substance that cries out to be released.

Nick watches calmly from his bed. 'Everything okay? You don't look too good.'

Gus starts to speak, and the jolt of the words in his skull causes it to thump even more. He finds he can only groan feebly.

Nick whistles softly between his teeth. 'You've got a hangover, I think.'

Gus can only nod. The sticking thickness in his mouth and throat refuses to go away. His eyes feel gummed up.

'It's best to get up and get on with the day rather than just lie there. We've got to go down to breakfast anyway.'

Nick's exhorting voice brings only a moan from Gus. The word 'breakfast' conjures up nightmare images for him.

'I don't think I'll make it. You go.'

Nick throws up his arms. 'You know how proud Mrs Morgan is of her cooking! If someone refuses one of her breakfasts, I can't think what she'll do. She'll be up here investigating. She'll probably call the police, or ambulance, or undertaker.'

Gus groans again.

'Come on, Gus. You've got to make the effort. Still three-quarters of an hour before breakfast. Best get up now. You'll feel worse if you just lie there.' Nick leaps out of bed and flings Gus's bedclothes violently aside. Gus bravely responds and totters to his feet, looking vaguely around for clothes. He feels as if large stones have been impacted into his head. When he moves or bends down the stones shift about inside his brain. His skull feels so heavy, he wishes he could just lift it off his shoulders and set it down beside him to rest.

'No! Just the thought of breakfast makes me feel suicidal. I can't go down. Perhaps she won't notice I'm missing.'

'Oh, she'll notice all right. She's preparing four deadly concoctions at this very moment. When she sees your empty chair she'll do a Macbeth with Banquo's ghost. I'll always remember that speech!' Nick backs dramatically away from his bedside chair, his voice rising in horror and disbelief. '*Avaunt! And quit my sight! Let the earth hide thee! The time hath been, that, when the brains were out, the man would die, but now they rise again!*'

'Yes. Well my brains definitely feel as if they're out,' Gus says faintly, 'and I can feel something rising again.'

Nick bites his lips in earnest thought. 'Listen, I've got a plan. Right. Get your clothes on, sneak downstairs, go out while Mrs M's in the kitchen and take a walk along the beach. The fresh air will revive you. I'll tell her you've gone for a run before breakfast. If you don't come back in time, we'll say you must have decided to run further - you're in strict training for the athletics team - and we'll divide your breakfast between us. That way, nothing will be wasted. She'll be happy, Dermot will be pleased at the extra food - and you'll have escaped without Mrs M suspecting anything.'

Gus looks at Nick uncertainly, but Nick's voice is insistent.

'You've got no choice! If you try to eat breakfast you could throw it up all over Mrs M's best pink tablecloth. Think how disastrous that could be! If you stay in bed she's bound to come up…'

'Can't you say I've got some deadly infectious disease?' Gus pleads as he limply puts clothes on. Nick ignores him. 'She might carry the breakfast up with her and try to force-feed you...'

Gus thinks as best he can in the circumstances. It is the only plan. He nods and moves towards the bedroom door. It seems to swivel somehow before his eyes as he is about to touch it. Nick springs to his assistance and opens it quietly, then steals noiselessly onto the landing. 'Okay, all clear! Do it now. Don't think about it. Watch the stairs. Now wouldn't be a good time to fall down them.'

Gus creeps out. Nick is busy making hasty calculations and muttering the results to him. 'Fourth stair down creaks. And the seventh - I think - or would it be the eighth? Just tread them all carefully!'

Gus grips the banister for balance and reassurance. With great care, like someone enduring the medieval torture of walking on hot coals, he negotiates each stair. Nick looks down from above, giving a stern thumbs-up at each successful step, though his encouragement is lost on Gus, who peers down as well as he is able with the stones in his head rolling agonisingly back and fore with the motion.

Suddenly, there is a creak on one stair. It seems terrifyingly loud as it pierces through the fragile armour of his brain. Gus is not up to counting, so he is not certain if Nick's forecast was correct. He knows he is further advanced than the fourth, so Nick is wrong on that one. He hovers on the incriminating stair, wondering if he has the strength to turn and dash back up into his room. He looks up and sees Nick urging him silently but frantically on. Slowly and fearfully, like a sinner descending into Hell, he continues downwards.

At last he is on level ground. The next obstacle is the front door. He's doubtful if he can open it silently. Damn Nick! Why hadn't he foreseen that problem? But now he knows he has reached the point of no return. He must go on. He proceeds carefully towards the door. He puts his hand on it. It seems to lurch slightly before him. He puts his hand on the knob. Strangely, he hears the door opening before he begins to turn it. More strangely, the sound seems to be behind him. How disorientated he is! No, it is not this door. He hears footsteps from behind…

'Ah, Gus, what are you up to?' Mrs Morgan asks cheerfully. 'Just getting your breakfast ready. Fried eggs, sausages, bacon, fried bread today.' She waits expectantly for Gus's face to brighten at the mention of food.

Gus turns slowly to her. He realises he has to make a quick decision. But his brain is incapable of making even the slowest decision. Can he act the part of the keen, fit, early-morning athlete? Even if by some miracle of inspired theatricals he could accomplish this, he is not dressed for the role. Nick should have made certain he had his running shorts and vest on. Damn Nick again for sloppy thinking and the supreme confidence with which he persuaded him to go ahead with the plan. Should he own up and say he is not well? Will she guess the truth? The effort of thought involved in each self-directed question causes a stab of pain inside his head.

Mrs Morgan makes his decision for him. She inspects him closely. 'Oooh! You don't look at all well, Gus, bach. Quite pale! What you need is some food inside you. I can do you two fried eggs if you want…'

Like a rodeo rider on a wildly bucking bronco, Gus is fighting a fierce battle to gain control of his rebelling stomach. Somehow, he succeeds and manages to speak normally, though his voice rasps in a throat that feels like a parched cave.

'N-n-no, thanks, Mrs Morgan. I think I've got a slight tummy upset. I might have to skip breakfast today. Perhaps I can eat double tomorrow to make up for it.' He curses himself for his last improvised remark, the vision of which has launched his head and gut into more wild protests. He smiles a painful smile. 'I think I'll take a walk along the seafront. All I need is some fresh air.'

'Ah! First I'll give you something for that stomach.'

'No, honestly, Mrs Morgan - I'll be fine!'

'Oh, you youngsters are so obsolete!' As if performing a citizen's arrest, Mrs Morgan marches him through the kitchen door and he has no strength to resist. He stifles a heave at the odours of fermenting food that seem to hit him from all directions and tries not to look at any of it. She reaches into a cupboard and produces an alarmingly ancient-looking bottle of white powder, pouring some into a cup and topping it up with boiling water. She hands him the fizzing cup at mouth level, which suggests that she is poised to administer the dose if he doesn't do it himself. The sickly effervescent mixture dances up his nose causing more somersaults in his stomach and making him splutter. He presses the bouncing bubbles of liquid down into his throat, his eyes blinking with the effort. Her loud cackling laughter rips through him like a burst of machine-gun fire.

'There! That wasn't so bad, was it?'

Gus feels on the brink of complete metabolic breakdown, but the prospect of imminent escape gives him vital last forces of resistance.

'Thanks, Mrs Morgan. That should do the trick. I'll go for a walk and then I'll be fine.' Suddenly, miraculously, he finds enough energy to stride briskly to the front door. He opens it with ease and is outside. He rushes across the road onto the promenade and jumps with surprising agility the short distance down to the beach. The softness of sand under his feet seems somehow comforting. He nestles down under the shelter of the seawall and in a sudden climactic movement ejaculates Mrs Morgan's mixture, white like ectoplasm, onto the sand.

He sits there hunched up against the sea air. For some reason he becomes obsessed with looking at his right thumbnail. Perhaps it is an instinctive attempt to focus on some detail, in the way that meditators and mystics repeat a mantra. The acrid taste of the night before nests stubbornly in his mouth and cannot be shifted. His headache clings like the barbed grip of a fish-hook.

Gradually, Gus's stomach calms. The stones in his head slowly dissolve, leaving an unpleasant but manageable throbbing sensation. Fortunately it is a dry October day. The keening winds of winter have not yet arrived. The sea is misty blue and the breaking waves spattering the sand, and the mustard-coloured sun rising in the sky, help to heal his bewildered body and soothe his head.

How long has he sprawled here? He has no watch, but he thinks perhaps an hour. It must be nearing nine o'clock. He can go back to Gwylan House, have a wash and continue his recovery. Thankfully, it is Sunday, with no lectures.

As he is about to get up, he notices Simon in the distance by the bandstand. Simon jumps onto the sand and strides purposefully towards the water. At the sea's edge he squats on his haunches. He stares intently into the water, as if he has lost something in it. Slowly he lifts his gaze towards the horizon. He picks up a pebble and flings it into the sea.

Gus doesn't want to meet him, so he hauls himself up and dusts the sand off his clothes. The shock of standing causes his head to thump with renewed force. Perhaps he should sit down again - but no, to talk to Simon requires an effort of which he is not capable. Nick or Dermot would be no problem, but Simon is a difficult person.

As he clambers onto the promenade, the surprise of what he sees makes his eyes dilate and his mouth open in that involuntary, stupid way that causes the victim to curse himself afterwards for dropping his guard of calm unconcern. Peter Strutton is walking towards him, smiling and chuckling. Alongside him is Fiona, also looking delighted. Peter Strutton looks the more embarrassed of the two as he recognises Gus and nods a little awkwardly as Gus is getting up from his knees. Fiona gives a loud 'hello'. Gus gazes at their backs as they stroll together like any couple taking in the morning air.

Could the two have met by chance, on the seafront, so early in the day? There is something about the way they step out together. Has Peter Strutton stayed the night in Alex? Isn't that dangerous? Forbidden certainly for a male student. Surely even more so for a lecturer?

Should he tell people? Gus dislikes the idea of babbling about such a sighting. In any case, if he has seen them, so have others.

Monday, 23 June

N ine days after the body has been washed up, family and friends are assembled in the chapel of the funeral home. The room sinks in its own sea of grey and black. The mourners face the dark oblong of the coffin at the front. There are low whispers of talk, restrained nods of greeting between relatives who may rarely meet, as they wait. When the Reverend Leonard Daly walks in, the subdued murmur drops abruptly to a heavy silence.

The clergyman, middle-aged, bespectacled, with a chubby face and small, solemn eyes, begins, 'We are gathered here today…' His gentle, measured tones peal through the chapel in a smooth tenor.

In the middle of the front row, directly before the Reverend Daly, the mother and father sit perfectly still. Her hand is clasped in his. They look attentively up at him, yet with eyes that seem curiously unseeing, as if the object of their vision is not the priest in front of them, talking steadily and evenly, but something invisible, intangible, but more present.

'...God's will can sometimes seem difficult for us to comprehend. We always want to know the reason for an event, an event that may devastate and bewilder us, but sometimes we may not be meant to know that reason. We have to trust in His will, have faith in His purpose, even though we as mere mortals may not be able to understand that purpose...'

The man and woman whose hands are clasped together try to listen to what is being said, but the words penetrate their minds only in brief fragments.

'...A young person, with so much to look forward to...has been snatched from us in the prime of life...'

'...blessed with intelligence, ability...'

'...the tragic loss of a bright young talent, with a whole lifetime ahead...'

The rest of the Reverend Daly's address is obscured by other persistent voices from inside the parents' heads. There is a mute debate taking place within each, silently addressing, questioning, beseeching. Why no communication with us? Was it a reckless, spur-of-the-moment action, or contemplated, planned, over a long period of slowly engulfing despair? We are the mother and father ....

And the Reverend's words find their ears again, like seaspray in the wind.

'...Now is a time of great grief, of incomprehension. We have to endure the grief, the bafflement, and look beyond it, difficult though it is, impossible though it seems to us here today…'

'…Disappointments, especially when you're young, can seem devastating and world-shattering. It can be difficult to see beyond a temporary heartache, an ephemeral sadness or disillusion, to the fulfilment and success that talent, ability, a gifted mind, will undoubtedly bring…'

'…All lives are precious, but young lives are especially precious…'

'…We are stricken with a sense of loss, a sense of waste..'

The inward voices haunting the mother and father are never silent for long. *Why*?

And they ponder again. Was it some unspeakable torment, building up with slow, relentless pain, or a hideous accident?..

Thursday, 24 October

Eight months earlier. A month has passed since his arrival. The thought of home has receded far into Gus's consciousness, but it is still there treading water in the back corners of his mind. He is reminded of it once a week, when a letter arrives from his mother with news of doings in the house and village and entreaties to him to ensure he wears sufficient clothing to combat the coming mid-Wales winter, which she seems convinced will reach Arctic proportions. In his dutiful reply he writes about his lodgings and meals and how well Mrs Morgan takes care of them, though without mentioning the strange white powder that she compelled him to ingest, which mercifully has had no after-effects. Gus gives some description of the other boys, brief details of courses, the weather and the sea. A letter from his thirteen-year-old brother Raymond made him smile with an account of Raymond's exploits on the football field.

Nick mentioned that one of the girls from Alex, Glenys, was suffering from homesickness. Gus replied that he felt homecured. Nick agreed.

The sea air is primed with promise and desire, dream and expectation. Time stretches ahead like the ocean - inviting, restless, expansive, frightening, in its beauty and awesomeness. Gus turns from Marine Terrace onto Terrace Road, the straight narrow thoroughfare running the town's breadth to link the sea and railway station. It is abustle with morning shoppers. He hears a mix of English and the melodic cadences of Welsh. He has this strange, exhilarating sensation that the town has suddenly been invented just for him, but at the same time he is alive to its ancientness and feels proud to take his place among the generations of eager young people who have arrived here and doubtless felt the same thing. If heaven exists, he thinks, the feeling on reaching there must be similar to his sentiments now - a beautiful freshness, along with a sense that it has displayed this shining burnished brightness for all time. A breaking free of the bounds of ordinary life into a new realm, and even more miraculous that a small town of seemingly normal streets and normal people should excite this wonder. And at the same time, this edge of anxiety, of entering into the unknown, that tells him it is not heaven, but real life.

At Terrace Road he turns right, onto the broader sweep of North Parade and follows it uphill as it merges with Great Darkgate Street, whose Welsh name, Y Ffordd Fawr, Main Street, is more appropriate than the gloomy English version. It houses small busy shops, of fruit and vegetables, clothes, crafts, books, with a smattering of banks, opticians, chemists. At its crest he walks down into Pier Street with its cafes and gift shops, the sea framed at its far end. He passes the Cabin cafe and turns into Galloway and Morgan's bookshop.

The shop is a large, rambling treasure-store brimming with books on every subject. Upstairs is a dusty, musty hideaway of second-hand volumes in closely-packed shelves on grey whining floorboards.

But its drab silence disguises its glory. The shelves between which its readers and rummagers squeeze and linger become the walls of a miracle timeship, snatching up visitors and transporting them spinningly through centuries and continents, to the Wales of ancient bards and Dafydd ap Gwilym, the England of Chaucer, Shakespeare, Tennyson, the Scotland of Burns, the Greece of Socrates and Sophocles, the Russia of Peter the Great, the America of Whitman and Washington.

Gus, perched on a rickety chair, has been spirited back to England at the start of the nineteenth century. A young medical student is taking notes at a lecture at Guy's Hospital. He is short of paper so he scribbles in between the lines of previously-filled pages. He watches operations, pressing in among the crowd of students where the patient, before the days of anaesthetic, screams in agony. He cleans and bandages wounds and stumps of severed limbs. In the evening, in shabby lodgings, he begins to write poetry.

He has endured his own emotional amputations. His parents ran a stables hiring out horses, but his father died from a horse-fall on the cobblestones of north London when the boy was eight. His mother died when he was fourteen. He and his two younger brothers and sister were put in the care of an uncaring guardian. The young man gives up his job in medicine, travels in Britain, catches a cold through sitting on the open roof of a stagecoach rather than the warmer inside, to save money on fares. The cold becomes tuberculosis - the same incurable disease that had killed his eighteen-year-old brother, whom he'd nursed and watched die.

Gus is aware of someone moving towards him. He glances up and Amy is next to him, gazing down at his book.

'Are you studying him?' she asks pleasantly.

Gus has no time to be nervous. 'Keats? Not at the moment - but probably later in the term I expect. I was just reading about his life.'

'He died young, didn't he?'

'Yes - twenty-five.'

'All the good poets seem to do that - apart from Wordsworth - he just went on and on.' Her voice trails off drearily.

'I think it was all that walking in the Lake District - obviously the recipe for a long life.'

'In that case, Fiona should be all right - she's from up there.'

'Oh - Fiona. She seems quite, um…'

'Refined? I know what you mean. She's okay, actually. Quite amusing. Clever.'

Gus feels reassured. Her words suggest that Amy doesn't think of herself as having those qualities, if she admires them in others.

He hasn't mentioned to anyone his sighting of Fiona with one of the lecturers and wonders if rumours are flying around Alex. Should he say something now? No - he doesn't want Amy to think of him as a prattler of gossip. Perhaps the meeting between Peter Strutton and Fiona was pure coincidence anyway, in which case he'll look silly if he inflates it out of all proportion.

Gus fingers his book. 'The good thing about Keats - he has youthful energy and freshness and yet he also sounds older and wiser. Like that line, *A thing of beauty is a joy forever*. I can't remember when I first heard it - ages ago, before I knew anything about poetry - but I've always assumed it was written by somebody middle-aged and sort of - staid and boring. It's a shock to learn he wrote it when he was twenty-one and he wasn't a bit like that. He was a lively, witty guy. And what "thing" did he have in mind? He didn't have much access to things of beauty.'

She is looking at him curiously, in an interested way. She doesn't know what to say in reply. She presses her lips together, nods seriously. He wonders if he has bored or alienated her. He is aware of the gap in conversation. Should he say more, or wait for her to respond?

Amy looks around. 'Any idea where Jack Kerouac is?' Her voice is light and likeable. They both smile at the obvious answer, which Gus promptly supplies.

'Dead. Somewhere in America.'

Amy continues her smile. 'They said downstairs it was second bay, on the right.'

They search together. Gus learns that Amy is from Gloucester and is doing English, History and American Studies.

'So what made you come to Aber - apart from being Welsh?' she asks.

'I came here on a sixth-form course and really liked the place - and the sea. I've just read that, whatever room Keats entered, he would instinctively sit nearest the window to look out. Think of what he would have made of Aber - a sea view like the one I've got.'

'You're obsessed with John Keats! Are you a poet? Are you going to write brilliant verse gazing out to sea?'

'Um, I don't know about that. I write a few things but…'

'Mmm, that's interesting. You'll have to show me some time. Have you seen *Dragon*, the University literature magazine? I'm certain they'd be interested in new writers.'

Cursingly, Gus feels his face reddening. Should he carry on down this path? It might be a way of engaging her interest, impressing her. No, best to leave it for now.

'Oh yes…I don't think I'm ready for publication yet. I just scribble a few things…' He looks up at her. Her hair is velvet ebony and looks freshly washed. Her large puppy-like eyes gleam down at him, beckoning him into their blackness.

'You're in Alex aren't you?' he asks. 'We stayed there on the sixth-form course.'

Amy gasps in imitation shock. 'Ah, so you've slept in Alex! That's illegal, you know.' Then more seriously, 'Aber wasn't my first choice. I wanted to go to Bristol but I couldn't get in. But it's okay so far. The sea's nice when you step out first thing in the morning. My room is at the back, though, so I can't see it. Fiona's room is in front. She says she's going to complain to the council about the noise it makes at night. Well, I can't find Jack Kerouac.' She looks around and purses her lips in an irritated, childlike way. 'I'll have to buy a new one.'

He has to do it, but there is no time to go back to his lodgings before the lecture on *Hamlet* at three o'clock. The toilets in the Old College will have to serve. Happily, there is no-one else in there. He goes into the furthest cubicle.

Anyone know any virgins? The question stands out in a slanting scribble on the wall. Underneath someone has responded with another question. *In Aber?* Below this a third hand exclaims, *Too bloody many!*

He leans against the wall and pulls his trousers down. He massages quickly, conscious of time elapsing, though he doesn't think anyone noticed his entrance. He fixes Amy in his mind, the profile of her body, her light gracefulness as she walks. His desire homes in on her face, so full of poetry and sensitivity, her shy sideways smile. That dreamy, heavenly face. Now she is naked, still smiling, her body pressed to his. Now he is clasping her, crushing her against him, her thighs firm against his.

Then it gushes out. He squeezes, squeezes, squeezes in an ecstasy of wresting and release, gripping and relaxing. His head stretches back against the cubicle wall with the effort and the relief. His eyes look up to the ceiling, as if in thankful prayer for the pleasure.

They are met by another pair of eyes, staring down at him from above the white tiled wall of the next cubicle. The eyes are wide, fixed in an unblinking gaze of calm, riveted concentration. They hold his own for what seems like forever, though it must be only a few seconds. Then they slither down behind the partition.

Gus is impaled against the cold hard wall as if held tight there by a spear piercing through his chest. He hears a soft thud as someone steps down onto the ground. There is a click of the next door's bolt followed by a rapid footfall across the floor.

It all happened so quickly, yet so slowly. The eyes held his for so long in the few seconds that they met. Gus did not see, but he can somehow imagine too vividly, a mouth beneath the eyes, a drooling mouth, lips being licked in gratification.

When did the watcher come in? He must have crept across the floor at some point. Gus had heard nothing, lost in his rapture. How long had the eyes been silently watching? Incredible to think they had been only a few feet above him, viewing every manipulation of his hand, looking down on every twitch of his mouth, every ecstasy on his face, to the blissful and tumultuous climax.

And the worst thing is, Gus thinks he knows who owns the eyes.

Friday, 25 October

Gus prepares himself for the ordeal that will be breakfast. He lies in bed thinking. Is there any way he can avoid it? He could say he's ill, but, as might have happened before, Mrs Morgan will want to know all the details if he doesn't appear. And he'll also have to feign illness to Nick, who at present lies snuggled in his bed across the room. If he doesn't pretend, then Nick will want to know why a perfectly healthy Gus doesn't want breakfast.

Sooner or later Gus will have to face this person. He has seen Gus exposed, physically and mentally; has gazed down on his secret shame. That look of rapt interest, as if the voyeur - is that the word? -was absorbed in a book. The engrossed eyes did not look horrified or shocked. There was an expression of cool intensity about them. How many times has he done it before? Does he spend his time climbing silently onto toilet seats to watch below?

Then, of course - it strikes him. The voyeur will be just as embarrassed as he is. He won't be certain if Gus had positively identified him or not. He'll be wondering - did Gus realise it was me? He could be in the same agony of shame and uncertainty.

But - was it who Gus thinks it was? The eyes revealed themselves for - how long? A second and a half? Two or three seconds? The eyes and the top of the head. And Gus, preoccupied with his own frenzied bliss, had only a brief worm's eye view. Could he confidently pick him out in an identity parade? He's not absolutely certain. He still can't believe it happened. He goes over those seconds in his mind. It seemed such a long time, the eyes hanging rigid there, he sprawled against the wall in suspended activity as if frozen. Then the eyes sliding quietly away.

So, two people will face each other across breakfast, both in a silent turmoil of infamy and disgrace. The rational thing would be for Gus to have a private word. After all, he has the lesser cause to be ashamed. He has never discussed the activity with anyone - it is something boys would not talk about, at least not seriously. He has never learned of anyone he knows indulging in it, but he read in a guide that it's 'almost universal' in adolescence. He liked the word 'universal' and wondered if beings from distant planets have also discovered its joys. Still, he finds it hard to picture anyone he knows doing it. Nick, for instance, he can never imagine. Dermot seems too intellectual to surrender himself to the pleasures of the flesh, with anyone or on his own. Simon, yes, definitely. Geraint - mmm, maybe.

Gus and Nick go down. The other two have not yet appeared.

'What's holding that boy up?' Nick says.

'Dermot? Probably frozen to death in his room,' Gus suggests.

Mr Morgan shambles in, bearing the large teapot.

'Not such a good day out there today, boys,' he says, nodding ominously towards the sea. 'Ah, it'll be winter soon!' A faint shudder seems to convulse his body, in anticipation of the event. 'And Mr Williams from two doors up left us all yesterday.' Mr Morgan sighs in sad resignation. 'Ah well. They do say he's gone to a better place.'

Nick turns to him in concern. 'What - dead?'

'No - Shrewsbury,' continues Mr Morgan in the same lugubrious tone. 'Got a daughter there, he has. Never been there myself - only passed through, but they do say it's a pleasant town.' He makes his way back out, as Nick flickers a silent laugh at Gus and Dermot appears in the doorway.

Dermot looks as if he has just tumbled out of bed. His yellow hair faces several directions at once. His eyes are crusted slits. He feels rather than sees his way to his place at the table.

'What a sight,' says Nick.

'A peculiarity of the English language,' yawns Dermot as he flops into his chair. '*Sight* and *vision* mean the same thing, right? But think of the difference in meaning between *what a sight* and *what a vision*.'

'I don't start thinking for another half hour,' Nick answers. 'Where's our fourth musketeer?'

'Anyone seen Simon this morning?' Mrs Morgan asks as she sweeps in with large plates of breakfast. There is a collective vague shaking of heads. 'Simon!' she hollers up the stairs, her voice building through the two syllables into a high-pitched alarm-like crescendo that would unnerve a gladiator and causes a suddenly-wakened Dermot almost to leap out of his chair. In the absence of an immediate response she can be heard stomping up the stairs and giving a cheerfully rhythmic knock on Simon's door. The boys just catch a feeble nasal reply.

Simon appears. Gus steals a glance at him, but Simon is not returning it. He gives a general sheepish grin as greeting.

Gus can't be certain. Rather than trying to compare Simon's eyes and brow with what he remembers, he is looking for evidence in Simon's expression and behaviour. Simon is not looking at him, or anyone, but then he never does. He hunches down over his bowl of cornflakes, spooning them in as if there is no other human within a thousand miles. His eyes are pale grey and his mouth wide and thin-lipped, his skin as soft and clear as a girl's.

Gus concludes that Simon, if it was him, is as anxious to avoid any communication about the matter as he is. In any case, unless he is certain, what could he say? 'Were you in the toilet at three o'clock yesterday afternoon?' Simon, he thinks, would be as happy as he is to make a silent agreement to pretend it never happened.

Monday, 28 October

He lies in bed in the shadowed darkness of early morning, the heckling of seagulls weaving in and out of his thoughts. He must try to make certain he is never first down for breakfast, in case Simon is second and they have to face each other alone. The one encouraging thing Gus feels certain of is that Simon will not tell anyone else what he saw. He is uncommunicative and in any case he can't disclose anything without admitting he witnessed it. But just the fact that Simon - if it was him - knows, is a humiliation. The disgrace, to be caught doing it, in the University. For someone else to know what he does. For someone else to see the beautiful, shameful pleasure on his face.

He tries to think how he can approach Simon. He cannot, because he can never be certain that it was Simon who saw him. And it is not the sort of conversation topic one can bring up indirectly. Hold on. Could he maybe follow Simon to see if he does the same thing again? No. He's not a private detective. Simon may notice he's being trailed. In any case Gus does not have the time. Simon may only do it occasionally and Gus could spend endless fruitless hours stalking him. What an absurd idea!

Should he tell someone? "Report" Simon? But he can't do that without revealing his own shame. Could he just say he was in the toilet, doing normal things? No. And Gus isn't certain it was him. Simon could just deny it.

Nick stirs in his bed, turns over, gives a heavy contented sigh. Yes, Nick, he is certain, would never have such problems to worry about. For some reason, Peter Strutton also strays into his musing. Gus is awed by the man's mind, his razor-sharp reading and insights into poetry, the evident pleasure he takes in teaching and explaining, the enviable life he leads which must be both satisfying and stimulating at the same time. To have proceeded through the trials of adolescence and studenthood, to be established permanently in this beautiful place of sea and sky and learning...

And for some reason he has a sneaking sympathy with Simon. He feels a bond with him. Perhaps it is his own sense of guilt. They are both doing ugly, forbidden things and enjoying them.

Hold on again. Why should he worry? If it wasn't Simon, he has nothing to be concerned about. If it was Simon, he will be just as humiliated and ashamed as Gus, if not more so.

Yes, he must think positive. Think it wasn't Simon.

But then - if it wasn't him, who was it? Could it be anyone else he knows? Aber is not a big place. There are no holidaymakers here now. Who ever saw him is almost certainly still around. He must be in the University regularly. He probably sees Gus on a daily basis.

Perhaps he's the type to tell others.

Gus is almost beginning to wish it was Simon.

Best, somehow, by some supreme effort, to pretend it never happened.

But every time he sees Simon now...

Tuesday, 29 October

Peter Strutton wonders once more about himself. He has done it again, almost before he realised it. He should have checked himself, thought for a moment. His mind goes back to the time, a fortnight ago. He had walked, late on the Saturday night, along the prom to "kick the bar." He'd told himself it was an innocent stroll, but in his mind must have been the thought of hovering outside Alex, looking up at its lighted windows, perhaps bumping into some students on their way back, not to talk with them, but just to gain a pleasant feeling from observing them, tasting the atmosphere of a group of young people together in comradeship. He had a scarf he could pull up around his face if he didn't want to be recognised.

He'd kicked the bar, turned and begun his walk back. Four or five girls were coming towards him, chatting and laughing. He hadn't bothered with the scarf, but had nodded to them, and then recognised some from his first-year classes - Tessa, Glenys, Fiona. They'd started talking. One, Fiona, spoke naturally, unselfconsciously. The general exchange was developing into a conversation between the two of them. Fiona had nodded to the others, 'you go on,' and they had turned obediently away. Fiona and Peter continued chatting for a while. Fiona was beginning to get cold, champing from foot to foot. 'Want to come back for coffee?' she'd asked.

And then it had happened. He should never have gone back. Did he really think he could just go in for a coffee? The feeling of pleasured anticipation, with that edge of danger, had enraptured, ensnared him again.

He should not continue with it. He should find someone his own age. But she seems mature. He feels he can be of help to her, not so much academically (he will have to be careful there), but in her development, her growth into a woman. And he loves to see a young person's eyes expand with awe as he shows them a poem or tells them a fascinating fact about a poet. They will remember, probably for the rest of their lives, the first time they came across that poem, just as he remembers the wonderful surprise of encountering Dylan Thomas's *Fern Hill* or Keats's *To Autumn* for the first time - the joy of the words and the satisfaction of the tutor's comments and explanation. Of course this can happen in seminars, but to do it on a personal level - in a pub, in a stroll along the seafront, in someone's small student room - is doubly rewarding.

And she can help him, keep his mind alive to the wonder and beauty of youth, while he is still sufficiently young to be accepted as one of them. He simply likes to meet with students, of both sexes. He dreads the prospect of declining into the position of people like Savage or Parker-Hurst, who deliver cold impersonal lectures. He sometimes shudders at the thought of at what point in life he will be forced to surrender the easy contact he has with students.

He mustn't become obsessed with her. He must take care to resist requests to help her with work. But she does not seem predatory. She is clever, intelligent, articulate and, he thinks, will do well without assistance from him. Already they talk about literature on an even basis. She makes shrewd, insightful comments with assurance.

Yet - he is twenty-nine, ten years the elder. A postgraduate, or a third-year student, might be acceptable, but a first-year, barely a month into the course...

As far as he is aware, the other lecturers have not suspected. His fear as always is that she might boast to other students. And of course they always seem to get wind of such things. One of his male students saw them the morning after that first encounter. How stupid of him to walk openly along the prom with her.

An awkward time will be seminars. Prof Savage decides on the groupings. If he says to the Professor that he doesn't want a particular student in his group, that will draw immediate attention. He will have to be careful not to look at her, not to speak to her in a special way. He will probably have to endure smirks and smiles from others in the class. But he thinks he can do it.

Wednesday, 30 October

The lecture-hall is a large, high-ceilinged rectangle, with light flooding in from the long far side that commands a view of the sea. The end row seats on this side are always the first to be taken, and generations of students have spent the whole of a lecture gazing dreamily out to sky and water. But Gus feels a pang of pleasure as he spots a vacant place at the end of a nearside row, because next to it sits Amy. She looks up with a restrained, wordless smile, but one that is more inviting, and sets his heart galloping more, than any voiced greeting. His eyes take in her fragile waist and neat breasts beneath the black glow of her hair. She is wearing a polo-neck sweater of bright light blue like the sky, with sleeves pushed up, unveiling smooth, trimly-contoured forearms. Her quiet response as he sits beside her seems to draw him into her, with invisible threads of energy, that a *hi* or *hello* might destroy. Thankfully, the lecture is about to begin, so he doesn't have to say anything to her.

Dr Parker-Hurst's voluminous black gown drowns his lankily meagre frame. Grey-faced and ancient-looking, he resembles an elongated, emaciated bat about to swoop, or rather, topple, on to the front row of students, who strain their necks to look up to his face or huddle over to scribble frantic notes that they will later pore over in a largely futile attempt to decipher or comprehend. He talks mainly from memory, glancing at his notes occasionally almost as an afterthought. He speaks in a sad, world-weary tone reinforcing the suspicion that he has delivered the same lecture word-for-word for several years if not decades. On the rare occasions that he looks down at his notes, his thick black spectacles, balanced precariously on the tip of his beak-like nose, sometimes plummet from it, and he catches them with sudden agility of movement, gazes at them in surprise as if not realising they've fallen from his own head, replaces them, and carries on.

'…Samuel Taylor Coleridge was, mercifully, not as prolific a poet as his friend Wordsworth. Wordsworth left a sonnet at every place he visited, just as a dog cocks its leg up on every tree it passes. He composed one at Devil's Bridge.'

He pauses, to add drama and to give students the opportunity to conjure up in their minds Devil's Bridge, a nearby waterfall and tourist spot. Then, in a flat expressionless voice, as if reading out statistics of potato production, he recites:

> *How art thou named? In search of what strange land,*
> *From what huge height, descending? Can such force*
> *Of waters issue from a British source…?*

There are titters from the students, and a hint of a smile on Dr Parker-Hurst's harrowed face.

All through the lecture Gus is aware of Amy's presence beside him, of an exhilaration inside, that still-new and pounding sensation that takes over body and mind, like some sublime emotional massage, channelled into his being among the dull rows of heads-down scribbling students. Amy seems absorbed in her note-taking. He wants to breathe in deeply to still his frantic heart, that hammers so fast he feels it will race clean out of his body. He thinks of the tingling moment when the hour will be up and of what he will say to her.

At the end of the lecture she continues writing for a few moments, then turns to him, contorts her face slightly and mumbles, 'Mmm, a bit boring.' They get up to leave. Gus is walking beside her, an embrace away. The sense of her next to him is overwhelming. He is about to ask her if she's going for coffee, but before he has chance she looks at her watch.

'I've got another lecture now - American Studies.'

Gus feels his heart sink at a missed opportunity. All he can do is mutter, 'oh, right,' smile weakly and nod.

'Probably see you this afternoon at the Shakespeare lecture.' She moves away. But...he is certain her eyes catch his for an instant and express something to him. He watches her neat walk, file and book cradled in her arms.

'Nice girl. Go for it. Don't hang around or she'll be snapped up by somebody else.' There is that mischievous, mirthful sparkle in Nick's eyes. Gus hasn't been aware of his approach.

'So - studying literature - do you think it makes you a better person?' asks Dermot as the boys stroll up Pier Street.

Nick tries to sound more assured than he really is. 'Yeh, happier, more fulfilled, more in control.'

Dermot turns on him. 'Then why is it that writers are very unhappy, disturbed, fail in relationships, commit suicide?'

Geraint throws back his long hair. 'Yes - but it's a better quality unhappiness than most people have.'

'Reading literature is a civilising influence,' puts in Gus.

Dermot swings round to face him, striding clumsily backwards up the street. 'You should've come to the Classical Music Society last night. Mahler's Fifth Symphony. Amazing! Yes, literature might be civilising, but music is a superior art form. Words analyse, music expresses. Music probes deeper than words. It gets underneath and beyond language to faithfully reproduce the sharp, pure emotion that words only describe. "Words are the ashes of experience." That's what Kafka said.' Dermot spins decisively round to face forwards again

'Hang on,' Nick yells. 'You just said words describe. Before that you said they only analyse.'

The last thing Gus wants is an intellectual discussion, but neither does he want to be intimidated. He thinks for a moment, then surprises himself with his reply.

'Literature is the most difficult to appreciate. All the other arts make an immediate appeal to the senses. You can hear music. You can see painting, sculpture, photography. You can watch films, plays and dance. But literature appeals to our sixth sense, the imagination, which means it has to work harder to communicate.'

Dermot nods sagely. Nick claps his hands. 'Woohey, Gus! What an answer! That's bloody silenced him!'

'A very valid point,' Dermot responds. 'We shall think further on't.'

In the afternoon, from the library, Gus looks out to sea. A placid, sunlit day. High-arched dreaming skies stretch westward. Far distant peaks of ghostly blue melt into the heavens. Waves tilt upwards and topple down in a spreading softness like cream upon the pebbles.

That mute, momentary but unmistakable appeal of her eyes to his.

Monday, 4 November

'Hey, Gus, you ever thought about the guy who first invented shaving?' asks Nick as he examines his face in the mirror of their room. 'It must've taken a bit of courage. After all, it made the men look like women.'

Nick puffs out his right cheek to inspect a spot critically. 'It was a lessening of the sex difference. It must've met with fierce opposition. They would have called him a pansy. He must have been ridiculed by the men and women of the tribe. Then a few women would have said, "Yeh, I prefer him without the beard."'

Nick stands back for an overall view of his face, like an artist appraising his canvas. 'You know, I remember reading about the first white men to visit Australia. The natives had never seen a man without a beard before. One of the white guys had to pull down his trousers to prove his manhood.'

Gus, stretched on his bed, looks up from his reading. 'From what I've heard, they do that every Saturday night in the Unicorn.'

Nick leans his head to one side and fondles his face with satisfaction.

'Now then, a dab of aftershave for the ladies and I'll be ready!'

'We're only going to a lecture, Nick,' Gus points out.

'Yes, but I don't know who I'll be sitting next to. With any luck, it'll be Lorna.' He gives his face a final affectionate pat.

'It could be Fiona. She might get a whiff and think you're sending out signals to her.'

A look of distaste comes across Nick's shining face. 'How could she possibly think that *I* fancy *her*? Anyway, from what I've heard, she's got her eye on someone else. One of the lecturers, no less.' Nick gives Gus a knowing look. He is waiting for Gus to quiz him, proud to show off his knowledge.

Gus returns Nick's look. 'Could it be - Peter Strutton?'

'The blond beauty,' says Nick. 'He certainly doesn't waste much time. But no, there's only one woman for me - I'm a one-woman man - and that's the lovely Lorna.' He thrusts his chin almost into the mirror and slowly rubs it.

'She smokes too much.'

'Oh, I don't mind that. I find it quite sexy. I imagine I'm that cigarette, being sucked by those exquisite lips. Did you do *Romeo and Juliet* in school? Remember Romeo saying, *Oh that*

I were a glove upon that hand, that I might kiss that cheek, or something like that?'

'Yes, but he didn't say, "Oh that I were a cigarette upon her lips." Doesn't sound quite so romantic.'

Nick is still studying his face in the mirror. 'I reckon we should all grow beards before the end of term. Whadda you think?'

Gus ponders. 'Mmm, somehow I can't imagine Simon with a beard. And Dermot would just look odd.'

'Oh, I can see Dermot with an arty little growth on his chin - but Simon - I don't know what to make of him. Came across a nice phrase in Shakespeare - *'Tis certain that his urine freezes.* Could apply to Simon.'

Gus thinks back. It is about a fortnight now. He has faced Simon across the table for breakfast, for evening meals - though never, so far, with no-one else present. Gus hopes the pain, like a bruise, will slowly fade with the passing of time. He guesses Simon feels the same. Still, he cannot help wondering about Simon. How often does he do that - if it was him? What's going on in his mind? At least Simon does not seem to have followed up his brief remark about Amy on the beach...

The lecture hall is already quite full when Gus and Nick arrive. Gus notices a group from Alex, including Amy, Fiona and Lorna, sitting together. He is disappointed that Amy doesn't seem to be looking out for him. She's waiting calmly, pen poised. No chance to sit near her. The seats around her are all occupied. Dr Erica Timms, a tall gangly Liverpudlian in her mid-thirties, strides in to begin the lecture.

The Cabin is a café of dark green walls with moody black-and-white photographs of Monroe, Bogart, Dean, Brando, McQueen. It is redolent of earnest or frivolous conversations on literature and politics, music and romance. At mid-morning students spill out of the College and wander up Pier Street into its pleasingly dim interior. The girls are already there. As the boys join them, Amy mouths a silent *hello* to Gus that seems intimate and exclusive to him, as if she is acknowledging a secret pact between them, and this instantly revives his spirits and hopes. Nick manoeuvres himself into a seat opposite Lorna.

The Cupid's bow of Lorna's lips purses and she leans her head indolently on her hand, her blond hair swirling to one side. '...You don't really, do you?' Her eyes widen in disbelief. 'This guy eats breakfast the night before to save time in the mornings.' Her loud voice pleases and alarms Nick.

'Yeh, only sometimes,' he says, casting a glance at Gus, who will know the truth, 'but I often find myself eating a second breakfast in the morning anyway, 'cos I feel hungry.'

'Doesn't that somewhat defeat the object?' Fiona asks.

'Well, I suppose to some extent. But if the object is to be happy and fulfilled, then I'm doing that.'

'He's a growing boy,' says Lorna, looking at him with cool blue eyes, suddenly motherly.

Fiona wears a white T-shirt, large hooped earrings like bracelets and a big socialising smile. Her T-shirt has several pictures on it - a pair of bees, an oar, a piece of knotted rope, followed by two more bees. She catches Nick looking at it.

'Can't you work it out?' she asks. 'Think of Shakespeare. *Hamlet.*' She gives a lop-sided smile resembling a lazy leer, that Nick finds unattractive. She points to her right breast, raising her eyebrows provocatively. 'Two bee -.' The rest of the group join in. 'Oar - knot -TWO BEE.'

Gus notices Amy's thin, elegantly-boned hands. That slight, celestial smile. Lorna stretches and flourishes her long brown fleshy legs and suddenly turns to Gus.

'I never expected you to have a Welsh accent.'

'Oh? Why not?'

'Your face doesn't look Welsh.'

'How does a Welsh face look?'

'Well - different from an English one.'

Dermot erupts. 'Don't be stupid! If Gus was Japanese, he'd look different. But Welsh and English are the same race.'

This draws an indignant response from Geraint. 'No they're not. The Welsh are Celts. They were in Britain long before the English came. They're the original British.'

'I'm not really Welsh anyway,' Gus says. 'I'm English Welsh.'

'English Welsh,' laughs Nick. 'That's a contradiction if ever I heard one.'

'Do you know the Welsh for *atomic bomb*?' Fiona asks noisily…'It's *bom atomig*.' She looks around for a response.

'I think it's good that a language doesn't have its own phrase for atomic bomb,' says Amy.

'Yeh, but Welsh borrows so many words from English, people must think it's English pronounced in a funny way,' Nick puts in.

'Ha!' laughs Geraint. 'Look how many words English borrows - from everywhere!'

'English is just French pronounced as if it's German, anyway,' declares Dermot. 'I studied German once - for about five minutes. I decided to give it up when I found there are three ways of saying *the* and only one is correct at any one time. How can you learn a language when your chances of getting *the* wrong are sixty-six percent? At least with French it's fifty percent. I'm surprised German kids don't do what everyone else does - give German up after a year and do Media Studies.'

'All languages are quite stupid and illogical anyway,' Fiona says. 'Like English. *Adore* and *abhor* couldn't be further apart in meaning, yet they sound virtually the same.'

Dermot flings back his rebellious hair. 'Broad daylight. Can you have narrow daylight?'

Nick watches Lorna smoking her cigarette, which she does in a magical, mystical way, drawing the smoke voluptuously in, as if she is being made love to, and then letting it slide out through her soft nostrils.

'How long have you been smoking?' Nick feels he has to say something, to explain his riveted gaze on her.

'Only since last summer. There were four of us sharing a caravan. At the start of the week only one girl smoked. Honestly, by the end of the week we were all doing it.' The smoke glides out again.

Gus, who has never tried smoking, wonders what devilish attraction there is about it that makes it spread so quickly, like an infectious disease, but one which its victims embrace voluntarily.

The girls get up to leave. Nick notices again the way Lorna takes her large springy steps, prancing like a delighted child. As she walks she seems to sway her entire body from her shoulders, through her torso and buttocks and legs.

As the girls walk back to the library, they exchange opinions of the boys.

'Dermot's weird.'

'He switches from one subject to another like a monkey swinging from tree to tree.'

'He's like a walking encyclopaedia.'

'With a few entries missing.'

'He comes out with some strange things. He suddenly said to me, *life is a mere dream that fades*. Apparently Napoleon said it.'

'He's a chameleon.'

'More like a comedian,' says Fiona, 'though I do like the way he takes his glasses off.'

'Nick's geography's not very good - he thinks Ben Nevis is a Scottish rugby player.'

'He only said that as a joke.'

'No - I think he was serious.'

The boys linger for a while in the Cabin. 'I reckon Nick is lovesick,' says Geraint. 'He looks forlorn - or should I say "for-lorna". She's not my cup of tea.'

'What don't you like about her?' Nick asks.

'Her lips are too thick and her mouth is floppy.'

'A damning appraisal,' says Dermot. 'How about Amy?'

Nick shakes his head in disapproval. 'I don't go much for the strong silent type. I prefer weak noisy people - you know where you are with them.'

Gus turns to Nick. 'I wouldn't say Lorna is weak. Definitely not the type to argue with.' He thinks of Amy. A shy half-smile. A pristine moment that caught his eye. A slim, sedate walk.

'I wonder why smoking is considered attractive in people,' Geraint ponders.

'Smoking and sex are very similar,' answers Dermot. 'Both are considered forbidden and dangerous and emblems of adulthood.'

'Ugh! It's disgusting,' says Geraint, 'breathing in smoke. Why do people do it? It's not logical. I mean, if a building's on fire, you get out. You don't stop to breathe in, thinking, wah, that smoke - it's great! How anyone can enjoy slurping up a thick fog of fumes like that I'll never know.'

'Have you tried it?'

'Yeh, but I think I must've been doing something wrong, like putting the wrong end in my mouth - I couldn't get any pleasure. It's like when I tried to play the harmonica - everyone said it was easy, but I couldn't do it.'

'It can't be different from - vodka, though,' Nick says with a grin, looking at Gus.

Gus smiles. 'Vodka's more dangerous, if it makes you want to swim across to Ireland.'

Tuesday, 12 November

Gus waits outside the cinema, watching his damp breath melt coldly into the evening air. Around him students mill in chattering groups or quieter pairs. Inside him is a blending of excitement and trepidation, each giving the other a sharper edge. He resists the temptation to shift from foot to foot, but wants to look calm and assured, even-keeled, for when she appears.

At last he sees her, at the junction of Bath Street and Queens Road. As she comes up to him Gus feels like exclaiming, *you made it!* but he doesn't want to betray his anxiety so he says 'hi!' as he smiles. The lack of the usual mechanical opening chat between them, as if they've known each other for a long time and don't feel the need of it, further eases him. All Amy does is tighten her shoulders, draw her arms about her and say quickly, 'Let's go in - it's cold!' She smiles, not directly to him, but to the world in general, it seems.

In the cinema they sit close to each other. He feels the warmth of her shoulder against his. She watches the film attentively. Now he can hold off no longer. He must slip his hand into hers. Her palm is soft and neat. Her lips stretch without opening into a brief, pleased smile, half to him, half to her front. She tilts her head towards him and her eyes meet his for a beautiful second.

Afterwards he asks her if she wants to go for a drink, but she says she prefers to go back to her room in Alex, as it's midweek. As they stroll along the prom they chat sparsely but easily about their courses, the lecturers, other students. At the entrance to Alex she turns from his side to face him. She has dark, strong eyes - unexpected in such a light and tender face - that seem to hold you forever in the brief moment that she looks at you.

She does not ask him in, but her face brightens towards him, her smile colouring her lips and eyes.

'I've enjoyed tonight.'

'Yes, same with me. We'll do it again?'

She nods with quiet enthusiasm. 'That'd be good. Well - see you tomorrow, I expect.' Her smile is meeker now.

They bid goodbye to each other and he watches her light movements as she flits like a bird up the stairs. That intoxicating sense of being away from home, free of the gravitational pull of the mother planet, in strange and exciting new worlds, watching a girl's soft tread up a stairway.

As he walks back to Gwylan House, powdery rain drifts lazily in from the sea along the prom. A fine mist of spray lingers in the air. Into his ears steals the sound of the incoming sea, swishing gently and relentlessly on the shingle. As he goes up to his room, he hears voices from inside it. Nick is speaking.

'Would you believe it? Some people our age are *married*, with *kids*? Can you imagine what that would be like?'

Gus recognises Dermot's voice. 'When you marry, you lose your identity. You're no longer an individual. It's no coincidence that the words "merge" and "marriage" sound so similar. Two people merge into one. Of course, some people are terrified of being individual, of being alone.'

Nick again. 'But if you really love someone, the thought of being with them for the rest of your life should seem like paradise.'

'No, it's totally unnatural to stick with someone for ever - romantic but unnatural. It's the idea of marrying for life, being with the same person permanently, that's so scary.'

'Swans do it. They mate for life.'

'Yeh, but all swans look the same anyway. Seen one swan and you've seen them all. There'd be no point in swapping one for another.'

'They can't be identical, otherwise swans would change partners without realising. They must have some way of picking their mate out from all the others.'

Gus can see the light on in Simon's room. He wonders if he should knock to say hello, but he is fearful of showing any interest in him. He knows he will face a barrage of questions from the two philosophers in his room.

'Ah! Here's lover boy!' Nick's warm-natured smile takes any mocking contempt out of his greeting. 'How did you get on? Good film?'

Gus tries to hold back a smirk that he knows will appear half-smug, half-embarrassed. 'Yes, fine. Interesting film.'

'And?'

'She's a nice girl. Yes, I like her.'

'And? Did you get into Alex?'

'No - she's got work to do for tomorrow.' Gus hints at disappointment, but feels more relief.

'Ah well, a lot of girls have this first-date embargo anyway. And I guess Amy's that sort of girl.'

'So when did you ask her out?' Gus detects a pleasing note of envy in Dermot's question.

In fact, it was Amy who'd asked Gus out. They were coming out of a seminar on Yeats yesterday, had fallen easily into a calm stride alongside each other, chatting about some of the poems they'd been discussing and their evocative titles - *The Lake Isle of Innisfree, The Lover Tells of the Rose in his Heart, He Wishes for the Cloths of Heaven*. 'Are you doing anything tomorrow night?' she had asked, almost as the tailpiece to a sentence.

'No, not particularly.'

'Well there's a film on at Bath Street cinema I wouldn't mind seeing.' She'd named the film but he hadn't heard of it and had forgotten its title almost at once.

'Like to come with me?' Her eyes had looked straight into his for a second. Too surprised to feel the immediate impact, he'd replied without fuss or wavering. 'Yes, sounds good.'

'Great. I've got a History seminar now. See you - outside the cinema - about seven-thirty tomorrow?'

She had marched off, smiling as she did. Gus noticed, he thought, a little more breeziness in her walk.

'Oh, a few days ago,' he says casually in reply to Dermot's question.

'This one's a dark horse,' Nick adds, but Gus senses that Nick feels happiness for him.

That night in bed, Gus thinks about Amy, re-runs in his mind, with pleasure and wonder, the sequence of her asking and moments in the cinema. The softened roar of the sea draws in and out, like the breathing of an all-present being, soothing itself into him. He hears in his mind the soft inflexions of her voice. He thinks of her smile - the sort of smile that conveys the news that all the troubles of the world have evaporated, every last person's burden has been lifted, and the whole planet is in celebration. Yet it is a restrained smile, not wide but modest, a smile that bares not teeth but a gentle spirit, that reaches quietly out to meet you. He remembers Byron's words from *She Walks In Beauty* :

> *A mind at peace with all below,*
> *A heart whose love is innocent.*

Wednesday, 13 November

E ight-fifteen in the evening. Nick and Gus have gone to an English Society meeting. Simon sits in his room. Nick had asked him to come with them, but he prefers the solitude of his own four walls where he'll try to finish an essay. He'd heard Dermot say he was going to a talk on 'The Cold War and the Conservative Party' at the Politics Society.

In the silence the ticking of Simon's alarm clock assumes a deafening loudness that begins to beat against his brain unstoppably, paralysing him against action and thought until all he can do is sit and listen to the tortuous tick-tock.

He cannot prevent himself from looking at the clock's face, cannot avoid following the red second hand as it thumps its way around the circle. His eyes are fixed immovably on it, like a man hypnotised by a rearing cobra before it finally darts forward. He sits straitened like this for long periods until time has lost its meaning.

Gus is going out with Amy. He's heard him talking to Nick. He saw them together, side-by-side, in Pier Street, just the two of them, and they both had that fulfilled, together kind of look on their faces. He thought when he first arrived that Gus was quiet and uncomfortable like himself, but now Gus is confident, gliding untroubled through the bleak far-from-home days.

This terrible shyness with girls he likes. He is unable to do anything about it. It's like a speech impediment. He is fine with people he's not attracted to. He can laugh and chat, make witty observations, just as the other boys do. But anyone he likes - he is totally disabled. He just can't pull himself together. He cannot see what is in him that anyone could like.

Girls hover in his mind. Annaliese is there for much of the time, though he has not seen her for eight weeks. Ann-a-lies-e. He whispers its syllables. Such a beautiful name. She was perfect for him. She is only a hundred miles away but is unreachable. When she comes back home at Christmas, how will she be? How will he be when he's with her? Flashes of Amy, too, settle into his consciousness, in a quiet, unperturbing way, but he can rouse himself smoothly when he thinks of her. And then there is Lorna, so achingly beautiful, who must be everyone's dream.

He chooses Lorna. He's had Annaliese for the past two days. Feminine sighs, soft exhalations of pleasure, low breathings of matchless bliss - he hears them all in the haze of his fantasy. He can see Lorna vividly, her image sharply focused in his imagination. He lies down and encircles in his arms his mental picture of her, blond hair against his. If only he had a photograph of her; he could kiss it. But he can see her well enough now. He works himself to the cusp of a climax. He holds it, teetering deliciously on its brink. He does this several times, holding back, hanging on the edge, the nerve sensations rippling outwards and through him. Then he surrenders. A torrent of fulfilled desire seems to gush through his entire body.

Then the satisfied, spent, uncaring torpor. The warm fluid seeping down to the back of his buttocks and thighs. The comforting tepid feel is followed by a sudden cold loneliness, a vague helpless shame, then a relaxation as he sinks back on the bed and closes his eyes.

The fantasy discharged safely from his body and his mind, Simon can concentrate on his essay on *Escapism and Acceptance in Keats's Poetry* for Erica Timms. Later, at night, he'll walk down to the sea's edge again and look across into the blackness.

Monday, 23 June

T he funeral is over. Family and friends gather in the parents' house. Faces, tight with grief, lean into embraces that do not console. The cloudless blue skies outside the window seem unwittingly to mock the darkness within, inside the house and inside people's minds. The air is heavy with the pain of confronting what has happened. Mourners steal among the different clusters of dark-garmented figures with slow, leaden movements, as if too sudden a motion would destroy the fragile atmosphere of endurance, of seeing this day through somehow and then coping with the days and years to come.

And among the groups of quiet-voiced friends and relatives beyond the immediate family, some begin to question.

'I was worried the Reverend was going a little too near the mark. All those things about disappointments, heartaches, disillusion. I know he didn't actually mention - well - suicide - but…'

'Yes. I found it a bit - unnecessary. Must have been upsetting for them.'

'I'll never believe it was suicide.'

'But who would go into the water, half-past twelve at night, with no-one else around, if they didn't mean to…?'

'But the doctors said they couldn't be certain how long -'

'But that man walking along the promenade said he saw someone in the water at half-past midnight.'

'It could have been somebody else. The students get up to all sorts of things.'

'And the amount of alcohol in the body…'

'And pebbles in the pockets…'

'That could have been just a prank. People do stupid things sometimes. At the end of term, after a hard year. It must be tempting, if you've had a few drinks…'

'But, on your own.'

'Other people might have been there. Perhaps they're afraid to come forward. Perhaps they didn't realise there was a problem. You know what people are like when they've been drinking. They may not have noticed somebody was missing.'

'But the witness only saw one person. Why on earth didn't he go and take a closer look?'

'We can't blame him. It was pitch-black. He didn't think anything of it at the time. He wasn't even certain it was a person. It could have been a shadow, or a bird. It was only when he heard about it the next day he remembered what he'd seen.'

'It seems so out of character.'

'Can we really say we know someone, even those we're closest to? But… we could think about it forever. Whatever happened, it was a terrible tragedy…'

Thursday, 14 November

Half way along Pier Street, after a morning lecture on Shelley droningly delivered by Dr Parker-Hurst, for which Gus managed to obtain a seaview seat, so he was able to gaze out and bask in the still warm glow of his cinema date with Amy, he and Nick meet Dermot.

'Let's go to a different café for a change. Somewhere brighter than the Cabin,' says Nick.

'Somewhere brighter than the Cabin?' Dermot repeats. 'You mean you don't want that moody, brooding atmosphere?'

'The Cabin's a great place, but sometimes I like to be able to see the coffee I'm drinking.'

'You're exaggerating as usual,' Dermot mocks. 'It's your eyes that are dimmed with the cumulative effects of alcohol.'

'It's good to see ordinary people from the town, not just students. Let's go to the Penguin.'

'Oh no. It's full of middle-aged and elderly ladies discussing their aches and pains, retired men who rabbit on about Wilson and Heath, prices, the youth of today.'

'That's what we need,' Nick replies, 'a bit of everyday normality. The real world. I feel sorry for the people of the town, having to put up with us lot, descending on them from far-flung places like - Essex. Weird, arrogant guys like Dermot.' Nick flashes a twinkling eye at him. 'No, seriously, can you imagine what it's like - you go into a pub and it's full of students - café, same thing. I'm surprised they don't rise up and throw us all out.'

'Aber wouldn't be Aber without the students,' Dermot says.

The Penguin is a small, busy port-of-call further up Pier Street, with white tables and light pastel walls. Gus, away from the cloistered invigoration of the Old College, finds himself dispirited by the atmosphere. Nick smiles.

'Nice to get away from the Uni. That quad seems like a monastery sometimes, when it's empty and your footsteps echo on the floor. Things seem too stern and *intellectual*.' Nick twists the word around his tongue and grimaces. The boys collect their coffee and head for the only free table remaining.

They see the back of a fair-haired man at the next table. Peter Strutton. With his blond features and debonairly casual cream jacket he looks out of place in terms of people and season, among the grey and brown November coats. The hearts of Nick and Gus sink a little. They will have to acknowledge him. Their awareness of his presence will inhibit conversation.

But he nods a friendly greeting, says 'Hi boys!' as if he is one of them. His amiable grin dispels any embarrassment on their part. He asks them if they've had a lecture and who gave it and when they reply that it was Dr Parker-Hurst they notice a hint of an amused smile on his face, as if he too has experienced the rigours of his instruction.

'Taking a well-earned break?' He smiles again.

'That's right,' Nick says. 'And yourself?'

'Same here. Yes - Shakespeare seminar for Year Three next, then the novel this afternoon.' He swivels round to them as he speaks. Gus pales a little at the thought of having to chat to him but Nick is at ease as he flops down at the table.

'How are you settling in?' Peter asks.

'Good,' Nick answers. 'But there's so much going on. There's a Society or Club for practically everything.'

'And there's the Arts Festival coming up,' Peter adds. 'Jazz, the London Symphony Orchestra, a folk concert, three days of experimental and classic films. When will I find the time to teach?'

'What do you prefer teaching?' Nick asks. 'Novels, poetry or drama?'

'Oh, poetry every time. That's my first love.'

'I don't mind some poetry - Shelley, Wordsworth,' says Dermot, scrutinising his coffee, 'but I hate a lot of it. All that fanciful, fluffy language. I remember having to learn *The Brook* off-by-heart when I was in school. *I come from haunts of coot*

and hern, I make a sudden sally. I used to think sally was a girl
and I wondered why he was suddenly making it with her.'

They expect Dr Strutton to frown at Dermot's joke but
instead he grins knowingly. 'That's the point. We come across
poetry for the first time in school and we get this wildly
misconceived notion of it. It doesn't seem to relate to our lives
at all. It seems to be all about nature, or declaring love for sweet
and virtuous ladies.'

Gus suddenly finds himself speaking. 'So what do you think
poetry is?'

'Oh that's a difficult one. I suppose, really, it's the recording
of what it's like to be human. It's all about the problems,
sadnesses, satisfactions, delights of living. We all have poetry
inside us - the capacity to feel and notice, to see wonder and
sorrow in the world. They are the raw materials of the poet, and
they're general human traits.'

'Poetry uses what we all use every day - words,' Gus says.
'In that way it's different from all the other arts. We don't all
paint every day or work on stone or clay like a sculptor or read
or write music. It's sad that poetry's regarded as a bit obscure
and inaccessible.'

'Very true,' says Peter Strutton, to Gus's relieved pleasure.

Nick breaks in. 'You know an awful lot of poetry from
memory.' Peter Strutton is prone to reciting poetry in seminars -
long pieces from Yeats, Keats, Thomas Hardy.

He thinks for a moment. 'That's the great thing about a
poem. You can carry it round inside your head, like a song or a
piece of music. You can repeat its lines to yourself. It becomes
part of you. You can dip into poems at odd moments. You can
hop from one short poem to another. Someone said it's like
taking a tablet for a headache. You just let it dissolve into your
brain.'

'Who's your favourite poet, then?' Dermot asks the obvious question, that Peter Strutton never likes to answer.

'I don't really have *one* favourite. I like, oh, Keats, Byron, Donne, Housman, Sassoon as much as Wilfred Owen as a war poet. Gerard Manley Hopkins you can't help but like, although he's a bit eccentric.' He realises he is trotting off a list of names largely meaningless to them.

And he realises, when he thinks of poetry, it's often individual lines and stanzas that come into his head rather than the poets themselves.

Beauty.

To bend with apples the mossed cottage-trees
And fill all fruit with ripeness to the core.

He hangs in shades the orange bright
Like golden lamps in a green night.

Mystery.

In Xanadu did Kubla Khan
A stately pleasure-dome decree:
Where Alph, the sacred river, ran
Through caverns measureless to man
Down to a sunless sea.

And, sometimes, his own fears for the future.

When summer's end is nighing
And skies at evening cloud,
I muse on change and fortune
And all the feats I vowed
When I was young and proud.

'Well, boys, I've got to be moving. Nice talking to you!'

The boys nod as he gets up. They're not certain what to call him. 'Sir' they use only for schoolteachers. 'Dr Strutton' sounds formal and at the same time calls for an adult confidence that they do not possess. So they just nod.

'Nice bloke, that,' Nick says.

'I can't imagine Sewage or Parker-Hurst chatting to students in a café,' adds Gus.

'Can't even imagine them in a café mixing with normal people.'

'From what I've heard,' says Dermot, 'he's quite fond of mixing with young female students.'

Nick leans forward over his coffee. 'I was talking the other day to Lorna. Yeh - him and Fiona. Fiona's really into it. But apparently he lives in a small flat in town. I thought he'd have a nice comfortable house in the country somewhere. He must be well-off - a lecturer and writer.'

Friday, 15 November

The sea is in angry, restless mood. The tide crashes on the shore in frothing white manes. Rolling surges of water boom against the beach re-echoing as they break along the shoreline. Sometimes the sea rears up and spatters the seafront in spray and spume.

The light is on in the breakfast room. Mr Morgan stands in its doorway with legs apart and feet firmly anchored, grasping the doorframe as if bracing himself against an imagined indoor bombardment of wind and water.

'A rough one out there today, boys!' he shouts. 'The wind's wicked. It'll cut into you when you go out.'

Mrs Morgan scurries in with two racks of toast. 'Do you remember - last year, wasn't it, Griff? - a boy was walking along the prom, and he was picked up by the waves - came over the top and carried him out to sea. A student, he was, from Ceredigion Hall just down the road. They found his body washed up on the beach next day.' She nods grimly as she places the toast racks on the table, snatching up just-emptied cereal bowls to make room.

'That's right,' Mr Morgan says. 'Just picked him up like a daffodil. He was in the sea before he could lift a finger. Never been known before. Must've been a freak wave.'

'It was Mrs Lewis from Hafodynys who spotted him, wasn't it? Walking along the prom next day with her poodle. Suddenly saw this body on the sand. Terrible shock for her it was.'

'Did she go down and examine it?' Simon asks, unusually speaking to Mrs Morgan.

Mrs Morgan shudders. 'No-o-o-o. She rushed away and phoned the police. She's still got an awful look about her to this day.'

'That might be the gin people say she's partial to a drop of, love,' Mr Morgan puts in.

'Well,' Mrs Morgan exclaims from deep in her throat, 'I think I'd go for the gin if I saw something like that - though they do say she enjoyed a drop before.'

'Yes, never knew what hit him. Water just came right up over the front, over the pavement.' Mr Morgan makes large sweeping gestures with his arms to demonstrate. 'So be careful when you go out today, lads. Make certain you've paid Mrs Morgan up-to-date.' He winks at them.

Simon picks up a limp-looking piece of toast. 'My mother bought me an umbrella especially to come up here. I don't think it's much use in this weather, though.'

'Umbrellas tend to be a bit redundant in Aber,' Dermot comments. 'At least until someone designs one that can cope with horizontal rain.'

'What a way to go, though,' Nick says. 'Walking along the seafront - and suddenly...Whoosh.'

Dermot takes a large gulp of tea. 'Might be a good way to go. You don't have time to think about it.'

'Perhaps it was deliberate,' Simon says. 'He walked into the storm knowing he might get swept away.'

'Yes,' says Gus. 'I read about Tchaikovsky. He drank a glass of infected water and died of cholera. But some people think he drank it knowing it was infected.'

Dermot shakes his head. 'No - sudden, violent and unexpected, that's the best way. Then you have no chance to regret things or feel miserable about dying.'

Simon leans forward earnestly. 'It's a funny thing - none of us wants to die. We all fear it - not existing. Yet we don't lament the fact that we weren't existing before we were born. We don't worry about not having been alive fifty years ago, but we're scared stiff at the prospect of not being alive in fifty years' time.'

'It's only because we're human that we think about it,' Gus says. 'Other animals are probably not aware of it at all. It's like Yeats said. *Man has created death.*'

'How can we accept death, though?' Nick asks, with that look of gravity that occasionally overlays his features.

Dermot spreads marmalade awkwardly onto his toast. 'Just think of the millions of people throughout human history who've died and the millions and millions who will be born in the future. At any given time only a tiny percentage of all those people are alive on earth. At the moment it's our turn. We're all *travellers between life and death*, to quote your friend Wordsworth. You can understand the fear of death, though. We think we're gods, because of our consciousness and intelligence and emotions, music, art - even poetry. When we think of death, the way we think of ourselves is suddenly diminished, from a god to an insect. The shock is too devastating for us.'

Simon speaks with confidence. 'When you're living you're also dying - that's the paradox.'

Dermot's piece of toast hovers near his mouth. 'Look at the waves that come onto the shoreline. Suppose each wave thinks it's special and unique. How absurd! It doesn't realise it's just one of billions of waves that rise and fall over the centuries. We're like that. We're just one wave in a series that continually falls. Billions have come before us and billions will come after us. You hear about people saving lives. You never save anyone's life - you just postpone death.' He takes a large, decisive bite on his toast.

'How would you want to die, Gus?' Simon asks.

Gus is momentarily surprised. He takes Simon's directly speaking to him as a further step in the process of normalising relations between them.

'Mmm, I don't know. I've often thought, I might get run over.'

There is general laughter. 'You make it sound like a decision,' Dermot says. He apes Gus. 'Mmm, I'm feeling a bit bored today. Think I'll get run over to liven things up.'

'To deaden things up,' Simon corrects.

'This conversation's taken a morbid turn,' Nick shouts.

Dermot takes a last gulp of tea. 'So how would you want to die, Nick?'

Nick looks around the table, that provocative grin on his face.

'Old.'

And he guffaws in his usual way.

Monday, 18 November

'Coleridge was a brilliant public lecturer, although somewhat unpredictable. He would suddenly go off at a complete tangent from his set subject. Sometimes he would lecture throughout on a completely different topic from the one advertised. Sometimes he didn't turn up at all - a course of action which, unfortunately, is not permitted to us.'

Dr Parker-Hurst clutches his black gown between his bony grey-whiskered fingers as if to reassure himself he has remembered to wear it.

'Coleridge sometimes signed poems under the pseudonym Nehemiah Higginbottom, a name even more improbable than - Samuel Taylor Coleridge. He seems to have had a predilection for highly imaginative pseudonyms. He broke off his studies at Cambridge to enlist in the Light Dragoons. He wanted to escape, to vanish without trace and not draw attention to himself. To accomplish this, he enlisted under the name - Silas Tomkin Comberbache…'

Laughter from the students, before Dr Parker-Hurst launches into the main part of his lecture. 'Today we will consider two of the most powerfully imaginative and mysterious poems in the English language, Coleridge's *The Ancient Mariner* and *Kubla Khan*…'

Two hours later, and lunchtime in the crowded canteen at the Students' Union. The juke-box thuds out music to compete with a buzzing welter of voices amid the clink of cutlery and plates. Gus's mention of the morning lectures on Coleridge and Shakespeare has fired Dermot's imagination.

'I'd like to be famous, say, four hundred years after my death. That would be great, to be talked about and analysed. Ordinary fame in my lifetime doesn't interest me. I'd like to be the stuff of legend, celebrated by posterity - or else I want no fame or achievement at all. I don't see a good job, salary, status as any goal worth aiming at. You end up just like everybody else.'

'That's right,' says Geraint. 'Supposing Jesus had stayed a carpenter, and not bothered saving the world.'

'He hasn't saved the world. Look at the mess we're in. No. I don't want to push a pen or tinkle keys on these new-fangled computers all my life. If I do that then when I die I'll feel complete despair. I won't have anything to show for all the thoughts that pass through my mind. I want to look up from my death bed and see shelves of books I've written - music, art, philosophy. Then I'll be happy.'

'What if none of them's been published?' ventures Gus, looking at his watch.

'It doesn't matter. I'll still feel a sense of achievement. Shakespeare hadn't published much when he died.'

'But you don't know if he died happy.'

'Yes, he must have.'

Gus checks his watch again.

Nick suddenly springs to life. 'Oh yeh, he died thinking, *I'm Shakespeare, people will still be reading my stuff in four hundred years' time, everyone will know about me.* I can't believe that.'

'Well,' puts in Geraint, 'if he knew he was dying, I can't imagine he was too chuffed about things anyway.'

'Okay, that's it,' Nick yells, 'I suggest that the Committee of Inquiry into the State of Shakespeare's Mind When He Died reconvene at a later date - preferably when I'm dead myself.'

A sense of pleasing tenseness is rippling through Gus's chest and stomach.

'I hate watching or reading Shakespeare anyway,' Geraint says lazily. 'It gives me a headache. Too many words. You get a verbal hangover afterwards.'

'Over twenty thousand,' says Gus, 'and half of them he uses only once. I think a committee must have written the plays. No one person could have all that vocabulary. And where did he get all those words? He wasn't an aristocrat - he didn't have a huge mansion with a huge library. There weren't even any dictionaries.'

'Course there were dictionaries,' laughs Nick.

'Bet you there weren't,' says Gus. He feels again that exciting anxiety in the pit of his stomach. Twenty minutes to go...

'You completely ignore the nature of genius,' says Dermot. 'You can't judge it in normal human terms. The whole idea of genius is that it accomplishes things that normal people find incredible and inexplicable.'

'Inexplicable,' Nick repeats. 'Love that word. I would have said "unexplainable".'

'Shakespeare couldn't even spell his own name properly. He spelt it in six different ways,' says Geraint, which prompts a fracas of opinions around the table.

'I'm not surprised. It's quite difficult. I went through a whole year in school when I couldn't spell it.'

'Yes, but he *was* Shakespeare.'

'And the amount of stuff that's written about him - all that criticism and commentary, about themes and characters and linguistic style and psycho-analytical studies - I'm certain most of it would have baffled him.'

'He would probably have failed an exam paper on himself.'

'Especially if he couldn't spell his own name.'

'If he was so clever, I'm surprised he didn't just change his name to something he could spell - "Jones", for instance.'

'But "Shakespeare" does have a certain ring about it. "The Royal Jones Theatre" doesn't sound all that impressive.'

'In fact, he's more likely to have changed his name from "Jones" to "Shakespeare".'

'Which explains why he couldn't spell it, if it wasn't his real name.'

'I'm surprised few critics seem to have commented on the erotic undertones of Shakespeare's name,' says Dermot. 'In fact, sometimes he's referred to as "Shakeshaft" - even more bawdy.'

'I'd like to write a comic novel,' says Geraint. 'To make people laugh is a higher skill than making them think.'

Gus gets up from the table, conscious of the others' enquiring looks. 'I'm going to meet Amy,' he says with as casual a tone as he can muster. 'We're going to do some work together.' It's odd - he feels almost guilty, as if he is breaking up the group of happy males. He almost wishes he could stay in this carefree passing of ideas.

'Hey, we're just about to play table football,' Nick shouts. 'You're our best midfield man. But...,' he lets out a mournful sigh, 'if Amy is calling, you must go to her side.' He wags his finger and gives an impure laugh. 'Don't do anything I wouldn't do.'

'Which means do practically anything,' says Geraint.

'He will anyway,' Dermot adds.

'Got protection, lad?' Nick asks him, quietly, in an almost fatherly tone, though it is a subject Gus's own father would never broach. Then he grins. Gus nods. He walks out, watching the banter continue through the window, Nick giving him a thumbs-up and a wink.

They stand closely side by side, staring out at the sea in front of the Old College, wanting but not yet quite daring to touch each other. A rush of wind tumbles Amy's hair about her face and she brushes it back, her hand pale in pleasing contrast to the darkness of her hair. As he leans his head towards hers, he has the sensation of very slowly falling, a silent steady melting into the thrill of her presence. Her hair is soft against his cheek and as he puts his arm around her he feels the reassuring firmness of her shoulder.

They turn to walk along the prom, and she puts her arm around his waist, her hand nestling snugly in the back pocket of his jeans. The wind tugs at them, pulling them along as they labour laughingly against it, their bodies tight together against its vehemence.

Gus is pleased and surprised that she has invited him back to Alex after one date, but there is an innocence, an openness about her. Her room is narrow and basic, but the furniture - a bed, wardrobe, desk, bookcase - is less ancient than at Gwylan House and the room is clean and uncluttered. The absence of photographs gladdens him. No parents or siblings means she shows independence and freedom, is not tiresomely tied to her family. Even more welcome - no evidence of a "boyfriend back home" reveals itself. On the wall are some posters - again good to see no male singers or bands, which might make him feel pressurised to achieve some standard. A picture of Monet's garden, all luscious greens and reds of grass and flowers, cool shade and luminous sun. A Renoir of white-sailed boats on the Seine.

Amy glides around the small room in a relaxed, undemanding way and he feels the tension slip agreeably from him. She smiles, not shyly, not expectantly, but in a free, friendly manner. Then a sudden decisiveness. 'Right. I've got to do this essay on Wordsworth...' She settles down with pen, paper and poems spread in front of her. Gus takes up his *Critical Commentary On The Odes of Keats* and watches her absorbed face, delicate as a peach, as she reflects and ponders then turns resolutely to write. He notes her smooth slim fingers gripping the pen, looks at her face again.

He longs to touch a kiss onto the nape of her neck, to start gently, with no force or aggression - yes, with supreme gentleness. It looks so soft and exposed and vulnerable. He wants to rest his lips on it, to show he will protect it from all the jagged shrapnel of life. He imagines as he kisses it, her head turning towards him, her lips stretching into that slight smile. Then he will hold her more tightly, press her to him...

But now does not seem the right time. She might think the less of him if he interrupts her while she's writing, or if she thinks his purpose in coming back with her was sex. Besides, it is daytime, which does not seem to favour passion or desire.

As he leaves she stands in front of him. 'I'll probably stay in tonight. I want to finish this essay. Then I'll have a cup of coffee with Lorna and Fiona. Their rooms overlook the sea so it's nice to go in them.'

Their faces are so close. Their noses rub and she gives a quiet, intimate giggle. His lips seek hers and brush them, then taste them. He feels her lips in response pressing then yielding against his. His arms circle her waist, drawing it to him. He feels the delicate weight of her arms as they close around his neck.

Her pleased eyes look into his, their bodies slip apart. 'Have a good rest of the day,' he says, their hands clasping each other's forearms. 'I'll see you tomorrow I expect.' She nods, contented. 'Take care.' It's a saying his family don't use, and he likes the sound of it from her lips that have the impress of his kiss upon them.

Gus arrives back at Gwylan House just in time for the evening meal. The boys are already in their seats waiting to be fed.

'Hey, we thought we'd lost you,' Nick exclaims. 'What you've been getting at Amy's obviously beats anything Mrs M can put in front of you.'

'Not much competition there,' comments Dermot.

Nick notices the faint simper on Gus's face. 'You look happy! One date and he's in! What's this guy got that we haven't?'

'Oh, we just worked on our essays.'

'Ah, this man's got it all planned out,' Nick says. 'He's taking it in easy stages. First he's in the seat next to Amy at lectures, then he's in her room, then he's in her undies, then he's in her...'

'Full stop!' Dermot laughs.

Simon says nothing. There is the hint of a reluctant smile under his combed-down hair.

The entrance of Mrs Morgan puts an end to Gus's ribbing. She looks agitated.

'Yes, the law's definitely not strict enough these days. Our son Brian was driving through Trefechan this morning,' she blurts forth, 'and a woman came out of a side street and hit him. Would you believe? The side of his car - well, apparently it's a write-off.' Her voice rises to a near-screech. 'And she'll probably get away with it. I'll wager she'll just get a warning. Yes, the law's definitely not strict enough these days. Brian says that, for things like that, people should be imprisoned. He says, if they're incinerated for a month, that will make certain they don't do it again.'

'It certainly will, Mrs Morgan,' says Nick as the others struggle to suppress smirks.

Wednesday, 20 November

> *Come to me in the silence of the night;*
> *Come in the speaking silence of a dream;*
> *Come with soft rounded cheeks and eyes as bright*
> *As sunlight on a stream...*

He reads the poetry, the letter pushed through the downstairs letterbox, and knows he will have to do something. Fiona is an intelligent, able girl, but not as mature as he first thought. She sees him as a prize she has won. He fears she is not discreet. At least she seems to understand that he can't come to Alex to see her. She comes to his flat in the afternoon or evening. He thought she might be put off by its meagreness but she seems to think it romantic - the struggling writer and all that. At least so far he has persuaded her not to stay overnight.

But sending poetry to him - it is something that makes him shudder. He feels a certain contempt for her but pity at the same time. She's pathetically trying to impress him. He can imagine her sitting in a library or buying books of poetry and poring feverishly over them for suitable verses. He recognised the lines from Christina Rossetti but not this one.

> *O love, that stronger art than wine,*
> *Pleasing delusion, witchery divine,*
> *Wont to be prized above all wealth,*
> *Disease that has more joys than health.*

'Only it's not a delusion or disease in my case,' she's written underneath.

Peter feels for her. He understands what she is going through. She has fallen too violently for him. She's someone whose ardour, once released, cannot be dammed up. He doesn't want to hurt her, but he fears the damage has already been done. He's led her on, flattered by her attention to him, by his effect on her, by the reassurance that he can still appeal to young eyes.

But he should have known this. First-year student. First love probably. She is tasting the exquisite sweetness of the fruit; buffeted by that passion-racking, peace-wrecking, exhilarating joy. Poignant and sad it is to think of her, the love-fervour, the infatuation, the frenzy that can turn to a fury that can destroy, both the self and others.

He will have to send her a letter, finishing things completely. He should have no trouble writing it. He can sound firm, but caring also. He can be sympathetic, can praise her but at the same time make it clear he has to end it. He can suggest there must be plenty of male students who will welcome the chance to go out with her. There is only a fortnight to the end of term. By next term, with any luck, her affections will have moved on.

But she has invited him to an end-of-term party. He would love to go, to mingle informally with the students, be part of the atmosphere, enjoy their acceptance of him. He should be able to do that without her thinking his presence means he is wavering in his denial of her. Perhaps it's risky. A party and drinks might exacerbate her emotions. But it is too much of a temptation - a one-off event, with the holiday soon after. As long as he treads carefully, avoids being isolated with her, he should be all right.

Monday, 25 November

O ne empty chair at the evening meal. The other three boys look at each other.

'He's never late.'

'I saw him in the library this morning.'

'He never loses track of time where food's concerned.'

Dermot's eyes stare down at the pink-and-white check tablecloth, as if searching there for some sign of the missing diner. 'I can only think of two things that would make him late for a meal.'

This prompts more speculation.

'He's dead,' Simon pronounces.

'Okay then!' Dermot nods impatiently, 'three things including that.'

'He's suffering acute memory loss,' Gus suggests.

Simon's turn again. 'He's had some kind of religious conversion. Seen a vision in Pier Street.'

'He's fasting,' is Gus's even more improbable idea.

'Okay, okay!' shouts Dermot. 'The vision in Pier Street is probably the nearest to my theory - but not the religious type. I was thinking of - a girl or alcohol.'

There is a thud as the front door closes. A look of relief passes over the boys' faces. Nick hurries in. He is breathing hard, his hair is dishevelled, his mouth is open, his face looks embattled.

But then a more placid smile smooths his features. He calmly pulls back his chair and sits, still smiling, almost more to himself than to the others.

'So where've you been?' Dermot demands.

'In the Cambrian…with Lorna…all afternoon.'

'There!' Dermot cries triumphantly. 'I was doubly correct!'

Nick does not appear concerned to hear what Dermot's strange exclamation might mean. 'Well, Lorna and about two hundred other people to be strictly accurate,' he mutters. 'Some kind of birthday party - forget whose.'

' "About two hundred" is not being "strictly accurate",' Dermot corrects. 'It's an approximation.'

'*It's an approximation.*' Nick mimics Dermot's voice, jerking his head curiously from side to side. 'Why don't you speak bloody English?' He laughs, a kind of hoarse growl that ends in a robust belch.

Mrs Morgan brings in the meals. Roast beef, Yorkshire pudding, onions, carrots, potatoes simmer invitingly on the heaped plates. Nick looks down at his in a puzzled manner, as if food is the last thing he's expecting.

'I'm drunk, boys,' he says softly. 'I can't eat this.'

There is such a note of sad finality in his quiet voice, all know immediately they cannot persuade him to sample even a mouthful. They also know that they do not need to remind him of the consequences of returning the plate untouched to Mrs M.

For a few moments, there is an awful silence. Dermot is the first to react.

'Somehow,' he says, pointing to Nick's food as if it is a dead body they have just appallingly killed, 'we have to get rid of *that*.'

Each surveys his own piled plateful. The thought of having to ingest extra gives each face a look of shocked alarm, as if the problem plate really were a corpse and they have been forced to confront the terrible prospect of cannibalism. Even Dermot, usually so fearless in the face of any culinary challenge, shakes his head.

'I don't think I can manage anything.'

Nick continues to gaze inertly at his plate. Although he looks fairly normal as he sits, it is obvious he is incapable of thought or action.

'How much have you had to drink?' Simon asks.

'As much as any man could desire.' Nick leans back in his chair with a contented, sated grin on his face, then adds mysteriously, 'unhoped for this side of Heaven.'

Simon thinks for a moment. 'Isn't that a quote from somewhere?'

'Don't worry about that now!' Dermot snaps, with impressive ruthlessness. 'We need to get rid of that food somehow!'

'Isn't it Rupert Brooke?' Simon continues.

'Shut up!' Dermot has taken control. 'Does anyone have a plastic bag on them?'

'Don't be stupid!' Gus protests. 'Why would we carry plastic bags around with us when we sit down to an evening meal?'

'Precisely for situations like this,' Simon says.

Nick comes faintly back to life. 'Perhaps we could each put some in our pockets, boys, wrapped in tissues.'

This produces a chorus of criticism.

'That would be messy.'

'Think of the gravy.'

'We'd all have to walk out of here with strange bulging pockets.'

'Strange bulging soggy smelly pockets.'

Gus has an idea. 'What we need is someone who's got a plastic bag upstairs to rush up and bring it down. We stuff the food inside, put it in that cupboard over there until later.' He points to an ancient-looking large three-drawer cabinet in the corner of the room, its wood pocked and marked.

'How can we get it back?' Dermot asks. 'What if Mrs M looks in there?'

'She'll get a surprise,' says Nick unhelpfully.

'I think we should fill the plastic bag and fling it out through the front door, across the road before Mrs M notices,' Dermot says.

'Don't be dumb!' Gus whispers heavily. 'Supposing it hits somebody? Imagine some poor soul out for a quiet evening stroll along the prom. Suddenly a bag of meat, carrots, onions and potatoes hurtles through the air and hits them on the head!' He prods his potatoes with a fork. 'And judging by the hardness of these spuds, they'd collapse on the spot with a fractured skull.'

But Dermot is insistent. 'They won't be able to trace it back to us. They'll think it's fallen from a plane or something.'

'People in planes don't throw food out of the window,' Simon points out.

'And Mrs M is always saying how well-known her cooking is in Aber,' Gus adds. 'They'll probably recognise the meat as being hers.'

'Wouldn't it be better if Nick just said he doesn't feel hungry?' Simon suggests.

Gus and Dermot look at each other in surprised silence, as if suddenly confronted with an amazing new possibility.

Gus shakes his head. 'No. That would draw Mrs M's attention to Nick. If she finds out he's drunk - she could throw him out of the lodgings or report him to the University. They can even dismiss you. No - we'll hide it in the cupboard. When it's safe we can *carry* it' - he stresses the verb, looking pointedly at Dermot - 'across the road, put it in a litter bin, or bury it in the sand.'

'That's a good idea, bury it in the sand,' says Simon excitedly. 'Then someone might find it in the future…'

'What a find,' Dermot mutters wearily.

'It'll be a historical relic,' Simon goes on, 'like a time capsule. I read once about workmen renovating an old house. They found a sandwich embedded in the walls, believed to be a hundred years old.'

'That makes it slightly more recent than the sandwiches in the Students' Union,' Gus says.

Dermot leans forward with passion. 'Or we could put it in a bottle and cast it out to sea. Put in a note explaining who we are, saying who Nick is. It'll be all over the newspapers. TV will carry stories saying where in the four corners of the world it's landed.'

'Probably Aberdovey,' says Gus.

Simon suddenly jerks up out of his chair. 'I've got a bag upstairs.' With uncharacteristic speed he rushes out of the room, while the others, except Nick, continue with their meal. Simon returns and pulls a jumble of bags from his pocket, first one, then another, then another…like a conjuror with rabbits in a hat.

'Jesus, how many have you got?' Dermot asks.

'Five altogether. I think we should wrap it in all of them, to reduce the smell and make it less obvious what it is.'

Gus sighs. 'We're not playing pass the parcel.'

'That's an idea!' Dermot exclaims. 'We could take it in to the Unicorn…'

'Right!' says Gus decisively. He seizes up Nick's plate and empties its contents into one of the bags. The food slides obediently off the plate, watched by four pairs of eyes. Nick looks on in a daze, without emotion. Gus pauses, thinks, then puts the remaining bags around the first. He moves across to the cabinet, opens the bottom drawer, squeezes the flopping, oddly-shaped package carefully inside, shuts the door and stands back with satisfaction.

'Right. That's it. Now let's all eat - except Nick, of course.'

'Actually,' says Nick, 'I wouldn't mind something now…I think my appetite's coming back.'

'It's too late!' Dermot gives a muted scream.

'What's in that cupboard anyway?' Simon asks.

Dermot's mouth froths with laughter. 'Probably a large collection of plastic bags containing remains of uneaten meals deposited by drunken students over the decades.'

Simon looks up. 'What if Mrs M notices that Nick's a bit…?'

'Blotto,' suggests Dermot.

'Yes. She often makes a point of talking to Nick because she gets more sense out of him than out of the rest of us.'

'Don't worry,' Dermot says. 'I'll engage her in conversation. Good point. I'll divert her attention from Nick.'

'Ask her about her grandson Eric or her son Brian,' Gus suggests. 'She's always talking about them.'

'That's right,' Simon adds. 'Brian works on a magazine. Oh - ask her about the car accident.'

Mrs Morgan comes in to collect the empty plates, and with desserts of rice pudding. She glances at the boys.

Dermot clears his throat. 'Lovely meal, thanks, Mrs Morgan. We all enjoyed it.'

Mrs Morgan is pleased and surprised at the rare compliment. 'Good. Well I do my best, as you know. All right Nick?'

Nick's mouth begins to move slowly in reply, but before anything can emerge Dermot's voice breaks in.

'Um, Mrs Morgan, I hear, um, is your son okay after the accident?'

'Oh yes he's fine. It's just his car. But he's had good news with his job. He's just been promoted on his magazine. They've made him insulting editor.'

Stifling his laughter, Dermot presses on, 'And, um, uh, didn't you mention he might be getting married?'

'Well, no, not at the moment. He does like a young lady, but she only wants to be friends with him. She said she only wants a botanic relationship. Ah! Sons! They're always a worry. I expect all your mothers at home are anxious about you, wondering what you get up to. Sometimes mothers ring me up to ask how their boy is doing. I always make it redundantly clear that if their boy wants a shoulder to cry on, he can come to mine. I'm a bit like that Mary Popout, really. And I must say, most of the boys who come here are as good as angels, like you. You do get one or two, of course, but, by and large, all good boys.' And Mrs Morgan waltzes happily out clutching four empty plates.

Nick is eyeing his rice pudding in the same baffled way that he'd contemplated his main course.

'Don't say it, Nick,' Dermot pleads with some aggression. 'Please don't say it.'

Nick is more conciliatory. 'It's okay. I can eat this.' Then he gazes at the others and his voice drops to a furtive whisper. 'There's a Yorkshire pudding lurking in the cupboard.' And he laughs like his old self. He looks around the table and his eyes gleam with triumph. 'And by the way, guys, I've made it with Lorna.'

Tuesday, 26 November

Dermot emerges from his attic room and takes his place at the breakfast table. The hairs in his nostrils trail coldly down like stalactites. '*St Agnes' Eve - ah, bitter chill it was,*' murmurs Nick, impressively remembering his Keats from last week's lecture.

'Dermot *limps trembling through the frozen grass*,' adds Gus.

'Ah, no poetry at breakfast, please,' Dermot pleads. 'There's a funny scraping sound in my room.' He reaches out a quivering hand for the toast while the others discuss his observation.

'Perhaps it's a mouse.'

'I should think it's too cold up there for any known creature to exist - with the possible exception of a polar bear.'

'Dermot exists up there.'

'Well, he's no known creature.'

Mr Morgan shuffles gloomily in with a large pot of tea. 'Cold one this morning lads! Ah, winter's set in all right. None of you have been up here in winter have you?' There is an ominous note in his voice, like that of a hardened Roman centurion addressing raw recruits on Hadrian's Wall. 'Well, we can say goodbye to the nice weather until May!' He wraps his arms around himself in a dramatic gesture of bleak exposure, although it is warm and cosy in the room. 'Mind you, it's not half as cold as some places. Did you know, in certain spots in the world, it's so cold that, if you sweat, the sweat freezes on your head?'

Leaving them to ponder his complex logic, he begins his shuffle back out, as Mrs Morgan scuttles in with brimming plates of fried breakfast. 'Twt! Stop your moaning. There's tea poured for you in the kitchen.'

'Tea good this morning?' he asks as always, though Mrs Morgan's tea provides as little variation in taste as aspirin.

'Well it's warm and wet.'

'Warm and wet, that's how we like it, love!' he says, winking to the boys.

Mrs Morgan leans over to Nick. 'Now then, tell me, Nick, are my fried eggs as good as your mother's?'

Nick thinks for a moment. 'That's a really difficult question. I think I like them both equally. Yes, they're both exquisite, perfect, and you can't have better than that!'

'A very tactile answer!' she says, laughing.

Dermot turns to Nick. 'So how are we this morning?'

Nick grunts.

'I don't think you were fully aware of the drama that unfolded around your person yesterday evening.'

'Oh, I was aware all right, but I felt a bit like in those stories you hear of patients who wake up from anaesthetic during operations, and they can see and hear everything that's going on but they can't move or speak. I remember the food, and the cupboard, and you were all talking about me as if I wasn't here -'

'Well, to all intents and purposes you weren't, but your meal was, so we had to dispose of it.' Dermot turns to Gus. 'By the way, how *did* you dispose of it?'

'Simple. I heard Mr and Mrs M go out about eight-thirty, so I got it from the cupboard and put it in a litter bin on the prom.'

Simon spreads marmalade sparsely on his toast. 'So all our brilliant ideas were in vain. No sensational discoveries in a hundred years' time.'

'Ah, but yesterday was definitely sensational!' Nick bursts forth. 'And I'm going round to Lorna's place tonight and there's going to be fireworks.'

Gus takes a swig of tea. 'So you're in with Lorna then?'

'Yep! Definitely!' Nick roars out the word, slaps his hand on the table. 'Oh she is one gorgeous girl!'

'Keep your voice down,' Dermot warns, 'or Mrs M might think you're talking about her...'

Thursday, 28 November

F ive o'clock on a cold evening. Gus and Nick sit in the English room of the library. From the window they can see the streetlamps of the promenade give an orange glaze to grey pavement. Behind is the black outline of the pier.

Nick gazes in weary dismay at the hill of books and papers strewn in front of him. 'I'm getting pissed off with this essay.'

'What's it on?' Gus asks.

'It's a quotation from Keats. *"Oh for a life of sensations rather than thoughts." To what extent is Keats's poetry about sensation rather than thought*? Got to do it for Gerald Bailey. I hear he's a tough marker.'

'Be careful with that word *sensation*,' Gus advises. 'It doesn't have its modern meaning. Keats meant he wanted to perceive the beauty of the world through the senses, through seeing and hearing it, through smelling, touching and tasting, rather than analysing and philosophising.'

'I know that, dumbo,' Nick says affectionately. 'Though I'm certain if Keats had met Lorna, he'd think, *bloody sensational!* Anyway, I fancy a pint.' He looks at Gus for response.

Gus is wary. 'Just one. Remember what happened a few days ago. If we both turned up drunk at Mrs Morgan's meal, I don't think the other two guys would be able to cover for us.'

'Or it could be twice the fun and excitement. Or imagine if we all came in pissed! That's what we should do, all four of us should go out for a few jars one afternoon and see what happens.'

'I know what would happen. We'd all get evicted. Anyway, I can't imagine Simon getting drunk.'

'That's exactly what he should do. He needs to loosen up. Though I remember him saying he wanted to be a writer - but then everybody thinks that. What if he's secretly observing us and writing down all our conversations?'

Gus feels a tremble go through him at Nick's phrase "secretly observing" and hopes Nick hasn't noticed. He tries to sound unperturbed. 'He seems such a mysterious guy.'

'Oh, I think he's just shy,' Nick replies. ' But I saw him last week coming out of the college toilets. He looked at me in a strange way, kind of startled, looked almost guilty. Weird!'

Gus is interested. 'So what do you think it was?'

'Dunno. It only lasted a second. Then he seemed to collect himself and he just said, "Hi!" and went. Then I saw him once sat on the sand against the bandstand wall, staring out to sea. Suddenly he rushed down and stopped right by the water's edge. Anyway, just be thankful we're normal warm-blooded males! Come on. Let's go.'

They decide for a change to go to the Marine Hotel.

'Hey, this is posh for us,' Nick says in a low voice, gazing about at décor rather more stately than that of the Unicorn or White Horse.

It is quiet, with a few early-evening customers. A familiar figure is at the bar buying a drink. He turns to them with a smile.

'We can't go on meeting like this! On your way back to lodgings?'

'That's right,' Nick replies. Both boys would prefer Peter Strutton to stay at the bar while they sit down, or for him to find a seat for himself.

'Care to join me for a short while?'

'Sure,' Nick answers, while Gus nods faintly. The lecturer leads them to a table overlooking the sea.

He carries a folder and a paperback. It's a title they've seen around the bookshops, *Small Rooms in Wales*. Underneath is

Peter Strutton's name as author. 'I've just been in a discussion group in Borth. Had to give a talk and answer questions on, um, my book.' He points almost apologetically to the neat volume of short stories. How strange, and fulfilling, Gus thinks, to be sitting in a pub with a book in front of him, and, alongside, the person who wrote it.

'I wouldn't want to be a writer,' says Nick. 'I expect people turn up on your doorstep wanting your autograph or wanting to punch you in the face. You probably get hundreds of letters and you have to open them all in case one's important.'

Peter sips his beer and gives a laugh. 'Well, it's not quite like that - certainly not at the present time.'

'Are you writing something at the moment?' Gus asks.

'I'm working on a novel. Almost finished it.' As he speaks, he thinks of the task ahead of him, securing the interest of an agent and publisher. His book of short stories has attracted attention and praise, but not huge sales, and he published it himself by using money he might have put towards buying a house, plus a contribution from his parents which he promised to pay back. His junior lecturer's salary is only slowly improving the situation. As a result, he lives in a small rented flat in the centre of town, with a bed-and-breakfast on one side and a kindly elderly widow on the other. He knows he will not be able to afford the luxury of further self-publication for the foreseeable future. But if his novel is accepted, and sells...

'Do you find it hard to fit in writing alongside lecturing?' Nick asks.

Peter snaps out of his reverie and glances down at his book. 'You do need time. But - I'm fairly determined. Sometimes you have to work at something for a long time without any encouraging results or improvement.'

'I imagine it's a bit like climbing Mount Everest,' Gus puts in.

Peter is pleased that someone appreciates that effort is involved. Most students seem to think he sits down cheerfully and reels off the words without toil or struggle.

'That's a good analogy,' he says. 'We all want to savour the spectacular views from the summit, but we don't want to endure the climbing - the hard graft, the uncertainty, the patience required. And sometimes it seems agonisingly slow as you edge along or look despairingly for a foothold.' He makes laboured creeping movements with his hand and smiles.

'It must be hard work,' Gus says. 'Sitting in front of a blank sheet of paper, having to fill page after page with combinations of words that will keep total strangers interested.'

'So how do you write?' Nick asks.

'By sitting down for a long time, I suppose. I explore, dig, toil away. Eventually I produce. It takes patience. You want to rush in and finish it in one go. But it's like,' - he searches for a suitable comparison - 'papering a room. You have to take it in stages. It's no use having one huge expanse of paper to cover a whole wall - you'll never get it up. You do the room strip by strip, making certain each strip matches and the joins show as little as possible.'

'I wouldn't have the patience,' Nick says

'Well, it can be fascinating. We call novel writing "creative writing" and people think of it in purely creative terms, but it can be as much about discovering as inventing. You discover what's inside you waiting to come out.'

'Sometimes you don't know what you've got to say until you've said it, I expect,' Gus adds.

'Precisely,' affirms Peter. 'In that way it can be exciting. Like a journey into a foreign country.'

'But it must be so complicated.'

Peter laughs. 'Yes, sometimes it feels like building a jumbo jet. There are hundreds of different parts, and they all have to fit together without the seams or joins being visible. Any cracks and it could fall apart and crash to the ground.'

'Don't you watch films and wish you could just take pictures with a camera rather than be limited to using words?' Nick asks.

Peter leans back in his chair and strokes his chin. 'I remember once, a teenager said what I thought was a very alarming thing to me. He said he couldn't see the point of anyone *writing* stories or novels. "Why don't they just make a film of the story?" he asked. "What's the point of writing it?" I could see why he was thinking that. He watched lots of films and television, but didn't read books.'

'That would be horrible,' says Gus. 'I can't imagine not reading…'

Peter nods in worried agreement. 'There was something I read this morning by the Irish writer Synge. It began, "a brilliant morning of April, and the green glittering waves…" If this was depicted in a film, without the words, something would be lost, no matter how beautiful the camera shots might be. It's because, when we watch a film, we're seeing someone else's pictures. When we read, we use our own imaginations and conjure up our own personal pictures. In a film, everything is done for you. You don't need to contribute anything yourself. And you know what they say - you can't judge a book by its film version.'

'*Conjure* is a good word,' Gus says, 'because there's something magical there.'

'Exactly,' says Peter. 'I think reading can give a sharper focus to something than seeing it on film or as a picture. I'm not against films or painting at all - the opposite - I enjoy them both and they can do things that books can't - but likewise there's a special delight in books that they can't capture. It's the delight of communicating everything in words. Words can describe and delineate with more impact, with perception and understanding - landscapes, cities, people, relationships. And words can also be just as effective as films in conveying suspense, tension.'

'Another thing about films,' Gus says, 'is that they're over too quickly - two hours or less and you've seen the whole thing. Books you read over a period, often weeks, so you absorb it bit by bit.'

'That's right,' says Peter. 'It seeps into your consciousness. Films look more convenient - you save time - but maybe it's too instant. Of course, a good film stays with you, and you can watch it again, but most films you tend to see once and that's it. As you said, they're over too quickly. You don't have chance to savour them. A novel takes longer to read, you normally do it over several sessions, over days and weeks. It can percolate through to you gradually - like good filter coffee, as opposed to the instant variety. Also, reading is a relaxing personal activity. It's nice in films that you are among a crowd all watching the same thing - but it's a little disconcerting - like going into a library or café, settling down to read a book, and noticing that the place is full of people reading the same book.'

Nick thumps Gus on the arm as they walk along the prom. 'Hey, we've just had a drink with an author!'

Gus is full of wonder. 'It's brilliant, the way he talks.'

'And he agreed with all the points you made. They were good ideas, Gus.' Nick's voice is keen with encouragement.

'Yes, but he's so fluent, the way he expresses himself.'

'That's his job, isn't it? He gets lots of practice in talking to people. He eats, breathes and sleeps *lit-er-at-ure.*'

'Mmm. He seems to do it so naturally.' Gus watches the sea mist smoulder along the beach like a long grey cloud. At the far end of the curve of seafront facades with their lighted windows,

Constitution Hill masses above Alex. The sky is boundless and black. That feeling again, of a huge space, waiting to be explored and filled, of freedom and uncertainty, hope and doubt.

Friday, 29 November

Twelve noon, and a grey wind blows solidly in, bowling along the beach and ballooning into their ears as they battle across the sand with a football. 'That's the trouble,' Dermot shouts against the wind, 'if you love someone, by definition you're tied to them, you can't let go, you're dependent on them for your happiness. In other words, you've lost control of your own life.'

Nick scoops the ball up onto his thigh with the flick of a heel. 'In the case of Lorna, I want to lose control, full stop. She's unbelievable.'

Dermot protests. 'No need to be facetious.'

Nick bounces the ball deftly on his thigh. 'Oh yes there is. You're taking things too seriously.'

'Know what's unusual about the word *facetious*?' Gus asks.

Dermot yells back, suddenly lunging at Nick to dispossess him of the ball. 'It contains all the vowels in alphabetical order. Just like *abstemious*.'

Nick, indignant, complains loudly. 'I'm trying to have a serious discussion here!'

'*Serious*? No, that doesn't quite make it. No *a*. In any case, you've just told Dermot he's too serious.'

Nick, lost in his own mental ecstasies, ignores Gus. 'Lorna! Oh, that body!'

'People aren't just beautiful in face or body,' says Dermot. 'They can be beautiful in the way they do things - the way they look at you, the way they think, the way they write...'

Geraint walks backwards against the wind. 'I can't love a woman's body unless I like her personality. If I don't love the person, I couldn't love the body.'

'If I love the body -' Nick pauses, boots the ball up into the wind - 'I make bloody certain I love the person.' He gives his loud explosion of laughter, looking knowingly to Gus for corroboration. Gus fears the assumptions that Nick may be making about him.

Dermot rushes forward to catch the ball as the wind boomerangs it back. 'Love doesn't exist. It's just an illusion. The amazing thing is, some people live together under the illusion for twenty, thirty, forty years. They should be congratulated, not for being married so long, but for keeping the illusion going for that length of time.'

Geraint knocks the ball out of Dermot's hand. 'Lorna's just a pouter.'

'Oh, she pouts all right,' Nick enthuses. 'She even walks in a pouting kind of way.'

Geraint and Nick pass the ball stylishly between them in time with their words.

'How can you walk poutingly?'

'Well, she kind of, thrusts her legs out, then her tits.'

'Mmm, nice face, ugly smile.'

'How can anyone have an ugly smile?'

'She bares her teeth, as if she wants to eat you.'

'I wouldn't mind.'

Dermot cuts in. 'They shouldn't be called The Opposite Sex. They're not opposite, not diametrically opposed. They should be called The Adjacent Sex.'

'Anyway,' Nick shouts, 'we've got the expert right here with us, who's hardly said a word so far. Tell us all, Gus,' and he whacks the ball towards an imaginary goal, 'have you *scored* yet?'

Gus has a sudden impulse to lie. He checks it. 'No, not yet,' he says cheerfully, 'plenty of time.'

Nick's voice rises in outrage. 'Plenty of time? After what we've done in poetry recently? *Carpe diem. Seize the day* and all that stuff. *Time's winged chariot hurrying near.*'

'Dragging his feet,' says Geraint.

'Dragging something bloody else as well.' Nick's eyes, with their look of well-meaning mischief, swivel like a telescope towards Gus. He receives a welcome respite from Dermot who pronounces, 'life would be better without sex.'

'Without sex, there'd be no life, Dermot. Sex *is* life.' Nick is emphatic.

'Yes, but life isn't sex.'

'Speak for yourself,' Nick yells, lapsing into his private thoughts. The sex-proclaiming sway of Lorna's shoulders and arse as she walks. That smile, those beckoning eyes. A high, flute-like voice, mellow, but surprisingly, *alluringly* - that was the word he wanted - soft, for one whose body was so raunchy.

Gus too is thinking. He must set himself a deadline, a target. Otherwise he'll just drift and put it off, and Amy will start to think there's something wrong with him, or he might do it on impulse and won't have protection. Amy has not pressurised him or even mentioned it. But there are unmistakeable signs from her - her large-eyed smile when she looks at him; the way they have kissed, with her giving herself to him, absorbed in the kiss's pleasure, ready for them to journey together into a new land. He has practised alone, face-down on the bed, when he knows Nick will be elsewhere - a laboured, messy process when he feels he is doing it to order, and pretending he is performing with someone.

Sunday is a good day because Mrs Morgan's main meal is at lunchtime and the evening feed is what she grandly calls 'high tea', of scones and cake at six o'clock, which should not leave him feeling too bloated and incapable in the way that a weekday meal might. Yes, it must be a Sunday. This Sunday.

Sunday, 1 December

Gus takes an afternoon walk around the castle and South Beach, then explores the cluster of streets that slope up from the beachfront at improbable angles, like the legs of an inebriated octopus, culminating in the unlikely summit of the Castle Theatre. Terraced houses huddle almost on top of each other like dominoes - you have the feeling that if the top one fell, the others would tumble down on to the beach. Penmaesglas Street, Custom House Street, Prospect Street - narrow clambering rows, whose silent front doors no-one seems to leave or enter. Gus likes walking these mysterious deserted pavements and peering through the windows. In one a fruit bowl bulges with apples, bananas, oranges. Another displays a hushed guitar.

This is the day he has set himself, and he is determined. All day he has beaten back the doubts, refused to think about them, negotiating each hour with a steely resolution that heartens him. He walks back to Gwylan House, eats his high tea without chaff from the others, escapes swiftly and is on the prom for the five-minute walk to Alex.

He knocks on Amy's door and hears her clear-voiced 'Come in!' She is standing at her desk, shuffling papers together. She wears dark-blue jeans and a black slim-fitting polo-neck jumper of ribbed wool, her shape satisfyingly visible through it. She moves quickly towards him and gives him a kiss, brief but on the lips, her hands lightly on his shoulders for the moment that the kiss lasts.

'What do you want to do tonight?' she asks. 'Want to go for a walk, or a drink? Or there are some one-act plays in the Barn Theatre, including one by Jean-Paul Sartre. Looks fine out, not too cold.'

'Oh, I thought we could just stay in.' His nonchalant tone pleases him, though his throat is tight.

'Okay,' she says pleasantly. 'Doing what?'

'Um, just relaxing.'

She looks out of the window at Brynymor Street that runs above and behind, bathed in its Sunday evening quietness, then turns back to him. Her movements are as soft, as quietly inviting, as her voice. 'Lorna and Fiona have gone to a meeting of the Environment Group. They asked me but I told them you were coming round.'

Gus wonders, suddenly, for the first time, if they ply her with the same questions as the boys ask him, make the same teasing references.

He sits on the bed, leaning forward. She sits beside him and looks at him with a closed-mouth smile, happy and harmless. In her hair and eyes, black assumes qualities of brightness and warmth, but retains its sense of mystery and enticement. He puts his arm around her, feels the firm yet feminine, unmuscular flesh of her shoulder, and draws her to him. They keel back onto the bed.

His heart begins to pummel in his breast. He looks down at the softly-contoured features of her face. He kisses her lips. That same flesh-to-flesh soft moistness but now they are lying together not standing. She reaches her hands to her neck. 'I'll take my jumper off.' Yes, she is willing. She peels it off in one agile movement. She has a pale blue bra and her body is slender with slim arms. He wonders if he should take off her jeans himself, ask her or wait for her to do it. He feels himself becoming big and firm and knows this is the moment. She undoes her jeans, pulls her knees to her stomach to remove them. Her thighs are pale, clear, girlish-fleshy. She straightens her legs. He kneels on the bed, strips his jeans down to his calves. He should have taken his shoes off, but no matter too late now to untie them. Only their underwear is left. Her eyes, concentrated but calm, anticipating, trusting, look up into his. He presses down on her. His body feels ready for the final step.

But then, something happens. Or rather, nothing happens. He can feel a steady, relentless weakening inside himself. The room is reverting back too soon to the ordinary and the everyday. He becomes aware again of things around him - the silence of the four walls, that seem to tower over the bed, the papers on the desk, the assorted books in the bookcase, the high, looming wardrobe. The seconds are endless. The peacefulness of the room is unbearable. She lies unmoving beneath him. He is aware that he is stretched uselessly over her.

'I'm sorry,' he whispers eventually. 'Perhaps I'm too - anxious.'

She is silent for what seems a long period. Then at last she speaks. 'It's okay. There's plenty of time.'

'I don't understand it.'

'Don't worry.' Her voice is soft, intimate, but it no longer feels as if they are the only two people in the world.

She continues to hold him closely to her. 'Mmm, it's really nice to feel your body.'

Is she saying it to comfort him? He should be grateful for that. But he wants her awe, her satisfied spentness. He wants to savour her feeling of fulfilment in him, his of fulfilment in her.

She looks up at the ceiling. He feels awkward, prone above her, as if they have both been thrown from a moving train and he has landed by chance on top of her. Should he lie with her, relax for a while, gather himself, try again later? But if he fails again…Besides, there is the sense of something being over, something ended, a close to this particular event, just as, in an exam, you cannot go back and start again once the time is up.

He wants to leave immediately, to turn and escape, but that would make him look even more humiliated, even more immature. He does not want to upset her by showing the devastation he feels inside, but a show of cheerful normality might give the impression that he doesn't care about his failure, doesn't care about her. Whatever she may feel inside, she chats easily about life in Alex, the work they have to do, lecturers, and he in turn talks about his lodgings. When he leaves, neither of them mentions it and he feels less desolate.

He stands outside Alex. And the misery returns. He is conscious of the huge black heave of the sea beyond the dim sands. Cold needles of rain probe across his face. He knows that Nick and Dermot have gone to the Folk Club, then on to the Students' Union for a drink. With luck he will arrive back before them. He will go straight to bed and pretend to be asleep when they come in.

Monday, 2 December

At quarter-past-seven Gus peers out from behind his bed sheets and sees Nick sleeping soundly. He gets out of bed, dresses quickly and silently. A wash might wake up Nick, so he leaves at once, down the stairs - no sign of the Morgans, fortunately - and is outside. He will go back as breakfast is starting, which means that at least he will avoid the threat of an intimate conversation with Nick in their room.

The water brims in on long rolling swells. Clinging rainflakes creep in from the sea through the vaporous air.

He feels stunned. He tries not to labour over in his mind the experience of last night but it is impossible to prevent himself. Why didn't it happen? Was he a coward? Did he lack the nerve? Lose it when it came to the test? Did the unfamiliar presence of another human being distract him? Does he not like Amy enough? Surely that shouldn't matter anyway? Could he have done it with someone else? Or is it a general failure?

Tomorrow there is a Christmas Party. He will have to face Amy. Will other people notice his discomfort, her hurt? What if she shuns him? What if she has told Lorna and Fiona?

He times his return well. Cereal-munching and conversation have just begun and Nick and Dermot, absorbed in both, barely acknowledge him, while Simon gives his usual bare trace of a smile.

'That's the trouble,' says Nick. 'I've experienced no drama in my life. There's nothing I can write about. I wish I could have a war, something traumatic, like all the stuff that's happening in Vietnam. But I've just had an ordinary, uneventful upbringing.'

'You don't have to experience war or amazing events to write books,' Dermot responds. 'Look at Jane Austen. She just wrote about ordinary life.'

'She's got soldiers and sailors in her books, though,' Simon points out.

'Ha! Can you imagine any of them leading a charge or blasting the enemy with cannon?' retorts Dermot. 'You know the most violent event in Jane Austen? Someone falls down a few steps. And all the men fly into a panic.'

Gus feels the need to come into the exchange and sound normal. 'Or take Kerouac. He didn't write about anything amazing. But he made it amazing. He made ordinary events momentous.'

Dermot doesn't even bother to look up from his corn flakes. 'Kerouac? His writing's just meaningless rambling.'

Nick looks perplexed. 'Who the hell is he?'

'Jack Kerouac.'

Nick is impressed. 'Great name. That's the sort of name I need.'

'If you were in a real war, Nick,' says Dermot, 'I'd bet you'd soon be wanting a peaceful existence.'

'That's right,' Gus adds. 'You'd be thinking - I can't put pen to paper with all these bombs going off. When is the war going to end so I can go back home and start writing?'

Nick turns to Gus after Mrs Morgan has brought in their breakfasts. 'Hey. You must have been exhausted last night! You were fast asleep when I came in. Expended all your energy over at Amy's?'

Gus is aware from the corner of his eye of a sudden glance up by Simon at the mention of Amy.

'Oh, I just felt a bit tired.'

'And you were up this morning and out of the room like shit from a giraffe. I thought at first it was another hangover, then I thought, no, he wouldn't have wasted time *drinking* at Amy's last night. What did Shakespeare say about alcohol? *It provokes the desire but take away the performance.*'

'*It sets him off and it takes him on,*' Dermot continues.

'No. Isn't it *sets him on and takes him off*? That makes more bloody sense. Then I thought maybe you'd had uncontrollable urgings and had hot-footed it over to Alex, forgetting they don't let men in until - what is it? - ten-thirty? Jesus! That place is like a nunnery. Not that I've ever been in one.'

'More like a brothel last night, I expect,' Dermot puts in. '*He offered his honour*.'

'*She honoured his offer*,' Nick adds.

'*And all night long it was honour and offer*,' Nick and Dermot shout together, then look around anxiously in case Mrs Morgan has heard. Nick's face takes on a grim expression as he wags his finger at Gus. 'Don't overdo it now, lad. Pace yourself. Don't want to burn yourself out.'

Gus is rescued by Mrs Morgan's timely entrance. 'I see you've got your cheque book with you, Nick. Good! You've still got to pay for last week.' Nick dutifully starts to write a cheque.

'Oh, another left-hander!' she proclaims. 'Just like our grandson Eric. But you know, Eric is wonderful! He can use his right hand for writing as well. His teacher is astonished. He said it was very unusual for a boy to be amphibious like he is. We're all certain he's going to go far, Eric.'

'How old is he, Mrs Morgan?' Nick asks politely.

'Thirteen. He's good at all subjects. He's already fluid in French, but what he really likes is Art and Design. He wants to be a Posterior Designer when he leaves school.'

The boys raise eyebrows, exchange stealthy grins as she goes out. 'We should definitely write a book about this place,' Nick says. 'It is incredible. You wouldn't need to be Jack Kerosene, or whatever his name is, to make it so.'

'You're as bad as Mrs M,' Dermot says, laughing with Gus. Simon joins in.

Tuesday, 3 December

The large back room of the White Horse has been hired for the end-of-term party. Dermot, whose birthday it is, returns from Gwylan House's shower to Gus and Nick's room, where they wait with Simon.

'So was this a special birthday present to yourself?' Nick asks.

Dermot is indignant. 'No. I shower once a week. You know that.'

'Ah! Your once-a-week ablution.' Nick appeals to the others. 'Can you believe it? Once a week! How do we manage to live with you?'

Dermot looks at himself warily in the mirror, as if to check he is still the same person. 'If you wash too often, you wash away all the natural, beneficial oils in your skin. Apart from that, I like a shower to be a significant event in my calendar. I like to appreciate it. I like to feel the difference in myself before and after. You can't do that if you shower too often. And it saves water.'

'Rubbish,' Nick answers. 'I shower every day and feel the difference. I feel a new me every day. Course, it might be because I'm in love.'

'Yes - in love with showering - and with yourself! You've been preening yourself in front of that mirror for twenty minutes.' Dermot's laugh as he speaks shows no malice. 'Elizabeth the First only used to have a bath once a year.'

'Whether she needed it or not,' Gus adds.

'No wonder she was the bloody Virgin Queen,' Nick says, studying his face in the mirror.

'What's Fiona going to think of you if you get really close to her without showering?' Gus asks Dermot with mock censure.

'I've no intention of getting really close to her. Anyway, it's never occurred to me what people think of me, especially Fiona. It's what you think of yourself that's important.'

Gus feels a sudden spearing of emotional pain. *It's what you think of yourself.* Anxiety gores at him. Amy will be at the party.

'So how do your friends back home think of you?' Simon asks.

'Shouldn't think he's got any,' Nick says.

Dermot attacks his wet hair viciously with a towel. 'Um…probably - crazy but harmless.'

Gus gives a grin. 'They said that about Hitler before he seized power.'

Nick jabs a finger at Dermot. 'You're one of those unkempt students Mrs M rants on about.'

'Can you get kempt students?' Dermot asks.

'Anyway, I think you'll be safe from Fiona,' Nick says. 'Apparently she's invited Peter Strutton to the party. That should be interesting.'

Gus checks his hair in the mirror. 'Do you think Mrs M counts the number of showers we take?'

'Oh, she doesn't miss a bloody thing,' Nick answers. 'She's got more eyes than Mississippi. She's probably got hidden cameras in the bathroom and she drools over our naked bodies.'

Hidden cameras. Drools. Six weeks have gone by, but still a picture flashes before Gus's eyes, piercing through his body, jarring into his mind.

'Can you imagine Mrs M naked?' Dermot's eyes widen in wonder.

The room at the White Horse is already filled when they arrive. In the centre bodies are dancing, their forms blending into a gyrating montage of movement. Around the edges people laugh, talk, sway towards each other. Josh and Dafydd nod to them.

'We'll get a drink.' Like a jungle patrol leader, Nick pushes his way through the ever-encroaching forest of babbling, lurching humanity, returning the smiles and 'hi's' of Rosina, Vivienne and Tessa, while Gus, Geraint and Rob follow in his wake. Eventually they reach their goal, a broad drinks table overflowing with wines, beers, lagers and a bowl of oddly-coloured yellow-pinkish punch of undefined mixtures, that no-one has yet had the courage to test. Gus has decided that he will not drink too much. He will take it easy and simply relax. He has seen Amy, Lorna and Fiona together. Fiona waved eagerly towards them. Amy's smile to him seemed subdued but not unfriendly. Lorna looks coolly beautiful, calm and in control.

'Wow, look at Rosina's skirt!' Nick exclaims. 'How does she move her arse and legs in that?'

'Generally speaking,' Dermot pronounces, 'the tighter a woman's skirt, the looser her morals.'

'I'm not certain why you use the plural when you refer to her morals,' Gus says. 'I don't think she's got even one.'

Nick stretches his body and arm over to secure supplies of beer.

'That's a nice bottom you've got there.' A girl with long straight cheek-caressing brown hair leans back to admire him.

Nick glances at her. 'Thanks. I find it quite useful, for various things.'

'I bet you do.' She slides her eyes from it to scrutinise his face.

'Hey, homemade gorse wine!' Geraint shouts. 'I might try some.'

'I'm not going to poison my guts with that stuff!' Nick bellows above the noise. 'You wouldn't eat gorse, would you? Why the hell drink it!'

Gus examines the bottle. 'From the thickness of it, you might have to chew it rather than drink it.'

Dermot is feeling uneasy among the crowd and the talk. 'The boring thing about typical students is that they all think they're unique.'

'That what makes them typical - they all think they're unique,' Geraint adds.

'But people can't help being boring,' Nick says. 'No-one sets out to bore other people. No-one says their ambition is to bore others.'

'That's the trouble,' says Dermot. 'Bores don't realise they're boring - if they did they'd stop being boring. All bores actually think they're very interesting people - that's what makes them boring.'

'You're beginning to sound,' Gus says, and he is joined by the other two - 'BORING!'

Peter Strutton is in a small circle of students. He stands relaxedly, in a loose-fitting casual fawn jacket, one hand in his pocket, the other clasping a glass of white wine. He leans backwards, laughing, and the students join in, the girls eyeing him in close fascination.

He spots the boys, says something smilingly to the circle and begins to thread his way through the dancing army towards them.

Nick greets him, more confidently now. 'Glad you could make it, Dr Strutton.'

'I promise no poetry talk today, lads. I'm off duty. How are things going?'

'Fine,' Nick replies, slapping his arm around Dermot. 'It's this young man's birthday.'

Dermot shakes his head in slow bewilderment. 'I just can't believe I'm nineteen.'

Peter Strutton laughs. 'Happy Birthday! I think people are surprised by whatever age they are. I'm surprised I'm twenty-nine. I'm certain people are just as surprised to be forty-two, sixty-seven, ninety-one, eight, whatever. By the time you've got used to being a certain age, it's your birthday again.'

'Twenty-nine,' says Geraint, adding with an irreverence prompted by the party atmosphere, 'now that does seem really old.'

Peter takes it in good part. 'I know what you mean. The gap between younger and older always seems huge - if you're the younger person. But if you're the older, it doesn't seem so big. I must seem decades older to you, but to me, you're only a few years younger than I am. It makes perfect sense if you think about it. Supposing someone is forty - twenty years older than you. To you, twenty years adds up to a whole lifetime, but to the forty-year-old, it's only half a lifetime. Also, he knows what it's like to be your age, but you don't what it's like to be forty, so it seems to you that he's on a different planet. I don't see myself as older, only as having been alive longer.'

Suddenly, for no apparent reason, a second-year student leaps onto his chair and blares out from his lungs a shout of:

Aber-Aber-Aber!

The group of males gathered round him answer in three sharp, ear-bursting shouts.

OY-OY-OY!

The sequence is repeated with an increasing frenzy, the yell-leader beating an imaginary drum with his fist.

Aber-Aber-Aber!
OY-OY-OY!
Aber!
OY!
Aber!
OY!
Aber-Aber-Aber-Aber-Aber!

'Ah! The famous Aber Yell,' Peter says. 'Very impressive.' He sees Fiona moving steadfastly towards him. She looks determined, but her usual boisterous confidence is not apparent, with the trace of a nervous smile on her lips.

Peter Strutton too looks a little apprehensive and embarrassed. He mutters a quick 'excuse me,' and he weaves his way towards her.

Nick jabs Dermot playfully in the ribs. 'Is that the same drink you started with?'

'I'm pacing myself,' says Dermot. 'I want to make it memorable. Not like you. Your idea of a memorable night is one that you can't remember anything about.'

Lorna and Amy appear through the press of bodies.

'Done your Christmas shopping yet, Dermot?' Amy asks.

'I haven't done last year's yet,' he replies.

Nick kisses Lorna hello, tilting forward and grasping her round the waist as she leans her head back. Arm-in arm they meander onto the dance floor. Gus is wondering if he should do the same with Amy. At least, above the music and the hubbub of voices, they will have little chance to talk compared with the less clamorous outskirts of the room.

Amy seems calm and unconcerned, quietly enjoying the occasion. They have one slow dance together and her body feels warm resting against him but they do not kiss. She tells him she will leave tomorrow for the holiday, as she can have a lift home with two second-year students from Alex.

They are interrupted by Rosina and Glenys rushing towards them. They look agitated.

'Amy, could you come for a minute! It's Fiona. She's crying.'

Gus sees Fiona, framed darkly in the doorway. She is leaning against it. Her arms are loosely at her sides and she is letting tears slide helplessly down her face.

Thursday, 5 December

'So, the end of term,' Dermot declares as they sit in the Students' Union. 'I feel a bit like a soldier from the First World War returning to his family on leave. They'll have no idea of all the things that have happened to us.'

'That is a bit melodramatic.' Nick groans. 'God, I'm bloody shattered.'

'I'm surprised you're still standing,' Geraint says. 'After that party on Tuesday night. Then you went straight round to Lorna's yesterday, and no doubt had it off with her.'

'That's the trouble - if you're a bloke, mate, you can't lie back and think of England - or Wales in our case. You have to charge forward and think of D-Day. Jump from the landing craft. Storm up the beach. Isn't that true, Gus?'

Dermot nudges Gus. 'Somehow I can't imagine Lorna's defences being as stout as the German Panzers'.'

'Or like the Charge of the Light Brigade,' Geraint says. *'Into the Valley of Death rode the six hundred* - or, if it was sperm, more like six million.'

'Nipples to right of them, nipples to left of them,' cries Dermot.

'Is that right?' Nick asks. 'Six million sperm? Yes, I suppose it did feel like that.'

'Into the jaws of Death, into the mouth of Hell,' Geraint declaims.

'That sounds like Lorna,' says Dermot.

'*I came, I saw, I conquered,*' puts in Gus, trying to match the others' mood.

'Ah, in my case it'd be, *I came, I came, I came.*' Nick rends forth a thunderous burst of laughter, looks at Gus for reaction, then says thoughtfully, 'I wouldn't mind being a sperm.'

'You might come back as one in another life,' Dermot suggests.

'You're one big sperm anyway,' adds Geraint with finality.

'Talking of which,' says Nick with a chuckle, 'there was a bit of a scene at the party on Tuesday - Peter Strutton and Fiona.'

Eager voices demand more information.

'Well, it happened outside, so we all missed the drama. Fiona accosted him - love that word - at the party. Apparently he's finished with her. He left but she rushed outside with him and clung on to him. He had to tear himself free to escape from her clutches. Lorna says Fiona was in a terrible state afterwards - threatening to throw herself into the sea and do all sorts of things.'

'I did notice Fiona being very friendly to Peter Strutton at the party,' Geraint says. 'Poor guy must've thought he'd put his underpants on outside his trousers by mistake.'

'So ends a beautiful relationship, by the sound of it.' Nick jerks violently back in his chair. 'But - hey, Dermot - that means that Fiona is free.'

Dermot glances up. Unexpectedly, he looks deliberative. A reluctant smile creeps into his face. 'Actually, she's not bad.'

Christmas Vacation

Gus decides to take the coach to Cardiff, which lops half-an-hour off the train journey time, but half-a-foot off the leg room in his seat. It still takes five-and-a-half hours to cover the one hundred miles as the crow flies. There follows a twenty-five minute haul by train up the valley to Nanthyfryd.

When he arrives there, in late afternoon, the village's main street is virtually deserted. The mist curls down from the mountain as he walks past the small dozing shops, their gloomy interiors bereft of customers. Everyone is probably in Cardiff or Pontypridd, revelling in the pre-Christmas bustle.

His family's house is old and narrow, but, because it is end-of-terrace, it stretches further back than other houses in the street. The three bedrooms upstairs are for his parents, his two brothers sharing, and himself, while sister Maxine's bedroom, which the boys are never allowed to enter, is in one of the three small reception rooms downstairs.

Gus has read about the odd effects on time that would beset space travellers if moving at high speeds. If they spent a few months away from Earth, they would find on their return that years had elapsed. This is the curious feeling that hits Gus as he enters the house. His mother looks strange yet familiar at the same time. His father looks smaller, diminished, older, but Gus feels pleasure at his father's genuine smile of delight on seeing him. They are like figures from his past. Years, rather than ten weeks, seem to have gone by, yet he also has the sensation of having been blasted back in time. He has forgotten home, the smell and the feel of it.

The house seems more familiar, less changed, than the people in it. His bedroom reeks of the past. His old bed - why does he think of it as "old"? - is comforting, in a nostalgic kind of way - yet how can a person of eighteen be affected by nostalgia? The bed feels as if it belongs to a past era he thought he had freed himself from but hasn't, just as, until that moment with Amy, he thought he had moved forward in life but hasn't. But, once snuggled deep in his old bed, he finds his half-dreams before sleep are sweeter, with lovely images of Amy floating before his inner vision.

His brothers Raymond, thirteen, and James, eleven, and his sister Maxine, fifteen, regard him strangely, almost, as Dermot mentioned, as if he is a soldier returning home from the wars. He has the unnerving feeling that his brothers look on him now as a man. Maxine seems to have changed the most. She is almost a woman. Odd to think his family have carried on their lives, for the ten weeks, without him, without him having thought about them apart from brief reminders in his mother's weekly letter and Raymond's occasional note. Now he feels guilt, even though he is the only one who knows of his lack of thought.

It is difficult to find privacy in the house. Yet there is less privacy in Aber, and it bothers him less. Perhaps it is because, there, the sea and sky give the illusion of space - but it is not an illusion. Stranger still, it is the absence of sea that he finds most pressing, and depressing. Why has he never felt it before in Nanthyfryd? Yet why should he have? Nanthyfryd is well inland.

The rooms of the house seem darker than he remembers them - surely another illusion? People sit or move about in a shadowy dimness. Perhaps it is the short sunless winter days. But he has been here all previous winters without this having struck him. There is a curious dislodgement in his mind. Aber, where he is not, seems to fill it. Nanthyfryd, where he is, seems distant and remote. He realises he regarded his life in Aber as permanent. To find himself back home comes as a sudden shock for which he was not prepared. Yet how could it have not entered his mind?

But soon the old familiar sights and sounds come back - his mother clanging the kettle on the stove, dusting, busily making mince pies and Welsh cakes; his father up to his elbows in suds at the washing-up bowl, or sitting in front of the coal fire, reading newspapers or thrillers. Gus notices he wears glasses now, awkwardly perched halfway down his nose. During the few days he has off from the mine, he lounges about the house, not knowing quite what to do with himself for much of the time.

By Christmas Day, Gus is feeling more at home in his home. The day itself is satisfying - safe, secure, stable. It too feels like something from the past, but Gus has made the journey back to it with no disruption to his mind. It is still a special day, with a timeless permanence, standing outside normal existence, outside the bewildering dislocations wrought by time and his life away. They have a family meal, with one set of grandparents coming over. The returning recognisable taste of his mother's cooking, the treat of turkey and Christmas pudding, overcome the odd feelings that dog him. They even all join in with simple games afterwards, - I spy, charades, an unruly enjoyable game of snap with playing cards. For Christmas presents, Gus gets a thick sweater from his mother, worried by his occasional references to the Aber cold in his letters, and gloves from his sister, doubtless from his mother's prompting.

Amy sends him a Christmas card, but no letter. She writes in the card, *Have a happy Christmas and a great New Year. See you next term.* He gets a breezy letter from Nick recounting how he and his mate Jason got drunk on Christmas Eve in Pontypool and walked four miles home.

By the time the month's vacation is up, Gus is firmly established back in his house and in time. Now it feels strange to be on the move to Aber again. Why does the university year have these breaks? There is a double dislocation, first in moving back to home, then in switching again to university. It is like suddenly veering to one side of the road, then, equally joltingly, being swung across in the other direction in a crazy zig-zag, before resuming the normal straight and even course.

Tuesday, 7 January

M r Morgan is on the phone in the hallway.
'We're just popping out to the supermarket after we've cleared the breakfast things, Brian.'

The boys listen with silent chuckles as he is prompted by Mrs Morgan.

'Only to get milk, tell him.'

'Only to get milk.'

'Tell him the presents were very nice again.'

'The presents were very nice again, Brian.'

Mr Morgan shambles in to the breakfast room and squints through the window. 'Weather's looking good. A bit windy. Yes - it'll be a dry day if it doesn't rain.'

'Did you have a good Christmas?' Nick asks them as Mrs Morgan gathers up the boys' empty plates.

'Yes, very good, thanks,' she chirps. 'We went to our son Brian's. And before Christmas we saw a wonderful Nativity Play in the school. Our granddaughter Bethan was Mary. She was so good in it. And our grandson Jonathan was one of the Wise Men. And he did look wise! And he had a big black beard - I almost didn't recognise him! And the three of them came in with their gifts, gold, frankenstein and myrrh. He gave such a lovely bow! And Bethan cradled the baby in her little arms!...'

Nick struggles to choke a laugh and succeeds in turning it into a passable cough. Simon hunches up, trying to swallow back his titters.

'Frankincense, isn't it, love?' says Mr Morgan with an eye towards the boys.

'That's what I said, didn't I? Oh, it was lovely! I was almost in tears -'

'Just like us,' Nick murmurs.

' - Then at the end they all sang "Away In A Manger". And Jonathan's beard almost fell off as he opened his mouth but he managed to catch it...that's right - gold, *frankincense* and mirth...' She marches out with the four plates.

'Did you buy Mrs Morgan anything nice for Christmas, Mr Morgan?' Nick, recovered, asks amiably.

'Bought her a shopping bag,' he says in a doleful tone. 'That's what she said she wanted. I don't know why. We've got loads of bags here. They're everywhere. I don't know what she does with them all.'

The continuous sigh, surge and suck of waves upon the shore. The sky dim white in the distance, merging into pale blues and greys. High above, a patch of cloud lit in a silvery gleam the only indication that the sun is present. A ripping wind brings in clouds of wheeling seagulls, who leap and whoop excitedly then bank and glide in serene effortless crescents.

Gus watches the water. Is he glad to be back? Again that tremor of anticipation, and apprehension. Amy's face and gentleness, so yearningly beautiful. Her smile, that you can feel as well as see. That line he has crossed with her, that he can never go back to; never pretend that it didn't happen and just start again. The month away from her could provide a convenient break if he wants to back off her, write it off as a bad job and start afresh with someone else. He doesn't know why he thinks of Lorna - of all the people he knows the most unattainable. He has seen her already from a distance. The way she walks, from her thighs, jaunting upon the street, her shoulders swaying as sexily as her hips.

No. He likes Amy and he wants her. It's a new year; a new dawn. He can do it, he is certain.

The sea hurling now at the beach, the wind brimming above, the chaotic crying of seagulls as they cut across the sky.

Thursday, 9 January

The walls of Fiona's room in Alex are festooned with posters of rock bands, a map of the world and an aerial photograph of a large mansion-like dwelling surrounded by green land. In the evening she switches on a reddish-pink light giving the room a strange psychedelic feel.

Gus and Nick lounge on the bed, Amy and Lorna sit on the room's two chairs. Fiona carries in a large tray of five coffees and disperses them expertly to her guests, then squeezes onto the bed beside the boys. An expensive-looking music system supplies a sleepy-voiced male vocalist.

'So, is everyone back and raring to go for a second term?' Fiona asks.

'Yes, everyone carrying on as normal - or in the case of Dermot, as abnormal.' Nick laughs. He points to the photograph. 'Is that your house?' Fiona voices an 'mhmm.'

'And I suppose you'll inherit it as lady of the manor.' There is an undercurrent of mockery and disgust in Nick's amicable tone.

'Oh no,' she says. 'Much too big. I don't know what I'll do.'

'Marry someone rich and famous,' says Nick.

She laughs a little embarrassedly. 'Well, that's not exactly in my head at the moment!'

There is a hush. No-one is certain how to react and each is wondering if Fiona is thinking distressing or harmless thoughts. Lorna breaks the silence.

'I was talking to Rosina the other day. She came up with this strange and amazing idea. When she leaves university, she's got to live somewhere, buy her own house or rent a place…'

She stops.

'Go on,' says Fiona.

'She's worked out that - if she hadn't been born, everyone in Britain would be living in a different house.'

Nick is puzzled. 'Whaaat?'

Lorna continues. 'If she hadn't been born, someone else would be living in the house that she would have bought or be renting. So someone else would be living in the house that that person is now living in, and so on. So everyone in Britain would be in a different house. Is there a flaw in that logic?'

There is another silence as each thinks.

'That could apply to any person who's born,' says Fiona.

'So,' continues Amy, 'whoever's born, it makes a difference to absolutely everyone else in the country.'

'Perhaps the world,' Nick adds gravely.

'I hadn't thought of that,' Gus exclaims. 'Each of us will make a difference to the world.'

Fiona thinks. 'And it won't be that we're living in different houses. It'll mean that some people will be living in different parts of the country, so they'll meet different people, marry differently, have different jobs…'

'What an amazing theory.' Nick is dumbfounded.

'So the whole course of human history is altered by the mere existence of each individual,' proclaims Fiona.

'That's why each human life is infinitely precious,' says Lorna.

Gus has been silent, and thinking. 'Hold on. If Rosina hadn't been born, the house that she's living in might simply be left empty. And if it's not that house, it'll be someone else's. So somewhere along the line - there's going to be an empty house, which means that everyone after that point will be in the same house as they're in now.'

'Not necessarily. If there's a housing shortage, there'll be very few empty houses,' Lorna suggests.

Nick turns to Gus. 'Trust you to destroy a beautiful idea.'

'No,' Gus replies. 'There's something in the theory. Depending on where along the line the empty house is, Rosina's non-existence could affect a few people, or thousands. And you can apply it in lots of ways. If I hadn't been alive to come to Aber, someone else would be sharing the room with you, Nick. Someone else would be in that person's room...Yes, it makes sense.'

'You could apply it to marriage,' Amy goes on. 'If I hadn't been born, the person who marries me would probably marry someone else, and so on...'

Lorna's face stiffens as if in reprimand. 'So you've decided to get married. You haven't mentioned anything about it to us.'

There is general laughter, prompting an embarrassed smile from Amy. She avoids looking at Gus. 'Well, I suppose we all will eventually,' she says, looking down at the floor.

Gus feels a sudden revulsion, at the very thought of marriage, of the future. Into his mind there intrudes a dark and startling picture, like a sharp bolt of lightning that makes the surrounding sky even more sombre. He and Amy in the future, together, working, living in a neat new house. Perhaps this was why he couldn't do it with her - a subconscious fear of what it might lead to. Or Amy married to someone else. Or him as a husband, in busy nine-to-five regulated society. The future, in the rare moments that he thinks of it in conventional terms, is an alarming prospect, almost like death. For most of the time you do not believe it will really happen, but the occasional realisation that it will brings on a sudden overpowering blackness, which, thankfully, just as suddenly vanishes.

And he is back in the present. To the calm, clear afternoon sea, as still as a painting framed through Fiona's window, the sky a thin sheet of winter-pale blue resting lightly on the water, one or two clouds cruising unhurriedly across.

'Some of us have enough worries in the present!' Fiona laughs.

Gus looks towards her, and her eye catches his. For a second, she seems to look into his, thinking.

Thinking what? And another bolt of lightning strikes him. Does she know? About what happened last term? Or didn't happen? Surely Amy wouldn't tell anyone? Or would she? Fiona and Lorna are people who have a way of encouraging others to talk, whose manner prompts confession. The girls live, eat, think, talk together, constantly in each other's company. And Lorna? She is with Nick. Nick? How many people know?

Gus suddenly feels conspicuous, exposed, a specimen to be analysed and appraised.

Or did she? Did Fiona's pondering, probing eyes scrutinise him, or did she just respond because his uneasy eyes happened to meet hers for a moment? And what is she thinking as regards Peter Strutton and herself? What could be happening there? Fiona seems buoyant, untroubled now, but she invariably is when in company.

There is a smooth camaraderie about the five of them. Gus had half-feared that Lorna and Nick would be all over and round each other, in which case he might feel obliged to pair off with Amy - he has talked to her only briefly in the four days they've been back, chatting to her about the Christmas each had. But Nick lounges happily back beside him on the bed.

Lorna and Amy remain in their chairs, perhaps to avoid making Fiona feel awkward among two couples. No. He's certain Amy hasn't said anything. She looks relaxed, unperturbed, after the one uncomfortable moment for her earlier. If it was Lorna or Fiona, they would be far more likely to blab or ridicule. But not Amy.

No, not Amy.

Saturday, 11 January

What awaits him this weekend? He didn't make any arrangements with Amy in Fiona's room on Thursday. Strangely, Amy wasn't at the seminar yesterday morning and he had no chance to ask anyone from Alex where she might be. Neither was she in last night's debate in the Skinner's Barn Bar, a lively affray on whether the expense of space exploration can be justified when there are so many problems in the world.

As Gus steps into the hallway of Gwylan House from the breakfast room, his eye catches sight of a white envelope by the front door. It has no postage stamp so it must have been dropped through the letter-box by hand. As he nears it he can see a short name in the middle. The three letters of his name, in small neat light-pressured handwriting.

Amy's.

There is that rippling of excitement through him. A personal note, to him. That suggestion of a private pact between them. Amy could have mentioned something on Thursday evening, in the public presence of Fiona, Nick and Lorna. But this is more intimate.

Something stops him opening the envelope immediately in the hallway. He wants to delay the sensation, feel the suspense for a few moments longer. And he is nervous. He can hear Nick and Dermot in animated talk in the breakfast room. He'll take the letter upstairs, lie on his bed and read it.

She must be inviting him round in the evening. She wouldn't have wanted to ask him in front of everyone on Thursday. Anticipation, wrestling with trepidation in his mind again. The thrill and the dread clashing within.

> Dear Gus,
>
> I'm afraid I've come down with flu, so I won't be able to see you this weekend. I felt it coming on on Thursday evening, and then yesterday I felt really horrible and found it difficult to get out of bed.
>
> The nurse has given me something for it. I didn't sleep very well last night and felt rough this morning so it's probably best if I'm in quarantine this weekend.
>
> Excuse the shaky handwriting. I'm scribbling this down quickly and I've asked Rosina to drop it into you.
>
> See you soon,
>
> Amy

The mixture of expectancy and anxiety that he felt before has given way to another jarring mingling, of disappointment and relief. Should he ignore the letter and go over to Alex to see her, and show his tenderness towards her? He would like to hold her in his arms, in her helpless state. The pressure would be off him. But somehow that would be too romantic, too daring.

Early evening. Nick is lounging on his bed after his usual Saturday afternoon football exertions in the Digs League. He thrusts a paperback over to Gus, pointing to a verse.

'I've found this brilliant poem. By Yeats.'

The Scholars

Bald heads, forgetful of their sins,
Old learned, respectable bald heads,
Edit and annotate the lines
That young men, tossing on their beds,
Rhymed out in love's despair
To flatter beauty's ignorant ear.

'Isn't that so true? People like Parker-Hurst or Sewage, analysing poems as if they're dissecting a dead rat, losing sight of the fact that they were written by lovesick, tormented guys - like you and me!'

Nick flicks idly through the pages. 'So, a weekend without Amy. What are you going to do with yourself? Disco in King's tonight - or there's always the Ballroom Dancing Club on the Pier. My mate Sam from the Cricket Club's started going and he thinks he's getting addicted. He reckons it helps him with his cover drive.' Nick suddenly leaps from his bed and performs an elegant, sweeping stroke with an imaginary bat. Then he squeezes his lips together in an expression of tearful glumness.

'But yes - no Amy.'

'Well I haven't known her that long, only a couple of weeks last term.'

'Yeh, but you really seem to be in there. You surprised us all. Dark horse, you are. Anyway, I'm round at Lorna's tonight. And - don't wait up for me. *I may be gone some time.* Who said that? Me! All bloody night I hope.' And Nick gives his guffaw.

'So - you're planning - a dirty stopover!'

'That's the plan. It's a shame Amy's not match fit. You could have been my accomplice. We can get sent down together! No - no-one's going to find out. And even if they do, you just get a warning. It would be worth it, just to spend the night with Lorna. That's the nicest thing - waking up with somebody in the morning.' Nick tosses back his head, breathes in with deep contentment as if he is inhaling Lorna's morning smell.

'So what do you do - hide under the bed?'

'No-oo-oh.' Nick draws the word out mockingly at Gus's naivety. 'The cleaners don't come in on Sunday morning, so you just have to stay in the room until ten-thirty, when guys are officially allowed in. The worst thing is going to be - if I have to take a piss in the middle of the night. I can either take a chance and sneak down the corridor -or, much easier - use the wash-hand basin.'

Gus envies the spirit of adventure that is captivating Nick, and feels a little alarm at the way events are developing.

'Listen,' Nick goes on, 'next weekend maybe, when Amy's recovered, if you feel like accompanying me...Great. I'll pave the way with tonight's mission.'

'What about breakfast tomorrow?'

'I've told Mrs M I'm staying with friends in Borth. No problem.'

'You've got it all worked out!'

'Ah! That's the secret - planning. As Alexander the Great might have said. Hey - Alex! That's appropriate. It will be Alex the Great tonight. Hey - you stayed there for a week in Form Six didn't you? You know the layout. You can even come along tonight if you want. You can be my scout. You could look in on Amy - maybe give her some tender loving care. And there's always Fiona - she needs someone to comfort her after Peter Strutton.'

'No - Amy said it's best if I don't see her. And I think I'll pass as regards Fiona.'

'Or there are plenty of other bods in there. How about Tessa, or the lovely Rosina or tall Vivienne? They'll all be in the White Horse tonight, I bet.'

'No - I might spend a quiet night in - save myself for when Amy is well.'

'Ah - your loyalty is touching. Yeh - next weekend. Definitely.' Nick stresses the final word with a dramatic wag of the finger, straight between Gus's eyes.

Tuesday, 14 January

> *There's not a fibre in my trembling frame*
> *That does not vibrate when thy step draws near,*
> *There's not a pulse that throbs not when I hear*
> *Thy voice, thy breathing, nay thy very name.*
> *When thou art with me every sense seems dim,*
> *And all I am, or know, or feel, is thee;*
> *My soul grows faint, my veins run liquid flame,*
> *And my bewildered spirit seems to swim*
> *In eddying whirls of passion, dizzily.*

The poem is written in large, fluent, unselfconscious handwriting, the hand of someone with large, flowing passions. Peter squats on his sofa. He finds he is leaning forward as he reads. He notices his wrists are stretched taut and his hands clasp tightly the paper. He tries to relax them. He admires the simple intensity of the verse.

And all I am, or know, or feel, is thee

Every word a monosyllable. He likes *my veins run liquid flame*. But it becomes profoundly disconcerting to realise that he is the object of this fervour. Where is she finding all this verse? It's not from the mainstream English poets. Fiona must be scouring the anthologies, hungrily selecting what she thinks will make an impact.

> *Won't you dream of me tonight?*
> *Please say that you will,*
> *In secret union, out of sight,*
> *When you're lying still.*
> *Breathing softly in the dark,*
> *Won't you feel that sudden spark*
> *Flood your sleeping mind with light,*
> *If you dream of me tonight?*

She cannot be harbouring seriously these sentiments. She may be wanting to demonstrate her knowledge, her enthusiasm for poetry. She may be just indulging her overflowing adolescent emotions. She is enjoying searching out the poems, showing him what strong passions she is capable of.

But it did not stop in the Christmas vacation. Apart from the card saying 'I miss you so much', as if they were an established couple, there was more poetry. He has made his position clear. He can do no more except wait for the inferno to burn itself out. Perhaps it's a warning to him. He's been fortunate previously, enjoying brief passions with girls, who then drift away and find boys. This clinging infatuation he has not been at the receiving end of before. And the scene at the party was embarrassing - and frightening. If Professor Savage gets wind of it, hears any rumours...Yet he genuinely wants to get to know the students, consort amongst them, make them feel he is their friend.

Perhaps he should not lament getting older and wanting to hang on to his youth through the reassurance of female students still finding him desirable. Perhaps it will be easier when he is older. Then they are unlikely to find him attractive. When he is forty...But the thought is revolting. And will his feelings have evaporated?

He has finished a second draft of his novel - but has begun to go through it again, striving for a perfection that eludes him as a sparkling wavelet slips through the hand that tries to hold it. He has conquered the main bulk of the book, established control over it after endless hours of struggle, sometimes arduous, sometimes exhilarating - but deep within its pages pockets of resistance still hold out, refusing to be elevated to the level of excellence he demands. This is like street fighting, and is painfully slow, but he perseveres. But this and the work of preparing and delivering lectures and seminars fills his cup of life without the shackles clamped around him by lovesickness.

Thursday, 16 January

Amy is in lectures, looking slightly paler than normal, but she stops to talk to Gus afterwards and invites him over to Alex for the evening. There is the flutter in his stomach again, that sudden surging of hope and desire through body and mind. It is the first time he will have been alone with her, in her room, since...

Then the uncertainty surfaces again. He hasn't told her of Nick's plan for the two of them to stay in Alex on Saturday night. If he doesn't mention it to her tonight, he will have to somehow spring it on her tomorrow or on the day itself.

On the walk to Alex, he is wondering if others experience this tumult that takes place in his consciousness. Human beings, so neat, so defined, so constrained on the surface. Is the upheaval of a universe happening inside each small figure? Or is it only him? No - he has the testimony of the great poets. Or are they freaks of nature?

Amy when she opens her door seems unperturbed. They give each other a quick kiss on the cheek, her hands lightly on his shoulders. Before he has time to decide about an embrace she takes her hands away and steps aside with that lovely lithe movement, holding the door for him to come in.

'How are the other boys?' she asks brightly. 'How's Nick, and Dermot - and Simon?' Does she hesitate before saying that last name, giving it slightly more emphasis?

'Yes, everyone's back in the swing of things,' he replies.

'Oh,' she sighs. 'I've missed a few lectures and seminars this week. That's a nuisance.'

'Do you need to borrow any notes?'

'No thanks. Fiona's lent me hers. She's got quite large manic handwriting, but she's really good. She sits with me and deciphers it for me. Simon said I could borrow his.' She laughs. 'He flashed open his book in front of me, but the writing was so tiny - microscopic. I couldn't make out a word.'

Did Simon, like Fiona, offer to decipher it for her? Would Amy tell him if he did?

'I politely declined.' She says this with no hint, as far as he can see, of feeling towards Simon. Gus relaxes again.

'Ah ! I'm so glad I feel better,' she sighs again, with a relieved smile at him. She sits down, stretching her arms in front of her and interlocking her fingers. If her words were a hint...But it has been over six weeks now. He cannot just resume where he left off, as if it were only yesterday. She would come and sit beside him on the bed if she wanted anything to happen - unless she is waiting for him.

They begin to talk, about their Christmases and New Years, in a friendly way. He can feel time, and Amy, and his chance and resolve, slipping away. Amy shows no sign of movement or longing. There is the occasional lull in conversation when both do not look at each other, but stare thoughtfully ahead or down. At least he has re-established contact. He can fix a time to see her soon and then prepare himself. And she has only just recovered from her bout of illness.

At last he gets up to leave. She give him the same swift kiss as when he arrived. He hasn't yet arranged a date with her.

'I expect I'll see you tomorrow,' she says. 'Don't know yet what I'm doing over the weekend.'

The weekend. He could now mention it. But no. And he could, now, put his arms around her waist, stroke back her hair and go for a proper kiss - but if she pulled herself away from him…

The weekend, and Nick's plan, is coming too soon. Gus feels increasing alarm. Not at the danger and the forbidden aspect of it - he could enjoy that. But at the thought of spending the whole night, and morning, with Amy. He knows, with that sense of helplessness again, and anger at his own indecisive spinelessness, that he will have to get out of it.

Saturday, 18 January

'Snow on the hills this morning, boys.' Mr Morgan gives a gloomy smile as he gathers up the breakfast plates. They hear his shuffle recede sorrowfully into the distance.

'It's funny,' Gus says. 'If anyone except Mr M had said that, it would sound quite romantic. It would conjure up a picture of white-capped peaks…'

Nick slurps his tea. 'What a pig of a meal. That would bloat a bloody camel. Don't really feel like doing anything now. That's my day finished.'

Simon yawns. 'Who feels like doing *anything* at eight-thirty in the morning?'

'I am surprised at the efficiency with which you waste time, Nick,' Dermot says.

'Ah, it's a skill that improves significantly with practice.'

'Hard work never killed anyone yet.'

'Yeh, but there's always a first time. No point in taking risks. Speaking of health, we need some more players for our Digs team, Promenaders. We got thrashed by Carp last week. We're playing Plyn today. You free, Gus? Simon? You're both pretty good at table football - if you can translate those skills onto the turf, you'll strike terror into the opposition.'

'I know it sounds hopelessly ambitious,' says Dermot, 'but I might go to the library.'

'I should go to the laundrette,' Gus says.

'Laundrette?' Nick glares at him in disgust. 'There'll be ladies looking on at the football. A chance to impress them with your bodily movements…'

Nick has not yet mentioned the visit to Alex planned for tonight. Gus hasn't thought of an excuse, still hasn't spoken about it to Amy. He could tell Nick he's quarrelled with Amy, but if Nick goes to Alex he's bound to learn the truth.

Dermot as usual takes the conversation off at a tangent. 'When you think of it, for every word that exists in the English language, someone, somewhere, must have made it up, invented it - even *the* or *or* or *examination*. Who were they?'

'My favourite word at the moment is *lascivious*.' Nick mouths it with heavy, drooling emphasis on the second syllable. Dermot leans over to him. 'I thought it would be *Lorna* - but then I suppose they mean roughly the same thing.'

'Watch it.' Nick gives him a playful glare. 'But I expect this young man's favourite word is - *Amy*.' He gives Gus a hearty pat on the shoulder.

'Funny thing about *Amy*,' says Dermot, 'it's only three letters, but you can make lots of words out of it - *may*, *yam*.'

'*Yma* in Welsh,' Nick says.

'*Mya*, except that it's spelt differently - *Maia*. She's a goddess,' Simon puts in, with a smile to himself, that does not escape Gus's attention.

Nick laughs excitedly. 'Oh well Gus would certainly agree with you there.' He turns to Gus. 'We're still waiting for your report on her.'

'Well, nothing to report so far. We're - going along nicely.'

'Nicely,' Nick repeats with disdain. 'You sound like a fifty-year-old.'

'Let him alone,' Dermot moans in exasperation, 'we're not all like you - faster than the speed of light.'

'I'm only joking,' Nick protests. 'He knows I am. Oh, by the way, Gus, I'm going to have to disappoint you about tonight. Lorna's going to Bangor overnight, with some of her Alex friends, for a Gymanfa Ganu - you know, a Welsh concert, even though she doesn't know a word of Welsh. Tried to persuade me to go as well. Course, there's nothing stopping you staying over in Alex, but you wouldn't have me as an accomplice.'

'Oh.' Gus feels the sudden glorious relief gush through his mind and body. He shrugs his shoulders sadly, squeezes his lips together to show disappointed acceptance. 'Mmm, don't really fancy going on my own. Never mind. Is Amy going with Lorna?'

Nick's voice is low and rebuking. 'Don't know, mate. You should know her movements, not me. If she's still here, go for it on your own.' Then his voice lightens. '- But, yeh, it's more fun with two of us. We'll arrange something, maybe for the end of term. Perhaps you two guys can come along. We'll organise a grand raid! Dermot, we'll team you up with Fiona. Simon - let's see - how about Rosina? Or Teresa? She's nice. I think she likes you.'

Simon smiles shyly.

Monday, 20 January

T his terrible, drowning, obliterating feeling that he is the only person in the world who is unhappy.

Simon sits in his room, silently with the light off, at least until the other boys go out for the night, to the Folk Club in the Skinner's, he'd heard them say.

Solitariness gives you odd feelings. You can see people all around you, but between you and them is an unswimmable sea. Sharks of your own imagination lurk there. This sense of a desert island, of being trapped within himself. He cannot communicate to anyone all that he knows and feels about poetry, literature, human history, the human condition. Is he condemned forever to hold these things in his head with no means to share them with others? He can debate, discuss things inside his mind, but when it comes to talking to other people...

Nick had asked Mr Morgan, 'how long you been taking in students, then, Mr Morgan?' A simple question, but he could never have asked it, at least not in the way Nick did - natural, relaxed, unforced, genial. The only way he could see Mr

Morgan was as the strange, wrinkled, middle-aged man, friendly but remote from him.

Sometimes he feels so worthless in the presence of the other boys, a smaller-than-life figure. But he's always felt this way. The rugby period in school. The first time he tried to tackle someone. He was brutally handed off. He can still feel the sensation of being flung down in the mud, like a soldier being shot, his collapsed body at the feet of rampaging boys, his face terrifyingly level with their greyed boots, as if he was about to be buried alive. 'Scrum'. Such an ugly word. How did it originate? Perhaps a mixture of 'scramble' and 'crumble'…

Now all his learning and thinking count for nothing when he's surrounded by them at breakfast or in the evening, listening to their inane chatter as they whinge over everyday superficial matters. But then other times he appreciates them, admires them, wishes he could be like them. Dermot is intriguing. His brain, like his feet, is large and untidy. Thoughts zoom through it with the speed of non-stop trains through stations. Jolting disconnected ideas but always thought-provoking. Nick, well, he would be the one doing the handing-off at rugby, the running with the ball, the skipping and side-stepping that he himself has practised in his bedroom but never achieved on the field.

And Gus…He and Gus are wary of each other, but he can detect in Gus, at least in part of him, something of a kindred spirit. Gus is the only one of whom he can feel, yes, he's had the same hesitations, maybe the same mental writhings, as me. But now Gus, it seems, is with Amy, going along untroubled.

Amy, who gives him kind, unlonging smiles. Amy…

This torturing loneliness that rears up in front of him, the cobra again, staring into his paralysed soul. The cobra has a hundred heads and a hundred pairs of ugly eyes trained on him. And the cobra faces him whichever direction he turns.

This morning, in Smith's bookshop, he saw a girl of beguiling loveliness browsing. He wishes he could have gone breezily up to her and said, 'Hey, we're having a party tonight. How about coming to it?' in a happy, careless way. Only, of course, he wasn't having a party, wasn't going to one and in any case he knew he could not bring himself to say anything to her. He nudged closer to her, hoping a reckless impulse would overtake him and he would suddenly start a conversation with her. But his heart began thudding like a drum. He knew that if he spoke he would sound breathless and nervous...

And on Saturday, there was a girl standing in front of him at the supermarket. Her hair was soft black and thick. He felt a desire to put his face into it, to lose himself in it. He was relieved when she turned her head slightly to reveal a mediocre face which did not attract him.

Amy...

He totters on the peak one last time before toppling, deliciously exhausted, and the warm fluid bubbles over the brim. He groans with joy and squirms with the effort and shock, like the recoil of a discharged gun.

But now he is growing tired of his lonely raptures between the sheets. The exquisite, ecstatic squeezing, the avalanche of fire through his body and the rush of the soft liquid onto his thighs, the easeful satisfaction, now followed almost invariably by a sudden cold aloneness and revulsion against the mind-images, or sometimes photographs, that had so enchanted him for fifteen blissful minutes.

He hugs to himself his unloved, uncherished body and descends into sleep.

Thursday, 23 January

'Today we will consider Shakespeare's so-called "Problem Plays", namely *All's Well That Ends Well, Measure for Measure, Troilus and Cressida*. Are they comedies? Are they tragedies? They seem somewhat diffused and ambiguous in their intent, like most of the essays that I've had handed in to me this week...'

Dr Parker-Hurst places his hands on his gown lapels and rocks alarmingly back and forth on his heels. 'Of course, *All's Well That Ends Well* was never considered a problem play until, uh, *I* edited it for the Albatross Shakespeare series...'

Amy is sitting two rows in front of Gus. She wears an enticingly warm-looking, snugly-fitting dark blue jumper. Her dark hair spreads loosely down over her neck and shoulders as she writes, and he can just see the pen held between her small smooth fingers. He likes this quietness about her; her contented unspectacular self-sufficiency. Lorna can be boisterous and extrovert, attracting boys' attention like a magnet. Fiona can be witty, opinionated, loud. Amy can just be there, can just be. Her complete unawareness and lack of acknowledgement of her beauty makes her all the more beautiful. She went to Bangor with the Alex girls on the weekend, so Gus ended up going with Dermot to the Film Society to see Ken Russell's version of Lawrence's *Women in Love*, while Nick and Geraint went to the Saturday night disco.

'I've got another lecture now and seminars this afternoon,' she says to Gus as they leave the lecture. 'Do you want to come round this evening?' Her expression is neither tense nor eager, but friendly and composed.

Gus almost hoped she would not invite him. But he cannot make excuses or show alarm, so he agrees with enthusiasm. He feels the disquiet gnawing at his stomach, but at the same time thinks he should grasp this chance, fling aside doubts, calm himself beforehand, focus, be determined and dauntless. It has been seven weeks now - surely enough time for them both to be able to brush it aside as a distant memory. This time he will do it.

'Anyone coming up to the Physics Lecture Theatre tonight?' Dermot asks. 'Astronomy Society - should be an interesting talk. *Are We Alone In The Universe?*'

'I wish I knew more about science,' Nick says as they munch on Mrs Morgan's evening meal of pork, swede, onions and potatoes. 'When the moon landing happened, me and my dad went out into the back garden that night, like lots of people, looked up at the moon and thought, there are men walking around up there, *human beings*. Just amazing. We should have a few science students as friends. Then we could ask them questions.'

Dermot looks suspiciously at his swede, probing it with his fork like an explorer wary of snakes in the jungle. 'What deep scientific questions, what riddles of the universe, have you been pondering?'

Nick examines his pork. 'Why is shit always brown?'

'In your case,' says Dermot, 'it's probably the alcohol.'

'Or Mrs Morgan's gravy,' Gus suggests.

Nick waves his knife in the air. 'And I've always wondered strange things like, are identical twins always exactly the same height?'

Dermot is impatient. 'Of course they are. They're identical.'

'But what if they're different sexes?'

'How can you have identical twins of different sexes? They're going to have different bits, aren't they, bugbrain?'

'Well, perhaps they both have the same bits from each of the sexes.'

'They wouldn't be identical twins then - they'd be identical freaks.'

'You can't have identical freaks - a freak is by definition someone who's unique.'

'This fascinating conversation is going round in circles,' Gus says.

'A good example of tautology,' pronounces Dermot. 'How can you go round in any other way?'

Gus turns on him. 'What should I say then, smartarse?'

'*Going* in circles.'

'That's stupid. That would mean going forward in circles.'

The rest of the meal is negotiated without too much effort, though Gus can feel the tension rising, like slow but remorseless flood waters, within him. Nick has to go straightaway to the library to finish an overdue essay and there are no comments on Gus's planned visit. He goes up to his room, cleans his teeth, reads and thinks for half an hour, then leaves.

Tight knots are gripping his chest, but Amy is relaxed, smiling, her normal pleasant self. She wears maroon jeans and her buttocks look trim and compact inside them. They talk as usual about their courses, lectures, essays to be written. Gus could postpone it. But he is in the room with her. They are together again. He has attempted it once, seven weeks ago. They can both forget that now. He wants to cement their relationship. And he might look cowardly, lacking courage and ardour, showing indifference to her, if he does not make another move.

Why is he thinking about it this way? It should be a simple, joyful matter. She is attractive and likes him. He likes her. It should be a natural result of that mutual attraction. Yes, just let it happen. Don't think about it. That is what Nick or Geraint would do. He can picture them doing it.

'Cup of coffee?' Her eyes are welcoming, with a caressive warmth as they look at him in unflinching unselfconscious innocence. Her body stands poised above him as he sits on the bed leaning back against the wall. She folds her arms idly, untroubled, waiting for his answer.

'Yes, that'd be good.'

'Stay there, I'll do it.' She motions him down, goes out into the corridor to the communal kitchen. He contemplates the room, the shining boats on the Seine, the multicolours of Monet's garden. He should have gone with her, for now he has the feeling of being in a doctor's or dentist's waiting room.

She returns with two full cups, hands one to him and sits on the bed beside him, slipping her light moccasins off and letting them fall. She draws her feet up and sits cross-legged, her feet in pale green socks giving Gus a pleasing feeling of homely closeness to her as they lean against each other. She playfully pushes her shoulder against his as she wriggles down beside him and he retaliates by nudging back. He feels the anxiety lessening with the healing power of her next to him, companionable, unthreatening.

They sip coffee in enjoyable cosy silence. She collects his cup and puts it with hers on the table then settles next to him again. He puts his arm around her and she nestles against him, her head on his shoulder. He doesn't have to go any further. He can sense her pleasure and contentment at being there beside him.

He feels too static. He must do something. He kisses her, puts his arm around her waist, draws her to him. Her hand clasps his arm. The touch of it on him feels soft and affectionate. Her lips respond to his in a long, lingering kiss. Afterwards her head presses against his neck and he kisses her dark hair as it brushes his face. He puts his hand to her breast.

'Shall we get into bed?' she asks quietly, looking up at him, slightly nervous but intimate, awaiting his answer. The sudden question takes him by surprise. He wonders for a moment if she has planned it. But why should it surprise him? It is an obvious thing to do. They must. He nods in agreement. He unties his shoe laces, tumbles his shoes to the floor and peals off his socks with a calm lack of fumbling that encourages him. They haul off their jeans and tops and Amy pulls back the bedclothes and jumps nimbly in. He slips in beside her. There is a warm, nestlike feel, more private, more personal, now they are together under the sheets and he can feel so closely but not see the bare warm flesh of her limbs and body against his. She unclips her bra. He slides onto her narrow, slight torso with its small firm breasts that he treasures. His tongue finds her nipple and twirls it, and it feels delicious, like licking heavenly ice-cream. She murmurs and groans with enjoyment. Now it must happen.

…Why can't he do it? Do the thing that both he and she want so much, the simplest, most elementary animal thing? He lies on top of her in the gloom, feeling helpless and hopeless, like someone trapped on barbed wire, naked, exposed. She says nothing, makes no sound, lying inert and still, with expressionless eyes fixed on the ceiling, as if she is in a coffin, and he the lid. He thinks of all the millions of men around the world who must be making love to women they do not love. He cannot do that simple act with the person he truly cherishes. This time he cannot even say he is sorry. He has no words.

He turns away off her, lies beside her in the narrow bed. The shame is as sharp as a physical pain. He could not feel more humiliated if a hundred people were gathered watching the wreck of his attempt. He curses himself for having tried. They were so happy, holding each other and kissing.

Their shoulders are faintly touching. Gus wants to hold her hand under the bedclothes, to affirm his commitment to her still, but somehow it would feel like a trespass. Or is he afraid she will push his hand angrily, scornfully away?

She does not demonstrate her upset. After a while she rolls out of the bed and puts on her clothes. He is not certain what to do. The room is painfully small and crowded with the two of them. It feels wrong to be lying here, in her bed. He gets up and starts to dress. Time stands still. It feels as if an age passes as he reaches for his trousers and steps into them and pulls them up, then zips and fastens them.

Then another age creeps by as he pulls his jumper over his head and stretches arms into it. Then, somehow worst and most self-conscious of all, sitting on her bed to yank on socks and shoes, even though he can turn his back on her to do it. The space between them is tiny, the silence huge. He longs for one of them to speak but all he can think of to say is sorry, which will sound so weak to him and so infuriating to her.

Amy turns to him and embraces him, resting her head lethargically on his chest. He hugs her in return. Some relief comes to him at the feel of her body against him once more.

'Sorry.' The word comes out of him at last, in a mournful whisper.

'I'd love to feel you inside me.' She is not angry, but placidly doleful.

'I think I'm a bit tense - about the projects and the course, and all that.'

She says nothing, just continues to hold him. He feels he has to carry on speaking. 'If we were doing it regularly, that probably wouldn't matter, but as we haven't done it before, I think it makes a difference to me.' He is doubtful as to whether he believes this, doubtful now what to believe about himself.

Amy shrugs her shoulders listlessly. 'We'll just have to wait, until you're ready. There's nothing wrong with me, is there?'

'No!' He shakes his head with emphasis.

They stand unspeaking in the embrace. He feels grateful to her for her patient effort to understand what he cannot understand himself. His black despair abates a little.

'Probably best if I go back now.' He hesitates. 'Thanks for the coffee.'

She walks out with him, to the main door. 'I'll see you tomorrow, at the first lecture.'

Gus turns onto the prom, glances back as he moves away, sees her faint smile as she waves to him.

He checks his watch. Eight-fifty. Nick will just be coming back from the library, or with luck may stop off for a drink with someone. It's too early to go to bed so as to avoid Nick, but he doesn't want to wander around or go into a pub until the time that Nick is asleep. He will just go back to Gwylan House, and endure whatever he has to.

Friday, 24 January

Gus had returned to Gwylan House relieved to find his room empty. A jumper, a pair of jeans and a book of Yeats's poetry were strewn across Nick's bed. There was a light under Simon's door, but Gus still does not feel comfortable in chatting to him, and knocking on his door to say hi would be unthinkable. Of Dermot there was no sign. For half an hour he tried to concentrate on some reading, but his mind refused to stop thinking about what had happened. He went to bed and heard Nick come in at quarter-to-eleven. He pretended to be asleep, while Nick attempted to move quietly about the room.

'Hey, partner-in-crime!' Nick mouths as they lie in their beds in the dim morning.

'What d'you mean?' Gus's voice is weary after a night's fitful sleep.

'I was in Alex last night. You must have left early.'

'How do you know I was there?'

'Amy came into Lorna's room just as I was leaving.' Nick's voice is raw with the early morning and his words are half-swallowed by the blankets that engulf his face. His eyes are not on Gus but sink blearily against his pillow.

Nick's tone is matter-of-fact. If Amy had looked bothered or miserable wouldn't he mention it?

'She's a nice girl. Nice smile. How're you getting on with her?'

'Good.'

Nick's face appears from beneath the blankets in a grin. '*Good.*' His monosyllabic echo is a comment on Gus's lack of description. Fortunately Gus can pretend semi-consciousness. But Nick is bound to be wondering at his early exit of the night before.

'I wanted to get back to finish my Shelley essay.'

Nick's voice is still cracked with sleepiness. 'Admirable dedication. You did what you had to do and then left. Yes, that's good. Lorna wouldn't let me go. Had to practically tear my underpants out of her grip.'

'Sounds painful.'

'Oh, excruciating. We'd better get up.'

Would Amy have said anything to Lorna? Why did she go into Lorna's room? Just for a normal late-night chat? Or to seek comfort or advice, pour out her feelings?

'No. Time travel just isn't possible. If you travelled forward or back in time, you'd alter that place and time just by being there as an extra person.' Dermot chews slowly on his toast as he speaks.

'Or you could go back and murder your father as a child,' says Simon ' -so how could you be born?'

'There could be infinite parallel universes,' Gus suggests. 'I wonder about people from other planets. Will they appreciate music? Will they have their own poetry? Will they even have the same five senses as us? Will they play games? Will they have a sense of humour? Will they have religion?'

'Will they have sex? That's the big question,' says Nick. 'Perhaps they'll be able to produce offspring without it. Can you imagine that? No longings, no romance. Can you imagine how boring life would be?'

'That's a weird thought though,' says Dermot, fumbling as he spreads his marmalade, ' - if there's an infinite number of worlds, somewhere out there, in a different galaxy on the edge of the universe, there could be someone just like me, my twin, eating crumbly dry toast. Except that he's countless millions of light years away, and we'll never meet. Perhaps at this very moment he's thinking, *somewhere out there, there's someone like me...* '

Nick leans earnestly over to the mass of disorderly yellow hair. 'Dermot, there's nobody else like you throughout the entire universe. If I thought there was, I'd bloody shoot myself.'

Gus drinks reviving tea. 'Imagine, somewhere in the universe there could be a planet populated entirely by Dermots...'

'Planet of the Dermots,' says Simon. 'That would make a good film title.'

'But,' says Gus, 'if time travel was possible, then surely people from Earth in the future would have discovered it and would already have travelled back to us, but we don't see any evidence of them.'

'Hey, this boy's sharp this morning,' Nick shouts. 'But then, he did have an early night last night…'

Gus feels a sudden stab of anxiety, but Simon unknowingly rescues him. 'Well they're not going to announce it are they? They'd be locked up if they did. They would *infiltrate* us quietly. They'd move among us with stealth.'

Mr Morgan shuffles in and squints anxiously through the window. 'Wind from the west today, boys. That's a bad sign.' He gives a melancholy shake of the head. 'Make certain you wrap up warm when you walk along that prom.' He peers through the glass again to confirm his forecast, sucks air in through his teeth and shuffles back out.

The boys look at each other in silence. Simon, unusually, is the first to break it. 'Yes, it's them.' He gives a dramatic pause. 'Mr and Mrs Morgan are definitely time travellers from a future world.'

Nick puts his cup slowly down. 'Of all the people on Earth,' he says, with great deliberation, 'I would say that Mr and Mrs Morgan are the least likely to be alien creatures from an advanced civilisation of the future. Their clothes are twenty years out of date for a start…'

Simon's voice drops to a thick whisper. 'But that's exactly what we're meant to think. Their clothes are a disguise. It's obvious when you think about it.'

'That could account for Mrs M's strange usage of English vocabulary,' says Dermot. 'So we thought we'd found nice friendly lodgings run by a harmless middle-aged couple, when in fact we've been captured by aliens.'

Mrs Morgan comes into the room, to be met by a table of silent curious faces.

'You're all very quiet today, boys,' she says.

Nick's head gives a quick shudder, as if shaking itself awake from a dream. 'Uh - just really enjoyed the meal, Mrs Morgan. It was - out of this universe!'

'Well! There's praise indeed!' she says, beaming.

'There's probably something in the food to make us servile and compliant,' Simon says after she has left.

'More likely to make us bloody constipated,' says Nick. 'I've got to move...'

Discuss D. H. Lawrence's portrayal of childhood and the process of growing up in 'Sons And Lovers' and 'The Rainbow.' Gus sits in the library, with commentaries on Lawrence and both novels open in front of him, staring at the essay title as if a prolonged gaze at it will automatically provide a script. Lawrence's bearded, intense-eyed, slight face stares back at him from two of the book covers. Gus lifts his eyes and looks at the far wall, where the shelves on Medieval Literature stretch from floor to ceiling.

How much does Lorna know? Gus feels fairly certain that Nick knows nothing, otherwise Nick's manner towards him would surely be more - probing, more suspicious? Wouldn't it?

But even if Nick hasn't yet got wind of anything, it can only be a matter of time. Matter of time? Why is he using that phrase? It implies this is a permanent situation. He will soon be able to sort things out with Amy. But now he feels the terrible plummeting in his stomach when he thinks of her and him together. It is like an approaching exam. He can feel his confidence leaking away. And a growing sense of despondency, of fear, is filling the gap.

Monday, 27 January

This would be the ideal time. He has thought about it all weekend. There is a university doctor and a welfare officer. Gus has noticed the doctor, a short compact man, late fifties probably, with a light grey suit and wrinkled brow and cheeks. He pictures the doctor sitting in his surgery and himself opposite, and the doctor noting his words with a sage nod of the head, speaking to him in a calm, weary, remote voice. He remembers visits to the doctor with his mother, for the occasional cold or cough, half a lifetime ago. The last time he went he must have been eight or nine. If he was suffering an immediate physical illness that obviously needed treatment...but no. A doctor would be official confirmation to himself that something was wrong. The problem would be heaved onto the surface, with all the attendant mental trauma.

No, no doctor. The service is confidential, but wouldn't the doctor make notes? His difficulties - his name? - would be recorded, preserved in the medical records. In any case the doctor is in Pantycelyn Hall, on the Hill.

Who else? The welfare officer? A 'Mrs'. He wouldn't feel comfortable talking to a woman - but then he would feel hardly more comfortable with a man. He imagines her swivelling in her chair, listening with sympathy - but how could she understand?

Nick? Nick would, he thinks, be surprisingly sympathetic. He can see Nick listening with a serious face. Then he sees Nick's face burgeoning into a smile and a laugh. He can see himself being slapped on the shoulder. A loud gruff 'C'mon lad! Let's sort this out!'

Dermot would be baffled by his worrying over a trivial thing, irrelevant to the grand wonder of the universe. Simon, Geraint, both unthinkable. Only one person left.

Gus files into the ten o'clock seminar. Rosina, Glenys, Dafydd, a boy named Colin, a girl with straight brown hair and a spindly body, whose name he forgets... No-one there who is his close friend, with whom he would feel obliged to walk out at the end of the hour. That's a good start.

Gus manages to make a few appropriate comments in the course of the session, which should lay a groundwork of friendliness between him and Peter Strutton. The hour is slowly pulling towards its end. He can feel the time elapsing, gradually but unrelentingly. At the start it had seemed not an overwhelmingly daunting task, but now that the moment is approaching...

'Right! We shall call a halt now. So for next week I want you to read the first section of Book Two. Thanks for your ideas.' Peter smiles at the group as he closes his copy of *Paradise Lost*. There is the scraping of chairs, the rustle of books and notepads being put into bags, a contrast to the seminar, where voices were the only sound that broke the silence.

Gus stands and puts his papers and book away dawdlingly. One-by-one the other students file out through the door. *I wonder if you might be able to give me some advice. You know we talk about relationships, love and so on, in literature - I'm having a few difficulties.* Once he starts, once he gets out the first sentence, then he's certain Peter Strutton will prompt and encourage him.

Peter looks up at Gus, with a slight expectant smile, his eyes a little wide in curiosity at Gus's apparent reluctance to leave.

'Everything going along okay?' His voice is cheerful. It's not really a question.

'Oh, yes.' Gus grasps his bag, uncertain whether to pick it up or remain holding it.

Students sometimes linger after the others if they want to discuss work they are doing, or, quite often, if they are not confident enough to say something in class but want the lecturer to know they are interested, so they express their idea privately afterwards.

Something bothering you? What can I do for you? Can I help? All sound a little remote, off-putting, receptionist-like. Usually the student finds it easier to talk if Peter leads him gently on.

'Thanks for your contribution in the seminar today. It's always helpful to have students with pertinent points to make.'

'Oh, it was a good seminar, yes.' Gus can feel his resolve weakening.

'Do you like Milton?'

If only Peter Strutton had asked something like, *What can I do for you?*, Gus could have begun his speech.

'Yes. You can't help but be impressed by his vocabulary, his style, the way he describes Hell.'

He should swing the conversation back quickly. Now. *Actually, I was wondering if I could have a word.* That's all he needs to say. Peter Strutton obviously doesn't have another lecture or seminar immediately, or he would be standing up, other students would be hovering outside his open door.

'Yes. We'll have a look at that next week. How are you finding the work generally? A bit different from A-levels?'

'Yes, but really interesting. At A-level, you spend so much time on a few books. Suddenly, we're doing so many different things...' Now he can't possibly ask. It was a stupid idea anyway. How could Peter Strutton help? It was only the desire to mention it to someone who might show sympathy and understanding, even if only to give him the encouragement to see the doctor or welfare services. But then, if Peter Strutton knew his secret ...No. It would be too much overstepping the mark, entrusting, encumbering a lecturer with his personal woes. And whenever he saw Peter Strutton there would be that sense of shame, embarrassment...

'Yes, well, you seem to be doing pretty well so far. And it's a great part of the country!'

'Yes, certainly is.' Gus makes to leave.

'See you next week, then. Have a good week.' Peter smiles in his cordial way. Gus hoists his bag onto his shoulder and trundles out.

Strange, indeterminate conversation, Peter thinks. Did the student want to ask something specific, or was he just sluggish in leaving? He's a good, intelligent boy. Seems a little dreamy, but Peter can identify with that...

Tuesday, 28 January

'Think of the world spinning on its axis. While it's doing that, it's revolving round the sun. Right? While those two things are happening, the sun itself is travelling around the centre of the galaxy. While these three things are happening, all the galaxies, including ours, are flying through space, hurtling away from each other.'

'What rubbish is he spouting now?'

'Fascinating rubbish.'

'That about sums him up - fascinating rubbish.'

Dermot presses on, undaunted by Nick's and Gus's comments. 'So we're actually revolving in three directions at once and at the same time shooting outwards through the universe.'

'And I thought it was adolescence that made people feel mixed-up,' Nick declares, stabbing at his bacon. 'And it was the Unicorn's beer that gave me a sore head. But no, I'm hurtling through the bloody galaxy. Do you feel as if you're moving, Simon?'

'Um, to be honest, no, Nick.'

'Or you, Augustus?'

'No, I must admit, I feel pretty static.'

'So how is it, Professor Dermot, that we don't feel as if we're moving? If Aberystwyth is flying through space at three hundred miles per second, how is it I look out of the window and everything is still and boring? How is it Mrs Morgan's breakfasts don't fly off the plate instead of sitting in front of us looking sorry for themselves?'

'Probably because they're so heavy they defy the normal laws of the universe,' Gus suggests.

'It might explain why her eggs always look such a mess,' adds Nick.

'Because everything is moving together!' Dermot shouts in exasperation. 'That's why we don't notice it.'

'If the earth revolved just a little more slowly,' says Gus, 'we'd have twenty-five hours in the day. We could all use the extra hour to do something creative.'

Nick turns to him. 'But we wouldn't be conscious it was an extra hour, would we? It would be the norm.'

'If the Earth revolved a little slower, it would be uninhabitable. End of conversation,' Simon declares with unusual decisiveness.

Dermot twirls a spoon between his large fingers. 'I've been working something out. If the entire history of the Earth - four point six billion years - is the length of a football pitch - about a hundred metres - then one metre represents forty-six million years. Humans are only present in the last two centimetres of the field.'

'Then they'd be offside,' says Nick wearily. His voice suddenly switches to the exaggeratedly spellbound. 'Now that is *fascinating*.'

'You're too myopic, Nick. All you worry about is Lorna, not these amazing truths about our existence.'

'Lorna is an amazing truth about my existence,' Nick answers.

Gus will have to do it. There's no alternative. It was folly to think he could tell someone. He has managed so far to avoid outright lying to Nick, but he has come close on several occasions. Once he begins to lie, the pressure on him will be too great, the fear of what Nick will hear from Lorna too afflicting. He feels the terrible sense of dread which swallows up his desire when he thinks of Amy. He feels the devouring anxiety when he wonders who she has told.

How will he do it? Speak to her? That will be hard. He's not used to saying unpleasant things to people face-to-face - grown-up things with calm, measured, well-chosen words. That also gnaws at him. He thought he was adult. Now he feels like a boy, thrust into an adult world, his development frozen. He is on a lower level, struggling to lever himself up to the required higher elevation. And failing.

A letter would be best. He can select the right words, hand it over to her, and go. He doesn't know if she will be sad or not. He will feel aggrieved when she starts going with someone else, but it will give him freedom to work things out, experiment a little, take his time. He thought he was ready but he wasn't, that's all. Dermot, Simon, Geraint, they haven't got anyone yet and they're not worried, so there's no reason why he should be.

Dear Amy,

I'm sorry to have to write this, but I don't think we're really suited to each other. Of course we can still be friends, but I don't think we should be 'going out' together any more.

I hope this doesn't disappoint you too much. It's not your fault at all and I've enjoyed being with you, but I don't think I'm really ready for a relationship yet.

So I will see you around, no doubt. Hope everything continues to go okay with you. I'll sign off now.

'Bye
Gus

It sounds a bit sloppy - he has always envisaged composing long, sad, passionate letters of farewell if he has to, with perhaps a short poem of his own - but it is all that's needed and he feels relief that he has written it quickly without too much heart-searching. He seals the letter and writes 'Amy' in large clear letters on the envelope, then holds it away from him to look at her name. It is short, uncomplicated, beautiful. He kisses it. He doesn't like the idea of handing the letter over to her in person. He will nip round to Alex, hoping he doesn't see anyone he knows, and put it in the large letter rack on the ground floor. Or would it be best to slip it under her door? She might not check the rack before bumping into him again, which would be awkward, but putting it under her door would mean going up to her room and risking being seen, and if Amy is there, perhaps with laughing friends, a letter mysteriously appearing will look silly, and she might have to read it in front of people.

The letter rack is best. It's near the entrance. He can dart in and out. If he can avoid her for today, she is bound to have read it by the time she next sees him.

He walks to Alex. Self-disgust is rising inside him like nausea and he struggles to keep it down. No - he is definitely doing the right thing. Or is he not cowardly, feeble, running away from the problem? It's only three weeks into the term. He has hardly given it a chance. He really likes her. He feels an ache, a wrench, as if he is cutting the sapling of a tree that could grow beautiful and fruit-laden.

But a third failure… The risk is too great. The crushing, annihilating shame he would feel…No, he's made a mess of things with Amy, and it's best to wipe the slate clean and start again with someone else. Who else? When he thinks of any other girls, the same anxiety surfaces. No it doesn't - not with everyone. He feels a pleasing sense of anticipation when certain faces and bodies and voices come into his mind. There is Adele, an attractive cinnamon-skinned girl, with brown elegant fingers. And Vivienne, with rich, dark brown hair shading into black, seems a thoughtful, considerate person. He has developed this fixation with Amy. As if she is the only fish in the sea! Next week is Rag Week. There are extra events, a few discos, fun promenade entertainments, where he might fall easily into chat with someone. Yes, he must do this. And if he tries with someone he doesn't really like, then there would be no loss if he doesn't succeed. But…he might hurt someone, and there would still be the humiliation. Plus, the more people he fails with, the more likely it is word will get around…

He's done it. Put it in the letter rack and walked out again, with a moment's hesitation before leaving it, quickly got over. He didn't see anyone he'd feel obliged to stop and talk to. He'll lie low for a few days and catch up with his work.

Wednesday, 29 January

G us comes down to breakfast to see a letter, resting on the dark brown table in the hallway, where Mrs Morgan places mail for the boys. No stamp again, so it must have been pushed through the letterbox in person. Gus's name is on the envelope, in small, neat, upright letters, in light blue biro, the pretty handwriting of Amy.

He is reaching for it as Mr Morgan emerges slowly from the kitchen, engrossed in reading a letter, head tucked into his chest, chin against his askew tie. Gus has grown to like his rumpled, shuffling figure. It reminds him of his grandfather's solid, almost immoveable presence, that sense of immunity to misfortune acquired by a lifetime's harshness. The boys may make fun of Mr and Mrs Morgan, but there is a fund of kindliness and warmth in them that Gus is only now beginning to fully realise.

'Had a letter from one of the boys who used to be with us - oooh - ten years ago. Lovely boy from Pontardawe. He loved his home - he always used to say, "I'm going *down home*", "I've had a letter from *down home*." In America now he is. Sent us photos of his two children.' Mr Morgan peers up, his face full of thought. 'It's funny. Some of the boys keep in touch down the years. Others, you never hear from again.' At the last sentence there is a note of sad disappointment in his voice. Gus looks at him. Life after Aber. Gus shudders at the intrusion of the idea. It would be like stepping off the edge of the world, falling endlessly into the void, as Columbus's sailors feared would happen to them when they reached the limits of the flat earth.

Dear Gus,

Thanks for your letter. I'm sorry you feel that way. Personally I thought we were doing okay. I know there are things you were worried about but, as I said, I'm certain things would work out between us and I have no trouble being patient. Anyway, this is the way you feel so I have to accept it.

Thanks for the evenings out, etc. We'll still no doubt see each other in lectures, the library, social gatherings and so on, and there's no need for us to feel awkward. Still friends? I hope so.

Amy

She must have come round early that morning to deliver it, because he went for a quick drink with Dermot to the Blue Bell last night and didn't notice it when he came in. It's a nice letter. It's friendly, but seems rather casual, written without too much thought and obviously no real torment or grief. But then, what does he want? Amy consumed with sorrow and rage, blaming herself? Amy mocking and belittling him? He reads it again. Yes. She refers to his 'problem', but doesn't call it that, and is tactful and without criticism. That's typical of her. And she would have been prepared to carry on the relationship. There's that sense of regret in 'I have to accept it.' The door is still open. And because they've exchanged letters, settled everything through them, he can meet her in a group or on her own, without feeling awkward, as she says.

After breakfast he goes out onto the promenade and looks at the sea. It is a magnificent monochrome grey, angry and restless, its edges foaming white like the mouth of a madman, clawing its way up the shingle, scraping and sucking back down but never relenting, beating again and again against the beach, thumping down and pulling away, the grey sky looking on with mean, frowning disapproval.

Saturday, 8 February

T he crowd on the prom, students and townsfolk, are cheering and laughing, in spite of the dull white mid-morning sky, moist air and cinder-grey sea. The seven boys of Carpenter Hall are heaving and pulling against the ten girls of Alex, who are proving surprisingly robust and resilient. The boys are working more as a team, united in their desire to avoid humiliation - there is a suspicion that they have trained and prepared beforehand, though each would probably deny the stigma if questioned. One or two of the girls begin to weaken in grip and resolution, and their line slips slowly forward. The boys sense the kill and tug harder, a broad and solid rugby prop named Jeff Thomas, last man in the Carp line, beginning to inch backwards. The girls' slide forward becomes a lunge and some topple onto the ground. The boys sigh violently with effort and relief, some shake their fists in triumph, the girls laugh and giggle. Everyone cheers, though even among the Carp supporters, there seems an ironic note at the earnest faces of their team.

Gus stands in the crowd, alongside Simon and Dermot. The last day of Rag Week, with the final of the tug-of-war soon to come, Carp against Plyn on the seafront, Plyn having beaten off a stern challenge from the boys of Pantycelyn from up the Hill. This afternoon will see the Rag Procession through the streets, which, from what Gus has heard of previous years, should be entertaining - a series of colourful floats, in lorries loaned by local businesses, on the theme of pirates and buccaneers. *Courier* included a piece warning people not to throw things from the floats or at them, but the procession is expected to be good-natured and to bring a large turn-out of spectators. This evening will see the Rag Hop in the Parish Hall followed by a torchlight procession through the town. *Courier* mentioned that the Aber Rag invariably raises more money per student than any other university in Britain, and Gus can believe that, noting the attendance and support at events from both students and residents. He feels pleased to be part of this atmosphere, festive yet for a worthy end.

It has been a good week. Gus went with Dafydd and Josh to the Parish Hall Hop last Saturday, and even to the Fancy Dress Ball in the Great Hall up the Hill on Monday. He didn't notice Amy at the first, and there were one or two girls he liked, though he could not somehow summon the ardour or elan to make progress with them. Then he saw her, attractively attired as a rodeo girl. She stayed mainly with the Alex group, but he saw her dancing with a chain-mailed medieval knight and later a boy in a Hawaiian shirt and a hat made of pineapples leaves, though as far as he could see nothing came of either encounter. He and Dermot dressed as pirates, with Dermot wielding an impressively long wooden sword which Mrs Morgan had borrowed from grandson Jonathan. She had also offered the beard from his performance in the Nativity Play, but both Gus and Dermot, in the interests of historical authenticity, and because it was too hilariously ill-fitting and kept slipping off, declined the offer.

Wednesday saw the Rag Debate in the Skinners' Barn Bar, on the subject, "This House Believes That Small Bangs Are Preferable To Big Ones", with Martin Swanson from Padarn Hall and Julie Poulter from Alex the main speakers. On Thursday Nick, Gus, Dermot, Simon and others went to the revue, "Pies Cold in Alex," in King's Hall. The "cast of thousands" promised in the publicity leaflet turned out to be based on the personified inclusion of individual chips as extras, even then grossly exaggerated, as Dermot estimated there were possibly only ninety such "actors", donated by the Bridge End fish restaurant in Bridge Street and afterwards given free, though somewhat cold, to the audience. Fiona and Lorna, dressed as waitresses in a nightmare café, impressively hammed it up, Fiona predictably extrovert alongside the cooler but confident Lorna.

On Friday morning, Gus, Nick and Simon joined the large crowd gathered down by the harbour for the Raft Race. Among the onlookers, Gus noticed a scarf-bewrapped head, with blond hair just visible from under a green bobble hat. Had Peter Strutton come to watch Fiona on the Alex boat? Gus observed him during the race, noticed the restrained but pleased smile on his face. Would he wait for Fiona afterwards? But no - he slipped away as soon as the final was over. A week later, Gus saw he had written an account of the day's events for *Courier*.

'On Friday morning at ten o'clock, the Raft Race, with the word "raft" liberally interpreted, saw a variety of seaworthless vessels battle it out in a Titanic struggle to gain control of the high seas of Aber harbour. Pantycelyn's entry, two beds strapped together with failed-MOT tyres on either side, miraculously stayed afloat to pip the more sophisticated cruiser from Carp. The ladies of Alex, in their puddle-going liner with what appeared to be knickers for sails, gained third place, heroically beating off the challenge of the Digs Driftwood Destroyer while simultaneously repulsing an attempt at boarding by the Viking crew of a double mattress. Plyn's "canal barge", an upturned wardrobe romantically claimed to have been found washed up on Clarach beach, bobbed about the water in inebriated fashion and eventually reversed, or rather, diagonalled, past the finishing line. A craft housing the boys from Hafodunos, with its name, "The Slug", proudly emblazoned on its starboard side, lived up to this appellation in shape, speed and aesthetic appeal, while Ceri's Crocodile slithered along, appropriately more submerged than afloat.'

The article continued. 'In the afternoon was "Tower to Tower", a race from the top of the Geography Department tower on the Hill to the West Tower of the Old College on the seafront. Competitors were not allowed to touch the ground or use any adult form of transport and could have a maximum of four helpers. The hair-raising, bone-breaking dash down Penglais Road in an array of ingenious contraptions, including several designs of pram or creative variations of it, was won by a team from Portland Street guest houses. Two teams were disqualified after making an unscheduled pit-stop at The Crystal Palace, though both protested that their competitor had not touched the ground at any time, one, it was claimed, having even been carried to the toilet and held in the air while he performed the necessary actions.'

The heightened energy of Rag Week, that sense of collective fun, collective endeavour, combined with doing good for charity; the spirit of team and of place; the seafront frolickings that gladdened the February sky; the cheering crowds at the harbour and ranged along Penglais Road all the way down the Hill, that lent a warmth to the late winter chill of the air - all have blunted the hurt. Gus is pleased he made the effort to go to the two dances, but he felt a sinking in his heart at both, a hollowness of enjoyment. Both felt incomplete. All through the week, the two emotions - of elation and of woe - have jarred against each other, like blue-white waves grating on grey rock. He has seen Amy several times apart from at the Fancy Dress Ball - at the tug-of-war, throwing back her head in laughter, her black hair tumbling about her shoulders, at the raft race, elegant in slim navy-blue jeans and boots, the yellow, maroon and blue stripes of her college scarf swathed round her neck - and each time he has felt that sad craving.

Sunday, 9 February

'The sea is great, beautiful to contemplate in the morning, as the sun goes down in the evening. I just wish somebody would remove it during the night.'

Fiona gives a firm nod. 'My sentiments exactly.'

'Mmm, that's a bit worrying,' Dermot responds. 'We agree on something.'

Nick makes to get up from his half-prone position on the bed. 'If you like, we'll all go and leave you two to carry on together.'

Fiona cringes, her hands fly to her mouth in sudden terror. 'Ah, don't leave me alone with him!' Dermot, for once, looks a little bemused.

Evening in Fiona's room. The pink light casts an enlivening, stimulating glow on the six people crammed into it. A copy of Fitzgerald's *The Great Gatsby* lies half-open on the pillow.

Nick stirs the remains of the coffee in his cup. 'I can't imagine it's difficult to write a novel. They say everybody's got one book inside them.'

Dermot breaks in. 'That doesn't mean anything. We've all got an appendix inside us. It's useless.'

'Yes, but a novel, you just sit down and write. Everyone's got a story to tell. Anyone can write it if they sit down for long enough. I just wouldn't have the patience.'

'If you mean filling pages with words,' Gus says, 'well, I suppose anyone could do it. But to write a good-quality novel, that people who don't know you will want to read, to keep them interested over two or three hundred pages, keep them wondering what's going to come next - that's different.' He sees Amy out of the corner of his eye, listening.

'In the old days, it would've been much easier to sit down and write a novel,' puts in Fiona, 'because there weren't all the trivial distractions we have today, like TV, radio, music, newspapers.'

'Yes, but there were other trivial distractions - playing cards, drinking, cock-fighting...' Dermot counters.

Nick smirks at the last example.

Lorna yawns. 'I don't know if I find life interesting enough to write about it.'

'Well in that case write about the boredom of life,' Dermot says.

'How can you write about something boring?'

'Jane Austen and Chekov managed it.'

'Sometimes you don't know what you've got to say until you've said it,' Fiona adds.

Nick is dismissive. 'Novelists are just piss artists anyway.'

Dermot is serious and deliberate. 'There's a reason for that. People who work in offices, who have nine-to-five jobs, can go home and escape from their work and their bosses. Artists, writers are their own offices, their own bosses - and sometimes they can be harder on themselves than the most tyrannical of bosses - therefore they have to escape from themselves - and that's the hardest thing in the world.'

To escape from themselves. Gus wonders. Can he do that? Amy is looking quietly at ease, enjoying the cut and thrust of the conversation.

Dermot continues. 'Writers are addicted to words. Controlled by words. Words govern their lives, just as drugs control a drug addict's life. Words determine how they live and how they think. Words are everything to them and everything else is nothing. I don't want to get into that state.'

'Exaggerating as usual,' Nick responds. 'And I've heard you say before, you want to be a writer. Of course they're not addicts. Take Peter Strutton. He's a writer and he's a great guy, much more human than people like Sewage and Parker-Hurst, who coldly analyse and dissect other people's writing like students dissecting rats and mice, but don't write anything themselves.'

There is sudden silence. Gus, Lorna and Amy look at each other and try not to look at Fiona. Her face has sagged and her gaze stiffened. Her whole body seems to tense. She is rigid in her chair and her hands clasp its sides as if she is on the edge of a cliff. She stands up and walks out of the room.

Amy gives a concerned look to Lorna.

'Best to leave her,' Lorna says. 'She's still a little fragile.'

'Jesus.' Nick slaps the back of his head in annoyance. 'I didn't think. I forgot I shouldn't mention the PS word in her presence. Shall I go and apologise?'

'No,' Lorna says. 'That'll make things worse. She'll be all right.'

Dermot rises with sudden resolution and strides out into the corridor.

Monday, 10 February

'Half-term already in school!' shrills Mrs Morgan as she waltzes in with the evening meals. 'Doesn't time fly? Eric stayed with us today. The things he has to do for homework! He had to find five interesting facts about an octopus. So I told him the first thing he should put down is that it's got eight testicles. He burst out laughing! I can't think why.' She leaves and the boys are still chortling with laughter as Mr Morgan shambles in.

'Something tickling you today, boys?'

Nick recovers enough to explain, his voice still shaking with titters, 'Mrs Morgan was just talking about…octopuses.'

'Oh! Octopuses. Very chewy.'

'Do you get any round here?' Nick asks in a bid to sound sensible.

Mr Morgan leans one hand on his hip, the other on Nick's chair, in an attitude of deep thought. 'Well, I've never seen one myself. We get all sorts of things - dolphins, people have seen. Some say they've seen sharks, whales, the odd mermaid. Mervyn Thomas - now he says he saw an octopus once in the harbour by South Beach. He's adamant he counted eight legs in the water. Mind you, he'd just come out of the Castle Hotel after a few drinks. People reckon it was a dog swimming, kicking its legs in the air, and Mervyn was seeing double.'

'Hey, you were the Knight in Shining Armour yesterday, Dermot!' Nick shouts. 'Or should I say the Knight in Shining *Amour*? Rushing out after Fiona. And what did you say to her? She came back smiling.'

It was true. Fiona had returned to the room, her face puffed and strained with tears, but she had looked around with a humble, embarrassed smile, announced, 'sorry, everyone,' blown her nose in a measured but decisive way, curled up like a cat on the bed, her legs tucked under her, and the talk had continued a little while longer, without incident, before the boys left.

'Nothing,' Dermot answers. 'Just told her there was no point in getting upset, tears wouldn't help the situation. I said she could be indulging in a dangerous fantasy. If PS has told her he doesn't want to carry on, she should accept it. There is no way you can force someone to love you. *If of himself he will not love, nothing can make him.*' Dermot's voice rises in volume and venom. '*The devil take him!* She laughed.'

Dermot hacks at his roast lamb and adds as he chews, 'she's an attractive girl.' There is a chorus of Ah's from the others. He cannot prevent his lips from widening into an uncharacteristically coy grin. 'There are dozens of guys who'd want to go out with her. No, don't look at me. All around me I can hear the sound of breaking hearts. Don't want to go *there*. Anyway, changing the subject, anyone coming to the Film Society tonight? They're showing the 1931 film of *Frankenstein*. I would have thought you English boys would be interested, as it was written by the wife of your beloved Shelley.'

'Shelley came to Aber,' Gus says. 'In 1812. I've been reading about it. He sailed into the harbour - didn't mention any octopuses, mind. *The quiet water sleeps within* - that's how he described it. He even referred to the visit in a poem. He called Aber a town with two dark rocks either side - that must be Consti and Pen Dinas.'

'Shelley was drowned, wasn't he?' Simon asks Gus.

'That's right. They found his body washed up on the beach in Italy. They're not certain what happened. They think it was a storm, but others think he was attacked by pirates.'

'Or he could have just jumped into the sea,' Simon says.

'No,' Gus answers with assurance. 'He was too full of life.'

'Sometimes people who are full of life are full of death as well,' Simon adds.

'Shelley's body is buried partly in Rome, partly in Bournemouth - that's where they took his heart.' Gus, as he speaks, reflects that this is the longest conversation he has had with Simon.

Nick explodes into laughter. 'You guys are such a morbid bunch. Now, I know you've just split up with Amy, Gus, but there's no need to go…overboard.' He chuckles at his own pun.

Simon's ears prick up at the news. Amy and Gus. If that is true...Could he...? There is a Valentine's party on Saturday night.

Nick meanwhile snatches up the saltcellar and croons into it as into an imaginary microphone, 'I left my heart - in Bournemouth.' He collapses into more guffawing.

'I wonder what it's like to be drowning,' Simon says. 'I mean, what it feels like. How long it actually takes.'

Nick folds his arms and leans forward to Simon. 'Well, if you like, we can experiment on you. We'll carry you down to the water, throw you in and time you. Nah, I think it's physically impossible to drown. I reckon, if you were drowning, you'd suddenly find you were swimming, even if you didn't know how - you'd learn how to do it, there on the spot, because you'd be so desperate to survive.'

'That's bullshit,' Gus shouts. 'If that was the case, nobody would ever drown.'

'Some people are just unlucky,' Nick says. 'The current is too strong for them, or if they fall overboard they get left behind and they become exhausted or die of hypothermia. But I think in a normal sea, you'd survive.'

Simon picks up the saltcellar and for a moment Gus thinks he is going to imitate Nick's singing - but instead he knocks it against the table. 'Not if you put stones in your pockets. That's what Virginia Woolf did when she drowned herself in the Thames.'

Nick shakes his head. 'What a way to top yourself.'

'I wonder what she went through as she was drowning.' Gus looks thoughtful. 'I wonder if she regretted doing it.'

'Did she wish she could stay alive to write down all the thoughts and impressions that flashed through her mind - or should I say, that *flooded* her mind?' Dermot asks.

Nick joins in. 'She pioneered the stream of consciousness technique, didn't she? - where a writer records all the thoughts in a person's mind as they occur? Get it? *Stream* of consciousness.'

'It's better to hang,' Dermot says. 'Just swing peacefully on a rope.'

'No,' says Gus. 'Some guys who are hanged can take twenty minutes to die. It's better to walk into a river - or the sea.'

'It must be quite exciting, going under water,' says Simon with rare enthusiasm. 'Like going over the top in a battle.'

'Well I'm not certain if that was especially exciting,' Nick says. 'But -yeh - walking into the sea -' he shakes his head - 'too wet and uncomfortable - and too bloody cold around here. You'd have to take a trip to the Med - and by the time you got there, you'd just feel like taking a holiday. That reminds me, boys. Our late night swim - don't forget - June, after the exams. The water'll be warmer then. To make it more interesting - we could even put a few pebbles in our pockets!'

And he bellows out his laugh.

Wednesday, 12 February

The black void of night outside Simon's small window seems to overpower the light of his room, hemming him in. Loneliness, emptiness, press in on him as people press against you in a crowded room. Gus and Nick have gone to a student poetry reading at the English Society. He had half a mind to join them, but thought he would be bored by it, or disheartened if the standard of writing was higher than his own attempts. Dermot, he thinks, is at the Philosophy Society or in the library.

Two things fascinated him as a boy - castles and ships. Looking back, he can see now these were symbols of isolation, of cutting himself off from others, of building fortifications, protection, impenetrable to the outside world. He would pore over pictures of castles and forts in books, spend long hours playing with models, bewitched by their battlements and towers, portcullises and elaborate guarded gateways. Or he would marvel at photographs of proud destroyers and cruisers, thrusting through the water with gun turrets ranged vigilantly.

Last night he lay in bed and wondered what it would be like with a woman beside him. He has started to do it again - clasping one hand in the other, or putting his hand on his thigh and making believe it is her he is touching. He carefully pouts his lips, moves slowly down to the pillow, and kisses it, pretending it is her lips.

Annaliese is tall and narrow, with long, slim legs, and she walks with her body tilted slightly back, giving an aura of grace and stateliness. There is regality in her posture. Her hair is beautiful, such an expression of her. It is light brown and flows around her shoulders and down her back. Everything about her is so much *her*. He imagines her in Aber, her hair curling waywardly about her cheeks in the winds of winter, or rippled by the breeze on tranquil days. Today her cheeks would be aglow in the frostfire of the wind. She would be insulated against the cold, a scarf caressing her neck, a pretty hat, thick coat and boots, like a present waiting to be unwrapped... But when he sees her again in the holiday, will things still be the same? Ten weeks of not seeing him. She is bound to get to know other boys.

And, in her absence, this uncontrollable desire. Yesterday, as he was walking along the prom, Lorna was coming towards him. That unmistakeable stride, hair in softly curling clusters. He wanted to greet her with a strong outgoing 'Hi!', engage her eyes with a flashing brief smile. But as they passed and he opened his mouth, all that emerged was a weak, one-second, high-pitched moan, a pitiful whimper like a cry for help, that might draw sympathy if it came from a kitten or an injured sparrow. Even Lorna looked slightly embarrassed and gave, for her, a muted smile, though it was still alluring to see. He turned back to look at her, noted her buttocks swaying lazily like palm trees, that lovely soft, relaxed way of moving her body as she walks.

Dermot had quoted from Shelley. What was it? *Youth is a vain and feverish dream of sensualism.* The senses. He can *see* girls all the time, everywhere he goes. He can *hear* their voices. He can *smell* them as they walk past him in the street, in shops, in the Students' Union, in the pubs. He can even very nearly *taste* their perfume as they brush past. But he can't *touch* them. That's taboo. Why should that one sense out of the five be outlawed? Touching them would be just as harmless as perceiving them through the other four senses.

But. There is the party on Saturday. Amy should be there. And she's no longer seeing Gus. Yes, if he could just take this opportunity…

Thursday, 13 February

He thought they had stopped, but they keep coming, usually pushed through the letterbox, with just 'Peter' written on the front, perfectly in the centre of the envelope, as if she is homing in on a target. It is as if the surrounding white of the envelope is silence, and the blue name is her crying it out, it stands out so. He wishes he could help her in some way. She is foolish, immature, but he feels he is to blame. He should have put out more feelers as to the personality behind her apparent solid confidence. He has this dread that one day he'll return to his flat to find her camped outside and refusing to leave. So far, she's used only letters. That suggests that she is not completely obsessed and has limits to what she will do - at least up until now.

> *You don't realise how special you are,*
> *Just as the brightest, most beautiful star*
> *Shines without knowing its own loveliness,*
> *Radiant with light to illumine and bless.*

If only she hadn't included the poem - did she write it herself? If she'd sent him a friendly reminder of the party, instead of the curt "Remember Saturday night, the White Horse. Please come," with its jarring note of desperation, he might have thought about it. But there is no way he can be there in response to that.

She won't let go. She is hopelessly infatuated. What more can he do to wrench himself free? Write her another stiff letter? She might then parade it to the students. Best to keep mum. If he ignores the invitation it should send the message clearly enough. He would love to go. If only it was a normal invitation. But then he would still feel uneasy, knowing that Fiona was there. He remembers what happened at the party before Christmas.

He noticed her in the Raft Race, dark hair swirling wild around her face, at one with the other girls, heedless and unburdened, and he felt the chasm between him, a university lecturer, looking down on the harbour, muffled in his scarf and hat, and her, in among the students, laughing in the freedom of her youth. He felt suddenly, with a pain razored by its rarity, older than his years, while she looked younger than - or perhaps more accurately, as young as - she really was.

He thinks, he is already four years older than Keats was when he died - and the same age as Shelley when he drowned.

And the book. He is halfway through his revision of the second draft. The slow process draws on. Another month or so, he hopes. Then it will be ready.

Saturday, 15 February

The Skinners' Arms bounces to the sound of loud rock. The boys reach the drinks table. Grasping precariously full glasses, they fight their way back, the shrapnel of conversation rebounding around them.

'I went to London for the weekend. Had it off with a Chinese Girl.'

'What was it like?'

'Too many shops, some good pubs.'

'He's a useless law student. He actually thought a suspended sentence meant hanging.'

Julian, a first-year biochemistry student from Geraint's lodgings, increases the volume of his voice, swivelling towards Nick, Gus and Dermot as they pass by.

'Arts students don't study anything important or difficult. The sciences are about the really big, important issues in life, new inventions and discoveries that improve the world and all our lives. We split the atom, you guys worry about split infinitives.' Nigel, another science student, nods approvingly.

'I suppose,' says Dermot, turning to them, 'everybody thinks his own subject is the most difficult because it's only our own subject that we study in detail, so we're aware of all its complexities, but we're not aware of the intricacies of something we haven't studied.'

Nigel swigs lager from his glass. 'I don't see the point of studying English. We all speak it anyway. Who wants to know about a poet who wrote four hundred years ago?'

'I remember reading,' Dermot goes on, 'somebody worked out that on average every person speaking English quotes Shakespeare every seven minutes. Science gives us a brave new world, but it's not the be-all-and-end-all. It doesn't examine hearts and minds, like literature does in its time-honoured way. I suppose it seems obvious, a foregone conclusion. I know some people have studied Shakespeare and said good riddance to it. We should be made of sterner stuff. We're a band of brothers.' At points in his speech, Dermot counts on his fingers. He has stopped at eight.

Julian laughs. 'What is he talking about. Are you crazy?'

'Ah, there's method in my madness.' Dermot has reached his ninth finger. 'Actually, Shakespeare wasn't too bothered about split infinitives.' He pushes his hair from his forehead. 'Science and the Arts are very similar. Both need inventiveness, vision, a new way of looking at familiar things, attention to detail, painstaking exploration -'

'Okay, okay,' Nick interrupts. 'I didn't come here for a bloody lecture.'

Fiona glances towards the door whenever there is a new arrival. He's not coming. And there is no point in her looking forlornly around. He'll seek her out if he decides to put in an appearance. She realises now that it is a disease, delectable when it has more joys than health, diabolic when its joys end. She appreciated Dermot's efforts to comfort her and she felt better briefly, but now she is back in its grip. She has moments now when she sees the folly and futility of it and she can only wait for them to increase and the times of distress to decrease, to bring her slowly out of the illness. She realises she is supping her wine too quickly and too frequently.

Geraint sidles up alongside her. 'So I bet you've got some vintage wines in your cellar, Fiona. What's the oldest one you've got?'

Her face creases with the effort of clear thought. 'I think we have some wines from 1953.'

Nick swills the last of a glass into his mouth and laughs. 'If people have put off drinking it for that long, it can't be much good. A bottle of wine doesn't last more than half an hour in my place.' He leans towards Fiona. 'It was a *joke*, Fiona,' and he mimics her accent, 'a little *below the belt*, I realise.'

She and her friend Clare giggle and totter a little unsteadily. 'I don't mind you going below the belt,' Clare says. She turns to Fiona and leans on her shoulder. 'In fact, you can do anything below my belt.' They both squirm and wriggle with amusement.

The girls are trying to persuade Fiona of the attractions of Dermot. 'He's funny,' they say.

'He's very witty.'

'He's very kissable.'

Fiona makes a face. 'Ugh! He has such a large mouth. And that hair that goes everywhere!'

Nick has gone over to talk to his mates from the cricket team. Gus surveys the activity on the dance-floor. Amy is dancing. With Simon. They're not touching, and she's not looking or smiling at him. Simon glances at her every so often but she does not catch his eye. But they're dancing. He must have asked her.

What if she knew what Gus knows - or thinks he knows - about Simon? What if she knew what Simon knows about him? No, Simon couldn't mention it without incriminating himself.

Or could he? No, ridiculous. But could Simon tell her without detailing the circumstances? *Do you know what Gus does?* No. He must not think that way.

He turns away - to find himself facing Lorna. She is calmly sipping at a red wine, cradling the glass to her breast, taking in the people and activity around her without overtly staring or examining. She smiles leisurely at him, leaning forward to make herself heard.

'Good party. I didn't expect so many people to be here.'

Gus has to tilt his body towards her in turn. 'Yes, looks like most of Aber's turned up.' He feels the scent of her perfume, and his eye drinks in her blonde hair, her naked shoulders, the swell of her breasts, her smooth fingers grasping the glass.

She reaches out to touch his arm. There is an easy, natural intimacy to it that he likes.

'Can I tell you something?' she murmurs.

'Sure.' He is wondering.

Still holding his arm, she leads him to a less crowded spot at the edge of the room.

'I was really sorry to hear that you'd split up with Amy. It's a shame.'

'Yes, well, I think it's for the best. I don't think we're suited, really.'

'She seemed to think you were getting on together well.'

How much does Lorna know? Everything? Has Amy asked her to have a word with him?

'We were, yes, in lots of ways, but - I just don't want a close relationship at the moment.'

Lorna can sense his discomfort. 'It's okay. She hasn't asked me to speak to you.' Her disarming smile shows immaculate white teeth. 'Amy's not the dramatic, histrionic type, but she was quite sad about it. I thought I'd let you know.'

'Well, thanks.'

'Want to dance?'

He quickly scans the dance-floor. Amy is still dancing, this time with Matt, another biochemistry student. At least she and Simon are not in some corner together, chatting.

'Okay.' He is surprised, honoured. Lorna is considered wildly desirable, the type who rivets eyes and stirs crotches when she enters a room. He has always viewed such a one from a distance, never been so close until now.

He holds her hand as she treads in front of him, her bare shoulders threading through the press of forms. As if on cue the music slows to smooch pace. Her blond hair is like sunshine in the dark shadows. She puts her arms around his neck as if she has done it dozens of times before and her body sways sleekly against his as his arms embrace her waist. He thinks of more manly, confident guys who must have done the same thing, and proudly claims his place among them. He looks around. Nick is still engrossed in conversation with the cricket boys, oblivious to the dancing.

He lies in his bed in the early hours of Sunday morning, recapturing in his mind the feel of her against him, his pride at her choosing of him, the exalted feel it gave him that others would have noticed them together. Was she educating him in some way, massaging his shyness, gently leading him into an enjoyment of the female body's pleasures, providing him with practice to make him feel more at ease? How much does she know? The question keeps on nagging at him. Has Amy told her? Or has Lorna's feminine intuition told her, if not the full details, at least the need in him of some initiation? She is one of those people who would know all she needs to know about someone without being told. She seems to perceive instinctively the inner person.

It was for two dances. Then they went their separate ways to get more drinks. He's not certain if Nick saw them together. If he did, he hasn't said anything. And Nick, he thinks, is not the type to fly into a jealous rage. He's too secure, too certain, for that.

He lies on his back and stares up at the ceiling. Light begins to filter through the curtains. She couldn't possibly find him attractive? Could she?

Wednesday, 19 February

G us watches a flock of seagulls speed across the water, as gleefully as children running after an ice-cream seller. They dip and glide above the waves. They soar and swoop and drop across the sky. What enjoyment they seem to be having, as if they are all trying out new wings for the very first time, as children delight in new toys and play for hours in a total relaxed absorption!

> *I would that we were, my beloved, white birds*
> *on the foam of the sea!*

But children tire of toys. The seagulls never tire of their wings, and every moment brings home fully to them the joy of life. They bob on the sea, riding the waves like pristine surfers, thrown upward on the water's crest and plunging down in its fall. They must do it for sheer pleasure. Why else would they squat there? They hover above the toss of the waters, now beating their wings enthusiastically, now gliding, as pleased with themselves as a boy who rides a bicycle with no hands.

Their total delight in their total mastery of their art and life fills Gus with wonderment.

> *For I would we were changed to white birds*
> *on the wandering foam: I and you!*

He is anchored by inhibitions. Images of so many confident people gleam in his mind. He overhears them in the Cabin or the pub, sees them strutting about the college and town. There is an articulate poise, an aplomb, about them when they speak, and a heedlessness of what others might think of them, that he cannot match. At the Debating Society both Dermot and Fiona have made contributions from the floor, speaking with assurance and unquestioning self-conviction. And the lecturers, whose knowledge, judgement, opinions, seem so huge and organised, as if each head is a library of neatly-arranged volumes that can be opened instantly and effortlessly. He can account for it in the older generation, people like Savage and Parker-Hurst. They have had a lifetime to accumulate the erudition. But younger lecturers like Peter Strutton, Erica Timms, Gerald Bailey, amaze and awe him.

Or is he only projecting on to all these people his own fantasies of what he desires to be? He longs to meet and know them, to move and mix in their circle. But there is a gulf between him and them like the sea. The sea is beautiful and beckoning, full, rich, enticing - but dangerous and unknown. Who could perceive what deadly currents lurk beneath it?

He looks seaward. Further out the colour changes from a brimming green-blue to a deeper, darker, stiller indigo. Sprinkled across the water are specks of white waves swimming swiftly in towards the shore.

The smooth curve of the horizon is filled with sea. To the south, shaded in on top of it, is the faint grey mass of the cliffs of Aberaeron and New Quay. To the north, Towyn, perhaps in the dim distance even, the long stretch of the Lleyn Peninsula.

Horizons are always out of reach and receding as you move towards them. Rainbows are illusions of colour in a dark sky.

But no. These are distant but real peaks that can be touched and climbed. The colours of the rainbow are not an illusion - they are there before his eyes.

Gus and Dermot sit on hard stools amid the aroma of slowly mouldering paper in the upstairs of Galloway and Morgan's bookshop.

The shelves of book spines seem to envelope Gus like a comforting cloak. 'I love the smell of this place,' he says. 'I'd like to be able to sit down in this bookshop, start at the first shelf, and read every book volume by volume. How long do you think that would take?'

Dermot surveys the long racks of books. 'Approximately three centuries, I would say - two if you take one of those faster reading courses. But I don't think that's the solution to life's problems. Reading is great, but not as a substitute for living. Not if it's an excuse for hiding yourself away.'

'You're so wise, as usual,' Gus says.

'Know the difference between wise and stupid people? It's not knowledge or intelligence, but awareness. Wise people realise how much they don't know. Stupid people think they know everything.' Dermot notices the pained look on Gus's face. 'Anyway, what's the problem, my man?'

Gus shifts on his stool. 'Oh, I wish I could be more confident, like Nick or Geraint. I've never even been able to blow my nose like they do - you know- that deep foghorn blast that Geraint produces. Or burp with the volume that Nick achieves.'

'Maybe their confidence is just on the surface. Maybe they're both secretly thinking, "I wish I could be confident like Gus."'

'Yes, but things like discos and parties - they thrive on them. I struggle.'

'Well you seemed to be doing all right with Lorna at the party on Saturday.'

Gus gives an awkward smile. 'I think that was a one-off. She wanted somebody to dance with as Nick was with the boys.'

'But I know what you mean,' says Dermot. 'The same with me. It's that atmosphere of compulsory enjoyment that pervades a disco or party. No-one allowed to be quietly and undemonstratively happy. Everyone compelled to exhibit their happiness noisily for all to see.'

'Yes - and the way people talk - in parties, in seminars, in the debates and the society meetings. It seems so easy and natural to them.'

'Do you know,' Dermot says, 'the creature with the biggest mouth - the dinosaur - also had the smallest brain? I think the same applies to most people. And who was it said something like, when we're young we're too lacking in confidence and wisdom and serenity to enjoy our youth? By the time we've gained that confidence and wisdom and serenity, we've lost our youth.'

'*Wisdom is the property of the dead, a something incompatible with life,*' Gus adds.

'Hey, that sounds very profound. Who said that?'

'Our friend Yeats.'

'That problem will be solved when medical science has advanced to the point where we can be youthful for hundreds of years, so we'll be experienced and young at the same time.

Once we conquer death, then we'll have heaven on earth. Think how wonderful that will be for our descendents.'

'But will they appreciate it, or will they just take it for granted and go on being restless and discontented like humans are now?'

Dermot laughs. 'Perhaps there'll be a drug they can take, literally a wonder drug, to make people see the wonder of being alive. But - at the moment - we're stuck with our short lives and our lack of wisdom. We just have to accept that that's what life is. If we become frustrated by it we make life more difficult. We should be grateful for our mere existence, for a start. We're all here as a result of a lottery. We could so easily have not been born at all. And people don't value freedom. They don't realise that you can't have freedom on its own. It's not an absolute. You can only have freedom *from* something - some restraint, some discipline, some unpleasant thing you might otherwise have to endure. And you can only enjoy and appreciate your freedom by continually experiencing or keeping in mind those things that you have freedom *from*. We have to be grateful for all that happens. We can still be sad at what doesn't happen. Look at me now. I'm sitting down, apparently doing nothing - but my whole body is working hard to keep me alive. I'm breathing in and out and I can never stop doing that. My heart is pumping the blood around all the time. My temperature is kept at a precise figure. If it goes more than a few degrees above or below I'm in trouble. I have to spend a third of my life asleep. I have to ingest food at regular intervals. A million things are going on inside me. And in spite of all that effort I'm the merest dot on the map of eternity, a pinprick on the surface of life, a sudden itch that appears and disappears in a moment of cosmic time, before lapsing back into the nothingness from where I came.'

Gus gets reluctantly up. 'I'd better be moving, I've got this essay on Pope to complete.'

'Ah, the niggling minutiae of everyday life. Don't forget - Physics Lecture Theatre tonight. There's a talk on the Birth and Death of the Universe. How did it begin? Will it go on expanding forever? Or will it contract to the position it was before the Big Bang? Has there been a whole series of Big Bangs, or only one? What happened before the Big Bang?'

'Well, the Pope essay's got to be done. I like to get things right. I want to do a perfect job.'

'Gus,' says Dermot, in the tone of a weary teacher, 'life's too short to be perfectionist. In fact, it's barely long enough to be slapdash.'

Friday, 21 February

Afternoon. The sea pummels the pebbled beach. Waves dash themselves to foaming fragments and spray out in liquid ricochets. On Marine Terrace the water bulges over the seafront. The constant soughing is ringing in Gus's ears, the moist salted air sifts through eyes and nostrils. A wall of snarling wind thrusts against his back, pushing him along up to the pier entrance.

A meeting of the English Society several weeks ago had suggested the idea of poetry notebooks, where students copy poems that have caught their attention in reading. Several lecturers, including Erica Timms and Peter Strutton, read from theirs.

Gus has started his own.

> *Whether to sally and see thee, girl of my dreams,*
> *Or whether to stay*

> *And see thee not ! How vast the difference seems*
> *   Of Yea from Nay*
> *Just now. Yet this same sun will slant its beams*
> *   At no far day*
> *On our two mounds, and then what will the difference*
> *weigh!*

The sun's presence is discernible only as a flared globe of illuminated silvery-yellow cloud halfway up the sky. Imagine a calm sunlit day. Two graves, perhaps a long way from each other. His and Amy's. Yes, then what will the difference weigh! In another poem, Thomas Hardy watches a lunar eclipse and sees the Earth's shadow outlined against the moon, a smoothly curving line

> *Of imperturbable serenity.*

> *How shall I link such sun-cast symmetry*
> *With the torn, troubled form I know as thine.*
> *That profile, placid as a brow divine,*
> *With continents of moil and misery ?*

> *Can immense Mortality but throw so small a shade ?*

Life and living, so muddled, so jagged and tangled, so vast in its pain and disorder, is, as Dermot said, the merest dot on the map of eternity.

The Earth is a tiny globe smaller than a teardrop on the surface of the universe. One of the moon astronauts said he could hold out his thumb from space and obliterate our planet behind it.

So, this agonising and fever, what is the point of it?

> *Life is beautiful… entrancing, enchanting to look at…*
> *Even so beautiful Earth; and could we eliminate only*
> *This vile hungering impulse, this demon within us of*
> *craving,*
> *Life were beatitude, living a perfect divine satisfaction.*

This demon within us of craving. How to eliminate it? He is aware of a presence alongside his shoulder.

'Hi!' Lorna smiles guilelessly at him, then looks for a moment out to sea. She holds her face up against the air as if to be massaged by the wind as it swirls around her. The profile of her full lips is smooth and sensuous as she draws the air in. Her sunlit-sandy hair flares back as the wind rushes through it. She looks directly at him, almost into him, when she speaks.

'So what are you doing this afternoon?'

'Oh, nothing really. Just watching the waves.'

'Well isn't it better to do nothing with somebody rather than on your own?'

She looks for an answer. Gus hesitates, watching the wind tormenting the water, thrashing it up into whorls.

'Come on,' she shouts, raising her voice decisively above the skirl of wind and sea. 'Fancy a coffee in the Cabin?'

She doesn't wait on a reply but turns, hunching her head down into her lilac scarf over which her hair plays softly, and pushing her hands deeper into her pockets for refuge, awakening in him the desire to put a protective arm around her normally unassailable body.

The Cabin is warm, darkened, intimate. Heads turn to scrutinise Lorna. She peals off her scarf and coat. Underneath, to Gus's surprise, she is wearing a white T-shirt. Yet the sudden contradiction between her wintry appearance on the seafront and this summer look indoors seems typical of her.

She leans her elbows on the table, idly displaying bare, shapely forearms, with their soft down of fine hairs. She has firm, assured breasts, thrusting themselves confidently out into the white T-shirt. The two cups of flesh seem to reach out personally, insistently, to him.

That quick, special thrill in the pit of his stomach, that only a girl can trigger. That sharp leap of excitement, like a second heart thumping, especially when the girl is sought-after. The arch of her wrist and hand as she brings her coffee to her lips. She sips its heat, squeezing her lips together gratefully for a moment, a little comically, like a child, then looks at Gus. Unlike her clamour against the wind on the pier, her voice is close and quiet.

'So what are you doing out, all on your own, on this horrible afternoon?'

Gus feels himself warming to the playfully motherly tone in her voice. 'Oh, I was trying to write my Keats essay in the library, but I couldn't get down to it. I ended up browsing through poetry books. Anyway, I could ask you the same question.'

'It can get a bit claustrophobic in Alex. Sometimes it's good to get away' - she tosses her head back a little, smirks her lips - 'not that you can get very far away in a place like this. I thought I'd brave the elements. Looks like I chose the right day for it.' Her eyes, just for a moment, quiz his. Is she thinking also of this serendipitous meeting? 'You had the same idea.'

A hint of connection between them? 'Yes, I like the seafront.'

'Hm, I get that impression about you.' Her eyes find his again. 'You enjoy being on your own. You're a bit of a loner.'

'Sometimes. As you say, it's good to get away.'

'Ah, but I think there's a lot going on in that brain of yours. You're the type who flourishes when he's on his own. You often seem bored in company.'

'Oh I wouldn't say that.'

'I've noticed you. I think you definitely prefer your own thoughts to those of other people. And you do some writing, don't you?'

'Oh, nothing special.' He shakes his head dismissively and feels a sudden twinge through him. Has he told Nick? He can't remember? Or is it only Amy? If Amy has mentioned to Lorna about his writing, what else has she told her?

Lorna's head slants sideways as she studies him, fascination in her eyes, her hair falling carefree to one side. Collar-length, in loose wavy fronds, its shortness makes her look more mature, more womanly, than other blond girl students whose hair invariably spills long and straight beyond the neck and down the back. 'We'll have to get together some time. Then we can bore each other.'

The invitation, more like a remark, is tossed off casually. Gus nods a tight-mouthed smile. He could say 'When?' but it might sound too eager and perhaps she is not serious.

'Seeing Nick tonight?' Gus realises as he speaks that his chat-a-long question might be seen as taking up her offer.

'Yes, he's coming round to Alex - but -' she speaks more carefully, '- tomorrow he's got a get-together with the cricket boys in the White Horse. I'll be on my own. The girls are probably going to the disco on the Hill, but I'm not bothered. So if you want to do something…'

Gus must try not to blazon his delight on to his reply. His voice rises to a 'Yeh' of unconcerned agreement. 'We could go for a drink.'

Lorna is suddenly animated, leaning low over the table to him. 'Let's go somewhere where there are no students.'

'That's difficult in Aber - apart from the library.'

She laughs, with a glowing smile that squeezes her eyes until the soft, smooth lashes above and below seem almost to meet.

'How about one of the pubs by the castle?'

His voice finds a sudden confidence. 'Yes - let's do a little exploring.'

Saturday, 22 February

'Fancy Mr Jones from Gwyntgwyllt dying like that! It was so sudden! He hadn't even been ill! Never had a day's illness in his life!'

'Well there must've been something wrong with him, love, or he wouldn't have dropped dead.' Mr Morgan turns to the boys and nods gravely. 'Mr Jones from Gwyntgwyllt, a few doors up. Nice old boy. Funeral on Thursday.'

'And I'm not too good myself,' Mrs Morgan croaks. 'Almost lost my voice.'

'That'd be a rare thing.' Mr Morgan winks to the boys.

'The doctor said it was something at the bottom of my throat, right where my acropolis is.'

'Oesophagus, isn't it, love?'

'That's what I said didn't I?'

Mr Morgan peers out of the window, stretches yawningly with an 'Ah' and proceeds to scratch his back.

'What do you keep on scratching for?'

'I've got an itch love.'

'No you haven't. You're imagining it. Don't do it in front of the boys. It's not good manners!'

'If you've gotta itch, you gotta itch!' Nick declares.

'Don't encourage him!' Mrs Morgan admonishes.

'*Mr Jones from Gwyntgwyllt.*' Nick mimics Mrs Morgan perfectly as the boys sit in the Cabin in mid-morning.

'He probably choked to death pronouncing the name of his house,' says Dermot. 'What was it? *Gwyyynnntgwwyylllltt.*'

Geraint stops midway through an intake of coffee. 'Don't you dare make fun of the Welsh language, and you being Welsh too. The guy was probably about a hundred and five. They all seem to live to that age here. Welsh is the oldest language in Europe that's still spoken. And it used to be spoken all over Britain.'

'Oh yeh, I've heard it in the streets of Kensington,' Dermot sneers.

'Not now, you idiot! Before the Germanic tribes pushed us back into Wales. Take *Dover* - that's from the Welsh word for water, *dwfr*. The River Avon is from the Welsh word for river, *afon*. *Adder* comes from the Welsh *neidr*, a snake. English often uglifies the Welsh, like *Splott* in Cardiff comes from *ysblad*.'

'What does *Gwyntgwyllt* mean anyway?' Simon asks.

Geraint looks to the window in the direction of the sea. 'Very appropriate. It means *wild wind*.'

'Okay, guys,' Nick shouts, 'speaking of the Welsh lesson, there's only one place anyone who's Welsh could be this afternoon. Students' Union. TV Lounge. Wales versus England. When you see those boys in red run out onto the field, that's when you feel Welsh. Doesn't matter if you speak the language or not. Simon, we can make you an honorary Welshman for the day if you want.'

'Thanks,' says Simon. 'I'm not really a rugby fan. Football's my game.'

'Apparently there's a great atmosphere in the Students' Union,' Nick goes on. 'It's pretty evenly divided between Welsh and English supporters. So it's a noisy affair.'

Gus has watched other matches there and revels in the atmosphere. Today it will prevent him being troubled by too much fretful excitement at the thought of the evening and his meeting with Lorna.

'And cricket reunion tonight if anyone fancies it!' Nick turns to Gus. 'Want to come along? Now that you've put Amy on hold, don't want you sulking in our room.'

'Oh, I'll be all right,' Gus answers. 'I might stay in and do some of my essay.'

'Do some of your essay?' Nick repeats in horror.

'Yes, just - throw myself into it.'

Nick lets out his thunderous laugh. 'I'd rather throw myself - into the sea! Makes sense, I suppose, though. But then, you're a sensible lad.' He puts his arm around Gus. 'In fact, Gus, you're too sane. If you were a little less sane you'd be a better-balanced person. Your New Year's Resolution should have been - become a little more insane. Why not go out in Aber tonight, and look for the most beautiful woman you can find?'

Gus smiles and says in a joking tone, 'Yes, okay, maybe I will.'

Nick gives another blaring guffaw and releases Gus from his hold.

Wales narrowly won the rugby match and there was high and raucous passion in the Students' Union. Now it is the quiet of evening, the lights of the promenade illuminating yellow shimmering strips of water, elsewhere the sea lapping darkly against the dim sand. Gus waits. Nick has already left. He watched him from the window, strutting away in that intent, determined stride. Gus hovers a little way up from Gwylan House, in case anyone there should see him. Simon and Dermot are ensconced in their rooms. He almost toyed with the idea of telling Dermot he was meeting Lorna for the evening, but his caution outweighed his pride in the revelation. He would have to swear Dermot to secrecy, or else Dermot would tell Nick. Or would he have to be that dramatic? Couldn't he just mention, with a hint of a frown, *'probably best not to tell Nick'*? He'd have to say something, otherwise Dermot would artlessly gush out at breakfast, *'Have an interesting time with Lorna last night?'* and Nick would stop halfway through an ingestion of Mrs Morgan's eggs, his eyes as wide as his mouth.

And if he'd simply said to Dermot, *'I'm seeing Lorna tonight,'* it would somehow elevate him to a rank he did not qualify for, though he wished he could attain - the status of the loose guy, either naïve or philanderous, who openly cavorts with whoever takes his fancy irrespective of any possible consequences or complications.

He can see her coming towards him. She is not looking nervously ahead, not looking out for him, but is neatly self-contained, unconcerned as she trips along, her bouncing walk not as pronounced as usual, perhaps because it's cold and misty and she is wrapped snugly in her scarf.

It is only when she nears him that she glances up, but there is no suggestion of anxiety, or of making a particular effort to greet, in her bearing, just a nonchalant friendly 'Hi!'. She does not slow down or change her stride and Gus has the impression that, if he did not fall in with her step, she would simply walk past him.

He merges in beside her and finds her calm businesslike air is both relaxing and a little unnerving. This to her is any other night, any other date that she's been on. She hasn't built up any hopes, so he won't bitterly disappoint her but probably won't make an impression either. But again this joy, this supreme feeling of achievement, that he's been admitted to her roll, almost as if - more words from Wordsworth come into his mind - he *worshipp'st at the Temple's inner shrine.*

And he is *close* to her, almost brushing her shoulder as they walk. They are *together*. Simple, huge words.

He wonders about Amy. What is she doing? Is she thinking about anyone? He can't ask Lorna.

She gives him a quick look and a sweet smile from the depths of her scarf. 'You okay?' It's not a concerned question to him but a reassuring greeting, as they march up the slight rise opposite the seafront apartments and the Chinese takeaway, to where Pier Street meets the prom. Then they head into the wind-embraced stretch in front of the Old College that rises above them.

There is no conversation, but this does not bother Gus because Lorna seems similarly unbothered.

'Shall we go to the Castle?' She speaks pleasantly.

'Sure.'

Four male students are lounging in a corner of the Castle Hotel - third-years, Gus thinks. Their eyes stalk Lorna as she unrobes and makes herself comfortable. Gus gets drinks from the bar. Lorna has changed her T-shirt for a smarter soft purple blouse and Gus feels flattered by this attention from her.

She lifts her drink gaily in toast, with a laughing-eyed smile. 'Well, here we are - ready to bore each other!'

Gus smiles, happy-go-luckily. He feels good now.

She leans towards him. 'No - I didn't mean that,' she laughs. 'I'm certain you're not boring.' She does not look around or show interest in the rest of the pub or its occupants, but settles her attention on Gus.

'What are the other boys doing tonight?'

'Nick left about half-seven for his cricket reunion. I think Simon is in his room. Not certain about Dermot.'

'What's life like with that mad bunch of boys?'

Gus talks about his lodgings, throws in some amusing tales about Dermot and Mr and Mrs Morgan, asks Lorna what

Alexandra Hall is like. She answers that she feels institutionalised, as if in a convent. He pictures the setting, and an excitement trembles through him at the thought of that seafront haven of so many girls together, far from home and parents.

'I've often wondered what boys talk about together. Is it really only football and girls - in that order?' A light inquisitive smile teases her lips.

'Oh no! You wouldn't believe some of the conversations we have - everything. Religion, war, time travel, whether Mr and Mrs Morgan are aliens from another planet.' Gus explains the last subject and they laugh as one.

'So what do girls talk about?'

Lorna lowers her head, looks at him through arched eyebrows. 'Football and boys - but in reverse order.' She rotates her hand to demonstrate - a beautiful, neat, soft hand. 'No. People worry about their essays, their boyfriends or lack of them. I don't think we've discussed whether the staff are aliens,' she adds in sham earnestness, wrinkling her brow. He loves the animation of her face, the different expressions that lighten or darken it. He is so delighted he can watch them close-up, one-to-one.

Then a picture comes into his mind. The girls talking. Two hundred girls together. Rumours would spread. If Amy has said anything…She's not the type to spread news around. But - she need only tell one person. That person would tell another. That person…

He should ask Amy, once and for all. But if she has said something, she probably wouldn't tell him. If she hasn't said anything, she'll feel insulted, cheapened, by his accusation…

Does Lorna secretly know? If so, she betrays no sign, though he's not certain what sort of sign it would be. He must be positive, trust Amy, assume Lorna does not know. This is stupid! He is with a girl of mythological beauty, all on his own. He has her to himself for the evening. Forget what's happened, or has not happened.

'You're looking thoughtful. Come on, I don't want you going off into that dream world of yours.' Lorna's eyes are wide alive, clear pale blue, her face gazing into his.

'What were you thinking about? Some poet?'

'No - just...relaxing.' Gus spreads his mouth into a wide smile.

'D'you mind if I smoke?'

Gus is surprised at her politeness. Normally Lorna simply lights up. She offers him a cigarette.

'Not for me, thanks.'

No condescending words from her, like *You're a good boy*. Her lips embrace the cigarette. Her sleek fingers close around it as she sucks in. He likes the fleshy arc of her forearm as it holds the cigarette up. She glides the smoke out through her mouth and nostrils. She turns to him and smiles in that breezy way that tells him she is perfectly satisfied, with herself and with him, at ease in his company.

They talk about courses and lecturers. He does not probe her background, but knows she is from near Shrewsbury. But, somehow, connecting a person to a background, to another life at home, with family, away from Aber, seems irrelevant. People, once they reach here, are shorn of their past existence and become fresh, pure creations, resurrected into a new realm.

The pub is filling. The buzz of voices increases as groups and pairs shuffle in from the wind. It is nearing half-past ten. Gus wonders what might happen next. He has enjoyed good, unforced conversation with her but has felt rooted to his chair, unable to move to her. The magical touching of any part of her seems out of the question. Will she want to go to one of the clubs? He's seen her dancing, with light, flowing movements and mesmerising sexiness, the swirling curve of her breasts, her shoulders and hips in such graceful harmony. Or will she invite him back to her room? She's given no signals of this, which brings him disappointment, but perhaps more relief. Or does she expect him to come back with her anyway, so no signals are necessary?

He leans over to her. 'What do you want to do now? How about a club?'

She is hesitant. 'Mm, if you don't mind, I think I'll go for an early night. I've got some work to catch up on tomorrow.'

He feels a little vexed at this respect and formality from her. No wild night out with the two of them letting go.

They emerge into the night. They can either walk through the streets or -.

Lorna flings her scarf around her neck and completes his thought for him. 'Let's walk back along the prom.'

This is the wilder, more remote way. The town will be more social with revellers. She's chosen the route where they are more likely to be on their own.

They set off into the wind. She slips her arm into his, without fuss, not looking at him, as if she has done it a hundred times before, and they march along. Her closeness is exhilarating and makes up for his earlier discouragements.

'I can't wait for the summer. This place will be transformed. Imagine what the beaches are like in the sun!' She adds a skip to her stride at the thought.

'The only trouble is - we'll have exams then.'

'Oh, don't worry about them! I can't wait to get the sun on my face!' She holds her head up, as if to an imaginary gleaming yellow globe. Her eyes smile straight into his, and for a moment, but one sublime, he feels he is the only person in the world to her. She has granted him the privilege of being alone with her, on South Beach promenade, their bodies united against a grumbling wind that tugs at them, hauling them along as they labour happily against it.

They reach Castle Point where the view opens out to the long panoramic line of the dark sea and North Beach and the beacon-like orange lights of the seafront. To hold her now, to put his arm around her, would be a glimpse of heaven. She is not now the goddess untouchable to mortals, but a beautiful girl-woman alone with him late in the evening, her arm snuggled in his.

But this is like a jigsaw where he carefully fits the pieces in one by one. He is not allowed a mistake, and though he tries desperately to judge the shape and colour of the next piece, he is not certain if it will slot in. An arm around signifies, not friendship or attraction, but oneness.

They reach the pier. Alex can be seen in the distance. They start to chat again.

'Are you seeing Nick tonight?' Gus asks.

'Nah, shouldn't think so. He's probably having too good a time with his cricketing mates.'

Is her voice saying, *it's all clear, no need to worry*?

They pass Gwylan House. No light in his and Nick's room, though Gus did not expect one. The towering outline of Alex is looming nearer. It's too late now for Gus to put his arm around her. That might be seen as a crude attempt to invite himself in.

They reach the front doors of Alex. Lorna turns to him.

'I'd ask you up for coffee, but I feel a bit shattered. I didn't get in till two last night.' She is suddenly coy, looking up into his eyes almost apologetically. 'It's been a lovely evening.'

The word *lovely* surprises him. And she does not normally exaggerate praise.

She is waiting. That seems unusual for her, too. She is waiting, for something.

Then, at almost the same time as he embraces her waist, she reaches her arms up and lingers them around his neck. They kiss. Not a long kiss, but neither a peck. A kiss where he feels her lips luscious against his. And then her head is on his chest and his hand reaches to feel the softness of her hair.

He touches a kiss on her forehead and holds her to him. 'Mm, I've enjoyed it.'

'We'll do the same again, shall we?' She is asking him, waiting for his decision.

'Yes, that'd be good.' They give each other a final farewell hug and she steps into Alex, flashing a little wave. Then he sees her hurrying in through the foyer and the elegant sway of her body as it mounts each stair.

He walks back along the prom, to the rhythm of the incoming water, the wind keening into him, and a dreaming moon high above.

Friday, 28 February

C hris Bowen, third-year physics student and Chairman of the Debating Society, immaculately attired in dinner jacket and bow tie, sprawls his long legs out in his seat on the stage of the Exam Hall. The two guests, local politicians from Plaid Cymru and the Conservative Party, have made their speeches on the motion *Wales Should Be An Independent Nation* and Chris has thrown the debate open to the audience.

This is the part Chris enjoys most. Contributions from the floor can be deadly serious, humorous or impassioned, but always unpredictable. A person with the mildest, most retiring demeanour might voice the most subversive, revolutionary ideas, or a wild-eyed, ragged individual might come up with bland and boring opinions. One never knows what people will utter until they open their mouths.

Gus, Nick and Dermot sit together halfway down the hall on the left side of the aisle. Gus can see Fiona, flanked by Amy and Lorna, across on the right side a row in front of him. Every so often during the two speeches, Gus turned to look at the girls. Fiona's head was held slightly down, but her eyes seemed to stare forward. Her mouth was serious and absorbed, as if listening intently to the speakers. Her shoulders and posture were more rigid than normal. Amy and Lorna looked more relaxed as they listened. Peter Strutton, one of the few lecturers to regularly attend debates, sits quietly attentive and at ease, three rows behind the girls and to their right.

Dermot is the first to rise to his feet. 'I want to say that, although I'm from Builth Wells -' there are a few languid cheers from the audience ' - I don't feel particularly Welsh - or English or any other nationality. I just feel human - and I don't even feel that sometimes.'

'Aren't you proud to be Welsh?' someone shouts out.

'No. I'm grateful to be Welsh. I ask myself, would I like to be any other nationality? The answer is no. I'm very happy to be Welsh. But I'm not proud. I was born Welsh. I had no say in it. I don't think people should be proud of something that's an accident. I wouldn't be proud of being any nationality.'

A girl with fair frizzly hair, sporting a colourful red and pink top, speaks in a rushed, haranguing voice. 'I don't see why we have to be exclusively Welsh, or English, or anything else. Why can't we be a mixture of both? I feel neither completely Welsh nor completely English, but why should there be a dichotomy between the two? They're both part of a larger whole, Britain. When you were young, didn't any of you write in your schoolbooks your name and address followed by Britain, Europe, The World, The Galaxy, The Universe?'

An earnest-looking, bespectacled male student springs up. 'The previous speaker misses the point. We're talking about two distinct places - England and Wales. Like her, I feel neither English nor Welsh. Unlike her, I don't feel comfortable with that at all. I feel I have one foot in both countries. If they begin to move apart, I feel I'm being pulled in opposite directions.'

'Sounds painful!' someone shouts from the back of the hall.

'Exactly. I travel, I hover, between the two, without reaching either.'

One student announces he is 'fifty per cent Welsh, fifty per cent English.' Someone adds, 'Thirty-two per cent idiot,' which prompts a melee of answering statistics and snippets of humour and opinion. The debate threatens to slide into chaos.

'I'm a hundred per cent Anglo-Welsh.'

'I'd just like to declare, I'm eighty per cent water, ten per cent carbon...'

'My friend here, at the moment, is seventy-five per cent alcohol.'

'Wales is just a region of Britain, like the Midlands or the North-East.'

'Rubbish! Do these regions have their own language?'

'Of course they do! Have you ever tried understanding somebody from Newcastle?'

'Wales is more than a region but less than a nation.'

'I'm a patriot of the planet, not of any one particular country.'

A flame-haired, ginger-bearded student lumbers to his feet. 'Who cares where I'm from? Originally I'm from Africa, like everybody else in the human race. So why worry about trivialities like English and Welsh? I'm on this planet. I'm pleased I'm here. I'm very fortunate to be here. We all are. We all breathe in the same way. That's no coincidence. It's because we're all the same species.'

'I agree. Language, national culture, give the appearance of being fundamental to a nation, but from the perspective of humanity, they're superficial,' shouts someone without getting up, to the visible annoyance of Chris Bowen. This prompts Geraint to leap to his feet.

'It's easy to think that way - as long as your own language and culture are not under threat. We're all speaking English here at the moment without any problem. But supposing English was in danger of dying out? Supposing it was being swamped by some other language that a lot more people speak? We wouldn't think speaking English was a superficial thing then, would we? We'd defend our right to speak it. Well, that's exactly the position Welsh is in.'

Fiona gets up. Amy looks straight ahead, a little nervously. Lorna glances up at Fiona as if making some mute communication to her.

'I just want to say…' Fiona's voice sounds strained, slightly crackly, over-deliberate, '…that I've listened to the debate with great interest…'

Chris Bowen dislikes irrelevant preamble. He likes speakers to come to their point quickly. His face begins to show a twitch of impatience.

'…and, it seems to me…'

Chris twitches in his seat again.

'…that the issue of loyalty has not been discussed enough. Loyalty - .' Fiona pauses to let the word take effect, but does not look around.

' - is one of the great virtues. It's underrated. It's like mercy. To paraphrase Portia, it is twice blest. It blesseth him that gives and him that takes.' On the last three words she jerks her head in the direction of Peter Strutton. 'Yes, loyalty.' Her voice wavers. She looks down, seeming to become less confident.

She takes a deep breath and lifts her head again.

'Loyalty to a country - and to other people.' She turns her head again towards where Peter Strutton sits. She stiffens and looks straight ahead, doggedly.

Chris Bowen's impatience grows. Should he be formal and polite - *Come to the point, madam* - or informal and humorous, though he can't think of anything suitably funny?

There is a peculiar sort of snarl in Fiona's voice. 'Now could I name to thee a man.'

Dermot nods knowingly. '*Julius Caesar,*' he mutters.

'Why the hell doesn't she shut up?' Nick whispers.

Her voice suddenly rises to a bawl, her arm shoots up and swings towards Peter Strutton as she repeats, 'Now could I name to thee a man - '

There is momentary fear on Peter Strutton's face. His head moves back a little as if he's been hit by the arm sweepingly extended in his direction. Fiona clambers in front of Lorna as if to make her way along the row of seated bodies, all now looking at her in a mixture of bafflement, amusement and alarm. Lorna stands up to bar her way. There is a brief struggle but Lorna appears to be better balanced than Fiona and, with Amy clasping her left arm, Fiona sinks back into her seat.

Chris Bowen judges it time to stand up. 'Thanks for that - rather original contribution.' He shudders his head in amused bewilderment. 'I think on that note we'll call a halt to proceedings. Now, time to vote.'

Hands are raised and counted. The vote is narrowly in favour of independence for Wales. Chris speaks again. 'I'd like to give a big thank you to our two guest speakers, and to the contributors from the floor, original and combative as always. Don't forget next week's debate, *Religion Is The Opium Of The People...*'

Lorna holds Fiona's hand and Gus notices Peter Strutton rising to leave, his face ruminative, eyes unlooking, before he is swallowed up by the general exodus.

Fiona appears to be giving forth little sobs.

'Is she all right?' Nick asks quietly as they meet in the aisle to leave.

'Yes.' Lorna is grasping Fiona's arm. 'She had some wine before coming here. But she's okay.'

Fiona's head is bowed. Amy smiles briefly at Gus.

'We'll take Fiona back to Alex,' Lorna says, leading her along. Fiona looks drained and helpless, with a quaint stupefied expression on her face.

'Poor kid,' Nick murmurs.

'I thought you didn't like her,' Dermot says.

'No - she's okay. She must feel so unhappy.'

Monday, 3 March

Lorna's soft sunflower hair brushes against her cheek as she sits down. She looks perfectly at ease as usual. The Unicorn is brightly-lit, comfortingly busy but not crammed. This time Gus is sitting beside her on a bench, so there is no barrier between them, which makes him feel even more that they are a couple. He can feel her closeness, see from behind her arm and hand as she reaches out to bring her drink to her lips.

'I've got to go home this Friday,' she says with a tone of nuisance. 'Even though it's so near the end of term. Family celebration. It's my parents' twenty-fifth wedding anniversary. Gathering of the clan.'

Again, Gus has difficulty imagining her as part of a family, in a family atmosphere. She seems so independent, so self-contained, so unbelonging and unbeholden to anyone or anything. He cannot see her surrounded by a father, mother, brothers or sisters. There is that calm defiance in the set of her mouth and the curve of her lips, often a look of cool disdain in her eyes, that seems to proclaim her gloriously free of those kinds of ties.

'Yes, my parents have been married about the same length of time,' he says. 'Do you get on with your parents?'

She is thoughtful. 'Yes, better now. We had a bit of a crisis last year. They were really nagging me. I wrote them a letter setting out my terms. Since then we've got on much better.'

'Oh? What did you put in the letter?'

'I thanked them for my upbringing, for their love and concern for me.' She thinks again. 'We did *King Lear* for A-level and the words of Cordelia to her father struck a chord with me. She said she loved him according to her bond, no more nor less. "You have begot me, bred me, loved me. I return those duties back." She loves him as a father, but she refuses to bow down to him. She asserts her independence. I did the same. I said I wanted to make my own decisions, stand on my own two feet - about everything - about what I do, wear, eat, my friends. And I'd take responsibility for my decisions.'

Lorna's tone is calm and even. 'I think we appreciate each other more now. Lots of young people just harbour a simmering resentment against their parents. They whinge, but don't do anything except negative things. It's best to come right out and say what's bothering you.'

Wrote them a letter. Gus cannot imagine confronting his parents in that adult way. Perhaps it would be easier if his father and mother were nastier to him, if they tyrannised and nagged him. Then he would have something against which to assert his independence. But they do their best for him. The umbilical cord, of ways of thinking, of looking at the world, is still there. It would be dramatic and very satisfying to cut it cleanly, as Lorna did with her letter. But he is gradually filing away at it instead of taking up the sword and severing it with one blow.

He is like a prisoner scraping an escape tunnel with his hands, bit by tiny bit, hoping he will not be discovered, instead of vaulting over the walls in one inspired leap. He has removed himself physically from them, but they are still with him, watching over him. Some part of them has infiltrated itself into his being, like a spy, into his brain. It sits there, reporting back on what he does, what he thinks and feels. And because it is in his brain he cannot break free no matter how far away from them he may be.

Now the increasing closeness of mind that he was feeling towards Lorna has been destroyed. Suddenly she is several steps ahead of him in life, almost as if she is an older sister and he is a little boy. She is the undaunted explorer penetrating into the interior, fording rivers that seem uncrossable, frightening in their torrent of waters. With his feeling of mental inequality and weakness comes a certainty of physical rejection also. She won't desire the body of a mere boy.

'My parents seem so -,' he searches for the word, '- unenlightened. They know so little of what I know. When I think, they left school early, so everything I've done in the last few years would be unknown to them. And they seem to lead such unexciting lives. I mean, it's difficult to think of them as having been young. I can't imagine my father getting excited over anything.' He laughs. 'Least of all my mother.'

Lorna smiles. 'Oh, that's a little unkind! But I know what you mean. Yes, it's difficult to envisage our parents as having once been the same age as us. Someone said that, when you're twenty, you think how little your parents know. When you're thirty, you realise how much they know. I sometimes think of my father coming home from work, on the August day when I was conceived. It might have been a beautiful summer's evening. And that night he made love to my mother. They could have had little thought that they were getting me started in life.

They could have had no conception - excuse pun - of what I would be like. And yet if they hadn't done it that night, I would never have existed.'

'You could have been born at a later date.'

'But then would it have been the same me? I'd have a different star sign for a start - though I don't really believe in all that astrology stuff. If my mother had conceived some other night, would I have been an entirely different person, with different thoughts and feelings, a different consciousness? And if I'd been born a year later, I'd have different friends, been a year later coming to university…'

She leans down to pick up her glass. Gus's earlier despair at her advanced situation in life compared to him lessens. He begins to feel a pleasant, comfortable desiring for her. He's been surprised by her depth and thoughtfulness. She will be energising to him. She will lead him forward, in patience and tolerance and understanding perhaps, with her wisdom and worldly knowledge. Yes, he feels stimulated by her decisiveness, her refusal to tolerate what she doesn't like. *Dismiss whatever insults your soul*, Dermot said to him once, quoting from Whitman.

'I had a shock at Christmas,' she continues. 'My mother showed me a photograph of my grandmother when she was a young woman. I've always thought of gran as having been born old - you think that of grandparents don't you? - as always having that thin scraggly hair and frumpy shape and wrinkled hands and face. But she was beautiful. A lovely bright thing, with beautiful clear skin, thick hair bunched back, lovely eyes.'

Gus feels like telling Lorna she has exactly those qualities herself, now. But he cannot bring himself to do it. It will sound like cheap flattery to gain her favour. Nick would say it with warmth and a touch of light-heartedness.

'Yes,' Lorna carries on, 'we tend to think old people have always been old. And I suppose we think we'll always go on being young.'

'It's difficult to imagine some people as young, though - like Parker-Hurst.'

'The Ancient Mariner! Yes I must admit the lecturers - some of them - seem frozen in time. Yet I can't imagine Peter Strutton as old.'

'Do you fancy him?' Gus is surprised that the question comes suddenly from his lips without conscious thought.

She hesitates. 'Well - he's very fanciable! But no - I wouldn't contemplate it. Too complicated.'

'How is Fiona, after Friday night?'

'Not good. We got her back to Alex - just about! She's still befuddled by him. I saw her sitting on the beach yesterday, watching the water. I went down to talk to her, but she wasn't very responsive. She just stared out to sea. Then she started crying again.'

They talk about Simon. 'He seems to be, somehow, swallowed up by life,' Lorna says. 'He's like a hedgehog, folded up into himself. His hair is like spikes to keep out the rest of the world. He's another one who seems to spend a lot of time looking out to sea, as if that will solve his problems. I saw him propped up against the bandstand wall, the other day...'

Should he take this opportunity to ask if Simon is going out with Amy? He hasn't seen them together. Simon hasn't mentioned anything, but then he wouldn't.

No. It would suggest to Lorna that he's still interested in Amy, more so than in her. But isn't he? But Lorna might take steps to try to bring them together, might drop an encouraging word into Amy's ear. He isn't ready.

She turns and looks at Gus directly, for the first time in the evening. 'Anyway, how's university life for you? We're almost two-thirds through the first year now.' Her eyes have an amused sparkle, a look of easy intimacy with him, as if telling him he has entered her valued inner circle of friends. Perhaps she's not thinking him weak, timid, worthless after all. He feels encouraged to express his thoughts.

'Ah, university life! Yes, it's been an interesting year so far. It's an adventure in every way, an adventure of the mind, of the emotions.' He almost adds 'of the body,' but realises this is his hope rather than accomplishment at the moment.

'Any further thoughts about Amy?'

Gus shifts a little on the bench. 'Uh - no!'

'Don't worry. I'm not pushing anything. She hasn't asked me to talk to you. But I think she's missing you. Just thought I'd let you know.'

'Thanks.'

And the gap between him and Lorna has opened again. He no longer means anything to her, if she'd be happy to see him with Amy. He is her acquaintance among many. He looks out on the rest of the pub. The volume of noise and drinkers is increasing. Being side by side he and Lorna have no natural eye-contact, so now his feeling of alienation from her begins to deepen. Suddenly in his heart is the sense of hopelessness, defeat, with her. She is being gracious, merely friendly, to him. Anyway, how could he have possibly thought she could feel anything for him? It was a wild fantasy.

Has she sensed, in a moment, the withering of his ego? 'Hey, why so suddenly glum?' She squeezes his hand. Her fingers are compact, soft but not fleshy. He feels their femininity, her smaller hand in his. He smiles and her smile is there ready in response, her marigold smile, as he thinks it, with her face and her eyes lighting up like a flower opening. She nudges her head playfully up against his and the touch of her hair on his cheek bridges the gulf in an instant's magic.

'Time to be moving,' she says.

This could be the day, Gus thinks. Second date. She will expect it. She will help and encourage him. She won't mock or dismiss him. She won't take it personally if he's struggling. She won't think herself a failure, because so many others have shown her how much she turns them on. She won't have her own sense of inadequacy to deal with. She'll be there to take him through it.

Lorna attracts admiring glances as she makes for the door. Gus feels exalted to be with her. He's on a level with any of the boys who eye her - above their level, because she's with him.

They emerge onto the slope of Corporation Street. In the quiet late evening they seem to be the only two people in the town, in the world. There is something about walking down the night-time middle of a town's empty street that gives an added enchantment. Their footsteps sound on the bare silent tarmac. As they turn left onto Terrace Road the parallel outlines of houses on each side of Bath Street stretch darkly ahead like a mystery, melting under the black silhouette of the mountain at its end. The wind begins to sidle in from the sea. Lorna swings her scarf more tightly about her neck, immerses her face deep in its warmth. Her gloved hands are buried in her coat. Gus puts his arm protectively around her and she accepts its shelter, glancing a smile at him. He can feel her shoulder nuzzled into his armpit, the contours of her back firm along his outstretched arm. The absence of words adds to the oneness. Yes, all the time he is edging closer to the moment, stealing into her presence, and she is moving with him. It is as if they are doing a slow, lingering dance together, slipping into the right positions, physically and emotionally. Now they are almost ready.

They negotiate the fifty yards to Marine Terrace. Lorna looks up at him. 'Gus,' she says softly, hesitating a moment as if she is loathe to speak further. 'I'm going to have to leave you now and walk ahead. I promised Nick I'd see him tonight. He might be looking out of his window - your window - for me. Wouldn't look good if I was there with you.' She turns her face up to him again for response and to hint at the release of his arm.

She sees the drooping of hope in his eyes and mouth but his arm tightens around her in protest. 'Sorry,' she says. 'I won't have much chance to see him this week.'

'How about next Saturday?' Gus asks. 'I think Nick's got a Cricket Club social.'

'Ah, I'm going to Stratford with the Drama Club to see *All's Well That Ends Well*. We won't be back till late. But we can have a coffee in the week, maybe.'

She reaches a kiss to his cheek. He kisses her lips and she responds but does not let the kiss persist, easing her face away and her body from his grip. He is left holding her wool-gloved hands lightly. She swings them slackly in his.

'Thanks for the evening,' she says. 'I'll see you tomorrow anyway, at the lectures. Take care.'

He says something about her sleeping well and she is away, quickening her step against the chill wind. He watches her forging into the distance, her firm tread moving swiftly away from him.

Easter Vacation

Gus's return to Nanthyfryd is less of a shock to him than at Christmas. There is not such a sense of strangeness and dislocation and his father and mother seem less like alien creatures and he less alienated from them. Although the cushion of the Christmas and New Year festivities is absent, it feels more comforting, sheltered. He is pleased for the days to be emptied of the ado of Aber, a few weeks' void. He feels a greater sense of harmony between himself and home. He reads Flaubert's *Sentimental Education*. He helps his brothers and sister with homework and goes for a walk with his father in the village and surrounding countryside. He is more prepared now for the repeated pattern of a term in Aber followed by vacation with his family.

What thrills him is a letter from Lorna, with bold, fluent writing that slopes slightly forward, in strong dark-blue ink. He can imagine her fingers clasped around the pen. The letter is chatty and unforced, with no poetry quotes or philosophical reflections. She talks about a shopping trip to Chester with her mother, whom Gus envisages as attractive, youthful-looking, trim-figured and like her daughter. She mentions nights out with old school friends and arguments with her older brother, whom Gus imagines to be manly, assured and handsome, the male equivalent of her. She reports on her attempts to read *Paradise Lost* and her greater enjoyment of D. H. Lawrence's *The Virgin And The Gypsy*.

There is no letter from Amy.

He decides to take a day trip to Cardiff on the train. Perhaps, in the bustle of the city, thriving and teeming with people, he will meet someone. He's not certain how. Perhaps the courage to fasten his eyes for a few seconds on someone who takes his fancy, the willpower to smile, perhaps in response to her smile. What could follow? *Would you like to go somewhere for a coffee?* He will take some books to Cardiff library to do some studying. There are bound to be numerous students there. Out of them all there must be one who will catch his interest.

At Pontypridd a young woman gets on the train and sits opposite him. She has dark brown long cascading hair. She wears glasses and Gus imagines himself removing them to study her fine dark eyes underneath. But she wears both a wedding and an engagement ring on her finger. So what would be the point of speaking to her? There's no purpose in talking for the sake of talking. But she might be an interesting person. They might have a good conversation. On the other hand, she could be boring, suspicious, hostile. Anyway, she's married.

But she might be unhappy. She might be looking for someone, anyone. In that case, though, why doesn't she take off her rings? Perhaps she's mildly dissatisfied. He might be just the kind of person she needs. But how can he talk to her? She is just sitting there opposite him, not doing anything. If she was reading a book, that might be an opening. But she's not. She doesn't show the slightest interest in him. But, then, he must appear like that to her. She might be thinking exactly the same things about him. There is an expression of slightly pained confusion on her face, the look of not wanting to be there. Sad lips. Sometimes she casts her eyes down, sometimes looks straight ahead.

Her hair glistens splendidly with a few raindrops from the drizzle outside. Gus has a mild thought of following her as she steps down from the train in Cardiff, but it seems pointless and soon she is lost in the flow of pedestrians.

When he arrives at Cardiff library, there are seven people in the reference section, five men and two women, neither of whom attracts his interest. He stays for half-an-hour, then looks around the music and book shops.

When the four weeks of vacation are up and he prepares to return to Aber, it feels as if time is about to start moving again after a standstill. As the coach reaches Aberaeron and the coast, the sea is an exuberant blue, the sky a quieter shade, and Aber a mist-haloed mirage in the distance, nestled under the green of the hills of mid-Wales. He feels like a galactic traveller viewing the home planet after a long, long voyage through the dark sparseness of space.

Sunday, 20 April

L orna presses the bell, her lips expanding into a gleeful beam. 'This is quite exciting, going to a lecturer's home!'

Gus is more nervous, feeling Peter Strutton and she will happily chat leaving him behind. He and Lorna had walked by the seashore after their first seminar of the new term, on Tuesday - Amy and Nick had not been part of the group - and been met by Peter, strolling along by the Pier in the opposite direction, watching the mellowing orange of the sun reflected in the water as days begin to lengthen lazily into summer. He'd asked them, in his amiable way, if they'd had a good vacation, and said they should come round to his flat for coffee some time. They had agreed, thinking it the sort of invitation that is meaninglessly uttered and promptly forgotten, but Peter had phoned Alexandra Hall on Friday, asked for Lorna, and suggested a time for both her and Gus to come on Sunday.

Peter opens the door. He is dressed casually in a dark-blue shirt and extends his arm in invitation to them to enter, giving a friendly 'Hi!' as he does. He looks at ease but not dominatingly so, and there is something about his smile, temperate, not too effusive, that gives Gus reassurance.

The living room is small but comfortable-looking, with a light-patterned sofa and armchairs. There is a tall bookcase behind the door with neatly-arranged shelves of books. In an alcove beside the window is another bookcase which seems to consist entirely of novels. Lorna leans across and reads the titles. Peter brings in mugs of steaming, aromatic coffee. The soft furniture, the books, the coffee, seem to provide for Gus an idyllic setting of serene, untroubled reading and contemplation. It is what he wants to achieve, and what he seems a long way from.

'So many novels,' Lorna says. 'What is there about novels that make them so interesting?'

Peter picks up his coffee, warming his other hand against it. 'If you think - most things in life are either fact or fiction. The beauty of the novel is that it's both. It's an invention, and at the same time it's true, in the most profound way. And the brilliant thing about a novel is that it gives you the opportunity to use the greatest quality we possess as humans - our imagination, the ability to see in our minds things that are not physically in front of us, to hear words that are not physically spoken to us.'

'It must be wonderful to produce something like that,' Lorna says.

'It's good to feel the novel growing inside you, slowly developing like an embryo. You feel the excitement a mother would feel, I should think. When you're writing and it begins to build momentum, it's the perfect combination. It's hard work and it's exactly what you want to be doing.'

Gus searches for the right word, can't think of one suitably technical and decides it might be the best word anyway. 'But do you ever get - stuck - so you can't do anything?'

Peter laughs. 'I spend a lot of time being stuck!' He uses the word without hesitation. 'Sometimes it feels as if you're waiting for a bus that never turns up. You sit there thinking, surely I can come up with something? But nothing appears. Your mind is wiped clean. It seems incapable of even the simplest idea. Then you begin to get tense and angry, which makes things even worse. I've devised a formula to help me. The three P's. Patience, practice, perseverance. You need patience when words are not coming; perseverance to keep at it, keep developing and improving it; and practice gives you familiarity with the processes involved, which makes it easier. You could apply it to anything in life worth doing.' He looks at them questioningly, as if waiting for confirmation.

Gus is thinking.

'I suppose one of the good things about English is that there are so many words to choose from,' Gus says, snapping out of his reverie and realising as he speaks how strangely stupid the remark sounds.

Peter chuckles again, but not, Gus feels, at his naivety. 'When you try to write you do realise how many words there are in the English language - and how few of them are in your head at any given time. You feel how inadequate words are. You have thousands of words at your disposal, but you can't find the one word that you want. You are like someone who has wardrobes full of clothes, but it's impossible to pick out something suitable for the evening. Then you feel sorry for yourself and wish you were a painter or a musician or a sculptor so you could express yourself without words. You think it must be so much easier for them than it is for you.'

'Is that your novel?' Lorna nods towards a thick sheaf of papers on the table.

Peter is uncharacteristically hesitant. 'Yes. It's a draft. I've gone through it and made revisions.'

'Can I have a look?'

'Sure.'

Lorna picks up the hefty mass of paper and browses through. She sees sheets filled with crossings-out, margins chaotic with insertions, words in circles with arrows pointing to their rightful place in the text, words circled then crossed through again.

'This does look incredibly complicated,' she says. 'So you have to type up all these hand-written revisions, and then it's ready to send to a publisher?'

'Yes. As I said, it's like giving birth. It's a messy business.'

'It must be really thrilling, though,' says Lorna. 'But it's funny - when you read books, you tend to think the author has just written it straight off, without any alterations or switching-around.'

'Ah, that's the trick,' says Peter. 'Hide the evidence of the mess. But no. You just couldn't do it straight through, in one draft. It's impossible to think all that you need to think, imagine and feel all that you need to imagine and feel, in one go. You need more than one stab at it. If you're going to kill a monster, you'll need several strikes.'

'That sounds like hard work,' Lorna says.

'Well - if you're an actor, you have to do a lot of rehearsing before you get it right. If you're filming you'll do numerous takes. It's the same with writing. You have to be hard on yourself. You have to stretch yourself to the limit, in every way - in your power of invention and imagination, in stamina in sticking at it, in tenacity when things aren't going well, in patience when you need to organise a rabble of notes.'

Lorna flicks through the pages. 'Doesn't sound very glamorous.'

'Definitely not! Often it doesn't even feel like being creative. It's more like systematic attrition, a hard slog, trench warfare rather than a glorious charge that carries all before it. You gradually wear down through willpower the opposing forces - fear, defeatism, lack of belief, impatience, distractions, temptations to do other things.' He spreads his hands with each obstacle he lists, as if illustrating how it can grow if not checked.

They chat on. After an hour or so, the conversation begins to flag. Peter reflects to himself that if they were in a pub they could go happily on in the more convivial atmosphere, but just the three of them in the concentrated surroundings of his flat makes it harder, and he has work to prepare for tomorrow. Lorna smiles and puts her hands on her thighs ready to rise. Gus looks more thoughtful but seems ready also for the opportunity to leave.

After they have gone, Peter takes up a large brown envelope from the top of his desk. Lorna's luminous presence, her eyes and lips and body, are in his mind's eye. No - he can't do it for a second time this year. He must hold off. He feels the weight of the envelope's soft bulk of paper in his hands. It is like a corpse. His name and address is on the front. He's already done the work he mentioned to Lorna, of typing his revisions into a new draft and sending it to a publisher. This is it. Rejected and returned by a London company. But it is early days yet. He can't expect to be accepted by the first name he approaches. Remember the three P's.

Wednesday, 23 April

'Isn't it strange? If you look at the moon and you didn't know any different, you'd think it was only a few miles up in the sky. It looks nearer than the sea's horizon, doesn't it? It's the same with the sun. You can see why ancient civilisations worshipped them as gods. It must have been good to feel they were so close - yet maddeningly frustrating that they had no means of reaching them. If the sun and moon had been the same distance away on land as they thought them to be in the sky, they could have walked to them in a day.'

Lorna responds to Gus's words with contemplative regard. 'That's an interesting thought. I just think the moon looks beautiful. Especially when it hangs over the water.' She nudges her body closer to Gus, giving a little shiver of intimacy. Gus feels a lovely, agonised yearning for her. They have just been for a quiet drink in The White Horse. They are standing on the seafront outside Alex. A boy and girl gazing up at the moon, savouring its reflection in the water. Somewhere in Gus's mind is the thought of how many times through the student generations this has happened before, in this very spot, and his mind feels connected to all those minds and bodies that have lingered here, clothed in fashions of different eras, listening to different music, hearing different news of world events, but with the same feelings coursing through them. He puts his arm around her and she gives his waist a hug and squeeze in return.

'Want to come up for some coffee?' Lorna's question must also have echoed down the decades.

Sitting in Lorna's room, Gus feels the comfort of her light, unselfconscious movements as she coasts into the communal kitchen and returns with full mugs. He feels a sense between them now of easy familiarity, that underpins his desire for her. She is no longer the unattainable diva, to be thirsted for from a distance. They are in her small room, the drawn curtains and closed door shutting out the rest of the world. The world is all contracted into this one space. Love, as the poet John Donne said, *makes one little room an everywhere.*

Gus finishes his coffee and gets up to place the empty mug on the table. Now that he is on his feet, he moves over to where Lorna sits. She smiles serenely up at him, a smile of such perfect purity, as if all other thoughts and experiences she has ever had have been erased from her mind and he has taken up all that vacated space. He puts his arms around her shoulders, his hand caresses up to her neck, he guides her head to rest against his stomach, gazing down at the loose waves of her hair and letting his fingers fondle through them. He puts his hands gently under her shoulders and she rises in response. Now his hands are clasping around the small of her back and he feels her trim midriff pressed to his, her breasts probing to his chest. All that he needs is for her hands to reach around his neck.

Her hands move up and grip his forearms, half an embrace, half a hold-off. 'Woa, slow down. It's best to stop now.' Her voice has quiet assurance. 'I don't want to make life too complicated.'

She gives a tired-looking half-smile, to add courtesy to her answer. For a moment Gus wonders if he should carry on, persuade her with words as he nurtures her body. Isn't she the type who would respond to determination, to male aggression that would trample over nicety and objection? He has seen it in films. The male simply carries on and the female's initial reluctance is won over and she returns his advances readily.

Her words stop his musing. 'I like you as a friend. I think you're a smashing guy.' She speaks to him carefully, like a schoolmistress patiently explaining a tricky point. 'But - I'm already going out with the person you share a room with, and Nick and I are getting on fine at the moment, so that would cause problems.'

Her hands are resting lightly on his forearms now, and he is grasping the sides of her waist, like a couple about to dance again. She gives his arms a squeeze and says in a way that seems both intimate and businesslike, 'Let's sit down for a minute.' They return to their seats, like a couple who've ended the dance.

'But also,' she carries on, 'I don't think you would really want me as a girlfriend. We're different types. You wouldn't like the things I like doing and vice-versa. And - apart from that, I think you could be using me for - practice.' The tone of her voice is not in the least condemnatory. It is calm and kindly. She understands and is not criticising or mocking. But Gus has difficulty keeping the horror out of his eyes. What has Amy been saying?

'What do you mean?' As soon as he asks the question he feels annoyed at his feeble attempt to pretend innocence.

'I'm right, aren't I?' Again there is no malice in her voice.

Gus protests. 'No - I really like you. I want to - do it with you.'

'I don't give my favours as easily as some people think.'

'I know that. I'm not thinking you're an easy lay or anything like that.' Gus finds himself using the unfamiliar phrase and its strangeness jars in his mind as he tries to utter it with panache.

Lorna looks directly at him. 'Would this have been the first time?'

It's a question he hoped no-one would ever ask. Amy hadn't. But Lorna says it softly, more like a statement of understanding. He knows she will not babble the news around. He doesn't even feel he needs to answer. He nods his head with a quiet 'Mmm.' He feels relief, does not feel he's confessing to something shameful.

She moves with sudden swiftness over to his chair and kneels beside it, clasping his hand. 'It's okay.' She speaks as if reassuring someone who has just woken from a harrowing nightmare.

'Has Amy said anything?' he hears himself asking.

'No - not a word. And that, of course, made me wonder anyway. I remember, one time, she came into my room after you'd been with her, and it was obvious she was upset. She just had that "down" look about her although she tried to sound okay. I could tell something disappointing had happened. I didn't ask her anything.'

Lorna moves away and sits comfortably on the floor, legs crossed. 'Other times she seemed sad and I would ask her if she was all right and if there was anything she wanted to talk about, but she wouldn't. She's not like some girls who just pour out all the grisly detail!'

There is silence, but it's a gentle, companionable, comfortable silence. Lorna does not look at Gus as she speaks. 'You guys - you think it's such a big deal to lose your virginity. As if it's all or nothing - or, more accurately, you think it's nothing, and then all. You're a boy, you have sex, then suddenly you're a man. I don't think it's like that at all. It's a gradual process. The girls are not really bothered if it's your first time or not.'

Gus shifts awkwardly in his chair. 'Well - I thought - we might do it together. I do like you. I like your body and I like you as a person. And - yes - I did think you could help me. But I wasn't just using you.'

Lorna nods reassuringly. 'I believe you. But listen. Amy's a lovely girl. She likes you. I think she wants to get back with you.'

'Isn't she going out with someone else?' Gus has seen her with Matt, the biochemistry student.

Lorna is dismissive. 'I think she's been out a couple of times with Matt, but that's nothing to worry about. I don't even know if they're still seeing each other. If you like her, why don't you get in touch with her again? And take it easy. There's no need to be in a hurry. Amy's not the type to judge guys by the way they perform. There's more to her than that. Just get together and, when you're ready, you'll do it together.' She throws her head back and laughs at the ceiling. 'I sound like an agony aunt talking.'

The water licks along the dark shoreline, sucking on the shingle. The moon is a luminous silver-white. Together the moon and sea have witnessed every relationship, every first love, every despair - sometimes, even, the waves must have embraced the ultimate despair. Gus stares out at the water. Then he turns and walks along the prom, hands in pockets, to Gwylan House.

Wednesday, 30 April

'Who was it said,' Nick asks Gus, as they and Dermot slice into spongy omelettes and flesh-pale pyramids of chips at lunchtime in the Students' Union, '*poetry is the spontaneous overflow of powerful feelings*?'

'Wordsworth.'

'I thought so. Yes, I like that phrase. *Spontaneous overflow.*' Nick chuckles. 'That's what I get when I'm with Lorna.' And his chuckle becomes an explosion of laughter. '*Spont-an-e-ity.* Love that word. We all should all be more spontaneous.' He pokes his finger playfully at Gus. 'That's what we need more of. Don't think, just do it. You two guys are just too sane. Stark raving sane.'

'No-one's ever called me sane before,' Dermot protests. 'It's an insult.'

'Ah, people are too cautious. Somebody told me about this guy - he used a condom with an inflatable doll. Ha! Can you imagine!'

'You're right, Nick,' Dermot says. 'Animals do the same things as us, but without any fuss or bother. They don't dissect or moralise beforehand - they just do them.'

'Yes, what's that poem by Whitman, about turning and living with animals?'

'And all the things we think of as human,' Dermot continues, 'they're really just to feed animal tendencies. Think of romantic love, poetry, music, love songs. Their only purpose is to produce a tiny human being, forced out through the legs of another human being, in the most undignified way, just as any other animal gives birth.'

'You have a lovely way of putting things,' Nick says.

In the evening, Gus and Dermot are in the Pier Hotel. They rarely find themselves together in a pub, but Nick is at cricket nets, and there is no sign, as usual, of Simon or, more unusually, of Geraint.

The midweek atmosphere is quiet. Gus feels empty and forlorn. He is still smarting from an afternoon seminar on James Joyce. It had been a subdued affair, with the lecturer, Dr Arfon Lewis, dominating and students contributing little. At one point, during a silence - perhaps Gus had opened his mouth in a certain way, perhaps he had stifled a yawn - Dr Lewis had turned sharply to him and said,

'You were going to say something?'

Gus had been caught unawares. 'Um, no.'

'One always hopes,' Dr Lewis had remarked, relaxing again with a faintly cynical smile.

Gus had felt humiliated, felt the silent smirks of some students. Later, attempting to make amends, he'd tried to express an idea but had floundered miserably. Fiona, more confident and articulate, had disagreed, and triumphed over him.

'I don't feel at ease in seminars,' he says to Dermot, 'where we're forced to argue against each other. One person says something, another says something else, you have to defend your position but you can't think of the words. The other person has more words and more assurance, so they win. I prefer to think things out for myself. It's like Yeats said - *Out of the argument with others we make rhetoric. Out of the argument with ourselves we make poetry.*'

'The good thing about arguing with yourself is that you always win the argument,' Dermot points out.

At a corner table is an unlikely looking couple. The man has a craggy, weathered face, chaotic greying hair that flares up around his ears and neck. The woman is younger, neatly presented in a smart skirt and shoes. Gus looks across to them.

'It always surprises me who people get together with. You look at couples and you think, how can they possibly get on with each other? How can they possibly find it a fulfilling relationship?'

Dermot clasps his hands in front of him, interlocking his thick fingers. 'Most people are terrified of solitude. They put up with the most unsuitable, disgusting companion rather than be on their own. And why this fear? Because they have no inner resources. *That content surpassing wealth, the sage in meditation found.*'

Gus completes the quotation. '*And walked with inward glory crowned.* What a beautiful phrase, *with inward glory crowned.* Not needing anyone else. Yes, contentment definitely surpasses wealth.'

'Most people think too much about what they want and not enough about what they've got,' Dermot says, taking a decisive swig of his beer.

'Yet,' answers Gus, 'we can't move forward, can't discover new things, can't push the boundaries of knowledge out, unless we're discontented. If we were content, we'd still be living in caves, and dying at the age of thirty.'

There is a brief silence between them, broken by Dermot. 'So, you been out with anyone lately?'

Gus gives a tired 'No.' His sense of emptiness increases.

'Sensible man.'

'How about you? Who takes your fancy?'

'No-one really. I think vaguely about one or two people. The trouble is - I don't really like other people. I wouldn't even like myself if it wasn't for the fact that it's me and I have to live with myself.'

Gus goes to the bar for more beers. Peter Strutton's three P's. He has shown none of them. All he showed with Amy was another P - panic. That is what prompted the letter. But, in order to fulfil them, he needs - spontaneity. There is a feeling welling up inside him, an energy, that is both desperate and exhilarating. A craving, a desire for a gesture that will carry him along before he has chance to think about it. He will drink this next beer, his fourth, quickly. That will fortify him without making him incapable. All week he has been thinking about Amy. He will leave Dermot and...

'Hey! You're knocking it back tonight!' Dermot watches the level of amber rapidly lowering in Gus's glass.

'Hope you don't mind, Dermot, but I'm going to shoot off after this pint.'

'You're not coming up to the Physics Lecture Theatre? They're showing a series of Russian classics at the Film Club. *Battleship Potemkin* tonight.'

'No. I've got to go somewhere.'

'You sound like a man with a mission.'

Gus's mouth remains open after a large last gulp empties his glass, to give Dermot a breathless grin. 'Ah, you could say that.'

'Well, don't let me stand in your way. In fact I'd better head back soon. Got my essay on German princedoms of the seventeenth century to complete before getting to the film. Riveting stuff.'

Gus touches him on the shoulder as he bounces up. 'I'll explain it later.'

And he is outside. The night air breezing against his face freshens him and threatens to remove some of the momentum he has built up, so he starts to walk quickly before he can ponder. A surge of energy seems to carry him along the seafront, deserted but for the occasional solitary stroller, none of whom is walking at his rapid pace. The dark air, with the chill of April still on it, bears down on him, but he feels buoyed up by a new fierce confidence. Desire illuminates the night like a dazzlingly white cloud above him. His heart is filled to bursting with the sudden fury that possesses him. He thumps along, past Gwylan House, past Carpenter and Ceredigion halls. He sees Dafydd at his desk in the window of his room in Ceri, books spread in front of him. Gus waves but does not pause. He can see Alex getting bigger in the distance and his march becomes more ferocious.

At last he is at its entrance. His heart is pounding and heaving as if he has climbed a mountain. A faint headache hums behind his eyes. He hesitates for a second. This is probably the moment when he is most at risk from doubt. But no; he maintains the impetus and rushes in. He is climbing the stairs, exulting in his drive and energy. He should have done this months ago, this instinctive, animal-like surge.

He swallows up the corridor in quick strides. She will be sitting quietly, reading or absorbed in an essay. Again he will not think, will say as little as possible, will surprise her with his vigour and resolution.

He can see the profile of her door along the corridor. As he nears it, he notices something white at eye-level on it. He reaches the door. A piece of paper is stuck on with tape. He recognises Amy's neat unflustered handwriting. It reads:

Dear Nick,

Sorry I can't be in when you're coming round. I <u>had</u> to go to the library to get some material for this essay on Byron.

Please forgive me. Perhaps we can fix a date for next week.

Hope to see you soon.

Amy

Gus reads the note. He stares at it, reads it again. *A date for next week.* That can mean only one thing. Why else would she want them to meet? Highly unlikely that Nick will go round to do work with Amy. And if he did, he would surely mention it? Amy and Nick. Amy and Nick. They seem an unlikely pair. But Amy is friendly and open. Nick has no inhibitions. Gus thinks back to the couple in the pub. He gazes again at the note. *Please forgive me.* That *Please* makes it sound so intimate. And what about Lorna? How will Nick handle that?

He folds his arms and stands with his back to the door. He looks along the corridor. There is no movement. He turns to the door again. Then he turns around and walks slowly down the corridor. He rushes down the stairway and is out on to the pavement. He walks at normal pace back to Gwylan House.

Thursday, 1 May

Seven-thirty. He has come out before breakfast to watch the sea. His life is full of changes, yet the same sea has been beating against the shore for millennia, mocking paltry, ephemeral humanity with its insistent presence. Sometimes calm, sometimes angry, yet always strong, all-pervading. Yet within its waters are the swirling currents, the upheaval, that seems to mark his existence. Perhaps that's a metaphor for the human race. The tumult that besets individual lives, but framing and enclosing it the huge smooth sea of life.

He watches a black gull voyaging the waves, riding on their swell and fall. Suddenly it is away, skimming over the water with an unthinking freeflap of its wings. His eyes follow it until it is a black speck in the distance.

Gus had returned to his room to find it empty. There was the question of whether Nick had reached Amy's door before or after himself the previous night. Amy was taking a chance by leaving the note for Lorna to see. What is going on?

He had gone to bed at half-past eleven, feeling drained yet with a tired turmoil of thoughts in his head. He dropped off to sleep but was awoken by the door being stealthily opened at midnight. Gus had stirred slightly and Nick had whispered a hoarse 'sorry' and laughed as he stumbled over while pulling off his shoes.

Nick views the two poached eggs on his toast. 'Christ! These eggs are not just runny. They're bloody sprinting - for the finish!' He dabs his fork into them, hunched up in a morning lethargy.

'So did you see Lorna last night?' Gus will approach the problem carefully, without raising directly the question of Amy.

'No - she's gone to visit someone she knows in Lampeter - staying overnight.'

So, that would explain the boldness of Amy's message on the door.

'Where did you go last night, then?' Gus tries to make the question sound innocent.

'The Ship And Castle, with the cricket boys. Really good night. Some of those guys are crazy!'

'Do you "cricket boys" ever actually play cricket?' Dermot asks.

Nick is outraged. 'We're building up to the new season. Getting our tactics right.'

'In the pub!' says Simon.

'Yep,' says Nick, undaunted. 'Very important to build up the team spirit beforehand.'

'Didn't go to Alex last night then?' Gus will note carefully Nick's reaction.

Nick hesitates for a second. 'What is this? A bloody interrogation?'

'Where were you last night?' Simon snarls in a not very good imitation of the menacing interrogator.

Nick shakes his head in innocent surprise. 'No, I didn't. Why should I? Lorna's away. Don't think I'd be going to see Fiona.' He returns to chewing his eggs, an expression of slight disgust on his face, though whether caused by the eggs, or the thought of Fiona, Gus is not certain.

Should Gus now mention he was in Alex last night, and gauge Nick's response?

He has no time to decide. Dermot looks up from his second egg. 'Hey, did you accomplish your mission after? Rarely have I seen a man so agitated.'

Nick looks up with curiosity. 'What's this?'

'We were having a quiet drink in the Pier. Suddenly Gus shoots up, says "I've got to go somewhere" and storms off. Never seen him move so fast. He was possessed.'

'Well, this is interesting,' says Nick.

There is an expectant silence. Gus is aware of three pairs of eyes on him. Never has he hoped so much for the entrance of Mrs Morgan.

The silence continues. Gus realises that his hesitation in supplying an explanation will suggest that whatever he eventually comes up with may not be the truth.

'I - suddenly remembered I had to give a five-minute piece on Browning for Arfon Lewis's seminar today, so I had to rush back here. Just managed to get something together in time last night.'

He hurriedly thinks of who at the seminar might have contact with any of the three and might reveal it wasn't him, but Tall Vivienne, who would be giving the talk. No - he should be safe. But would Simon have been in his room?

Nick leans his chin on his hand, looking thoughtful and not entirely convinced.

'My gosh, you do all look glum this morning!' shrieks Mrs Morgan as she carries in the teapot. 'First of May, summer on its way! There should be big smiles all around! Oh you boys do live in a bubble. In a bubble! Reading all the great authors through the centuries. Studying history - Greece, Rome - philosophy. Everything done for you. Meals prepared, rooms cleaned. Money given to you. You don't appreciate it at the time. Even plates collected from your table.' She whisks Dermot's plate away, narrowly avoiding a collision with his still downcast nose.

'Getting worried about the exams, Mrs Morgan,' Nick explains.

'Ah, exams!' Mrs Morgan draws the word out in an almost luxurious tone. 'You'll be all right, don't worry! I've seen generations of you boys. They all get through. You've got brains! Yes, you'll be all right!'

Gus goes into the toilets after the first lecture of the day. So much for his spontaneity. If he hadn't careered forth in his wild emotion to Alex, he wouldn't have seen the note, wouldn't be in this tumult. But isn't it better for him to know?

On the wall is a new piece of graffiti.

> *To do is to be* - *Descartes*
> *To be is to do* - *Sartre*
> *Do be do be do* - *Frank Sinatra*

Where has he heard that before? Wasn't it Dermot, all that time ago in the first term? Doing? Or being? Just be. *Etre*. Human beings, not human doings.

He notices more on the opposite wall.

> *Anyone can be a success. It takes real guts to*
> *be a failure.*

That's what he lacks, isn't it? His name with one extra letter.

He should go to the library. Instead he takes a walk along South Beach promenade, where it feels more open, less populated. The water lies silvery, with glints of gold from the sun. The sky is vast and empty. The beach is deserted, but inside his head thoughts crowd and jostle with each other. Could it be true? He would have thought Amy more wise, more circumspect, than to fall for Nick. And Nick? He would certainly love the flattery of having two girlfriends. Gus has not noticed any signs of affection between Amy and Nick, but with Lorna still in tow, of course they would have to hide it. And Lorna? Wouldn't she suspect something was going on? Should he tell her? No, that would look mean and underhand. In any case, she is so much more worldly-wise than him, she would know how to handle the situation. Or would she? Perhaps she too is in turmoil.

Nick is the sort of person who would always have a choice of girlfriends. Gus cannot compete with him there. Any girl, including Amy, would easily come under his spell. But the thought of them together revolts him. Nick, leading innocent Amy on, feasting on her attractiveness and open friendliness, then probably dumping her, perhaps using her to make Lorna jealous. Perhaps he can counter by getting back with Lorna, if she too is aware of Nick's behaviour and is also suffering? No, in any battle of that sort with Nick, he'd be bound to come off worse.

He has a duty to protect Amy. But she must know that Lorna is still with Nick. Perhaps there is more to her than he realises. Perhaps she enjoys being 'the other woman.'

But, if Nick is going with Amy - what can he do about it? After all, it was he who rejected Amy in the first place. She owes no loyalty to him. She is free. But the vision in his mind of her and Nick together...

The best thing would be for him to tell Nick that he went to Amy's room and saw the note. Then Nick could give his answer. If they are going together, it would be good if Gus knew one way or the other. But, oh, the thought of it.

Yes. It's the only way.

Saturday, 3 May

'I heard on the news this morning - that what's-his-name - that famous actor - he's getting divorced again. That's the third time. And there was someone yesterday - they found out he was married to two people! That's bigamy. It's disgusting what people get up to these days. No, I definitely believe you should only marry once, and stick with that person through thick and thin. These people who do bigamy or have lots of wives -it's wrong. Yes, I believe in monotony in marriage!'

'You said it, love,' adds Mr Morgan, winking.

'So how long have you been married?' Nick asks Mrs Morgan.

'Ooh, thirty-nine years, coming up to!'

'Thirty-nine years, five months, twenty-two days...seventeen hours.' Mr Morgan pretends to count, rather dolefully.

She grabs his arm. 'And going strong! He's still the object of my affliction!' She marches him into the kitchen.

'Mrs Morgan ushered me into the front room when I went to pay my rent last week,' Nick says. 'There's a photo of them on the mantelpiece on their wedding day. They actually look in love. She looks quite attractive, and Mr M's quite good-looking too. It's like with my parents. We don't think they used to be young like us.'

Dermot gives Nick a look of disdain.

'Come on, then!' Nick goads. 'Make a cynical comment! Love doesn't exist! It's all airy-fairy!'

'I was just thinking,' Dermot responds, 'if you fall in love, you think that person is the most wonderful in the world. How absurdly illogical! Think how many people you've met in your life to that point - even if it's several hundred, a thousand, what percentage is that of all the women in the world? Infinitesimal.'

Nick indicates Dermot with a contemptuous outstretched hand. 'There speaks a man who's never been in love. That's the whole point about love. You can't apply logic to it. It's not maths or physics.'

Gus thinks, there are no rules, at least for some people. He hasn't yet found the courage to confront Nick about the note on Amy's door.

Dermot carries on as if Nick has said nothing. 'And another thing. People say, *I'll love you forever*. How can they possibly know that? How do they know what the situation will be in twenty years' or forty years' time?'

'Or in four days' time,' Nick adds, seeming to contradict his stance.

Yes, Gus is certain now. Nick believes in freedom to love whomsoever he loves when he wants to. If it's more than one person, so be it. In a way, he envies Nick this capacity.

Nick goes on. 'But you can't say to someone, "as far as I know, I'll love you forever."'

'That's the trouble,' Dermot answers. 'Love demands absolutes. It demands fantasy. You have to sound unrealistic in order to sound convincing. No. Love doesn't exist. It's like religion. It's a human invention, an illusion. We all have to pair off with someone of the opposite sex, stay with them to provide a stable background for rearing kids. So we invent the idea of love to make it more bearable.'

'You are so bloody old and wise,' Nick says. 'Why can't you act your age like the rest of us?'

'Well I tried being adolescent,' Dermot retorts. 'I tried being confused and desperate and yearning for sex. But I failed miserably - or should I say happily? So I decided to skip that stage of my life.'

'But I really want to love someone,' Nick persists. 'I want to *fall in love.* It's nothing to do with having kids. In fact, kids would be a bloody problem.'

'Yes, but once the first frenzy of love is over, you get bored just being with the same person. So, for variety, you have to have kids,' Dermot adds.

Or another girlfriend, Gus thinks.

Simon, as always, seems to have been immersed in his own secret thoughts. But now he suddenly looks up.

'Why do people talk about *falling* in love? Apart from in that phrase, we never use *falling* to mean anything other than going down, stumbling, hitting the ground - falling off a cliff. We don't say *falling in happiness* or *falling in enjoyment.* Shouldn't it be *rising in love* ?'

'Yeh, because if you're in love, you rise physically as well as mentally.' Nick laughs and puts his arm around Gus. 'Come on, Gus, support me. We believers in love should stick together in the face of this onslaught from the forces of darkness. "Love doesn't exist." What piffle! It's all around us! Take a walk out on the street, you'll see couples together, *in love.* Come to the

Saturday night discos in King's, or the cinema in Bath Street. You see couples - loving couples - necking, *embracing*. Look on the beach - not now, it's pissing down with rain - but you'll see two people there, holding each other in each other's arms. You can see the poetry in their souls, man.'

'Well, they couldn't really be holding each other in somebody else's arms,' Dermot remarks drily.

'Shut up. Hey and I've just thought of something, Dermot, you middle-aged sceptic. I saw Fiona in the Marlowe lecture on Monday, and she asked about you. "How's Dermot?" she said.'

'Ah, Fiona, the face that sank a thousand ships.'

'Dermot, I swear, I'm going to get you and Fiona together before the term is out,' Nick thunders. Then his voice quietens. 'It's strange, though. The other day - right? - I was in Alex, and I'd just - you know - and I got up off the bed. And I dangled the condom in front of me. It looked like gob, spit. And I thought, to this white, slimy looking mess was owed the whole of existence, all life on Earth, through hundreds of millions of years. If it didn't exist, then neither would I, or anyone, or anything else.'

'And a lot of heartache, suffering, suicides,' Dermot adds wearily. 'But that's very philosophical, Nick. This was with Lorna, I presume?'

'Who else?' asks Nick, his face all innocence.

Sunday, 4 May

Sunday morning on the seafront. Peter Strutton waits in front of the College. She's a little late. He hopes she will show up, for them both to get it over with, now that he's arranged it. He is taking a calculated risk, phoning her - perhaps he's been foolish. On the phone he tried to sound firm and neutral, but Fiona may still be highly-charged emotionally, or perhaps may have seen his call, despite his measured tone of voice, as a pretext, a hint that he might want to resume their relationship. People beset by infatuation can misinterpret anything so that it accords with their fantasy. In fact his phone call, asking her to return the several books he's lent her, was meant to accomplish the opposite - seal the official close of their relationship.

He gazes the length of the promenade's sweep back to Alex. There is no sign of her. Has she decided, in order to spite him, to keep the books?

It's a still, peaceful morning, with few people about. He looks out to sea, to the hazy pale blue horizon. Then suddenly, Fiona is beside him. She must have come through the town and down Pier Street.

Her smile is restrained, bashful. She looks at him and she feels the distance between them. She can see why she was attracted to him, but he is no longer the magical, marvellous figure sweeping her up, only a good-looking, well-preserved lecturer. His frame has shrunk to the size of an ordinary man. The gulf of years between them, that seemed so inviting and exotic, now seems cold and dispiriting. She does not stand close to him, but observes the conventional distance between lecturer and student, extending her arm out, as if across a deep crevice, to hand over the plastic bag of books. She says nothing, but keeps the slight smile on her face.

He thanks her and asks if she found them useful, to which she replies that she did. She's hoping he won't ask her if she wants to go for coffee or a walk. She wants it ended now. She's not sorry, or embarrassed, about the poems she sent him. They belong to times of fire and heat, and she is certain he won't ridicule her, silently or to others, but will respect her passions.

Still she finds herself saying, 'I'm sorry.' She adds, '...about the poems.'

'That's okay.' His voice is quiet and understanding, but brisk. Then, more slowly, 'they were a good selection.'

She casts her glance down, then looks out to sea, as if not knowing where else to put her eyes, as if waiting for him to make the next move or snippet of speech.

He looks at her. All her confidence seems to have ebbed away. She no longer appears exceptional, but rejoins the ranks of attractive first-years. Again, he finds himself thinking, when she is third year, or postgraduate - but that seems far into the future.

'Thanks for the books,' she says at last. 'They were very useful.'

' Glad you found them so. How is the work coming along?'

'Good.' A slight pause. 'I've been reading Gerard Manley Hopkins.'

'Ah.' Peter sheds some of the stiffness of his stance. 'A good poet.' His neck muscles move more easily as he nods his head. If either wanted, this could be the start of a conversation.

'Well - I'd better go back now.' She stands still and erect, as if waiting to be dismissed by him.

'Yes, me too. Got some work to do.' He turns slightly to leave, but looks at her and their eyes meet and momentarily engage, with a warmth that makes both feel more comfortable.

'See you around, then,' he says, cheerfully, as if they are two acquaintances who have just met by accident.

'See you,' Fiona repeats in the same tone.

As she turns and walks away, there seems more buoyancy in her step. He looks at the dark cascade of her hair around her neck and shoulders. He knows that, with that turning away, she has deposited him as a memory in her mind, still painful perhaps, but tamed and tucked away. Now her gaze is all in front of her, the open light blue sky, the long arc of the promenade, and Alex small in the distance at the centre of the painting.

She has told him about her family and, for brief moments over the months, he has thought of himself and her together in a flourishing relationship, meeting her parents, talking to them about his book, his plans, her father nodding with thoughtful interest. He would not want a huge sum. He imagines her father could easily afford a loan to get him started…But that would be a betrayal, a mean manipulation of her feelings for him, which in any case might prove themselves short-lived.

He watches her diminishing figure moving swiftly away along the promenade, walking into the immense canvas of sky and beach, seafront and sea around her, a darker speck among those soft, Sunday-morning colours.

Tuesday, 6 May

Nick peruses his face in the mirror, checking minutely for spots, while Gus lies on his bed, legs crossed at the ankles, his fingers tapping his chest, looking at the ceiling.

'Right! I'm off to Lorna's soon. Her friend Gina's boyfriend has a car, so the four of us are going for a drive - probably to Tal-y-bont or Devil's Bridge. There's some great places to explore round here now that summer's arrived. What's Gus up to tonight?' Nick's cheerfulness for once sounds forced, a deliberate bid to crack the coldness that seems to have enshrouded Gus of late.

'Oh, nothing planned. If Dermot's around I might go for a drink with him. Or maybe I'll just stay in and read. Not long now till the exams.'

'Now that sounds really exciting.'

Gus puckers his lips.

Nick is suddenly less brash, more thoughtful. 'Is everything okay? You do seem a bit - uncommunicative - recently.'

Gus nods, continuing to look at the ceiling.

Nick's voice is louder. 'Hey, we should get together for a drink sometime. We haven't done that for a while.'

'Haven't seen much of you recently. You seem pretty busy in your private life.'

'Now that sounds a bit like an accusation.' Nick looks at him earnestly, but there is still that hint of good humour in his eyes and the touch of a smile on his lips.

'I didn't mean it that way. You're free to do whatever you want.'

'What the hell does that mean? When people say that, it normally means they don't approve of whatever it is they think the person's doing.'

Gus's lips are pulled tightly together.

'Come on. Something's eating you. We've got to share this bloody room and we can't have one of us moping around with something obviously on his mind. And don't come out with a bloody poem.' Nick laughs and then his voice takes on a deep, menacing, interrogator's tone. 'I want answers.'

Gus hoists himself up to a sitting position on his bed. 'Remember a few days ago, you had a go at me for being so cautious and not being spontaneous?'

'Ye-e-s-s.' Nick draws the word carefully out.

'Well, I took your advice and decided, well - I didn't decide, I just did it on the spur of the moment - .'

Nick eyes light up. 'Ah! Is that when you suddenly went on your mission that Dermot was talking about?'

'That's right -'

'Now - let me guess where you went.' Nick strokes his chin in pretence of deep thought.

'I'll tell you. I went to Alex. I was going to burst in on Amy and - well, I'm not certain what I would have done - but I felt good, full of something.'

There seems to be the dawning of some kind of recognition on Nick's face.

' - But when I got there she wasn't in. There was a note on her door. To you.'

'Ah!' Now Nick's face has the full light of understanding on it. He detonates into laughter. He rolls and curls up on the bed, clutching his feet. He stops for a moment, looks at Gus, then rolls on his back and continues laughing.

'What's so funny?'

'And you thought? Oh yes, I can see it now. You would think that.'

Gus waits.

Nick abruptly ceases to laugh and sits on the edge of the bed. 'You think - I'm going out with Amy.'

'Well that's certainly what it looks like.'

'And you've been suffering the pangs of love all these days! That's why you've been so mopy and off with me. Christ! Lorna would cut off my balls with a rusty razor if she thought I was up to something.'

'So you're not, then?'

'Listen. I'll explain. We're going behind your back a little bit - but we think it's in a good cause. Me and Lorna are worried about you, and about Amy. We think you should get together. Lorna says Amy is still very interested in you - though Amy doesn't say much - and I think you'd make a great couple. I can't see why you broke up to begin with. So Lorna's been having a quiet chat with Amy and the two of us planned to go round and see her, to plan our strategy. Lorna couldn't make it on the day - was it last Wednesday? - but I said I'd go anyway and see what I could do to help the situation. Of course, when I got there after the cricket nets, I found that note. *The note.* Sounds like the title of a film or short story. So I caught up with the cricket boys in the Ship And Castle.'

'So what were you going to talk about?'

'I was going to make certain Amy was still interested in you. I've never seen myself as a matchmaker. I feel like something out of bloody Jane Austen. Lorna's the driving force. But - yeh - it's definitely a good cause. Amy's a lovely girl, you're a great guy. So - if Amy was for it, I was just going to mention to you - that Lorna and I had been chatting to her and she really wants you back. I was going to suggest you write her a letter, or start talking casually to her. I didn't think you'd storm the bloody citadel! Good for you! What a shame she wasn't in. What a scene that would have been when you got there! Like something out of a D.H. Lawrence novel.'

'You really think she's interested, then?'

'Definitely. And Lorna will back me up. She sees her all the time and knows these things. Now -' and Nick's voice slows down and quietens ' - that's not to say that Amy is pale with love, shrunken with desire, not sleeping, not eating, etc. But she's definitely interested. So get down to it and write that letter, or get your carcass off the supine position - love that word - and start having some friendly conversation with her.'

'But you still haven't talked to her?'

'We went round last night. In fact, if you'd done your dramatic entrance then, you would have burst in on the three of us having a chat about you. That would have been interesting!'

Thursday, 8 May

'*We few, we happy few, we band of brothers!*' declaims Nick, looking at the waiting mouths around the table, as he struts in for the evening meal. 'Great seminar on *Henry V* today. Parker-Hurst excelled himself. He's not such a bad bloke after all.' Nick contorts his face into something resembling the grey-faced lecturer's grizzled countenance, imitating his clipped accent.

> ' ... *'Tis true that we are in great danger,*
> *The greater therefore should our courage be.'*

'You could apply that to the exams coming up,' he adds grinning, as he collapses into a chair.

'Did you read the bit about all the arms and legs and heads chopped off in battle re-assembling themselves on Judgement Day, crying for the wives and children they left behind and condemning the king?' ventures Dermot. 'What did Shakespeare say - *few die well that die in battle?*'

'Yes, we went through all that as well. That's the great thing about Shakespeare. He sees all sides of the argument.'

'And what about where an English soldier robs a French one, or takes his money in exchange for his life?' Gus asks. 'That's not quite so glorious either.'

'And there's that stirring speech, *Once more unto the breech, dear friends.* That's followed by a soldier wishing he was in an alehouse in London, saying he'd give all his fame for a pot of ale and safety,' Simon adds.

'But it was a brilliant victory,' Nick enthuses. 'They were outnumbered five to one and they still won. Has anybody seen the Olivier film? I remember the tremendous *swish* as all those arrows flew through the air.'

'I wonder who was the first guy who hit on the idea of putting feathers on arrows,' Dermot muses. 'He must have looked at birds' feathers and thought, they fly so gracefully through the air, if we put feathers on our arrows, they'll do the same. The first attempts must have been failures - just like humans' first attempts to fly. People must have laughed at him - but someone somewhere must have had enough patience and self-belief and vision to persevere.'

Mrs Morgan has a puzzled look on her face and a piece of paper in her hand which she pores over. 'I need your educated brains, boys,' she says. 'I'm helping Eric with his homework. He's got a list of countries and he has to find out the capitals. I've got most of them. Let's see…France - Paris, Italy - Rome, Norway - Oslo…' She pronounces each name slowly and precisely. '…Sweden - Stockport, Spain - Madrid, Poland - Walsall…'

'I think you're a bit out with a couple of them, love,' Mr Morgan shouts as he follows her in.

After Mrs Morgan's list has been successfully revised and the Morgans have returned to the kitchen, Nick is in thoughtful mode.

'Sometimes I wonder about education. I mean, what is really the point of it? Like Mr and Mrs Morgan. They haven't had the education we've had. But they're just as happy, they feel as fulfilled, as in control, as anyone who's well-educated.'

Gus clears his throat. 'I suppose, with education, you take a broader outlook, see things from a wider perspective. You're not limited to your own thoughts and experiences - you can take account of those of other people whom you've never met, who might even be long dead. You're less inclined to make narrow, prejudiced judgements.'

'The good thing about education,' Dermot puts in, 'is that it teaches you uncertainty. People who haven't studied don't understand this. They take uncertainty as a sign of weakness and lack of confidence. They think certainty means strength and are too easily impressed by it. But it's the reverse. Uncertainty is strength. It's being certain that shows weakness. You're afraid to face your doubts, afraid to face uncomfortable truths, so you suppress or ignore them.'

Nick responds. 'The only thing is - if you're uncertain, you're not going to oppose people who are certain, because you think they may be right, which means they're going to get their way. Look at Hitler. You have to be certain in opposing certainty.'

'Not necessarily,' Dermot answers. 'If you treat uncertainty as a positive thing, then you value your uncertainty. You're not frightened by it. You accept it - welcome it, even.'

Simon chips in. 'That's right. It's like the stuff we did with Keats - his theory about negative capability. I've memorised it. *When a man is capable of being in uncertainties, mysteries, doubts, without any irritable reaching after fact and reason.* He said it was the quality Shakespeare had. If you're certain about things, your mind is closed to other ideas. If you're uncertain, you're open to new experiences. You're not afraid to move forward and do new things.'

'I must say, the level of conversation around this table is taking on new intellectual dimensions,' says Nick, looking at Gus in a pointed, deliberate way, as if to say, take note of this. Or is it, Gus wonders, that Nick is silently boasting about his own sense of confident adventure?

'Ah!' exclaims Dermot, leaning back in his chair with arms outstretched, 'someone said living is like learning to play the violin in public. You make all sorts of mistakes, and everyone's watching.'

'Right.' Nick nods his head vigorously in agreement. 'If you waited until you were certain before doing anything, you wouldn't do anything at all.' He is looking at Gus again.

'If you could wake up one morning and be instantly capable of doing something,' asks Dermot of the others, 'what would it be?'

Simon squirms nervously. 'I'd like to wake up - having written the greatest novel of the century.'

'I'd like to wake up, being able to speak six different languages,' says Dermot.

'I'd like to wake up and be instantly capable of bloody getting out of bed,' Nick says.

'And you - Gus?' prompts Dermot.

'I'd like to wake up to - .' He hesitates, to a chorus of, 'Come on! Come on!'

He knows what he wants, who he wants to wake up with. But he can't say that.

'To - the sound of the sea in my ears!'

Monday, 12 May

Gus hurriedly gathers up his books and file. His eyes have just followed Amy's steps through the library and out of its broad wooden door that always reminds him of a medieval fortress. Now will be the moment. He'll catch her up as she goes down the stairs. He mustn't think about the uncertainty in his mind, mustn't be frightened of it.

Amy is standing outside the entrance to the library, looking down on the quadrangle where students criss-cross, hover and chat, almost as if she is waiting for him. She looks composed, unruffled, as always. She wears a black T-shirt and her arms are bare and beautiful. She smiles at him in that sensuously shy way, her books cradled to her chest.

'How are you?' she asks, emphasising the last word. She casts her eyes down for a second, and that and her taut-lipped smile show anxiety mixed with her expectation.

'I'm fine - and you?'

'Good.'

He leans beside her on the wall overlooking the quad. He mustn't flounder now. This is the vital moment. He must keep the conversation going, naturally, unforcedly. 'Started your exam revision yet?'

Both find a distraction to their initial discomfort by peering down at the comings and goings below.

'Oh, I'm not looking forward to them. I'll be glad when they're over.' Her voice sounds wonderfully more comfortable, more natural now. Her eyes, sparkling black, suddenly flash expectantly up to his. He feels borne along, not in the breathless way he felt impelled to race to her room on the night he found her note to Nick, but in a smoother journey, spirited through by some gentler but insistent impulse.

'Are you still seeing the biochemistry student?'

'No.' Her headshake is vigorously dismissive, as if it's a ridiculous question. But there is no ridicule in her eyes, more of an inviting warmth.

'Well, in that case - like to see a film - tonight?'

'That'd be nice. I could do with a break.'

After the first awkwardness, it is almost as if they have a script prepared and the words each says are reassuringly familiar. Not the sense of unknown wild adventure in his heart any more, that is exhilarating and frightening in equal measure, but something more peaceable but no less satisfying. In the cinema he feels an ease and confidence sat next to her, a togetherness, that seems new and familiar at the same time, as if they've had a long-running relationship that he had to leave for a while and has now returned to. He holds her hand and he feels thanks and something near content, but with the added spice of anticipation of good things in the future.

A powdery pink haze suffuses the sky as they walk back along the promenade, the sun as it steals out of sight lending a silver glister to the water's horizon. They stop by 'the bar' across the road from Alex to watch, silently together, the spectacle of splendour. There seems never to have been a sun like this before.

'I'll go in now. I'll have an early night,' Amy says, but with a comfortable assuredness that has no sense in it of sending him away. Gus does not experience the mean, alarming desire he felt for her before. It is somehow different, a more secure, enjoyable longing.

'I'll see you - again?'

'Sure,' she replies, as if the question is so obvious it needs no reply.

Tuesday, 20 May

'So let's have a look at this poem. Everyone read it?' Peter puts a galvanising gusto into his voice and his eyes roam the room to include every one of the seven. Some students face him with ready, eager looks. Others' eyes hover with less assurance, on the brink of being cast down. Peter smiles with understanding. 'Okay then, take a few minutes to read it. Written by Yeats in memory of his friend, Robert Gregory, who was killed in the First World War.'

An Irish Airman Foresees His Death

I know that I shall meet my fate
Somewhere among the clouds above;
Those that I fight I do not hate,
Those that I guard I do not love;
My country is Kiltartan Cross,
My countrymen Kiltartan's poor,
No likely end could bring them loss

Or leave them happier than before.
Nor law, nor duty bade me fight,
Nor public men, nor cheering crowds,
A lonely impulse of delight
Drove to this tumult in the clouds;
I balanced all, brought all to mind,
The years to come seemed waste of breath,
A waste of breath the years behind
In balance with this life, this death.

Peter enjoys the silence, the peace in the room, as the students read. He looks at the young faces taking in the words. He himself has always been puzzled by the poem. He knows that Yeats admired Robert Gregory, regarding him as the perfect man, moved by his courage in enlisting to fight, yet something about the poem makes Peter uneasy, particularly those last four lines...

'Any immediate reactions?' Silence. Peter scans the room. Lorna's eyes meet his. 'I think it's a very negative poem. He doesn't hate the people he's fighting against, he doesn't love the people he's fighting for.'

'That's not negative, though, that's positive, isn't it? It means he's not a blind patriot, just saying it's love of his country and all that. He's honest.' Dafydd looks across to Lorna as he speaks, not at Peter. Peter likes it when students speak directly to each other rather than looking to him for sanction before talking. It means they have ready opinions and the discussion is likely to be more lively, and he knows he can step in and control and guide it when he needs to.

More silence. Then Rosina, addressing her question to Peter: 'That's a strange point. Why doesn't he love the people he's fighting for?'

Peter spreads his hands, palms outwards. 'Possibly because he's an Irishman fighting for the British Empire, perhaps thinking he's only protecting the rich English, not the poor Irish people who are his real *countrymen*. Also of course he was killed in Italy, fighting to protect the Italian nation. It's sadly ironic that he probably died accidentally in the end. It's thought he was shot down in error by his own side.'

He leans back in his chair, inviting further ideas.

'I think it shows the futility, of war,' Gus says. 'Whatever the outcome, it will make no difference to the poor local people. He can't see the point of giving his life for no reason. It will be a complete waste, yet he feels he has to.'

'But, according to the poem, no-one's forcing him to fight,' Rosina counters.

'That's a good point,' says Peter encouragingly. 'Why *is* he fighting?   What does he mean by *lonely impulse of delight*? Why should he be delighted?'

'Perhaps it's the sense of daring, the courage that's needed to fly up into the sky with people up there trying to kill each other,' Gus suggests.

'It's strange that he uses the word *lonely*,' Josh says. 'You'd think there'd be a great team spirit, a sense of camaraderie, among the pilots, like there was at the Battle of Britain.'

There is a lull. Peter looks around, seeking to include those who haven't yet spoken.

'Any thoughts, Simon?'

Simon peers up, as if suddenly realising where he is. He glances at his book, then up again. 'Isn't it really a poem about suicide? He says in the first line he knows he's going to die, and *death* is the last word of the poem. He embraces it. It's suicide dressed up as heroic death in battle. It seems strange because we never think of suicide as happening in the sky.'

Another thought strikes Gus. 'It's strange that he doesn't mention - heaven - at all. Even though he's talking about death, and the sky.'

'In fact,' puts in Lorna, 'he doesn't even mention *sky*. He just refers to *the clouds,* twice. That's negative. He could have mentioned beautiful blue sky.'

Gus feels his confidence increasing. 'Also - we don't know if the airman actually thought and felt these things. He didn't write the poem. It's the poet's view of him. Could the poet be projecting his own view of life onto the airman?'

'That's a question worth examining,' Peter responds. 'The difficulty with that view is that Yeats does not appear to have had that attitude to life or to Robert Gregory. Yeats lived to a ripe old age. And he saw the man he was writing about, Robert Gregory, as the ideal man, a man of outstanding qualities, *soldier, scholar, horseman, all he did done perfectly,* to quote from another poem Yeats wrote about him.'

Josh looks up again. 'Isn't he saying his death is a waste, just as his life is? It's a waste because he's not dying for any worthwhile cause. It's about the futility of life. Look at the last four lines. He's saying life itself is a waste. Therefore it's not wasting anything if you give it away.'

'The only reason for his death is as a test of his own courage and heroism,' Gus suggests.

'That's right. It's the *lonely impulse*, an ecstatic, apocalyptic moment,' says Simon, impressing everyone with his vocabulary.

Peter swivels in his chair. 'I think what Yeats meant by that was that Gregory focussed all his attention on, became totally absorbed in, that one moment, so that everything else, what had happened in the past, what was to come in the future, was obliterated in his mind. When you think of it, if you're fighting in the sky, you can't think of the past or the future, you have to concentrate all your mind on the present moment.'

'I don't see anything heroic about it.' Lorna shudders. 'It's a horrible, inhuman poem. It's so clinical, cold and rational.'

'But is he saying, if you look at life rationally, it isn't worth living? All this anguish and pain for just a short lifetime, and death at the end of it,' Simon says.

Lorna face shows repugnance. 'But he seems so casual in dismissing life and death, as if they both mean nothing.'

'But is he casual?' Peter asks. 'He says he *balanced all, brought all to mind.*'

Gus is suddenly reminded of an earlier seminar. 'It's like - *to be, or not to be.*'

'Interesting comparison,' says Peter. 'He does seem to be weighing his life up. One of the striking things about the poem is the sense of balance, the way that phrases are matched against each other, with the word *balance* used twice in the last four lines. It's full of repetitions and contrasts.' His eye works down the poem that he knows so well, yet does not know, picking out and speaking aloud the relevant words.

'Those that I fight - those that I guard; *love - hate*; *country - countrymen*; *Kiltartan Cross - Kiltartan's poor*; *bring them loss - leave them happier*; *crowds - lonely*; the repetitions of *nor, all, waste of breath*, then more contrasts - *to come - behind*, and finally-' he looks around again, '*this life - this death.*'

Saturday, 31 May

Three weeks have passed since their reunion and the days have sparkled into summer. The daytime sky is often a bold blushing azure, with sky and sea blending into one expanse of blue. In the evening, as the sun lowers slowly out of sight, the sea shines a glistening indigo, with a wavering, narrowing pathway of bronze across the water, the sun a ball of flaming deep pink where it meets the horizon.

These are the days for wandering along the beach after lectures, the summer seeming to siphon its air through the purity of sunlight and sea. The sun's warm breath glows against Gus and Amy as they saunter by the sea's edge, arms coupling each other. They scamper in laughing panic from the tide as it gushes up, and watch it gurgling along runnels and mingling with pebbles and sand.

These are the days of a calm togetherness, an easeful awareness of her presence beside him in his life, as they sit side-by-side at lunchtimes, or in the Cabin at mid-morning. For lectures Amy sits with the group from Alex, and he likes to watch the dusky flow of her hair, the profile of her forearm and neat hand as she writes.

Some evenings he goes to her room and they talk or work, separately but with the consciousness of each other's company. Not that crushing sense of compulsion now, more a feeling that they will both know, without discussing it, when they want it. A sense of a steady, unhurried moving forward to the day.

That time is now. It is ten in the evening. They have come back from the Film Club, preferring that to the offer of a group night out in the Angel. The curtains of Amy's window are open and the moon shines approvingly through. He loves the slim caressible curve of her neck as he rests his lips on it. Her face, with its clear fineness of features, as if softly fashioned and sculpted from the most exquisite materials, brushes warm against his.

Suddenly she has become, in look and in feel, a woman, her girlish innocence overlaid by something strong and insisting. Their claims upon each other begin to fuse into one. When he holds her and draws her backwards onto the bed the ready appeal of her eyes into his tells him all is right. Her dark hair, smouldering around her face, those large eyes of liquid black, seem to merge into him. When he pushes and slides inside her it is with power yet with supreme ease, effortless yet with wonderful heaving effort. It is so natural, so simple, so right and intended, he cannot believe it, yet he believes it more strongly than anything before. He is in her, part of her. They are one being, he in her and she in him, a perfection. He delights in her beauty afresh, as if for the first time, with every thrust. When he comes, in that flooding forth of all his joy poured into her, and she arches her back and he can see the rapture on her face and hear the soft moan from her mouth, she holds on to him so firmly that it really does feel that she will never let him go.

She draws a deep breath and smiles as she sighs the air out, then closes her eyes, contented and spent, as he kisses their lids. She opens them, looks into his eyes and his lips taste hers. He loves the way her lips respond to his and linger on them. He falls beside her into a sleep that is not sleep, a kind of delicious doze, like some blissful drug.

Her voice is whisperingly soft against his ear as he wakes. 'Shall we go for a walk?' Her eyes as she lies back are dark-lashed and brilliant, black irises floating in large creamy whites.

They hold hands across the beach under the starlight, the dark blueness of night and sea swirling around them as the warmth of her hand meets his, her fingertips lacing smoothly into his own, palms pressed together. They do not talk and this seems to draw them closer.

Conscious of the ceaseless sough and tumble of the water, he knows others must have done this before him, treaded the soft sand fronting Alex, gazed on the dreaming sea, after the first time. He feels pleased to be part of that pageant through generations, yet at the same time is aware of the absolute uniqueness of the event in his life.

He doesn't want to go back tonight. He wants to feel the warm naked firmness of her buttocks against him, feel her breasts and nipples pressing to his chest as his arms clasp her round in the darkness, her breath soft on his shoulder, her hair feathering his face. He wants to wake in the middle of the night and feel her to him, scan dimly the outlines of her bed and furniture and breathe in their unfamiliarity, knowing it is her room in Alex, not his.

They kiss to the sound of the sea as the breeze steals over their bodies. Then they slowly make their way, arms resolutely around each other, to Alex.

'You'd better go back,' she says gently as he holds her to him in her room. Her voice has a special quiet intimacy about it, that she would use for no other person, lightening the disappointment he feels. Yes, best not to take chances, though it would be glorious to lie with her all night. That will come. He should be wondrously satisfied with what has happened.

When he arrives back in Gwylan House, Nick, unusually, is already asleep. Gus slips into bed. The sheets feel strangely, starkly cold in the tepid night. Cold and empty. Yet as he settles in, the darkness folds around him, the warmth infuses into him, with the thought of Amy cosied in his arms.

Sunday, 8 June

A my has gone home for the weekend, saying she needs to "recharge her batteries" before the exams begin. She will be back this evening. But it has been a good week. Gus went to her room on Wednesday evening and they made love again. It did not have the monumental, achievement-like feel of the first time, but was beautiful, more measured, more enjoyable, less frenetic and convulsive. Afterwards she lay snuggled on his breast, her head nuzzled against his neck and shoulder. He almost forgot the time and had to leave hurriedly before curfew.

Lorna came up to him after the Tennyson lecture on Friday morning and said how pleased she was that he and Amy were back together. Again, Gus wondered, though this time with a lighter heart, how much she knew. She mentioned that Peter Strutton had phoned her again and asked if she and her "friend" would like to come over for coffee on Sunday. They've decided to go, despite the first of the exams looming tomorrow.

'Well, you're bloody privileged,' Nick had said, but his tone had been jokey rather than jealous, with no hint of concern over the possibility of the lecturer's interest in Lorna.

'What do you like least about writing?' Gus has mentally prepared some questions in advance, and this as it comes out of his mouth sounds more negative than when it was in his mind - but Peter Strutton only looks thoughtful as he stirs his coffee.

'The worst part of writing is the non-writing part. The writing you at least have control over. The non-writing is in the hands of other people.'

'What do you mean?' Lorna asks.

'Having to deal with agents, publishers, publicists - that sort of thing. Selling your book.'

'But you'd think,' Gus says, 'if it was a really good book, it would just sell itself.'

Peter crosses his ankle over his knee and leans back resignedly in his chair.

'That's what you think at first. You assume that people will be queuing up to publish what you've spent so much effort writing, what you find so fascinating and important. But it doesn't happen like that.'

He moves suddenly to the table, picks up a thick slab of A4 sheets, all neatly printed, and waves it in front of them.

'This is it,' he says, with a note of fatalism rather than pride in his voice. 'You think - how could anyone not be impressed by this? That's not being big-headed. You've given perhaps years to the project, devoted hours of time, effort and thought, written and re-written until it's as perfect as you can make it. It means so much to you, you automatically assume it will mean something to other people. But that doesn't follow. They haven't put in all that effort and dedication, so naturally it can't mean anything to them.'

He wonders, as he speaks, if he should be displaying his feelings to students in this way.

Lorna looks at the manuscript. 'It must be heart-breaking when a publisher rejects your book.'

The sad solicitude in her voice persuades him to go on. 'You feel quite bitter and angry. You think, someone's probably just glanced at it, read a couple of paragraphs, a few pages if you're lucky, and tossed it to one side. You think, I've spent years of my life working on that, how could they be so insulting? But we all do it with other people's books. Haven't you gone into a bookshop, picked up a book, read the first paragraph, and dropped it down again? I do it all the time. But it's not so nice when someone does it to me!'

'But at least those books have got themselves published.' Lorna means her response to justify Peter's casual rejection of them. She realises too late it could be seen as a put-down, a comment on Peter's failure to get that far. She glances at him. She thinks she sees suddenly an immense sorrow in his eyes, lasting a moment, but devastatingly intense, like an earthquake that can obliterate in a second.

'But you must really love writing,' Gus says. 'To be able to sit down day after day and work at it. That must be a reward for its own sake, regardless of whether you're successful in the eyes of others.'

Peter breathes in. His elbows are tucked in behind his chair's backrest, hands hanging down, as if he has been tied there. His eyes have a pained expression, as if something is being forced out of him. He is thinking, that anyone who has sat down as long as he has would write a book, as good as, if not better than, his.

He speaks slowly. 'Well, strangely enough, a lot of the time, I don't like it. Sometimes I hate it - but - I hate not writing even more.'

'You've had some more rejections since we last came round?' Lorna asks.

His nod of the head barely conceals glum embarrassment, so different from the bright assurance he normally displays. He is relieved that so far they haven't asked how many rejections he's had.

He thinks to himself, if he's not writing, he is like an empty shell, an empty, forlorn, useless shell of a man. From the outside he looks completely fine. But for himself, viewing from the inside, there's a vacuum at the centre of him that no-one is aware of. Some part of him feels dead, as if a limb of the spirit has been amputated or left trailing useless. He feels disabled but somehow has to adapt and carry on living without it.

He will do all sorts of things to try to keep at bay his consciousness of the vacuum inside. He will watch TV, make notes on poems. He will read, rearrange furniture or books in the house, re-read things he's written, to convince himself they are good. He will read his favourite writers and tell himself how privileged and fortunate he is to have had the chance to study them. But still he knows of the emptiness, the purposelessness, inside.

'So where do you go from here?' Lorna asks.

'Well, I do wonder that.' His face brightens. 'But that's not your problem. I'm sorry to be telling you all this. Unburdening myself to you, in this unseemly way.'

The talk switches, more agreeably, to poetry and literature but less pleasurably to the exams starting tomorrow. Peter tells them that, from what he has seen of them in seminars and from the essays they've submitted to him, they should have nothing to worry about. Their answering smiles look less convincing. He thinks of his own first-year days, when he revelled in the discovery of all those writers who have been his firm friends since. He thinks of Southey's poem, *The Scholar*.

> *My days among the dead are past;*
> *Around me I behold,*
> *Where'er these casual eyes are cast,*
> *The mighty minds of old...*

He recalls too its ending, where the poet expresses his hopes for himself.

> *Yet leaving here a name, I trust,*
> *That will not perish in the dust.*

After they've gone he stares at the sheaf of papers on the table. Seven rejections now, all polite, saying they've read his work with interest but do not think it suitable for their lists at the present time. But then, they would never say they found it sub-standard, poor, unpalatable - just in case he's accepted by another publisher and becomes a runaway success.

His apology to Lorna and Gus was true. He was sorry. He wishes he hadn't spoken to them as he did, exposing himself like that to raw undergraduates. He has almost certainly destroyed their pristine image of him. What had made him do it? He knew. He had to tell someone, just had to get it out sooner or later. He hadn't intended it to be them who would be the recipients of the confession. It was like a sudden attack of vomiting. You don't want it to befall you, can't choose who will be with you when it strikes.

And he thinks, if Lorna had been on her own, what might have happened. She is definitely more mature, more steadfast and stable, than Fiona, with a mesmeric beauty. She could be fierce, perhaps, strong-minded - but that glowing smile that flowers across her face, like a pure white crescent moon. He likes her insistence on the positive that she shows in seminars - he remembers Yeats's *An Irish Airman Foresees His Death* from a few weeks ago, in which she abhorred what she saw as negativity.

But no - that way madness lies.

Monday, 9 June

As you enter the long rectangular Main Hall your eyes are dazzled by the multiplied starkness of the scene. Seemingly endless columns of desks, each wooden surface a bare square of mid-brown, with thin metal legs on a bare polished floor of mid-brown, stretch away from the front into the distance. One has the impression that, if the back wall of the Old College building did not prevent it, the columns would carry on until they reached the sea.

There is a stage, but the only scenery is an unadorned table for the supervising lecturers. This will be a play with no spoken words, except Professor Savage's quiet command at nine-thirty, 'You may turn over your papers.' A drama of silence, exactly three hours long, will follow. There will be words - thousands of them poured into twelve-page answer books, which the examiners are now placing with pointlessly neat alignment into the centre of each desk, with a face-down question paper equally precisely positioned in each right-hand corner. Thousands of silent words flooding, spilling, limping out of each tautened mind onto the white sheets, like blood from a wound.

The echoing silence of the hall gives way to a subdued buzz of conversation outside, as the students wait to file in for their first of eight three-hour exams, on Elizabethan Drama. People shift from foot to foot, chuckle nervously at jokes. Hands fidget with pens and minds with concepts. Heads are bloated with hastily memorised quotations, opinions and ideas.

'Someone compared this to the moments before going over the top in the First World War,' says Simon, as the Gwylan group and others hover near the entrance. 'I can see what they mean.'

'You do get that feeling,' Gus adds. 'Like we're all going to be mown down by machine-gun fire as we walk in.'

'I heard that a giant consignment of toilet rolls arrived last week,' Nick says. 'Apparently they always do that before the exams, in case there's a run on them. Get it? - Ha! - a run.'

Gus spots Amy in a posse of Alex girls - Lorna, Fiona, Rosina, Vivienne. She looks apprehensive as she gives Gus a little intimate wave, fluttering her fingers to him. Lorna looks poised and unconcerned, extending him a fuller, more luminous smile, and even from this distance he can see the blue brilliance of her eyes. Fiona, unusually, is quiet. He wonders if Peter Strutton will be one of the supervisors.

Two hours later, deep in the vast silence of the examination room, Gus looks around at the bodies slanted over desks, heads bent in thought, pens pounding soundlessly on paper. He has done, he thinks, reasonably well on two questions, and now he is about to start his third and final answer. '*The real protagonist of "Julius Caesar" is the Roman mob.*' *Discuss.* He sits adjacent to Nick, who seems to be going well, turning his bowed head sideways to Gus every so often and twinkling an impish grin. Amy and Lorna are in the far column and in front of them. Amy's back inclines gracefully forward, her hair splaying onto her shoulders as she writes.

Gus is aware of someone brushing past him. A figure is walking briskly to the front of the hall. It's Simon. Is he requesting a second answer book? Surely he can't have written such a prodigious amount already? Nick and Gus exchange glances. More likely he's asking permission to go to the toilet - frowned on by the examiners but treated with understanding tolerance in the circumstances - in which case a member of staff will have to accompany him.

But no. He veers right, past the stage and towards the exit. He has not looked up at the examiners' table, where an impassive Professor Savage perches, nor at any of the other students. Gus sees Simon's face in profile as he approaches the door out. It is set rigid. Now Gus and Nick exchange surprised and troubled looks. Simon has walked out, with an hour still to go.

In the crammed cafeteria of the Students' Union at lunchtime, there is no sign of him.

'Simon must have blown it,' Nick declares. 'But it was a real armpit of an exam!'

'You seemed to be doing a lot of writing.' Gus's tone sounds almost like an accusation.

'Was any of it any good? That is the question. No - I think I got by.'

Gus, too, reckons he has "got by." Amy, in the brief moment he had to speak to her before she went back to Alex for lunch, told him she thought she might have fluffed the question on *Macbeth - 'This dead butcher and his fiend-like queen.' Is this an accurate description of Macbeth and his wife?* - but otherwise she feels happy with her efforts.

'Where is Simon? That's the big question,' says Nick.

'Back in his room,' Dermot suggests. 'He always retreats there if things are not going well.'

'Or...could be somewhere else,' Nick says as he tucks into steak pie and chips.

As soon as he's finished eating, Nick jumps up, wiping his mouth with a tissue.

'Right, boys, I'm going to look for Simon.'

Without waiting for a response, he marches off, leaving Gus and Dermot looking at each other and at Nick's quick footsteps past the tables and chairs.

After lunch Gus wanders past the mini-golf course and through the ruins of the castle. Mercifully, he has no exam this afternoon, but has plenty of revision to do before the one in history tomorrow morning - "The Making of the Western World," a huge canvas covering in summary all of European history from ancient Greece to the two World Wars. He contemplates his choice of venues. There is the library, sure to be full to bursting with students, furiously making notes or wearily lounging back, hands on brows, attempting to absorb information. Or he can go back to his room, which will be the opposite, if Nick's not there - silent and isolated, a view of blue sky and strolling promenaders through the window. Or -the greatest temptation - the beach, where one can study to the soft andante of the sea, watch the summer waves and the sun glinting on the water. There will be other distractions - sparsely-clad girls stretched on the sand, growing numbers of tourists, children splashing noisily in the paddling pool or building elaborate sandcastles.

Amy said she will stay in Alex after lunch to prepare for her two exams tomorrow, and on reflection this is best. He would dearly love to be with her, but, despite the contentment he feels when they are together, he doubts if he'll be able to concentrate one hundred per cent on studying. Next year, perhaps, they will have reached a stage of more manageable equilibrium in each other's presence. And thoughts of the long summer vacation, now only three weeks away, parade mouth-wateringly through his mind. He will invite her home, although he has a few qualms about it. She will perhaps ask him up to Gloucester, or maybe they can meet somewhere away from both homes. Even before then, in the fortnight of term that is left, they can enjoy themselves together. He thinks of them prancing in the summer sea, the sun burning amber, the water tinglingly fresh on their skin - or, perhaps, for one night he will stop over in Alex, and feel her against him through the warm tranquillity of the night-time hours and they will wake to the dawn sun gleaming on them. Lines from John Donne's *The Sun Rising* have found their way into his poetry notebook:

> *and since thy duties be*
> *To warm the world, that's done in warming us.*
> *Shine here to us, and thou art everywhere;*
> *This bed thy centre is, these walls thy sphere.*

Or more cheekily from another poem:

> *'Tis true, 'tis day; what though it be?*
> *O wilt thou therefore rise from me?*
> *Why should we rise? Because 'tis light?*
> *Did we lie down because 'twas night?*

From the castle he crosses the road for a stroll along South Beach. He remembers how he walked here at the start of the academic year, before the dance in King's Hall. He remembers an angrier sea foaming and frothing on the sand, waves strafing the shoreline and billowing onto the beach. He looks seaward, where now in the distance sky and sea melt gently into one. The beach is speckled with students and holiday makers.

There among them are Simon and Nick. Simon sits leaning forward head down, Nick alongside with his arm around him.

Wednesday, 11 June

'God, I've spent a lot this term.' Nick speaks with unusual glumness.

'So have I,' moans Geraint.

'But we've had a bloody good time!' Nick's tone changes in an instant. He slaps Dermot on the shoulder as they sit down in the Cabin, his mouth opening wide into his riotous laugh.

'You know,' Dermot says, 'there were a couple of boys, they got their money for the summer term, and decided not to come back to Aber. They went to Spain for a month and blew it all.'

'That's the best way to cut down on spending - not having any money. Anyway, back to the exams. Three down, five to go,' yells Nick as a large group gathers at quarter-past-five, cramming into tables under the brooding black-and-white figures of Dean and Bogart. 'I didn't mind that exam this afternoon. I actually enjoyed the question comparing any two of the love relationships dramatised in *The Rainbow*. I was going like a bloody train! And at least I haven't walked out of any so far.' Nick turns his head and looks down his nose at Simon in pretended censure, the familiar genial sparkle in his eyes.

'Yes, that was rather a heroic gesture,' says Fiona. 'We all secretly admire you, Simon. I've never had the courage to do that.'

Simon grins sheepishly, looking anything but heroic.

'So what happened?' Lorna asks. 'Did you write really brilliant answers, so you could afford to leave early?'

Simon laughs. 'No - the opposite. I realised halfway through the first question I should have chosen a different one to answer from Section A, so I abandoned it and started again, and then - oh I don't know - I just lost it.'

'Where did you go?' Lorna asks

Simon looks uncomfortable yet pleased by the attention he is getting.

'Went down on South Beach. I felt pretty depressed. Fortunately, this man here' - he indicates Nick - 'found me and gave me some words of wisdom.'

'You wonder why we're sitting these exams anyway,' Dermot says. 'Why are we putting ourselves through it? Are there any real rewards at the end of it?'

'A decent job, I hope,' Fiona answers. 'A reasonable amount of money.'

'I'll never make money,' Dermot replies. 'I would feel guilty about it. I can't help thinking that you can only make money by taking it off someone else.'

'Nonsense!' Fiona cries. 'You can create wealth, create money. Money is not a finite amount. It can grow. Everyone can become more wealthy. That's obvious if you look at history. If you get richer, it doesn't mean that someone else is getting poorer.'

This prompts a tennis rally of retorts between her and Dermot.

'Yes, but you can become richer than other people, so relative to you they're getting poorer.'

'That may be because the richer people work harder, are more motivated.'

'Oh here we go. The old argument that the poor are poor because they're stupid, or lazy, or somehow inferior to the rich.'

'There'll always be people in charge, and they'll always live better than the people under them.'

'Yes, that very phrase, "the people under them," shows you regard those people as inferior.'

'Where I come from,' puts in Nick, 'if somebody goes to the doctor, we say they're "under the doctor." Can you imagine that literally?'

'Wouldn't you like to get rich quick, though?' Geraint asks.

Dermot is emphatic. 'No.'

'Why not?'

'Well for a start it's grammatically incorrect. It should be "get rich quickly."'

Fiona returns to the fray. 'You say that nothing can be made out of nothing - but there is evidence all around you to the contrary. If you cut your grass so it is an inch high - a few months later it's six inches high. Where's that extra five inches of grass come from?'

'That's biology not economics. Anyway, you can pursue what you're interested in - money. I pursue what I'm interested in - reading and thinking. They're both necessary - we need money for prosperity and good living conditions - we need reading and thinking for a civilised society.'

'I'm not especially interested in money,' Fiona almost shrieks in exasperation. 'I agree with what you just said.'

'Woah, Fiona and Dermot agree,' shouts Nick, and he leads a discordant cheer.

Dermot seems oblivious to the noise. 'All I'm saying, is that money is like food. Up to a certain point it's necessary and beneficial. Beyond that point it's not only useless but harmful. It's like, everybody needs three meals a day; but that doesn't mean that six meals a day gives you twice the benefit.'

'Wealth is not very good value for money,' Gus says. 'Someone who's ten times as rich as you is unlikely to be ten times as happy. The ratio will always come down on the side of happiness rather than wealth.'

'The weight of your thoughts should matter more than the weight of your wallet,' says Nick.

'We say, "for love or money,"' Dermot adds. 'Well love is definitely more important.'

'I never thought I'd hear you say that,' exclaims Nick. 'And agreeing with Fiona as well. What is happening?'

There is general laughter.

'Speaking of *lurv*,' Nick, drawling the word out in a poor American accent, turns to Gus. 'Where is Amy?'

Good-humoured eyes from around the table focus on Gus. He saw her briefly as she came out of the exam and assumed she would come with everyone to the Cabin for a recuperative coffee. She exchanged a few friendly words with him, saying she thought she had done all right. Unusually, she hadn't wanted to join the group.

'She said she was worried about the nineteenth century poetry exam tomorrow,' Gus tells them. 'She wanted to do some revision before the evening meal.'

As they walk down Pier Street and onto the seafront, Simon, Fiona and Dermot are ahead talking together, Gus, Nick and Lorna in the rear.

'What exactly did you say to Simon?' Lorna asks Nick.

'I had a feeling he would go down by the sea, and there he was, sitting on South Beach. He said he wasn't going to do any more of the exams. He was pretty miserable. I just told him to persevere. If he sat the exams at least he'd have a chance of passing. If he didn't sit them, he'd bloody definitely have no chance. I told him to forget the failure and just focus on the next exam. He did that and he thinks he's done a lot better in the last two. He's okay now - and he's going to join us for the midnight swim on Friday!'

Lorna laughs. 'You're still going ahead with that?'

'Of course. You're coming, Gus? All of us Gwylan boys will be there. Geraint, Rosina, Vivienne - they'll all be there. You can get Amy to come, can't you, Gus? A few jars in the Angel, a barbie on the beach, some celebratory wine, then -into the water. It'll all go - as Fiona might say - *swimmingly*.'

'It *is* Friday the thirteenth, Nick,' Gus reminds him.

'So what?' There is disgust in Nick's voice. 'It's mid-June. It'll be a beautiful night. Have you ever known me to be bloody superstitious?'

Mrs Morgan is happily dusting the hallway of Gwylan House when the boys arrive back. She greets them beamingly.

'And how was it today?'

'Not too bad, thanks, Mrs Morgan,' Nick answers, followed by affirming nods and okays from Gus, Simon and Dermot.

'That's good!' Mrs Morgan looks genuinely pleased. 'Oh, Gus, there's a letter for you. Must have been pushed through the letterbox.'

There is a small white envelope on the hallway table. From the three letters of his name, Gus recognises the handwriting immediately.

Thursday, 12 June

The sky a soft summer-morning blue. Far away, high snowdrifts of cloud. The sun slanting rays of mustard-orange onto the sea. Gus has been sitting on a promenade bench for twenty minutes. Almost time to face breakfast. He got up early, after a peaceless night, while Nick was still sleeping. Last night he lingered in the library until closing time, then wandered by the sea in the darkness. One small mercy - no exam this morning.

'What's happened, Gus? Something's happened. Is it to do with that letter?'

Gus sits on his bed as he and Nick get ready to go down to breakfast.

Nick persists. 'Have you lost your tongue, man? You've hardly said a word since we got in yesterday. You were very quiet at the evening meal, rushed straight upstairs afterwards, then I heard you go out straight away. Come on - you can tell me! Even if I can't do anything, I bet you that telling me will make it feel less bad.'

Gus crushes his lips together and passes the letter to Nick, who reads it to himself, with a look of intense concentration.

Dear Gus,   Wednesday, p.m.

This is a difficult letter to get started. As you know, I went home the weekend before last. The truth is I have a boyfriend at home. He's at Liverpool University, but he's from Gloucester and we used to go out when we were in school. When we went to different universities, we made an agreement that we could both see other people if we wanted. Michael (that's his name) says he's been out with a few people.

We've seen each other at Christmas and Easter and at the weekend we decided we wouldn't go out with anyone else at the moment. We'd have the summer vacation together, just enjoy the holiday and not worry about the future. Therefore it would be best if you and I didn't get together in the summer. With Michael around, it would be awkward if you came to visit me, and I'd prefer to stay at home rather than come down to visit you.

This is nothing personal, of course. I like you a lot, but I've had this kind of on-off arrangement with Michael for a while, and coming up to the vacation we've decided to stick with each other.

I hope this doesn't sound too horrible. You and I have got on well together, particularly this last month, so I really hope that this doesn't come as too much of a blow to you.

Please don't think I'm being mean or insincere. As I say, I've enjoyed our times together. But we've never made a firm commitment to each other, so I don't feel I'm being disloyal in any way. It's probably best if we stop now, before we get too involved with each other.

Apologies also that this is in the middle of the exams. I should really have done it before - but I think it's for the best.

Michael is coming to Aber - he's got a car - and giving me a lift home, so I may not have chance to talk to you properly until next term.

So, I just have to say, have a really good summer. See you next term! Give my love to Nick and Dermot in case I don't see them.

Amy

'Well,' says Nick emphatically, 'bit of a surprise, I suppose. Yes - I can see why you'd be upset. But - hey - if that's what she feels, that's what she feels. Look, mate, there are plenty of other fish in the sea, literally and metaphorically - love that phrase - especially round here!' Nick's eyes glint. 'Yes, that's a blow - but tomorrow night you can do some "fishing" at the barbie and swim. I can name you a few class catches. Rosina, Vivienne - you like tall girls - she's like a bloody lighthouse - or how about Adele? - she's gorgeous.'

Gus remains sitting lifeless on the bed. Nick puts his hand on his shoulder.

'It's no good moping about it. *If of herself she will not love, nothing can make her. The Devil take her!*'

There is silence. Nick continues. 'I know I'm sounding harsh, but it's a harsh world. Amy's obviously thought about it. And can you honestly say you feel the "L" word for her? You feel hurt because you feel personally rejected. You think you must be lacking something because she's turned away from you for someone else. But it could be that she's the one who's lacking. She's lacking the ability to appreciate you. Other girls won't lack that ability and you've got to find them. As simple as that.'

'Marvellously put, Nick,' says Gus, with a mixture of sarcasm and admiration.

'Just get out there and find someone who appreciates you. Midnight swim tomorrow - golden opportunity.'

'You think I might find someone in the water?'

'No need to be frivolous. Come on, let's get one of Mrs M's egg delights inside us. Exam this afternoon. Can't afford to mess it up.'

Friday, 13 June

I balanced all, brought all to mind,
The years to come seemed waste of breath,
A waste of breath the years behind
In balance with this life, this death.

D arkness. The rhythmic crashing and clashing of waves on sand and shingle. The sea besieging the shore, like Death besieging Life. The sea's never-ceasing movement, like a shark that never sleeps, always waiting. The water looms as black as outer space and seems to stretch as far, endless black pulsing through a million years.

You gaze down into the dark swaying mass and you are staring into the liquid mirror of your soul. You are sinking into its silent depths and the water closes above your head like gates that open just enough to let you enter, then shut secretly and ghostlike about you, so quietly that no-one notices that you have slipped away into its sunless sanctuary.

There is only one way for certain that Gus can demonstrate to her the pain he feels. Only one means of convincing her. All he wants to do is express his sorrow in a way that she will understand. There is one, ultimate act. Words of Keats beat against his brain.

> *Darkling I listen; and, for many a time*
> *I have been half in love with easeful Death...*

Easeful Death. But Keats was only "half in love" with it. To be - or not to be?

Etre. To be young...was...

Love. He slides the word silently on his tongue, like a wine-taster. He breathes it to himself. Love. So easy to pronounce; so hard to say. So hard to know.

In recent weeks he has discovered a poem by Rupert Brooke. For some reason the whole poem has dissolved itself into him and he's found he knows it by heart almost without conscious effort.

> *I said I splendidly loved you; it's not true.*
> *Such long swift tides stir not a land-locked sea.*
> *On gods or fools the high risk falls - on you -*
> *The clean clear bitter-sweet that's not for me.*
> *Love soars from earth to ecstasies unwist.*
> *Love is flung Lucifer-like from Heaven to Hell.*

Then the lines that haunt him the most.

> *But - there are wanderers in the middle mist,*
> *Who cry for shadows, clutch, and cannot tell*
> *Whether they love at all, or, loving, whom:*
> *An old song's lady, a fool in fancy dress,*
> *Or phantoms, or their own face on the gloom;*
> *For love of Love, or from heart's loneliness.*
> *Pleasure's not theirs, nor pain. They doubt, and sigh*
> *And do not love at all. Of these am I.*

Is he crying for a shadow? Clutching? He cannot tell whether he loves at all. Is it for love of Love, or from his heart's loneliness? There is somehow a surprise, yet no surprise, when you realise at the very end that the poet is talking about himself. The word *I* is used only at the beginning and end of the poem. And the simple rhyme of *sigh* and *I* is so strangely forceful...

He'd walked past the Marine Hotel and seen older people sitting in its windows, looking placidly out to sea. He had suddenly felt a sharp stabbing mental pain. If he and Amy stayed together, they might be sitting there, viewing the water, in thirty years' time. The thought of it sinks uncomfortably into him. He doesn't want to think about that prospect. It seems wrong to feel this way, unless he doesn't love her. But the feeling refuses to leave him.

He looks across at the long seafront, Marine Terrace silhouetted against the night sky, with the warm orange-yellow of lit windows and streetlamps and the dark hump of Constitution Hill above Alex. Behind him the towers and eccentric shapes of the Old College soar into the sky. A fire dances and glows on the beach and he can see dim figures at the barbecue, just up from where the waves curl in along the shoreline. Beyond is the black glimmer of the water.

'Hello!' A light, clear voice piercing the night's quiet, suddenly rifling into its emptiness. A lithe, graceful shape beside him.

'Contemplating the water?' She leans down as she speaks and gazes too into its dark mystery in a gesture of companionship. She wears a soft, swishing skirt of blue and purple.

'I'm really sorry, Gus,' Lorna says. 'I didn't know Amy had anyone back home. She's mentioned once or twice there's a boy she sees, but it didn't seem serious. But don't blame Amy - or yourself. It's just one of those things. I can tell you Amy was quite cut up about having to break the news to you. It might be because Michael insisted on coming up here, she felt she had to tell you.'

'You mean she would have carried on deceiving me otherwise?'

'*No.*' She gives an emphatic shake of the head. 'I don't know if it really is serious between them. But obviously she had to tell you about him if he was coming here. Why don't you come down on to the beach?'

'Will Amy be there?'

'No. In fact Michael's already arrived. They've gone away for the weekend - to Borth, I think.'

Nick yells a welcoming 'Ah!' and toasts Gus with his can of beer. 'We were getting worried about you! Lorna spotted you and we thought, what the bloody hell is he doing up there? He should be *here*!' Nick plunges his forefinger down towards the sand in the exaggerated gesture of someone whose brain is agreeably coated with alcohol. He looks at the barbecue and then at Gus. 'There's one sausage left!' He lets rip his familiar hoot of laughter. 'But you're just in time for the swim. Okay, lads and ladies!'

The black water laps lukewarm around Gus's throat. His head is all that remains above the surface. In the dark, the sea appears thick and heavy, like oil, but it is light and soft against his body. He turns onto his back and lies there as in a coffin. He can see lights in the windows of Alex. The waves sway up to him and back, sluicing against his flesh. Above him moonlight sifts through the night clouds.

He wonders what Amy is doing at this very moment, just before midnight. Is there any thought of him at all in her mind? Is she "cut up" as Lorna said? Or have all her thoughts about him evaporated with the arrival of Michael?

Water is sidling and slinking around his body. He can feel it licking at his legs and shoulders. The sea's surface is glassy black with the gentlest of ripples, but he is conscious of its dark depths further out. He feels unbloated, light, almost weightless as he floats, and wonders about those who have eaten and drunk. The feasting seems to have had no effect on Nick, who looks the most energetic of the group, by turns treading water, floating on his back, then swimming vigorously in great splashes, a little further out each time.

Simon too is entombed in water up to his neck, and he regards Gus thoughtfully. Dermot has decided not to come in and squats down at the edge of the sea, looking every so often towards Fiona, who had started alongside Lorna but now drifts on her own, her head at an awkward angle, gazing up at the sky. Although he is at a distance from her, Gus fancies that her face bears the same drained and doleful expression as on the night she turned her wrath on Peter Strutton at the debate, as if the sea is some monster who has swallowed her body up to her neck and she is painfully and helplessly waiting for the inevitable completion of the deed.

There are about a dozen bodies in the sea. The beach echoes to laughter and chatter and shouts from shore to water as people scamper along the sand or sit and swallow beer or sip from plastic cups of wine.

Gus feels the water rilling against him and tries to catch in his hand the ripples of moonlit silver that nudge its surface smoothness. He tries to stifle the image of Amy nestled into him as they float carefree together looking at the stars…

There is a sudden half-shout, half-choke, from further out in the water. Another follows, higher-pitched and longer, then what sounds like a gasp. There is a bawl of 'Boys!' Gus turns his head in the direction of the noises.

Then it comes again. 'Uuuh! Boys!'

Where Nick was swimming Gus can see the crown of a head. It resurfaces. Nick tries to shake his head, but his mouth goes under again as he does so. His arms flap up as if trying to hoist themselves onto a solid surface, but they meet only water and sink down through it. Then, where Nick was, there is a black unbroken smoothness.

Saturday, 14 June

F our-thirty in the afternoon and Gus is on his way back to Gwylan House. He spent most of the morning in the library, attempting to study for the remaining exams on Monday and Tuesday. He watched television in the Students' Union, then walked by South Beach, the harbour and the castle, trying to stave off the swirl of thoughts in his mind.

Outside one of the guest houses of Marine Terrace, underneath its white walls and pastel blue window-sill, a baby gull is squatting. The thing Gus notices first is its head. It is straining forward, towards him, its mouth wide open, as if it's trying to speak to him. Its mouth is moving, as if it's trying to form words, as Nick did last night. It can't get up.

It must have fallen from the roof.

It is a warm day. The little gull is covered in grey down. It must be uncomfortable, helplessly prone in the glare of the bright heat.

Its mouth continues to silently plead.

Gus looks down at it. Where are its father and mother? Do they know their offspring lies suffering, in need of their care? Or have they heartlessly abandoned it? What is the relationship between seagulls and their children?

Should he tell someone? Phone a vet? Can anyone do anything? Would it be worth the time and effort?

He will go on a little way and come back later. He walks along Marine Terrace, on the buildings side, under the shadow of the tall fronts.

He never thinks of seagulls and dying. Somehow they seem timelessly enduring.

Thou wast not born for death, immortal Bird!

Like Keats's nightingales, seagulls don't seem individual. They are a species, and the species goes on irrespective of individual deaths. They remain the same through the centuries.

No hungry generations tread thee down;
The voice I hear this passing night was heard
In ancient days by emperor and clown.

The seagulls of Aber are likewise immortal. They carry on making the same relentless raucous squawks, as if it is the same bird continuously, through generations of students. They are like the sea that is their home: one substance, the millions of drops that make it up having no individual existence.

He has not walked as far as he intended. But he turns back. The pale blue window-sills of the guest house draw nearer. Half-reluctantly, his eyes scour the pavement ahead. He can't see the baby gull. It's gone. It can't have been as badly injured as he thought. Perhaps not injured at all. It must have flown away. Or perhaps someone saw it and phoned for help.

But no. It is hidden in the corner formed by the bay window and the wall. It must have crawled there to find some shade. Its beak is still open, its mouth still moving, but more slowly. It's still straining upwards, perhaps to him or perhaps to the sea-rich air that is its home. It is prone on this alien hard grey pavement, not riding on the soft sky above the waves.

He treads past it again.

When he returns, twenty minutes later, it is lying peaceful in the sun, its head untroubled by the solid concrete that is its pillow.

How sad that all it has known of Aberystwyth, all it has known of life, is this grey floor outside a guest house, for a pitifully short period of time. It dies unaware of the magic and beauty that surrounds it. It has had no chance to taste the enchantment. It has lived and died with no knowledge of poetry, art, music, no awareness of the universe or the immense number of years the world has existed.

'We really thought you'd gone last night,' Simon exclaims as they sit for the evening meal.

'Well I'm bloody back!' Nick chortles. 'Had you all fooled for a minute.'

'I could see you were messing about,' Gus puts in. 'I have to admit it did look and sound convincing. Personally I thought it was some kind of monster from the deep.'

Nick reprises his choking-gasping howl of Friday night. 'I notice nobody immediately swam to my rescue.'

'I thought, let him drown, maybe I'll have the room to myself next year,' Gus jokes.

'It was a good night,' Nick says. 'And not even a late one. What time did we come back here? Half-twelve, wasn't it? And I still managed to get in some studying today.'

Dermot slumps down in his seat, pushing a swathe of marauding hair back from his eyes. 'Have you heard the news? A body was washed up on the beach this morning.'

Nick, about to drink his tea, abruptly checks its progress to his mouth.

'Dafydd mentioned it lunchtime,' Dermot goes on. 'Something about Geraint and Rob, he thinks, finding somebody - some body - on the sand.'

'Quite a to-do outside today,' says Mr Morgan as he shuffles in. 'Police coming and going all morning. Somebody washed up, just outside here.' His voice rises with incredulity.

Mrs Morgan speaks with breathless speed. 'We saw the police cars outside. We went out to look but the police wouldn't let us near. Oooh - there was red and white tape all around - you know, the kind you always see in films but you can never buy it in the shops.'

'Why would you want to buy it, love?' laughs Mr Morgan.

'I'm just saying you never see it. But anyway, the police were there all morning. We watched it all from the window.'

Mr Morgan laughs again. '*You* watched it, love.'

'I tried to make out who it was, but I couldn't see anything. The police kept standing in the way. But I spoke to Mrs Evans from Fron Hyfryd and...she didn't know who it was either. Such a lovely day as well.' She shakes her head in sad bafflement. 'You wonder why people do these things. Might have been suicide, might have been an accident, I suppose.'

When the Morgans have gone, the boys gaze at each other. Nick answers their unasked question.

'Couldn't have been any of our lot. We're all here. And I think I've seen all the other boys today.'

'What about the girls?' Gus asks.

'I think I've seen them all.' Nick sounds less certain

Monday, 16 June

The final two days of the first-year exams will go ahead despite the tragedy. Professor Savage said a few words this morning and there was a minute's silence before the exam began.

Through the day the usual silence in the examination hall seemed to take a tighter grip, the supervising lecturers somehow more watchful, their eyes full of unspoken thoughts. And it felt strange, eerie, that the life of the university should go on with Peter Strutton no longer existing. Only one person missing out of hundreds but that one absence representing a priceless life. And the great authors that Gus is studying - Shakespeare, Wordsworth, Shelley - seem to lose their value because one person is no longer there to read them and take inspiration from them.

Another beautiful afternoon, the sea bejewelled with sparkles of sunshine, the sun's rays beaming against their bodies as Gus, Lorna and Dermot sit dangling their bare legs on the promenade shelf above the beach. In front of them, a little boy stamps delightedly about, bladderwrack popping and bursting beneath his feet as his steps sink crunching in the shingle and sand. The beach is dotted with clusters of holiday-makers, local people and students stretched face-down, propped up on elbows, with the sun on their backs and a stack of notes below their intent or wandering eyes.

'It must have been suicide,' says Lorna, 'and it must have been to do with his writing.' She turns to Gus. 'Remember he told us he'd had rejections from publishers - he didn't tell us how many, but I looked into his eyes as he said it and I could just see this huge disappointment in them. He must have thought he was a failure.'

Gus kicks his heels against the wall. 'But he wasn't. He was such a good teacher. I envied him so much his knowledge of literature. He was brilliant.'

'Rejection letters are nothing,' Dermot says. 'Sometimes people get twenty or more. Then one publisher accepts them and they never look back.'

Gus stares seaward. 'That's what's so tragic. He didn't follow his own teaching.' He turns to Lorna. 'Remember the three P's? It's that sense of utter hopelessness, I suppose. A despair that pushes you over the edge - literally.' He looks at the water and beach, at the spot where Peter's body was found.

'Why do people have to strive to achieve things?' asks Lorna, gazing at the glinting sea. 'Why do they think they're failures if they don't achieve them?'

'It's what keeps the human race moving along,' Dermot says. 'We have to try things. Other animals are content with just *being*, but we're not. We should aim to enjoy the state of just being. We should also aim to achieve what humans are capable of achieving. But that doesn't mean we have to destroy ourselves if we don't reach our goal.'

Lorna shakes her head slowly. 'Such a talented person. His whole life ahead of him. Yet to him the future must have looked so bleak. On such a beautiful night, as well, in this marvellous place.'

'How's Fiona taking it?' Gus asks her.

'Very upset. Shocked. She knew how much he wanted to be a successful writer. But she didn't think he could do this. She can't believe it was a planned thing. She doesn't think he was that kind of person. She thinks it was a temporary mood of despair that just overwhelmed him, like some freak wave that can burst over and sweep you up. She's so sorry that he couldn't have seen any way out of that mood of desolation.'

'He had so much to offer,' Gus murmurs, almost to himself.

Lorna clasps her hands together. 'Maybe if someone who knew him had come along on Friday night, as he was thinking - of doing it, and just said a kind word to him, he might still be here with us.'

Gerald Bailey formally identified the body. Peter Strutton, unusually, had put on dark clothes, a dark blue T-shirt, old jeans and black shoes - perhaps so as not to be seen on the beach, or perhaps to match his state of mind. When the police entered his flat, they found on his coffee table, piled neatly on top of each other, a file of eight rejection letters from publishers and agents, the last dated 10 June, probably received by him on Thursday or Friday. They were placed conspicuously in the centre of a table otherwise clear apart from a half-empty bottle of Scotch whisky. There was no note, but on top of them, in Peter's handwriting, were four lines of a poem by Yeats...

Tuesday, 17 June

G us is about to leave the cool dimness of Gwylan House for the bright early afternoon sunshine outside and a walk along the prom to his final three hours in the examination hall, for the second exam in Classical Studies.

Mrs Morgan emerges from the front room as he is in the hallway.

'Ah, Gus - the last exam today, Nick was saying. I expect you'll be glad when it's over!'

'Certainly will, Mrs Morgan.'

She pauses, slants her head a little to one side and regards Gus thoughtfully from this new angle.

'Is everything all right, Gus?' Her words are spoken more carefully and gently than normal. 'I can't help noticing you seem a little - quiet - recently. I know the terrible thing that happened to the lecturer must be a shock, but even before that you seemed, well - quiet.'

She pauses again before continuing.

'Now I don't want to interfere at all, but -,' she moves closer and places her hand on his arm, '- if there's anything I can do - just ask.' She smiles - a kind smile that surprises Gus with its air of unintrusive concern.

He hesitates a moment, uncertain what to say.

'Thanks, Mrs Morgan - um - yes, I did have a bit of - trouble- last week - but it's okay now.'

Her smile modifies into one of knowingness. Suddenly, she reminds him of Lorna. Mrs Morgan too seems to have acquired knowledge of him without the burden of his having to tell her.

'A young lady, is it?'

Gus nods.

'Oh Duw!' She gives a dismissive flap of the hand. 'Young ladies are two a penny! You don't realise how lucky you are. The place is swarming with them! You're spoilt for choice. You'll soon find someone - mark my words!' Her voice rises in pitch. 'Enjoy your freedom while you can! Anyway, get this exam over first.'

'Thanks, Mrs Morgan. I will.'

'And remember, if ever you want to talk about something, I'm here.' She moves away, but in a gesture of restoring his space rather than withdrawing her offer.

'Thanks, Mrs Morgan. That's very kind of you.'

She moves back to the front room entrance to let him go by. 'Twenty-three years we've been taking in students - all boys. Good boys, most of them. You get to know what goes on in their minds, what sort of things concern and worry them. And every year they think they're the only ones it's ever happened to.' She sighs and shakes her head slowly. 'As I've said before, you don't realise how lucky you are, having the opportunity to study and read all sorts of books. I wish I'd had your chance! But, I know -' she pats him gently on his arm - 'it's difficult to appreciate it when you're your age. Everything comes at you so quickly, doesn't it? But don't worry about the young lady, Gus bach. Plenty more where that one came from.'

He passes her with a more assured smile.

Walking along the prom, he thinks about Mrs Morgan's words. Yes - what seems to him novel and unique must have been re-enacted scores of times. Mrs Morgan has that in common with the sea, the moon and the seagulls - witnessing wave after wave of young men coming and going at this one phase of their lives. She possesses a wisdom that he can only glimpse. He almost felt he could hug her back there.

The exam went surprisingly well. Gus thinks he gave a good account of "the tragic technique of Sophocles" and a full answer to *Trace out the main lines in the development of Roman comedy*, though he is less certain of his writing for *How do the satires of Horace illustrate the principal features of Roman satire?* After it is over, he decides to go for a stroll on his own past St Michael's Church and around the castle. It is peaceful, apart from some laughter from the miniature golf course, and the air carries with it that faintly dreamlike aura of a summer's early evening, the peals of laughter mixing in with the blue tranquillity of the sky and the warm smell of sea and beach, all cleansed in soft lemon sunlight.

As he walks along the footpath separating the two areas of cemetery, he sees, at its far end outside the toilets, a few people gathered. He hears voices. Two men are side by side. Another is facing them, but Gus's view of him is obscured by the other two. They are talking. The two seem agitated. The third seems in the act of backing away slightly - but he can't because he is up against the walls of the building. As Gus draws near, one of the two grabs the third and clasps his hand around his jaw, pinning him against the wall. Gus sees it is Simon. Simon is lifted slightly up, his neck racked up by the man's big untidy hand. Simon's eyes gaze down in silent fear. His hands are free but they hang forgotten at his side and make no attempt to break the hold.

As Gus continues his walk towards them, the voices become clearer. The owner of the hand grasping Simon is doing most of the talking.

'What d'you think you're up to?…We're gonna nail you for this!'

'Do you think we should go to the police?' The second man, who stands behind and to the side of the first, has a more moderate voice.

'Nah! Let's deal with it here!' The first man tightens his hold on Simon's perspiring neck and lifts him further up. 'Bloody pervert…So that's how you get your kicks, hey?'

'What you going to do with him, Clem?' the second man asks.

'Told you!' He rubs his hand in Simon's cringing face. 'We'll make certain he thinks bloody twice about doing it in the future. Go and get Marty.'

'Here he comes, Clem.'

A big man, in a large, loose, grey T-shirt, is lumbering up the path alongside the golf course.

'What's going on?' Gus asks.

The first man turns abruptly, as if he did not expect to see anyone else in this part of the world.

'You a friend of his?' He jerks his head in contempt towards Simon's frightened frame.

'Yes I am.' Gus is surprised by his own firmness of voice.

'Well you'd better clear off, son. This is between me and him.' He turns back to Simon. 'Spying down on people in bloody public toilets…eh!'

Gus has to make a quick decision. He strolls closer to the man and puts his hands casually in his pockets. 'Well, perhaps we can talk about it.' Again Gus surprises himself, this time by how natural and relaxed he manages to sound.

The man opens his mouth to answer. He has no time to speak. Gus stamps his right foot down sudden and hard on the man's. The man makes a curious sound, somewhere between a groan and a yelp. He stoops slightly and his hand releases its grip on Simon.

'Run, Simon!'

Gus turns as he shouts, shoulders past the other man, glimpses the surprised look on his face, glimpses Simon out of the corner of his eye lunging forward to start his run. The two dash up the path, back the way Gus had walked, through the entrance to the cemetery, past the Students' Union. Gus, with Simon at his heels, sprints left down Laura Place.

A contemplative Josh, trudging up past the church, turns in surprise at the two flying figures. 'No time to stop!' Gus bawls as they flash by.

'Okay, lads,' Josh says calmly, resuming his meditation, only to have it interrupted again by three more bodies, heavier in bulk and breathing, one of them hobbling slightly, who jolt down the slope with looks of extreme stress on their faces as their feet thump on the concrete.

Gus and Simon veer right onto King Street, the Old College spinning giddily past, then left onto Pier Street, almost crashing into the wall of the Theological College as they negotiate the slope and narrow pavement, then across the road and onto the promenade. It is busy with strolling holidaymakers. People sit on benches or lick white-topped cones as they dawdle along, and there is a queue in summer colours of yellow, light blue, pale green or pink at the ice-cream stall by the Pier.

'Okay!' Gus gasps. 'Best to slow down now. We'll look too conspicuous if we run.' He turns his head anxiously back, but there is no sign of the pursuing trio.

'I think we've lost them,' he pants as he gulps in air. 'Must have turned up Pier Street rather than down. Probably best to go back to lodgings anyway.'

They walk mingling with the crowd, each too breathless to say more. Simon looks around, but his breathing calms and he moves more easily.

'Thanks,' he says.

Gus looks at him. 'You okay?'

'Yes.' Simon's faint relieved smile gives way to a look of sheepish shame.

'Let's get back,' Gus says.

All is quiet in Gwylan House. Mr and Mrs Morgan seem to be out, as do Dermot and Nick.

'Want to come in?' Simon asks as he opens the door of his room. Gus follows him in.

Simon looks at Gus as if waiting for him to ask something. Gus looks back.

'Thanks for doing that,' Simon says eventually. 'Bit of a tight situation.' He rubs his neck.

Gus folds his arms. 'I heard what they said.'

'About me - in the toilet?'

'Yes…Have you done that …before?'

'Yes.' There is a look of weary calmness on Simon's face. He glances up at Gus, searching for a response. 'You probably know I have.'

'Yes. University? Back in October?'

'I'm really sorry, Gus. I'm really sorry. I couldn't help it. I didn't know it was you in there.'

Gus smirks. 'It was a bit embarrassing.'

'Yes, I realise. I didn't mean…but, yes, it was awful. I've thought about it a lot since, wondering whether to speak to you about it. But I couldn't bring myself to. And I wasn't certain if you'd recognised me.' He looks up again at Gus, some hint of pleading in his eyes.

'So, do you do that…regularly?' Gus asks.

'No. not really. It's just, when things get a bit on top of me, I just do it, I'm not certain why. Like when I did it with you, I was really missing my girlfriend and I was feeling…not good. And today, the exams, the Dr Strutton thing, not seeing Annaliese - that's my girlfriend. But I'm not going to do it again. I know it's wrong.'

'I didn't know you had a girlfriend.'

'Yes. She's at university in Dublin.'

'Dublin? So that's why you keep -'

' - looking across the sea? That's right. I'm not certain why - I don't think she's going to swim over to me.' Simon grins rather foolishly.

'You should have told us.'

'Yes - I'm too secretive. That's my trouble'

'You write don't you?' Gus asks the question he has been wanting to ask for some time.

'Yes, I've got a few things. How about you?' Simon's voice is cordial, almost eager.

'Yes, I try as well. We'll have to, um, have a look at each other's work some time.'

Simon nods. 'I'd like to do that.'

'And next year - no secrets,' Gus says. 'And you're right - it's not a good thing to be doing. Apart from anything else, you could have got beaten up back there - or arrested.'

Simon nods again, with a repentant smile.

'Yes. Definitely not again. Thanks for stepping in.'

'I didn't realise how fit I was.'

'Nor me... You - won't tell anyone will you, Gus?'

Gus shrugs his shoulders. 'Not if you don't tell on me.'

'Done!' Simon offers his hand; Gus shakes it.

There is the noise of someone tramping up the stairs. Nick is singing to himself. He sees Simon and Gus through the open door. 'Well hi boys, what are you up to?'

'Oh,' says Gus, 'not much.'

'Hey, you guys look pretty hot!'

'Yeh - we've just been for a run,' Gus answers.

'Oh? Why wasn't I invited?'

'Um, it was snap decision. Spur of the moment thing.'

Nick claps his hands. 'Hey that's good. End of the year and you're finally doing something spontaneous. Feel good after it?'

'Yes,' says Simon. 'Good!'

Thursday, 19 June

The last but one day of term, and a final party in the White Horse, with a mixture of students studying different subjects. Some feel a shocked gloom still, but the mood is diluted by the presence of others who had not even heard the name 'Peter Strutton' until the news of a lecturer's suicide broke. The prevailing atmosphere is of the jovial lightness you would expect at the end of the academic year with exams safely negotiated.

'This could be the sort of party where you have to wait till morning to know who you've slept with,' says one of the boys, with a bravura laugh that might cast doubt on his ability to act on the intent.

'What's known as Love at First Light,' his friend adds.

Colin swirls his beer in its glass. 'Gareth reckons the exams have dampened his libido.'

'What does that mean? Speak English not Latin.'

'Made him less horny.'

'*Libido*. I've heard that word,' Nick says. 'So that's what it means. I thought it had something to do with books.'

'Imagine -' laughs Josh ' - Nick going into a library and asking, "Have you got anything on libido?" !'

'Funny people, librarians,' says Colin. 'Do you think they eat the food on their plate in alphabetical order - beans, carrots, parsnips, peas, potatoes…?'

'What about meat? Would you eat it under c for chicken, l for lamb or generically under m for meat?'

'What about gravy? Would you slurp it up all at once when you get to g?'

Colin waves his arm to signal a halt. 'Okay! Okay! It was only a joke!'

The Aber yell is heard from one corner, the name thundered frenziedly out by Geraint, balancing precariously on a chair, and answered by a raucous chorus.

> Aber-Aber-Aber!
> OY-OY-OY!
> Aber-Aber-Aber!
> OY-OY-OY!
> Aber!
> OY!
> Aber!
> OY!
> Aber-Aber-Aber-Aber-Aber!

The party begins to liven up, becomes more crowded, noisier, the conversation buzzing louder to compete with the music.

'...*Ulysses*? That's on my list of Books I Should Read But Know I Never Will.'

'It definitely conforms to Mark Twain's definition of a Classic, "a book that everyone wants to have read but nobody wants to read".'

'I've heard this rumour about Parker-Hurst, right? Apparently he keeps newspapers for a month before reading them, so as to avoid ephemeral items.'

'He's not such a bad old stick though, is he? Great name as well.'

'He is a stunningly dull person, though.'

'It's really strange - surnames - you get lots of people named Hill, but no Mountain or Valley. You get Bush but not Tree.'

'Lots of Wests but not many Norths or Souths...'

'And no North-Wests or South-South-Easts,'

'I don't see why you couldn't get a North-West. It could be a character from a Waugh novel.'

'First World Waugh or Second World Waugh?'

'Enough of this profound speculation.'

'Inane chatter, you mean...'

Fiona has come, and Dermot is enduring some taunting.

'Go on. Go up to her,' Nick urges. 'No need for a passionate declaration of love- .'

Dermot cuts in scornfully. 'If someone were to come up to me and say, "I love you," I'd be inclined to doubt either their sincerity or their sanity. And as regards Fiona, we have diametrically opposed views on everything.'

'Opposites attract,' comments Simon.

'If you're lumps of metal, maybe. Not if you're human.'

'Just talk to her. Say you're excited by her opinions being different from yours and you think you could have some really good arguments together,' Geraint suggests.

'I don't want her to think I'm even more crazy than she already thinks I am. Besides, she's bound to be upset over Peter Strutton.'

'Exactly. She needs someone to take her mind off him,' Nick counters sternly. 'And in any case, it's time to expand this strange life you lead.'

Dermot's speech is rapid and passionate. 'It doesn't seem strange to me. It only appears strange to other people because they don't lead it. If enough people led it, it wouldn't be considered strange at all. Most things that are thought to be strange or silly or objectionable or disgusting or sinister are only reckoned to be so because not many people do them. Most things that are thought good and normal and reasonable are only that way because lots of people do them. We should never persecute people for being different. We should ask what harm they're doing. If the answer's none, then there's no reason to persecute. Besides, I think she's ugly.'

'She's not really ugly,' Geraint replies. 'She only looks ugly.'

Dermot thumps his hand down on an imaginary table 'But that's what ugliness is all about.'

'Exactly. Appearances, which means nothing. I thought that was supposed to be your philosophy anyway.'

'Unattractive girls can be just as attractive as attractive ones,' Gus puts in.

'Bloody hell!' Nick exclaims. 'You're beginning to sound like *him*.' He points disgustedly in Dermot's direction. 'Just go over to her. She's very good at breaking the ice.'

'Especially when other people are walking on it,' Dermot answers.

After an hour or so of desultory dancing, chat and leisurely imbibing of alcohol, Gus strolls out for some fresh evening air. He finds he is followed by Nick. 'I'll join you,' Nick says. 'Nothing to stay in there for. I've done my good deed. Did you see Dermot and Fiona? They were dancing together. Lorna's gone home. Let's take a walk by the sea.'

They walk along Marine Terrace towards the Old College, conscious of the expanse of sky above and sea before them, as sunset dyes the water a spreading pale crimson-gold. Gus is surprised to hear Nick say softly,

> *It is a beauteous evening, calm and free...*

'Why did Wordsworth write *beauteous* instead of *beautiful*, I wonder? Was it just to be different and "poetic"?' Nick asks

'It sounds smoother, forms a nice rhythmic blend with *evening*.'

'And why is the evening *free*? Maybe because it makes you feel free, unencumbered by human worries.'

'That's right,' Gus answers. 'It's just *there*, just being, rather than doing.'

They recall the opening of the poem, reciting quietly together in a strange but strangely-pleasing unison, Nick, less sure of the words, slightly more hesitant than Gus.

> *It is a beauteous evening, calm and free.*
> *The holy time is quiet as a nun,*
> *Breathless with adoration; the broad sun*
> *Is sinking down in its tranquillity.*
> *The gentleness of heaven broods on the sea...*

'If anyone could hear us they'd think we were bloody mad,' laughs Nick. 'But, *the gentleness of heaven*. I like that phrase. *Heaven* could mean literally the sky - it looks so peaceful -'

' - but it might also refer to the carefree state of being in Heaven.' Gus carries on Nick's thought. 'He's already said that the time is *holy.* '

'I remember in that other poem,' Nick continues, 'Wordsworth wrote *heaven lies about us in our infancy.* When you think about it, it's not just in our infancy. Heaven lies about us all the time, if we can only see it.'

Gus is thoughtful. 'Edward Thomas wrote a poem called *Roads*. He said,

> *The next turning may reveal*
> *Heaven.* '

'Yes,' nods Nick, 'Heaven could be just around the corner. That's my philosophy. Feel that life is just beginning - all the time. Every day it starts anew. Every day we stand on its threshold, as if we're about to touch down on a newly discovered planet.'

'I remember we discussed that poem in class with Peter Strutton.'

They lean on the railings in front of the Old College. Nick looks out across the bay. 'He might have stood near here, on Friday night, in all this space, and yet he felt hemmed in, felt the darkness closing in around him.'

The half-descended sun arches across the water. The shining sea lies peaceful in the spreading blood-orange sunset. Gus looks too, at this bearer of so many moods through the year - angry, agitated, violent, cold, gentle, tranquil, warm, serene. And with the sadness, something rapturous beats within his breast, the indefinable Promise, huge as the world and endless as the universe, opening out before his inward vision as the sea spreads itself before his eyes. He looks forward to tomorrow, the last day of term. He will gaze at the water again after breakfast, feel the air morning-fresh against his face: a new morning, clean, unused, unexperienced, succulent and juicy, like a fruit ready to be tasted and savoured. Then he will catch the train for the long journey home.

Monday, 30 June

GODOLPHIN PUBLISHNG LTD,
63 COURTAULD STREET,
LONDON WC1
Telephone : 01-961 9437

Dr P. Strutton,
Flat 2,
7 Livingstone Place,   27 June
Aberystwyth
Cardiganshire

Dear Dr Strutton,

RE : GOLDEN LAMPS IN A GREEN NIGHT

Thank you for submitting sample chapters and a synopsis of your novel, *Golden Lamps in a Green Night*, to us. We apologise for the delay in replying: several of our staff have been visiting the Cincinnati Summer Book Fair.

We have read with interest your submission and would very much like to see the rest of the manuscript with a view to taking the project further. Please mail it to us and it will receive our prompt attention.

Yours sincerely,

Douglas Maynard

Douglas Maynard,
New Manuscripts Department

POETRY EXTRACTS QUOTED